FERAL NATION
RETALIATION - OPPOSITION - TENACITY

FERAL NATION

RETALIATION - OPPOSITION - TENACITY

Feral Nation Books 10-12
Scott B. Williams

Lightning Struck Press

Copyright © 2023 by Scott B. Williams. All rights reserved. No part of this book may be reproduced or transmitted in any form or by any means, electronic or mechanical, including photocopying, recording, or by any information storage and retrieval system, without permission in writing from the author.

This is a work of fiction. Names, characters and events are all products of the author's imagination and should not be construed as real. Any resemblance to persons living or dead is purely coincidental.

ISBN: 9798872498452
Cover and interior design © Scott B. Williams
Lightning Struck Press

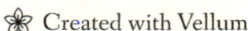 Created with Vellum

FERAL NATION
RETALIATION

SCOTT B. WILLIAMS

ONE

Eric Branson waited another ten minutes after the four Humvees disappeared down the narrow gravel road before giving his diversion team the signal to go. The two women accompanying the uniformed man who walked a few paces ahead of them were taking a huge risk, but though they were both aware of the consequences of the plan going sideways, they had volunteered without hesitation. One had friends and relatives detained behind the gate they were about to approach, and she understood that the success of this operation was the only hope those on the inside had. The other woman had never even met the prisoners, but Diane Lambert had little left to lose, and was determined to do everything in her power to avenge her slain husband and prevent other residents of the region from meeting the same fate. While she knew that the soldiers posted here weren't directly involved in the attack that led to Joe's death, they *were* working in conjunction with the organization of hired killers that were, and as such, were guilty by association. Furthermore, all of them were traitors to the nation they'd sworn to defend, and all were guilty of working to bring about that nation's demise. Diane wouldn't let him down, Eric knew, and Cindy Delacroix had already proven her mettle that day on the river when she made herself the bait to lure the crew of the stolen military gunboat into a deadly ambush.

Eric and the rest of his volunteers, the half dozen shooters that made up his small assault team, were spread out in position around the perimeter of the outpost, watching and waiting to see if the ruse he'd devised would create the desired effect. Eric didn't like launching an offensive like this in broad daylight, especially in the morning, when those posted to guard duty were likely alert and watchful, but after confirming the size of the detachment stationed there the evening before, he'd determined there was little alternative. He simply didn't have the manpower or equipment to take on nearly three dozen trained soldiers inside a defensive position, so he'd waited to see if most of them would leave for the day, as Sergeant Davis had assured him they would. When he saw the vehicles actually roll out shortly after sunrise, just as Davis predicted, leaving only a small detachment behind to stand guard, Eric made his decision to go ahead with the risky plan he had developed during a long night of observation and discussion with the others.

"We'll have you covered," he told Diane and Cindy," during a final briefing to make certain they knew exactly what to do. They both assured him they did, and Eric wished them luck before turning to Sergeant Davis with a stern glare and a warning: "One wrong step and you're a dead man! Got it?"

Eric didn't trust him, of course, and he had no qualms about having to kill him on the spot if the man gave him the slightest reason to do so, but getting him to cooperate would make this whole operation go smoother. Eric had gotten pretty much all the intel the sergeant had to give him by this point, and most of it had been quite useful, especially the detailed information about this remote outpost that would have been time-consuming to pinpoint otherwise. Located in a heavily wooded stretch of state hunting lands along the Red River, several miles above its confluence with the

Atchafalaya and the Mississippi at Simmesport, this was the base from which the stolen gunboat and the converted *Gulf Traveler* had been operating before Eric and his crew had taken both of them back. The former headquarters for the wildlife management area had everything the soldiers needed, including docks for the boats, and workspace and equipment storage in the small, cinderblock office and larger metal-sided building behind it. But the most impressive feature was the much larger structure on the side facing the river. Built some 12 feet above ground level on massive wooden pilings, it was a guest lodge, finished in a rustic style with board and batten cypress siding and a galvanized metal roof to mimic the style of the local river camps. It was obvious at first glance that no expense had been spared in its construction, and Davis said the big lodge contained nearly a dozen separate guest rooms with small, but cozy cabin-like interiors, and that the prisoners would probably be confined in one or more of those if they were indeed here, because it would be the easiest place to secure them. After observing that several of the exterior windows along the sides of the elevated building were indeed boarded up with heavy plywood fastened from the outside, Eric believed the sergeant was telling the truth.

Access to the lodge was by way of a two-flight staircase of wooden steps set back in the middle of the building. It was impossible to see all of the layout from where Eric was observing from a distance, but Davis said the stairs ascended to a wide, central breezeway under cover of the roof, from which there was access to each of the individual rooms. He said the troops were using some of these rooms too, so if the prisoners were there, escape attempts would be practically impossible. In addition to those soldiers with quarters up there, there were two sentries keeping watch over the entire outpost from a covered observation deck atop the main lodge roof that was accessed by a smaller stairway that couldn't be seen from without. The deck had obviously been built for lodge guests to climb up and enjoy a sweeping view out over the river and surrounding woodlands, and as such, it was a perfect watchtower for monitoring boat traffic approaching from either direction. To control the comings and goings of that traffic, the soldiers had placed a tripod mounted M2 machine gun in the middle of the platform, protected by an encircling ring of sandbags. The two sentries on duty there right now had rotated out just before the bulk of the soldiers left in the Humvees. Eric had seen them make the change when they suddenly stepped up onto the deck and the two that had been there disappeared down the steps that led into the building. The hidden access to and from that deck made it all the more ideal for the use to which they'd put it and created one of the challenges that Eric knew they had to deal with first in the assault.

As far as ground level defenses went, it was obvious the soldiers had been operating here long enough to dig in and set up perimeter fencing around the entire property and build dirt berms for hard cover across the exposed entrance to the post on the side opposite the river. A couple of old armored trucks that had probably been in the inventory of some national guard depot were parked on either side of the front gate, where they could be moved into position to block vehicle entry. The wide gravel road that led in from the west was the only access to the site other than by boat, so it wasn't a particularly difficult position to defend, and required only basic operational security to ensure it wasn't a soft target.

Now that the sound of the departing Humvees had faded away into the distance, the two guards assigned to the front gate would grow bored as they anticipated what was sure to be another long and uneventful day of waiting for their return. Taking them out would be a simple matter, but Eric knew there were still a few other soldiers inside the buildings besides those two and the two up there with that machine gun. He estimated another six to eight were inside in total and figured half of those were probably off duty for the day and completely at ease. They all had to be neutralized quickly though, and to do that, they had to be drawn outside of the buildings first. Eric had hit upon a plan to do just that, after satisfying himself through direct observation that everything here was pretty much as Davis had described it. Given that he had no choice, the sergeant had cooperated so far, and Eric's new plan would require him to do so again.

Eric's interrogation of Davis had provided him with lots of answers to other questions besides the details of this base of operations, including the truth behind the disappearance of Sergeant Patterson and his men that were stationed at the *real* Army post at the Simmesport lock and dam. When Eric and Jonathan found Patterson's post abandoned, shot-up and ransacked, it was obvious there had been an overwhelming attack there and all the evidence Eric found indicated that whoever did it used government-issued ammo identical to what Patterson's men would have carried. And after getting Davis to talk, Eric knew why. This new military force that Davis was a part of had sent him and his men into the region to hunt down insurgent forces, and they'd been told that Patterson's unit was part of a dangerous resistance effort that had gained control of the Mississippi and Atchafalaya and access to the Gulf by way of those two rivers.

It was a twisted story that someone far higher up had used to manipulate what remained of a few fractured national guard units in the isolated parts of Arkansas and Oklahoma, to the northwest, from which Davis had come. Eric now knew that several high-ranking generals were involved, and it was easy to piece together they had been working with their counterparts in the military forces of the foreign powers involved in the recent multi-pronged attacks on the integrity of the nation. Apparently, they'd coerced an untold number of former officers farther down the chain of command into helping them build this so called *North American Interior Defense* force that Davis had described when Eric pushed him for answers. Some of the enlisted men serving under them did so no doubt because they were afraid to question the authority of their superiors and had been led to believe they were on the right side of the fight. Others were pressured into it by offers of protection for their families and homes and other properties, but a large proportion of the soldiers doing the dirty work were foreign nationals that had been trained and funded by the same coalition of powers behind the takeover. Eric knew it mattered little where they were from, what uniform they were wearing, or what equipment they were using though. What mattered was that the men that were posted here had massacred an entire Army unit. Eric knew for a fact that Patterson was legitimate and that he served under the command of Lieutenant Holton, who in the end, had helped Eric get to Colorado, and that fact alone was justification for attacking this outpost and killing every man that was a part of it.

But making them pay for what they'd done at Simmesport wasn't the mission that brought Eric Branson and his team here today. This was far more personal, because the raids on civilian homes and communities in the river basin were the reason Eric's new friends and allies had been hiding out in the swamp in the first place, and the reason why their leader, Sam Necaise, along with several others, were missing. Eric already knew they'd been taken from the river at night while attempting to move people and supplies down to Keith's place, where Eric was to meet them. He'd learned that much from Debbie, the teenaged girl who was the only one that managed to escape when they were intercepted by a boat load of armed men. But Eric had no idea what happened to those who were captured until Sergeant Davis filled in the rest of the story during his interrogation. According to what he told Eric about their handling of the prisoners, Sam and those men arrested with him on the river were put in trucks to be brought here to this outpost.

"They're lucky they lived long enough to be taken in. They would have all been gunned down right there on the river if they'd attempted to put up a fight or run," Davis assured him, when telling Eric about the incident. "But since they didn't, we took them alive so they could be questioned about the extent of their operations and the locations of their hideouts. It was obvious they were part of the organized resistance we've been dealing with out here; since they were all armed and were sneaking down the river in the dark. And since they were captured in the same stretch of river where our gunboat crew went missing a couple of days before, we knew they were probably involved in that too. They are prisoners of war now, and as such, they are subject to military trial and swift punishment to suit their crimes as soon as they are found guilty."

Eric didn't bother to argue that Sam and those with him on the river were simply refugees, trying to survive and find safety, and that was the reason the group captured that night included three women and two boys who were too young to be a threat to anyone. It didn't matter what the man thought of them now though, because what was done was done, and Eric had no reason to doubt that Sam and everyone taken away with him were in grave danger after what he'd seen since returning to his collapsed homeland. He knew they didn't have much time, and so he had moved immediately to put together a small team and get into position to get them out if they were still here. Davis hadn't brought them here personally, but he'd given the order and he'd seen them taken away shortly after the boat he'd commanded dropped them off at the dock on Whiskey Bay Pilot Channel.

"Insurgents or domestic terrorists associated with these resistance groups are handled differently than the more compliant civilians that are being relocated to the refugee camps in Texas. Those that have already proven they are dangerous by their actions are segregated and removed from the larger population, then questioned until all the useful intel they have regarding their associates and their operations is extracted from them. What happens to them after that depends on the extent and nature of their specific crimes."

By the way he said it, Eric knew this illegitimate military organization that Davis was now a part of wouldn't comply with any recognized international conventions regarding the treatment of prisoners of war. Any force that would hunt down civilians, drive them from their homes and burn their towns and villages wouldn't respect the rights of those accused of actively resisting its incursions. With no national infrastructure or central command to answer to, these "soldiers" could do whatever they wanted, and Eric knew they would rid themselves of the burden of feeding, housing and transporting prisoners any longer than necessary to get the information they wanted from them. And Davis had to know that he faced a similar fate too now that the tables had turned for him and his unit, because whether he would acknowledge it or not, he had to know that *he* was the real terrorist and the real traitor to his country. That he was still alive and here today was due only to his usefulness in this operation. As far as those soldiers behind that gate knew, Sergeant Davis was missing in action and likely presumed dead. His sudden reappearance in the company of two civilian women would surely get a reaction, and Eric and the rest of his team intended to use that reaction to their advantage momentarily.

The sergeant had been instructed to walk a few paces ahead of Diane and Cindy, not only to give the appearance that he was leading them there to the outpost, but also to create the space Eric needed for a clear shot if the man tried something stupid. Davis knew before he left the concealment of the woods that Eric's red dot would be centered between his shoulder blades for the duration of his short stroll towards the gate. And he knew too that both Diane and Cindy were carrying concealed pistols and that he would have to contend with both of them as well if he attempted to turn the tables and use them for hostages. Davis knew the situation, and Eric expected him to comply up to a point, at least until the shooting started. If he dropped to the ground and stayed put when it did, he would live. But if he tried to run or join his comrades in the outpost, he was going to die with the rest of them.

When the three of them stepped from the woods and onto the road at Eric's signal, and began walking slowly towards the gate,

Davis shouted ahead to the guards to identify himself, holding both hands high where they could be seen. The startled soldiers raised their rifles, just as Eric expected, and studied the three figures through their optics to ascertain whether or not they were a threat. Eric was counting on the guards to hold their fire, but if they didn't, his two best shooters, Bart and Willis, had them in their sights from the perimeter tree line at 45-degree angles to either side of where Eric watched. He had more shooters in position to engage the two sentries on the upper deck with that machine gun, and to pick off the other soldiers that were somewhere inside the buildings and would surely emerge to respond if the fight went hot sooner than expected. If Eric's plan worked as he hoped, there wouldn't be enough of them left to call it a fight, but there were always variables that couldn't be controlled, and Eric knew his team was about to be put to the test.

There had been no time to work with them in advance or plan every detail of the mission, because the plan couldn't come together until Eric and the rest of them got here and did the recon. Of the eight men that were watching and waiting for Eric's first shot that would kick things off, Keith and Bart were the only other two that had real military combat training and experience, while all their adversaries here were soldiers. The men here may not have served in overseas wars like Eric and his brother and father, but they were presumably trained and disciplined, and Eric never underestimated an enemy's capability. His team had the element of surprise, but to really gain the advantage, they needed to draw more of their targets out in the open, and that was the purpose of this diversion he'd concocted. He was putting Diane and Cindy in a dangerous position, but they were willing volunteers and if it worked, the rest of the team would act with simultaneous, decisive action that would neutralize the defenders' capability before they even realized they were under attack. Eric knew they weren't expecting a surprise assault at this remote base so far upriver from where they'd encountered resistance. If they were, all those men that left in the

Humvees earlier would have stayed put. The truth was that after taking out that Simmesport post, these men had been operating purely on the offensive, using their superior numbers and equipment against unorganized and untrained civilians. Eric was determined to give them a taste of the other side of war today.

He saw that the two guards had lowered their rifles slightly now and heard one of them shout back to Davis. The sergeant was still wearing his uniform of MultiCam pattern BDUs that matched those of the guards behind the wire, but he carried no weapon. A length of rope trailed back from one of his raised hands, leading to the bound wrists of the two women who stumbled along side-by-side a dozen steps behind him. The distance from where he'd stopped to the gate was more than a hundred yards, making conversation with the guards difficult, so as Eric had expected, Davis was waved forward. But when he started walking again, Diane and Cindy appeared hesitant, forcing him to pull harder on the rope by which he was leading them. They stumbled on behind him for a few more steps, and then on cue, Diane seemed to trip and fall to the ground. Davis turned to see what was the matter and yelled at her to get to her feet. Eric kept his focus on the three of them, knowing that Bart and Willis had the two guards covered and that Keith, Trey and Lenny were in position to take out the two up there on that deck with the machine gun. The rest of the team, including Cindy's husband, Steven, Sam's nephew, Hal Necaise, and a fellow named Elroy Roberts, another of Sam's friends that had evacuated their camp on one of the ATVs, were watching from the woods on the north side of the compound.

But Eric didn't want any of them shooting when the soldiers first came out of the buildings. For this to work, they needed to draw as many of them as possible not just out into the compound, but outside the fence as well. That way, they'd have no cover and little chance of getting back inside to barricade themselves in the buildings or use the prisoners as human shields. That was why the two women were perfect for the diversion. The missing sergeant was returning from out of nowhere, but returning with a prize. Even from a distance, it was obvious Diane and Cindy were attractive females. Their sex appeal was enhanced by the shorts and tight T-shirts they were wearing, as they'd stumbled along behind the sergeant on bare feet. And now that Diane had fallen, she used the fact that she was barefoot to make it look more authentic, feigning an injury as she sat there apparently helpless, holding one of her feet in her free hand. Because her right wrist was bound to Cindy's left, at least to all appearances, the other woman had to sit down next to her, making it all the more difficult for the sergeant to get them up and moving again. Eric heard him cursing as he tugged on the rope, and he studied the man's face with the red dot of his Aimpoint, watching his expressions. Davis was a decent actor and so far was following instructions to the letter. As he appeared unable to get the women to cooperate, he turned back towards the gate, waving his other hand and shouting for assistance. Eric knew he was about to find out for real if his plan was going to work.

It took another minute, and then Eric saw one of the two gate guards turn and trot back into the compound, heading straight for the big lodge building. Eric watched as he disappeared up the stairs leading to the central breezeway on the main level, and time seemed to drag by while he was hidden from view somewhere in the corridor. Sergeant Davis was still trying to urge the women to get up and move out, but Diane remained defiantly on the ground, clutching her foot to emphasize that she couldn't. When Eric saw movement again from the lodge it was the returning guard descending the stairs, followed by four more out-of-uniform men who looked like they'd just rolled out of their bunks and grabbed their rifles. As they approached the gate, Eric saw the guy that waited behind swing it open for them to exit. A glance back towards the roof of the lodge confirmed that both men up there were focused on what was going on out front as well, and one of them was behind the weapon now and had swung the barrel around in the direction of Davis and the two women. Eric wasn't concerned about that gunner though, because he knew he could depend on Keith to take him out and that Lenny and Trey would back him up and get the second guy. Jonathan had already attested to the abilities of those two when he related to Eric the story of how they'd taken the gunboat back yet again, and how effective Lenny had been with his compound hunting bow. But as much as he wanted to watch everything that happened as it went down; Eric knew he had to keep an eye on what was going on at the front gate. And what was happening there now was that the guard that had gone to fetch help was leading the four that came back with him outside of the compound, exactly as he had hoped they would! And to make it even better, the idiots were bunched together in a cluster as they quickly walked towards Davis and the two women. Eric couldn't help but smile. *They were falling for it!* While he knew those four probably weren't the only ones that had been inside before the setup, getting that many out in the open was better than he'd hoped for and killing them and the guards would decimate the resistance.

Eric watched Davis for a second to confirm that he was keeping his distance from Diane and Cindy. While they appeared to be bound together when Davis was leading them out there, the reality was that the rope at their wrists was only loosely wrapped. The women were free to run or able to fight depending on what became necessary, so Eric switched his focus back to the approaching five to select his first target. Because of the way the plan was falling into place, he would have the satisfaction of kicking things off with the first shot that would be the signal for the rest of the team to take out their own targets. Eric picked the uniformed guard from among the five men heading towards Davis. Like the other guard posted at the gate with him, he was wearing no plate carrier, and Eric dropped him with a single round to the center of his chest.

TWO

Sam Necaise woke with an excruciating headache and squinted through half-open eyelids in the direction of the door. With the outer windows boarded up the room was mostly dark, but enough light was coming through the gap at the bottom of the door to tell him it was morning. It wasn't the light that woke him though, but rather the sounds of frantic commotion in the breezeway just outside his room. Shouted orders and slamming doors jarred him back to awareness of where he was, and the yelling was followed soon after by the sounds of boots on the wooden deck of the corridor and the steps leading down to the ground. Sam didn't know what it meant, but morning usually meant more pain was sure to follow once he heard the padlock coming off the hasp on the other side of the door behind which he was confined. Sam was determined to get to his feet before that happened, even though the agony of completing that simple task was nearly more than he could bear. The bruises seemed worse than they were before he'd slipped into unconsciousness sometime during the night, but Sam forced himself to roll over on the floor and then he managed to lift himself onto one elbow. From there, he gathered himself into a kneeling position on the hard cypress planking and using the nearest wall to steady himself, managed to stand. They weren't going to kick him while he was down again; not unless they knocked him down first. Sam was determined to meet the bastards face to face this time and every time. And if this was the visit during which they intended to finally kill him, he was going to die on his feet, and not curled up on the floor like a dog begging for mercy.

Sam was sure they *would* kill him at some point, along with Marcus, Darryl, and Charlie, his three friends they'd brought here with him. For all he knew, the other men were already dead. If they weren't, Sam assumed they were confined alone in separate rooms like him. He hadn't seen any of them since they'd all arrived here, but the interrogators kept telling him the others were indeed here and that unlike him, they were cooperating. They told him that if he would just do the same, he too would get the easier treatment and special privileges they now enjoyed. Of course, Sam didn't believe a word of it. Maybe one, or maybe even all three of them had broken under the pressure and the pain, but if they did, Sam doubted they had benefited from it. And if they *did* talk, doing so probably brought an end to their usefulness. Sam had heard pistol shots from out in the direction of the river the afternoon before, and there was no way of knowing whether he was hearing the executions of his friends just outside the compound or if one of the bored soldiers was simply popping off a few rounds at an empty can. He also heard vehicles coming and going during the daytime most days and knew his friends could have been taken away in one of those to someplace else to be disposed of or imprisoned elsewhere.

The reason Sam thought it unlikely any of them would get out of this situation alive was that they were accused of being involved in the disappearance of the gunboat on the river not far from where they'd been captured. The boat had gone missing while patrolling that stretch of the Atchafalaya, and other soldiers from this base from which it had been operating had discovered the bodies of the dead crewmen hung up in the brush along the riverbank. Of the four of them that were accused, Sam and Marcus *were* indeed involved in the clever ambush devised by Eric Branson. Sam didn't regret it for a minute either, because it was the first opportunity he'd had to strike back at this invading force of uniformed thugs that had uprooted the lives of him and his family and so many more in the area. He would never tell them he was there though, no matter what they did to him, because he knew for sure that admitting it would mean a death sentence for him and his friends. The gunboat wasn't in their possession when they were captured, of course, and Sam had no way of knowing if they knew where it was or knew of Eric Branson and the militia he and his young partner said they were building.

Sam hadn't seen Eric or Jonathan since they left on the captured prize to take it downriver to their hidden base of operations that Eric had called Sierra Zulu. For all he knew, Eric and those from Sam's group that went with him, including his nephew, Hal, and his friends Steven and Cindy Delacroix, could have been captured later too, or even killed. Sam didn't know if Eric came back to meet him as planned or not, because he'd never reached the agreed-on rendezvous point Eric had told him about; the property belonging to his brother, Keith, a sheriff's deputy down there in the next parish to the south. If Eric *did* show up, he would have found no one there, and likely wouldn't know what to make of that. Eric knew where Sam's camp was of course, and Sam figured he would go there to check too if he could, but after what had happened that night on the river, Sam didn't know if that was possible. He wouldn't have guessed there was more than one patrol boat, but apparently all of them, including Eric Branson, had underestimated the scope of what they were dealing with, and how hard it was to travel anywhere in the region now without running into trouble.

Sam had taken care to wait until well after dark when he set out on the first trip down to the rendezvous. The plan was to shuttle several people and as much gear as they had room for in the two big john boats and two pirogues they had available at the camp. While he'd originally wanted to get the other boats some of the men still had stashed at their abandoned homes and fishing camps so the entire group could move in one trip, by the time they were ready to move out, they'd deemed it too risky. Getting to them and moving them back to the river would involve using roads. Sam decided it wasn't worth it and most of the group supported his decision. As it turned out, his more cautious approach didn't fare any better, and they'd been discovered and taken captive at gunpoint anyway.

Sam hoped that those he'd left behind at the camp to await their turn to go downriver hadn't been found and taken in too. If they hadn't, there was a good chance that Marcus' girl, Debbie, had made it back there to tell them what happened and warn them just how dangerous it was to use the river now. But even if she hadn't, at least *she'd* escaped when the pirogue she was riding in capsized and dumped her into the dark waters of the river. Sam knew Marcus was worried about her being stranded alone like that in the middle of nowhere at night, but it was still better than what befell the rest of them at the hands of these soldiers.

"She can take care of herself in the woods," Sam had whispered to him shortly afterwards, as they were huddled together under guard on the deck of the wooden river cruiser that had intercepted them. "She may have complained some about being stuck out there all summer, but you know as well as I do that she can find her way back upriver to that camp. You've been bringing her out to the swamp huntin' and fishin' since she was old enough to keep up."

Marcus listened to Sam's reassuring words, but both men knew that anything could happen to an unarmed teenaged girl alone in a world of utter lawlessness and constant danger. The camp could have been found by another group of the soldiers before she had time to get back there, or she could have walked right into a patrol of them somewhere along the way. But even if she made it back and found the others still there in time to warn them they needed to move, they had no boats now and no safe way to get down to the planned rendezvous point other than laboriously bushwhacking through the swamp on foot, which meant their chances of doing so were slim to none.

Sam had contemplated those possibilities several times since that conversation with Marcus. He'd had plenty of time to do so because he'd spoken with no one else but his interrogator since the four of them had been brought here and separated upon arrival. But though he thought about the plight of Debbie and the others back there in the swamp, Sam was much more worried about the women and the two boys that had been captured with them that night. His own wife, Suzanne, was among those taken, and Sam feared he'd never see her again, even if he somehow avoided the death sentence he expected for what he was accused of by his captors. He and the other three adult men of the group were the accused insurgents. The women and boys would be relocated out of the contested zone, to one of those detention camps Sam had been hearing about. He was told they would have food and shelter there, and that they would be better off than those folks foolish enough to continue hiding out and fighting the inevitable.

Sam didn't know what to believe, or what would happen to his wife and the others, and the hardest part of his entire ordeal was knowing there was *nothing* he could do to help her. He wished like hell now that he'd left her back at their camp, because they *had* managed to stay hidden and *had* avoided trouble out there, at least until Eric Branson came along. He'd only brought her along because they were trying to shuttle as many people downriver as they had room for in the boats, and Darryl and Charlie were taking their wives too. Charlie's boys, Brian and Cameron, were just eight and ten, so he and their mother, Brenda, weren't going to leave them behind, of course. Because the boys were so young, they weren't accused of being terrorists, but Charlie had to be sick with worry, just as Sam was over Suzanne and Darryl over his wife, Phyllis. It was enough to break any man, knowing his family was in the hands of these ruthless invaders and there wasn't a damned thing he could do about it. Sam wouldn't blame either Charlie or Darryl if they *did* talk, but the truth was that none of them knew much of anything about Eric Branson other than what he and that young fellow named Jonathan that was with him had told them. They couldn't tell the interrogators what he was planning next or where his hideout was, because none of them knew, other than a vague idea that it was somewhere deep in the swamp to the south of I-10.

Sam wondered if he'd made a mistake by throwing his lot in with the likes of Eric Branson, but every time he considered that he had, he stopped to ask himself what was the alternative? Sure, it was dangerous to join a militia or participate in any resistance to what was happening to them, but what kind of life were they going to have if they didn't? Even though they'd done it successfully so far, they couldn't just hide out in the woods indefinitely, cut off from the outside world and surrounded by an enemy intent on hunting down anyone remaining in the region. While they had essential supplies for now and the equipment and know-how to hunt and fish, Sam knew the supplies would run out and even the game and fish wouldn't last considering their limited ability to move to new areas once resources in the immediate area were depleted. They had no access to medical help if someone in the group fell ill or was seriously wounded, and everyone there knew it was just a matter of time before one of them faced the consequences of that reality. The truth was that joining forces with others outside of their little group would eventually become necessary for their long-term survival, but until Eric Branson came along, they didn't really have the option. The man talked a good plan and seemed to have the background and skills to back it up. Sam had been willing to throw in with him because he was certain that turning this predicament around was going to take men willing and able to do the kinds of things Eric Branson said he was prepared to do. And after seeing how he set up the ambush of the gunboat and pulled it off without a hitch, Sam was convinced he wasn't just a bullshitter.

But no matter how much of a badass the former Navy SEAL was though; Sam was disheartened after seeing the extent of the invading forces they were facing. This wasn't just random gangs of looters or desperate opportunists like they'd seen in the early days of the collapse. This was an organized military operation manned by merciless killers bent on treating the local population like the enemy. Sam didn't know why or how they'd become what they were, but the reality of what he was seeing backed up the worst reports and stories he'd heard recently. These thugs were in Army uniforms and were using Army equipment and vehicles, but they were acting more like a foreign invasion force than anything else. And Sam had heard some of them conversing amongst themselves in languages other than English, so maybe they *were* part of a foreign force. Most of them were quite young, and several appeared to be from Hispanic or Middle Eastern ethnic groups. Sam figured they could have been recruited from among the countless migrants that had been pouring in for years before the campaigns of terror ramped up. But though he'd seen much diversity in the ranks, most of his interactions had been with one or two men that were older and clearly as Southern as he was. The first was that sergeant aboard the boat that intercepted them, and the other was the interrogator that had asked most of the questions since he got here, always accompanied by a couple of the young grunts that held Sam while he administered the beatings.

Sam expected no mercy from any of them, and knew that whether he gave in to them or not, it was unlikely to help the other three men that had been brought here with him, or Suzanne, who was no telling how far away from him now. There was no reason to believe they would keep him alive after they extracted all the information they could get from him. His sentence would be carried out swiftly and with no opportunity to appeal. Sam saw no hint of mercy in the eyes of these men and he entertained no illusions he could expect any. If they were going to kill him, he would die with dignity though. That was in his control, and it was that thought that gave him the strength to stand up again despite the pain, ready to meet whoever came through that door.

For a moment, he thought maybe no one would. After hearing a number of men running down the stairs, slamming doors shut behind them, he wondered for a moment if maybe everyone in the building had gone down there. But he hadn't heard anyone on the steps leading down from the roof, and Sam knew there was likely at least one guy up there with that machine gun he'd spotted as soon as he'd arrived here and was led away from the truck. The gunner up there would have a commanding view of the river and the entire compound. Sam knew this firsthand, because he'd been up there before himself, during one of his visits here to the wildlife management area headquarters in years past. He'd hunted in the vast acreage of this place often back in the good old days, when the only thing people around here were shooting at were ducks, deer and wild hogs. Sam had realized where he was being taken when he noticed the route the truck took after leaving the pavement. He immediately recognized the headquarters buildings and the big, rustic lodge, even though the soldiers had made lots of changes, installing fencing and barricades, and parking military vehicles in the spaces usually occupied by the pickup trucks and SUVs of the game wardens and other staff that had worked here. Sam had noted every detail he could, right up until he was escorted up the steps of the lodge and locked into the small, empty room from which he hadn't emerged since.

Sam's thoughts that they'd all left the building and that maybe he'd gotten to his feet for nothing were interrupted when he heard boots on the floor of the breezeway once again. This time the footsteps sounded like they were getting closer, and Sam knew his hearing hadn't fooled him when he heard the click of the padlock snapping open on the outside of his door. Sam stood his ground where he was, some six feet back from the entrance. When the door swung open, he saw it was indeed the interrogator, and he was alone this time. In his hand was one of the large bottles of water Sam had been getting every day along with barely enough food to keep him alive.

"Drink, so you can loosen your tongue and talk! It looks like Sergeant Davis has finally returned, and this is your last chance to answer the questions I have been asking you. I'm not kidding about that either. You either talk to me now, or you'll never be able to again if I have to go out there and tell him I still don't have the information he sent you here to give me!"

Sam knew he was talking about the sergeant that had been in command of the boat that intercepted them that night. Sam had already been questioned by him directly, right after his capture, as had everyone else with him. But the sergeant had been in a hurry to attend other business after dropping them all off at a dock on the Whiskey Bay Pilot Channel, where they had a small number of troops occupying an old road maintenance building. That was before Sam and the other three men had been separated from the women and the two boys. That sergeant had given orders for all of them to be sent away for interrogation, and Sam had heard him say he would be coming the next day to follow up. But only the four of them were brought here, and days had passed and still the sergeant didn't show. It didn't matter much to Sam one way or the other, because he didn't see how his situation would change whether that sergeant was back or not, but apparently, his interrogator was concerned. He'd failed to get a detailed confession and had extracted little useful intel from the prisoners, despite that he'd had days to do it. Now he was going to have to admit that failure to his superior. Sam knew things were about to get real with this guy, and he tried not to tense up and betray his concern as he took the bottle and kept his eyes locked on the other's while taking a slow swig of water.

Aside from the finality of his new threat, the one thing that was different this time was that the interrogator had come alone, which was a first. Every other time, his two helpers had been there carrying rifles, as well as their sidearms. Sam didn't know why so many of the men had hurried down the steps like they had just because the sergeant had returned, but whatever the reason, it apparently left the interrogator shorthanded, causing him to come alone to try his persuasive tactics on Sam once more before reporting he had nothing of value. This was a dangerous moment, Sam knew, because the man had an intensity about him today that made him unpredictable. Would he literally beat him to death or simply draw his pistol and shoot him if he didn't get his answers? Sam didn't know, but he did know the man was overconfident, and it was probably because he'd already beaten Sam so badly that he felt he had nothing to fear.

And Sam knew he must have looked beaten and defeated too, with his swollen black eyes and other bruises. At 64 years old, Sam was probably twice the other man's age. There was no reason for a strong, young soldier like that to fear an older fellow like him, especially in his battered and weakened state, but Sam thought about his options as he swallowed the last of the water. Would he ever get another opportunity like this, one-on-one with just one man? What if he could somehow manage to overpower him and take the guy's handgun? Could he find Marcus, Darryl and Charlie and free them too, assuming they were still alive? And could any of them get out of the building, much less out of the compound without being seen and shot? Sam doubted it, especially with that machine gun up there on the roof. But the adrenaline rushed through him as the possibilities filled his thoughts. Sam could either go for it, or he could do what he'd refused to do up until now, and concoct a bullshit story just to tell this guy something he wanted to hear. He decided that was probably the better idea and was just about to open his mouth to speak when a new sound surprised them both and stopped him short before he could utter a word. *It was gunfire;*

one distinct rifle shot first and then many more, almost in unison and seemingly coming from many directions at once....

The interrogator turned to face the open door behind him, no doubt to look out and see if he could tell what was going on, and that was when Sam made his decision to act.

THREE

The echoes of Eric's first shot were drowned in a barrage of nearly simultaneous rifle reports that erupted from multiple directions around the compound. Eric saw another of the men behind the one he'd dropped go down hard, as did the lone guard standing by the gate. A quick glance in the direction of the deck atop the lodge confirmed that the machine gun was sitting there unfired and unmanned. Keith, Lenny and Trey had taken care of the two up there and would now look for any other targets that appeared on their side of the compound, as would the three guys covering the north perimeter. Eric trusted that Willis and Bart would finish the other three men that had left the security of the compound and were now prone on the ground, trying desperately to hide behind the bodies of their fallen comrades. They simply had no chance, pinned down as they were with no cover in a crossfire between two expert shooters, so Eric turned his attention back to Sergeant Davis and the two women. While he'd given the man his word that he wouldn't shoot him in the back as long as he complied and followed the plan, Eric had doubted he would do so in the end, and now he saw that the sergeant had proven him right.

In the seconds it took Eric to kick off the assault and ensure the team had followed his lead, the desperate hostage had managed to engage Diane and Cindy in a life-or-death struggle. Somehow, he'd moved fast enough to throw himself on top of them as soon as the shooting started, closing the gap and entangling himself with them in such a way that it was impossible for Eric to get a shot that wouldn't endanger at least one of the two women. Eric realized then that he probably should have shot him first, instead of the other guy, but it was too late to second-guess that decision, and all that mattered now was preventing him from killing Diane and Cindy or using them for cover to try and escape or get inside that compound.

Eric knew the women had already freed their wrists from the fake bonds used to create the illusion they were the sergeant's captives. When Diane pretended to fall, Cindy only went down with her to make it look as if they were still bound. They should have had time to access their concealed handguns, and maybe one or both of them had, but Davis had still managed to get within grappling distance before either one had time to aim and fire. While he knew they were armed, he really had little to lose at that point and had gambled on being able to subdue them without getting shot. Eric would have done the same had he been in Davis' position, as few handgunners could pull off a successful defense against a truly determined rush launched at such close range. Both women said they could shoot, and the day Eric met her, Diane had killed one of the C.R.I. contractors in that house with his own pistol—the same one she'd carried today—but they were no match for the bigger and stronger sergeant in a hand-to-hand struggle.

Eric broke cover to sprint across the open ground towards the three of them, counting on Bart and the others to keep the heat on the remaining soldiers so they wouldn't have an opportunity to open fire on him. As he closed in, Eric saw that Davis had Diane face down on the ground and pinned under his weight as he attempted to get to the pistol that she had clutched beneath her with both hands. He would have already succeeded if not for Cindy, who was on his back and attempting to choke him with a forearm locked around his throat. Eric saw her pistol on the ground several feet out of her reach and figured she must have dropped it and couldn't risk letting go of the sergeant to try and retrieve it. Unfortunately, the way they were positioned and thrashing about made any shot Eric might attempt with his rifle still too risky, even from a much closer range, and he knew he was going to have to get up close and personal to put Davis out of the fight.

None of the three were aware of him running towards them, engrossed as they were in their struggle, and Eric already had his knife in hand as he focused on his target and considered how he would dispatch the sergeant in the fastest manner possible without hurting either woman. But he was robbed of the opportunity just before he was close enough to put steel to flesh. Diane had managed to maintain her tenacious grip on the pistol beneath her, even if it was of no use in that position, while Cindy suddenly remembered the short length of rope that was still looped around her left wrist.

She'd been using her left hand to reinforce the armlock she had on Davis' throat, but she wasn't strong enough or in the right position to apply an effective choke with just the forearm. What she did next was a brilliant flash of inspiration. She risked losing her grip by letting go with that left hand momentarily, but in doing so, she was free to then bring that arm briefly over the top of his head and encircle his unprotected neck with the rope. Eric saw her follow up the new grip without hesitation by suddenly rolling herself over and off his back suddenly to put all her body weight into tightening the stranglehold of cord she now had around his neck. Davis let go of Diane to claw at the constriction cutting off his air supply, as he threw himself backward onto Cindy. Eric's focus had narrowed like that of a charging predator about to pounce as he was certain he would plunge his blade into the man's chest as soon as he closed the 20-yard gap that remained. But he was stopped short before he could leap by the sudden crack of a 9mm pistol. Davis suddenly tensed and then went limp, and Cindy's face was splattered with blood. *Diane had taken the shot!* Her pistol was shaking slightly in her two-handed grip as she fired twice more from where she'd rolled up into a sitting position as soon as Davis' weight was off her. Cindy was shaking now too as she wiped the splattered blood off her face with one hand and pulled her leg from under the dead man's body.

Eric put his knife back in its sheath and announced his presence, as both women had been so focused on the fight with Davis, they were oblivious to all else. When he reached Diane's side, he steadied her hand to keep the barrel of the Sig P365 away from them both, and then checked her for injuries. Davis had slammed her to the ground hard, and she would have bruises, but nothing seemed broken. Eric likewise checked Cindy and when he was sure they both could move out, he helped them to their feet and urged them towards the wood line. After verifying that all of the soldiers that had followed the guard out of the compound were out of the fight, Eric trailed Diane and Cindy into the woods to where they'd left their rifles and other gear. Eric hated that he wasn't back there in the thick of the assault, but the way it worked out, Diane and Cindy were his first priority until they were safe. The two of them had made this operation possible, and both were the heroes of the day in his book, and he didn't want them exposed to more unnecessary risks at the moment. Keeping them well out of sight of the clearing, he led them around the perimeter to Bart's position to see what the old man's assessment of the situation was at this point.

"There's a couple shooters holed up in those two corner rooms at the front of that lodge building," Bart said, when Eric reached his father's side. "I thought it was just one at first, because I saw muzzle flashes from the room on the northwest corner, but a little later I saw some from the southwest corner too."

"In the window opening?"

"No, under it. They must have reinforced the front walls and made a bunker out of those two rooms. It looks like they've got shooting ports; take a look...."

Bart handed Eric his .308 with its 1-10x variable optic and Eric could clearly see the narrow, slotted shooting ports in the front face of both walls. It made sense, considering those walls faced the front gate, but Sergeant Davis hadn't mentioned them, and Eric and the team missed them in their recon, probably because they'd been closed and were obscured by the early morning shadows on that west-facing wall. As he studied them now, Eric figured the rooms probably weren't elaborate bunkers or anything of the sort. The men had probably just fastened some heavy steel plate behind the existing walls and cut a few slots to shoot through. It did make sense, since those two walls faced the gate and the road leading in. Eric passed the rifle back to Bart.

"It makes clearing that building a pain in the ass," Bart said, "especially since that's probably where Sam and the rest are. I've put some rounds through those ports, but I couldn't tell if I hit anything. I figured I haven't since they're still taking shots now and then. Can't really send a bunch of stray rounds everywhere, or risk grenades, so it'll have to be done the hard way. The only way in is up that staircase. If they have a way to cover it from where they are, it'll be sporty."

"What about the other buildings?" Eric nodded to the small cinderblock headquarters building and the metal-sided one behind it. "Have you seen anything moving down there?"

"Yep. Keith or one of those boys with him opened up in the direction of both buildings right after they took out the guys up on that top deck. I couldn't see what they were shooting at from this side, but there was some return fire from outta the smaller one in front, so if they got somebody, they didn't get them all at first, there may still be one or more of them in there now."

Eric considered the options. The operation had gone as planned, but there was simply no way to know the exact number of men in the compound because of all the buildings, and the number of individual rooms in the lodge. He still didn't know for sure where the prisoners were, or if they were even still there. All he had to go on was what Sergeant Davis had told him, and the evidence he saw in the form of those boarded-up windows on the side of the lodge building. Getting to them to find out was going to require eliminating the barricaded shooters. Eric didn't know if the surviving defenders of the post would correlate this attack with a rescue mission, but if they did, it was possible they would try to use the prisoners lives for leverage if given the opportunity.

The presence of the prisoners had limited Eric's options from the beginning, as was always the case with this sort of rescue mission. Those limitations had guided his planning for carrying out the entire attack with deception and surgically precise shooting, rather than overwhelming force involving heavy machine guns, grenade launchers and other explosives. It had mostly gone well, but flushing those last guys out was going to be dicey.

After seeing most of their force decimated by an unknown number of excellent shooters, those last guys left alive weren't going to do anything stupid to make themselves targets. They had to know they were surrounded and had no hope of thwarting the attack or escaping into the woods from which this unknown enemy appeared. They would hang tight where they were barricaded behind cover, hoping they could survive the onslaught until the four Humvees carrying the rest of their unit returned. Eric didn't know if the vehicles were in radio range or not, but if they were, it was possible they were even now hurrying back to join the fight. Sergeant Davis had told him the patrols would probably be gone all day, especially if they were looking for him and the other missing men that had been with him, but Eric had never assumed he had that much time, and as with every mission, the goal was to get in and accomplish the objective and then extract as quickly as possible. He'd hoped to avoid the need for room clearing, especially in two separate buildings, but there was little choice now, and the clock was ticking.

Eric was confident he could get inside the compound and reach the exterior of any of the structures without getting shot as long as he had Bart and enough of the other shooters to cover for him and suppress any fire from the defenders. Even the narrow shooting ports in those two upper rooms would be ineffective with the threat of precision fire incoming. But getting to the buildings was only the first step, and going inside to clear them would be trickier. It made sense from a tactical perspective to start with the two ground level buildings first, eliminating the possibility that someone in one of those would get a shot when he was ascending the steps to the lodge. But while he was doing that, the shooters up there would have time to round up the prisoners if the thought occurred to them that doing so would be beneficial.

What Eric needed was two teams of specialists with training and experience at that sort of thing—six or eight guys that he could split up and assign to the two ground structures and another four or five to go with him to storm the lodge. But wishing for what he didn't have would get him nowhere, and Eric didn't entertain the thought for more than a fleeting second. The only real door-kicker he had was his brother, Keith, an experienced combat Marine and veteran lawman. Keith was good to go, and Eric had already made up his mind to take Willis as a third backup, having seen the young man's gun-handling and shooting skills and cool, unflinching efficiency under pressure. The three of them would have to suffice, because there was no one else out there today that he knew he could fully depend on other than Bart, Diane and Cindy, and there was no way he was taking any of them, despite Bart's protest when Eric told him so.

"You know I'm depending on you more than anyone out here to keep us covered, Dad. You're the best shooter we've got."

"Looks to me like all those boys in Sam's bunch can shoot too! Hell, they've all been hunting every day since they had to move out to the swamp."

"Yeah, but you know damned well none of them have your

experience with targets that can shoot back! Besides, we've got to move fast, and you'd slow us down too much."

"Like hell I would! I may not be as fast as I used to be, but I'll still run you and your little brother down and smack some sense into both of you if I see that you need it!"

"You did it for years and it never did any good, so I wouldn't bother with it now, if I were you," Eric laughed. "You know I'm kidding, Dad. Of course, you'd do a great job going in, but somebody's got to be the backup team leader if something goes wrong. You're the only one out here that knows what to do."

"What about us?" Diane wanted to know. "Don't forget us. We can shoot too, and we want to do our part."

Diane and Cindy were still eager to help, despite all they'd been through, and Eric couldn't help but be impressed.

"Of course!" Eric said. "But I don't want you going inside, because you've both taken more than your share of the risk in this operation, and besides, it's my turn to get in on the action. Hell, I'm feeling left out, especially since you didn't even need my help with Sergeant Davis!"

"I wouldn't have minded if you'd shot him, but I didn't have any problem pulling the trigger, I can tell you that! He would have killed me in a heartbeat if Cindy hadn't gotten that rope around his neck."

"Yeah, about that..." Eric turned to Cindy. "That was a pretty slick move, the way you rolled off him to put the leverage on that stranglehold. Where did you learn that?"

"I don't know. I guess from all the wrestling I used to do with my brother growing up. It just came natural."

"Well, I'm glad it did. It worked beautifully, but I should have shot him first off, instead of that other soldier. I knew I couldn't trust him."

"He's served his purpose and he's not our problem anymore, that's the main thing," Bart said. "We've got enough to worry about without keeping up with prisoners."

Eric agreed. It simply wasn't feasible to hold him. Eric wouldn't just kill him in cold blood though, especially since he'd talked and mostly cooperated, and he hadn't made up his mind before the assault what to do with him. It would have been a problem, because if he'd just let him go, the sergeant would have found his way back to the survivors of his unit or another one and continued his business of running over the civilians in the territory his organization was invading.

Eric grabbed one of the spare handheld VHF radios from his bag and gave it to Diane. "I've got the perfect job for you," he said as he checked the channel of his own unit to make sure they were still in sync. I need the two of you to cut back through the woods to the place where you came out on the road before. Follow it a little further out, so you'll be in a good place to look and listen for vehicles, but make sure you're out of sight! If you hear anything coming down that road, give me a heads-up! I may not hear your call if we're in the thick of it in there, but keep trying until I do! Can you do that?"

Diane and Cindy both assured him that they could, and both of the women seemed satisfied that they'd been assigned another important role.

"I know you want to get more of the bastards, and I don't blame you, but whatever you do, don't get excited and shoot at anyone in the vehicles if you see them. There are too many of them and you'll have no hard cover out there if they open up on you, and we may have our hands full inside and not be able to help. I'm hoping it's just a precaution anyway, and that we'll all be out of here long before they come back." Eric turned to Bart. "I'm going to work my way around to the north side to get Willis and to update Steven, Hal and Elroy on the new plan and reposition them if I need to. Then, we'll get Keith and figure out the best angle to go in. Lenny and Trey are probably good where they are. We'll still have enough people around the perimeter to prevent anyone from slipping out."

Eric found Willis eager and ready when he reached his side

and explained to him what they needed to do. Willis had impressed Eric from the start, and he knew he'd be excited to be a part of the final mop-up. After stopping to tell Steven, Hal, and Elroy what he had planned, Eric led Willis around through the woods to get Keith. The soldiers had eliminated any vegetation within 200 feet of the perimeter fence they'd installed, so getting into the compound was going to require sprinting across open ground no matter which angle of approach they took. The open front gate was the easiest entrance, but it was the most exposed too, in full view of those shooting ports Bart had pointed out in the front rooms of the lodge.

"Let's go from back here," Keith said, when Eric and Willis reached his position and told him the situation.

"Do you have cutters?" Eric asked him.

Keith opened the small, but robust wire cutters in the multitool he carried in a pouch on his duty belt. "Not the fastest, but they'll do."

Eric nodded. The fence was standard cyclone wire—nothing special—but enough to slow down anyone wishing to get through it, while the razor wire at the top discouraged attempts to climb over it.

"Let me go first and cut it," Willis volunteered. "I can run faster than either one of you."

Eric figured he probably could. The fact that Willis was tough and very fit was another reason Eric liked the kid and saw so much potential in him. Keith said he'd exchanged fire with a guy shooting from a window in the back of the block building and didn't know if he'd hit him or not. He and Keith would hold back until Willis reached the fence and cut an opening for them, and then follow separately at intervals to avoid presenting a cluster of targets. Eric gave him the go ahead and Willis made it across the open ground to the fence without drawing fire. He made quick work cutting his way in, and as soon as he was through, he ran for the back corner of the metal building, which was the nearest cover available. Keith went next while Eric covered him, and Eric was about to follow as soon as his brother reached the fence when he was stopped short by a burst of gunfire from the cinderblock headquarters building. He saw Keith diving for cover behind the corner where Willis waited as bullets kicked up dust in the yard and ripped into the metal siding of the other building in front of them.

Eric aimed where he saw the muzzle flash from a window and unleashed a long burst from his own M4. He was uncertain if he'd hit his target, but the shooter dropped out of sight and now Keith and Willis were in position to cover him so he could follow them in. Eric was just about to sprint for the fence when he was interrupted by an urgent voice from the radio clipped to his chest rig. It was Diane:

"THERE'S A VEHICLE APPROACHING! I REPEAT! I CAN HEAR A VEHICLE APPROACHING ON THE ROAD!"

FOUR

Sam Necaise knew it was now or never if he was going to make a move and have any chance in hell of surviving the predicament he was in. The gunfire outside was intense, and as the interrogator peered out from the doorway to his room, Sam heard a heavy thud on the metal roof above. He was certain someone had fallen from the deck up there where they'd placed that machine gun, because it wasn't being used, even though the outpost seemed to be under attack. Sam knew if that was the situation, then every soldier there would be preoccupied with fighting back against whoever was out there trying to kill them. He knew he couldn't take the younger man in a fair fight, and he wasn't planning to try. There was nothing in the empty room he could use as a weapon, but he decided the door jamb itself would suffice, seeing how the man stood there looking out with his head about six inches from it.

Sam took a big step and lunged forward with all the strength he could muster in his state of exhaustion, gripping the guy's head with both hands and using his momentum to slam it into the unforgiving edge of the rustic cypress casing that framed the opening. If he'd been his usual self, Sam could have probably killed the man with the force of that blow, but even as it was, his opponent's skull still struck the wood hard enough to stun him and drop him to his knees. The interrogator hadn't expected the attack at all, focused as he was on the gunfire outside. Before he could recover from the disorientation and searing pain, Sam reached down to his waist and ripped the pistol out of the holster at his side, and then raised it to bring the baseplate of the weapon's magazine down like a hammer to the top of his head. This had the desired effect of putting the man completely on the floor and bought Sam time to step back and create distance, before he could recover. Sam leveled the weapon as he took a deep breath and stabilized his stance. By now the shooting outside had erupted into a two-way exchange from both sides that included full-auto bursts, mostly out in the direction of the front gate, where Sam knew the one road led in from the west. It sounded like someone was firing from inside the lodge too, so he knew that not all the soldiers had left the building. But regardless of their close proximity, Sam figured there was enough noise that a single pop from a pistol would hardly be noticed above the din, so he didn't hesitate to squeeze the trigger. A merciful bullet to the back of the head was hardly just revenge for all the torment this man had put Sam through since his arrival, but it was better than no revenge at all.

Sam grabbed the dead soldier by the boots and pulled him inside far enough that he could shut the door after reaching out there to grab the padlock off the hasp. Then, he searched the man's pockets until he found the key ring with a key that fit it, as well as several similar keys that he figured might work with the locks on the other rooms. Sam had to locate his friends and release them too, and he knew he had to move fast when he did and not waste time fumbling with keys in the process. He kept the ones that were similar pinched between a thumb and forefinger, and approached the door to crack it open again, this time just enough to have a look out into the breezeway and listen for any sounds of people in the other rooms of the building.

The shooting had slacked up by now, but there was someone, maybe more than one, still firing a rifle from up near the front of the lodge, and to Sam it sounded like it was coming from the corner room on the opposite side of the central breezeway, the one that faced out to the west and the entrance to the compound. That seemed to be where most of the incoming fire was originating, and every time shots went off from that room, Sam heard multiple rounds of return fire in answer. He could even hear the impact of the bullets smacking the wooden walls and wondered how whoever was inside up there had managed to avoid getting hit. The attack was intense, and it seemed those responsible had quickly gained the upper hand, based on the limited response Sam was now hearing from elsewhere in the compound.

The fact that he'd never heard the big machine gun up on the deck above the roof was telling, and Sam was certain now that it had indeed been a falling body he'd heard earlier, leaving the weapon up there unmanned and useless. The attackers had planned well, so it seemed, and Sam knew he had to be careful to avoid being seen by them too, because whoever they were, it was unlikely they would distinguish between him and the defenders of the outpost. But he would worry about who they were and figure out how to avoid them later. His more pressing concern was keeping out of sight of any of the defending soldiers still inside the building or pinned down somewhere nearby.

The rifle fire from up at the front of the building continued sporadically, and Sam was pretty sure there were two shooters up there, from the way the reports overlapped. He knew they were focused on whatever targets they were seeing outside, and he considered that if he could slip up there and enter the room behind them, he could dispatch them like he'd done the interrogator before anyone realized he'd escaped. But the thing that gave him second thoughts was the possibility that it could go wrong, and he could be killed before his friends had a chance to escape. Considering this, Sam determined he needed to find and free them first. And as long as those guys were preoccupied with the gunfight, Sam had an opportunity to slip out into the breezeway and look around.

He opened the door just enough to step out and then replaced and locked the padlock on the outside behind him, to make anyone passing by think he was still secure inside and to prevent them from finding their dead comrade. There was another closed door on the opposite side of the corridor, directly adjacent to his, but that one wasn't fitted with an outside hasp, so Sam dismissed the room behind it as a potential location for his friends. He followed the breezeway towards the rear of the building, passing two more doors without padlocks before getting close enough to see the last two, on opposite sides of the corridor at each corner where it ended and opened onto a wide back porch. He was hopeful, because from where he stood now, he could see that those two were locked, the same as his had been.

Sam could see the river in the distance behind the lodge, but there was a narrow strand of woods between it and the back of the compound, and he was certain some of the incoming rifle fire he'd heard had originated from that direction too. He knew that if he walked directly up to those doors, situated so close to the end of the breezeway, he'd likely come into view of any snipers concealed among those trees. Since he figured they'd probably shoot at any target they saw moving in the building or anywhere else in the compound, Sam wasn't taking any foolish chances. The only way to safely approach those doors was to drop to the deck and crawl down there on his belly, staying close to one wall. He'd be screwed if one of the defending soldiers suddenly stepped into the breezeway from one of the front rooms or from the stairs, but he had to take that chance. It would also be painful, bruised and sore as he was, but Sam pushed the pain out of his mind and lowered himself to the rough planking. It was better to abuse his battered knees and elbows than to take a bullet to the head.

When he reached the first door, he pressed his body as close to the wall as possible as he raised himself to one knee and tried the first key, and then another and another until finally, the lock popped open. Sam had no reservations about quickly scooting into the dimly illuminated room while staying low to the floor, since it had been locked from the outside and obviously wouldn't be occupied by the enemy.

The windows were boarded over like those in his own room, but with the door still ajar behind him to let in some light, Sam could see a figure backing away from him on the floor, terrified at his sudden entrance. It only took a glance to recognize that it was Charlie, from the short, stocky shape of his body and the bushy, full beard. Sam couldn't risk leaving the door open any longer, so that the two of them could see each other, so he called out to Charlie as he quickly pulled it shut behind him.

"It's me, Charlie! It's Sam! Are you okay?"

"I don't know anything!" Charlie replied with panic in his voice. "I've already told you everything I know!"

"It's okay, Charlie. I'm not one of them. I told you, it's me: *Sam!* No one's going to hurt you! We're getting out of here!"

"We're not getting out! They're shooting everybody! They've been shooting all morning! Can't you hear it? They've already shot everybody but me!"

"No! That's not what you heard, Charlie! They didn't shoot me, and they're not going to shoot you, either. Someone is attacking them! That's what you're hearing, and that's why I'm here! I got out of where they had me locked up and I got ahold of the keys so I could get you and Marcus and Darryl out too. But we've got to hurry! We've got to find both of them and then we've got to figure out how we can get out of this building!"

Sam crawled closer to reassure Charlie it was really him. "Are you okay, man? How bad are you hurt? Sam knew they must have beaten him the same as they had him, which was why he was so terrified at someone entering the room. But the truth was that Charlie was much worse.

"My knee!" He stammered. "It's busted up good! I can't walk. I can't even stand up. One of those guys kicked me in the knee with a heavy boot while I had all my weight on it. Kicked me so hard I heard something break. It's killing me, Sam! It hurts so bad I can hardly take it!"

Sam moved closer now until he could just make out Charlie's leg in the poor light. His friend wasn't exaggerating. Charlie's right knee was swollen to double the size of the other one. It really did look as bad as he said it was, and this was bad news for all of them. If Charlie couldn't even stand or walk, he damned sure couldn't run or fight. He was going to need help just getting out of the room, and especially getting down those steps to the ground. Sam could help him, but in the pain he was in himself, it wouldn't be easy, and the best they'd be able to do was hobble slowly along. Moving fast was out of the question. Sam knew the only thing he could do was leave him where he was for the moment so he could go look for Marcus and Darryl and hope like hell they weren't in the same kind of shape. With any luck at all, they were both in that other locked room across from Charlie's.

"I think Marcus is over there," Charlie said, when Sam told him about the other room. "I heard screaming and yelling that way several times and I'm pretty sure it sounded like Marcus. I don't know about Darryl."

"I'll go see," Sam said. "But don't worry, I'll be back to get you whether I find them or not."

Sam stopped behind the closed door to listen before exiting Charlie's room. He'd been so intent on determining his friend's condition that he'd barely noticed the extended lull in the shooting outside. *Did it mean the resistance inside the compound had been eliminated, and that the attackers were about to move in? Or did they pull back for some reason and leave?* It made going out there in the breezeway again a riskier proposition than it had been the first time, because without the occasional rifle shot from up there at the front of the lodge, Sam couldn't know where the one or two guys he'd heard up there before were now. If they weren't pinned down in that room, they could be anywhere, including right out there in the breezeway. It was a tense moment when Sam, with pistol in hand, pulled the door open far enough that he could peek outside and check. But the way was clear when he did, so he dropped to the floor and crawled out, keeping pressed to the wall while he closed the hasp behind him and placed the lock so that it appeared secure but was really open so he could quickly remove it upon his return. He knew Charlie wasn't going anywhere on his own with that shattered knee, so it wouldn't hurt a thing to make it look as if he were still locked in, just in case.

Sam kept as low to the deck of the corridor as possible and crawled across to the opposite door. When he got there, he moved in tight against the wall as he'd done on the other side and sorted through the keys while glancing down the breezeway for any indication of movement. This time, the second key he tested was the one, and the lock was off and in his pocket in seconds. Sam pushed the door open and peered inside. It was as empty of furnishings and other objects in there as his own room had been, and to his dismay, it appeared unoccupied as well.

A sudden wave of anxiety washed over him as he remembered those pistol shots he'd heard the day before. *Could they have really done what he'd feared they would do?* Sam pushed the door open a bit wider so he could crawl the rest of the way in and get out of view of the corridor. If the room was empty, he wouldn't waste any time there, but he wanted to at least check for clues as to who had been there. But he had barely gotten his head fully inside when he felt the door slam into the side of it hard enough that he was seeing stars as he went down. A weight landed on top of him as soon as he fell, and Sam realized that it was a person. *He was being physically attacked!* He had dropped the pistol when the door hit him, and he couldn't even feel around on the floor for it because his most pressing problem was protecting his head and face from whatever his attacker tried to hit him with next. He managed to get one hand over the back of his head just in time, but the blow he was prepared for never came:

"*Sam!*"

Sam was dazed and barely understood as he heard his name repeated again and turned his head enough to look up at the man who had quickly moved off of him and was now apologizing profusely. *It was Marcus!*

"I didn't expect it to be *you* coming in here, of all people, Sam! I thought it was one of those soldiers! I heard all that shooting and knew something big was going on. When I heard the lock opening, I figured this was my last chance if I was going to do anything to get out of here. I hid behind the door and as soon as I saw a head come in, I slammed it! I'm sorry about that! I'm glad it didn't knock you out!"

"Me too!" Sam said, as he pulled himself the rest of the way into the room and rolled over, still a little addled and in a lot of pain from the new blow to his already battered head. "Shut that door quick, Marcus! I don't know who's still here in the building, but there was at least two of them up there shooting at whoever is out there in the woods!"

Marcus did and then he knelt next to him to help Sam sit up.

"Are you gonna be okay? I know I hit you pretty hard. I was planning to kill whoever came through that door! When I saw it open and saw something coming in, I just reacted without checking who it was!"

"I'll live," Sam said. "It's not the hardest I've been hit since I've been here, I'll tell you that."

"You too? I'm not surprised," Marcus said. "I thought they were going to beat me to death the first time it happened. How in the world did you get out? And where did you get this?" He handed Sam the pistol he'd dropped. "What about Charlie and Darryl? Are they out too?"

Sam told him what he knew. "I don't know where to look for Darryl now since this is the last room I found with a lock on it. He must not be in the building unless he's up front somewhere close to where that shooting was coming from. I didn't want to go that way until I checked the rest of the rooms first. I was hoping to get you all together first so we could find a way out without having to deal with those guys, but now it looks like we don't have a choice, unless they've already been hit by whoever's been doing all that shooting at them.

"But if that's the case, we've got to worry about them shooting us too. I doubt they'll differentiate between us and the men trying to defend this place. They're going to be coming in here to hunt down the survivors, I'd imagine. I don't know how we're going to hide from them, and sure don't know how we'd ever slip out of here without them seeing us, but we've got to take this thing one step at a time. The two of us working together can help Charlie, but it won't do any good if any of those soldiers still holding out in here see us. The way I see it, I've got to try and take them out if they're still up there in one of those front rooms. If they are, they won't be expecting trouble from inside. If they already got hit, we won't have to worry about them, but we won't know without checking. Either way, there's a good chance of getting our hands on a rifle or two, and that's a start!"

Sam checked the magazine in the Beretta M9 he'd taken and confirmed that it was only down one round. He still had fifteen more available counting the one in the chamber, and if he needed more than that his plan probably wasn't going to work anyway. He intended to slip up to the door of the room where those guys were and shoot them from behind. A stealth attack was the only way to even the odds, and it was a quicker death than any of these men deserved, but the priority now was eliminating the threat. Marcus tried to argue that both of them ought to go, but Sam cut him off. "I don't need any help pulling a trigger, and you're unarmed anyway, so there's no sense in both of us going. If it goes wrong and something happens to both of us, Charlie and Darryl won't stand a chance, so keep that in mind. I'm going to pass right by the room where I left Charlie. He's bound to be getting anxious after seeing me and then being left alone again. You can go in there and wait with him and tell him what's going on. It'll be the third room on your right heading towards the front. You'll see where I left it dummy-locked."

Marcus didn't like being left out, but reluctantly agreed that Sam was probably right. Sam asked him to wait until he was closer into position near the last door at the front end of the breezeway before going to Charlie's room. He wanted to be in easy handgun range if the soldiers that had been shooting or anyone else suddenly stepped out into the corridor. When he started that way, he kept as close to the wall on the right side as possible, the pistol held at high ready in a two-handed grip in front of his chest. Sam kept his breathing slow and deep in an attempt to control his racing heart rate during the nerve-wracking approach. It was impossible to know what he was going to run into, because it had been quiet up there for several long minutes now. He had just about convinced himself that the last soldier in the lodge was dead when a sudden rifle report from within the walls broke the silence and told him otherwise.

This time, he could tell for sure that it was coming from right where he suspected, in that corner room looking out towards the entrance to the compound. Sam moved as quickly as he could, hoping to get to the shooter while his attention was still focused on whatever he'd just fired at. When he reached the outside of the door behind which he knew he would find him, Sam could see out of the breezeway past the front gate to the road. Several inert bodies were sprawled where they had fallen in the gravel out there, some of them wearing the camouflage that was the standard attire of the soldiers on the post. Sam's gaze followed the road farther out to where it disappeared into the woods, looking for any sign of the attackers, and as he did an approaching vehicle caught his attention. It wasn't a military vehicle like the one he'd been brought here in though; it was an ordinary dark gray, full-sized SUV, and considering the timing, Sam figured it was associated with whoever had mounted this attack on the outpost. He saw it slow and come to a stop well short of where the bodies would have forced the driver to detour around them in order to reach the gate. But as much as Sam wanted to see what happened next, so he'd know what was going on out there, he knew he was running out of time.

He twisted the knob quietly with his left hand and cracked the door just enough to see inside. The soldier behind the front wall was on his knees, his rifle clutched in front of him as he sat with his head back and away from a small slotted opening through which he'd apparently been shooting. Empty cartridge cases littered the floor around him, and the man appeared tense and strained to the limit. Whether he heard the opening door or simply sensed the danger lurking behind him, he suddenly turned his head to look, but Sam had already taken aim and as the soldier's eyes went wide, he squeezed the trigger.

FIVE

"Can you see them yet? Is it the convoy that left this morning?" Eric asked, as he keyed the transmitter of his handheld in response to Diane's frantic message. He glanced back into the perimeter at Keith and Willis, waiting until his brother looked his way to hold the radio up to his ear as a signal to let him know that something was going on. Eric wanted desperately to move in there with them and clear those buildings as planned, but he had to know what was coming down that road first. If it was the convoy, then Keith and Willis were going to have to pull back too. Eric didn't want them caught in there in the middle of the intense firefight that would ensue, and he wasn't sure how they'd handle the situation since they hadn't secured even one of the buildings yet or even verified the presence of the prisoners they came to get out. He looked back at the radio, impatiently waiting for it to come to life again so he'd have some answers. A few moments later, it did:

"It's not any of the Army Humvees," Diane said. "It's just one vehicle; a gray SUV. I think it's a GMC, maybe a Yukon? I can't see who's in it, because the windows are tinted really dark."

Eric considered the implications of this new development. He doubted some random civilian had turned off the highway and gotten lost on the intricate web of backroads that led to this isolated place. Maybe that could have happened a few months ago, but the way things were now, folks weren't out wandering the roads anywhere, and especially not around here, where these soldiers and their contractor cohorts were working so diligently to round them up and move them out of the area. Besides, Diane's description of the vehicle led Eric to suspect that it wasn't driven there by accident. The contractors and the cartels working with them favored those kinds of big SUVs, as well as the four-door pickups he'd already encountered so many of when dealing with them. Eric didn't know why one had come here now, but the timing was unfortunate, at best.

He pointed to the radio again and waved to Keith and Willis to proceed without him after indicating that he was going to remain outside and head around towards the front of the compound. Keith would know it had to do with something Diane and Cindy had seen out there, and that it didn't warrant having him and Willis withdraw. If it had been the convoy with all those returning soldiers, then it would have been a different story, of course, but as it was, Eric figured one SUV with a few C.R.I. contractors or similar unsavory characters wasn't enough to make them scrap the mission and withdraw. He moved back quickly to where Lenny and Trey were concealed to tell them where he was going and to let them know it was up to them to provide backup for Keith and Willis and to keep the river-facing side of the perimeter secured. Eric kept the conversation brief. It was a long way around to the road the way he had to go, keeping within the cover of the woods, and he was already on the way and about to call Diane back when her voice broke over the radio again with an update.

"They drove past where we're hiding and then slowed down and came to a stop when they saw Davis and those other dead guys in the road."

"Did anyone get out of the vehicle?"

"No, they just sat there with it running for a minute, but now it's backing up, coming slowly back this way along the road."

Eric was thinking fast as he picked his way through the underbrush. He didn't want to let these guys get away, after seeing what they'd seen, because he still hadn't finished the mission here and didn't know how long it would take to do so. If those contractors or whoever they were turned around and left, they'd likely get word to someone that something had seriously gone wrong here. It would result in a response as soon as they did, either from more of their guys or another unit of soldiers, and that could be in addition to the patrol he already knew would be coming back by the end of the day. It was crucial that those guys didn't get away, but he hated to put Diane and Cindy in that position. He was just about to ask her if she thought they could stop the SUV by shooting out the tires while still remaining out of sight when her voice broke the squelch of the radio again.

"They just stopped, almost right between where Cindy and I are hiding! They backed the vehicle into some bushes off the side of the road to hide it. The front doors are open now and I can see them!"

"How many?" Eric asked.

"Two men. The driver and one other. They have rifles and it looks like they are checking their gear and discussing what they're going to do. I think they are C.R.I. contractors, like those that attacked my aunt's neighborhood..." Diane said. "And like the ones that killed Joe...."

Eric knew by the tone in her voice what Diane wanted to do, but if those two were indeed with C.R.I., it was possible they were more useful alive, even if they only lived long enough to tell him the purpose of their visit. "I'm on my way and I'll bring Hal and Steven with me," he replied. "Try to keep an eye on them and let me know which way they go when they leave the vehicle. But be careful Diane. You don't know that there aren't more of them in the back seats. I don't want you and Cindy getting into a firefight with those guys. I sent you there to be a lookout, and you're doing a great job!"

Eric was backtracking around the north side of the perimeter the same way he'd gone when he'd left Bart and stopped to get Willis. It was the shortest route to the road out there and would take him past the positions in which he'd placed Hal, Steven and Elroy. None of those positions were as critical now with most of the compound secure. Bart was watching the lodge and Trey and Lenny would prevent anyone from slipping out back towards the river. One man was sufficient to watch this side, and Eric decided to leave it to Steven. Since he was Cindy's husband, he was the most likely to compromise them in a firefight by reacting on emotions, so Eric thought it best to keep him away from it. Eric would take one of the other two with him and send the third around to the other side to update Bart. He knew his father would have seen the SUV pull up and stop there at the end of the road and then back away again, but since the old man had no radio on him, he would have no way of knowing Eric was on his way to investigate. Bart could have easily taken the occupants out had they exited the vehicle and appeared to be a threat, but since they didn't, he must have simply watched and wondered, while still keeping an eye out for movement in the lodge. And while Eric would have much preferred to have Bart go with him, as he knew nothing of Elroy's abilities and only a little more of Hal's, it was more important to keep Bart and his rifle where he could pick off any targets he saw in that building. Eric knew both of the other men were experienced hunters though, and he'd witnessed Hal moving with care and stealth the morning he met him, when he slipped up quietly behind him and subdued him in order to question him and find out who he was and why he and so many others were living out there in that hidden camp that he and Jonathan had discovered.

Eric reached Steven first and didn't have to tell him the full story, since his position was farthest from the road and he hadn't seen the approach of the SUV. Eric just told him to hang tight where he was, explaining that he was headed out to check on Diane and Cindy. When he got to where he'd left Hal and Elroy, he asked Hal to come with him and explained to Elroy that he needed him to go and inform Bart of the situation. Then he set out to lead the way and had barely gone another 50 yards before the sound of gunfire erupted from exactly where they were headed, somewhere out there on the road just beyond sight of the compound. Eric glanced back at Hal and Elroy, intending to signal to Hal that they'd better hurry to the scene and was shocked when he saw what Elroy was doing. Eric had expected him to follow the two of them all the way west until they reached the point where the road entered the woods. From there, he could work his way back around to where Bart was set up without exposing himself to fire from anyone still watching from inside the lodge building. But instead of taking that sensible precaution, the idiot had already broken cover and was running across the open ground where Sergeant Davis had been shot dead. Since he was already nearly halfway across, there was no point in trying to stop him and Eric didn't want to risk a shout that would give away his presence until he knew what had happened that resulted in all the shooting he'd just heard.

"What in the hell is he thinking?" Eric asked Hal, who looked just as baffled as Eric by his buddy's dumb move.

"He ain't thinking! That's his main problem. Elroy's pretty good in the woods, sitting still, and keeping quiet and all, but the stress of all this gunfire today has gotten to him. I guess I should have mentioned to you when he volunteered that he gets like that sometimes."

Eric was speechless. Shots rang out, and he expected at any moment to see the guy go down to a round fired from one of those little shooting ports in the front of the lodge. But it didn't happen, and now Eric realized it was Bart that had opened fire, shooting at regular intervals, no doubt aiming at those same slots to cover for Elroy after seeing him out there in the open like that. The fool somehow made it all the way across without incident, and Eric just shook his head. Either he was incredibly lucky, or Bart had already taken those shooters out, perhaps without even realizing he'd hit them. Eric would have to find out later. Right now, his priority was getting to Diane and Cindy. The shooting from their direction had stopped as abruptly as it started, and he didn't know whether that was good news or bad.

He tried the radio but got no response from Diane. He knew that didn't necessarily mean the worst though, because as close as she apparently was to the two guys she was watching, she would have turned it down or all the way off once they got out of the vehicle. Eric didn't bother to keep calling. He cautioned Hal to move carefully and stay watchful as they slipped through the woods past the place where the clearing narrowed to the single road. They had paralleled the road but a short distance when Eric spotted the front grill of the gray SUV, the only part of it that was visible the way it was backed part way into the roadside brush. He turned and motioned to Hal to sit tight and cover him, and then he slipped in closer alone. Movement in the shadows of the trees back there behind the vehicle caused him to abruptly stop and shoulder his weapon, but as he swept the undergrowth through his lens, he saw it was Cindy, walking cautiously out to the edge of the road, where she stopped as if looking for something or someone in the direction of the outpost. Cindy had her weapon at ready, and Eric didn't want to get shot, so he called out to her in a low voice before stepping out into the open.

"ERIC! I was just looking to see if you were coming! We need your help! Diane's got one of them at gunpoint back there in the woods!"

Eric whistled back to Hal to signal him to follow and then quickly crossed the road to Cindy's side. From where she was standing, he could see the body of one dead man lying face down in the leaf litter that covered the ground behind the SUV. The front doors of the vehicle were still open, and there was an urgency in Cindy's voice that couldn't wait, so Eric only glanced inside to verify it was empty as he walked by. After following Cindy past the dead guy and into the heavy woods, he finally saw Diane standing with her back to him among the trees some 30 yards in from the parked vehicle. She had her rifle to her shoulder and was pointing it downward at something in front of her that Eric couldn't see until he reached her side.

"I gave them both a chance to just stop and surrender," Diane said, as she became aware of Eric's presence and Cindy's return. "This one seemed to be complying at first, but then his partner made a quick move and turned around firing his rifle, trying to kill me. I'd be dead right now if Cindy hadn't shot him from behind from across the road. They didn't know she was with me, because she was still over there out of sight when I ordered them to stop. I knew you wanted to question them, so when this guy tried to run, I shot him in the leg instead of in the back. I'm glad you got here fast, because he's bleeding a lot more than I thought he would."

Eric stepped past her to where the wounded man was curled up on the ground in the fetal position, grimacing in pain as he tried to stop the flow of blood welling through his soaked trousers and between his clenched fingers. His rifle was nearby where he'd dropped it, but he was too focused on stopping the bleeding to try and make a move for it, and besides, he already knew Diane was willing to shoot him. Eric asked Hal to secure the weapon and then he moved closer and squatted near the desperate man.

"If you want to live, do exactly as I say and don't try anything stupid, or I'll finish what my friend here started the second you do. Got it?"

The wounded man nodded, and seeing that Eric was pulling a RATS tourniquet from its pouch on his belt, he became a little more cooperative. Still, he was so desperate to stop the bleeding that he was reluctant to relinquish his two-handed grip on his leg.

"Move your hands or I can't get it in place! You've already lost a lot of blood, but this will stop it ASAP!"

Hal had the fallen weapon, and Diane was standing by with

her rifle still covering him, but Eric wasn't concerned the man would try anything now in his injured and helpless state. Eric's more pressing concern was whether or not he could keep him alive long enough to ask him the questions he needed answers to. Diane's bullet had hit him about six inches above the knee, probably nicking the femoral artery, considering the amount of blood he'd already lost. He wouldn't have lasted much longer without help and Eric knew he might still succumb with the limited assistance he could provide.

"I'm sorry," Diane said. "I had the drop on both of them before they saw me, and I thought they would realize that and surrender when I ordered them to. But I guess it totally freaked them out that someone was out there in the woods so close by. It was a good thing I was behind a tree, or I probably would have been hit when the other guy started shooting. It was also a good thing Cindy was over there to back me up. When she got the first one and this guy realized I wasn't alone, he panicked and took off straight into the woods. I yelled at him to stop, but he didn't, so I had to shoot him."

"You did good, Diane. Both of you did. If he dies, it's not your fault. He's getting what he asked for."

"I don't know who you people are!" The man said. "I wasn't trying to kill anyone, but we saw dead guys in the road up there and we backed up, trying to get out of here! Anybody would have! When she yelled at us, we freaked out. Anybody would have, after seeing all that!"

"I'm sure you two were just out riding the backroads, enjoying the scenery, right? You come upon a bunch of dead guys, so then you back up only a short distance away to hide your vehicle and then get out with rifles? Yeah, that makes sense! That's what anybody would do, right? Well, at least you won't die right now, as long as you stay still and don't lose too much more blood." Eric stood and glanced at Hal, who along with Cindy and Diane, had been watching him work.

"Bart's probably getting anxious to know what happened after

Elroy told him we were heading out here. Go back and tell him we've got it under control and see if they need any help. I've got this, and I'll be on my way in a few minutes."

Hal headed straight east through the woods, avoiding the road, and Eric walked back to the SUV after asking Diane and Cindy to keep a watch over the wounded man on the ground. Eric wanted to look closer inside it, as the dark-tinted windows of the still closed back doors could be hiding some clue as to what the men had come there for, and he was also planning to confine the survivor in the back until he finished his business at the outpost.

Eric had little concern of finding anyone else hiding out in there after all that had happened, figuring if anyone was riding in the back, they would have joined the fight or fled the scene during all the commotion after the shooting started. Still, he approached the front of the Yukon with his finger on the trigger of his M4 as he swept the second-row seats through the windshield with his weapon light. Confident they were unoccupied, he opened the passenger's side rear door to check the floorboards, which were clear and uncluttered. A pull-down partition separated the main passenger seating from the third row or rear cargo compartment though, so Eric went to the rear gate to make his final check. He thought it plausible the men were transporting drugs or something else of value to the outpost, but the possibility that he would find what he did when he opened that rear gate had never crossed Eric's mind. As the darkness within was displaced by the flood of daylight the open door let in, Eric was shocked to see that there was another person inside the gray SUV! It was a woman, jammed in there on her side with her hands tied behind her back, her ankles likewise bound, and her mouth gagged. The woman's eyes were wide with fear as she saw Eric standing there with his weapon pointed in her direction, but he quickly lowered the muzzle and pushed the M4 to one side on its sling to reassure her he wasn't going to use it.

"I'm not going to hurt you," Eric said. "You're not in any danger now. Let me get that rag off your face so you can talk and then I'll help you out of here."

As he moved closer to untie the gag, Eric thought that the frightened woman looked vaguely familiar. She was around 40, by his estimation, but it was hard to be sure in the condition she was in, with her hair disheveled, her face bruised and dirty and her clothes grimy with dried sweat and ground in dirt. When the woman saw that he really didn't intend to hurt her, she relaxed a little and allowed him to reach for the knot securing her gag without cringing as she had when he first discovered her. And after the gag came off and she coughed and struggled to get her voice, Eric saw something change in her eyes as she watched him cut away the cords around her ankles.

"I know who you are," she said. "You're that guy from the woods! You're the reason all this happened!"

Eric looked back at her more closely. That's why she looked familiar. He must have seen her at Sam's camp! Was she one of the women taken captive that night when Debbie escaped? Eric was certain that she must be, but he hadn't met her personally because there were lots of folks in Sam's camp, and he and Jonathan had been preoccupied with planning the gunboat ambush and then getting out of there soon after. Most of his conversations had been with the handful of men who'd been a part of that, and many others he'd only met in passing. But this woman was one of Sam's friends, of that he was certain.

"What's your name?" Eric asked. "Were you with Sam Necaise the night he was taking the boats down the river?"

The woman was reluctant to say, but Eric could tell by her reaction that she was indeed one of those taken that night. "Look, you are correct, I am Eric Branson, and it's true that I'm the reason Sam decided to move everyone down the river, but neither he nor I had any idea that those soldiers had another patrol boat. I'm sorry it happened, but the reason I'm here now is to find all of you and take you back to where the others are waiting. My intel source told me that Sam and those captured with him would be brought to this place that those soldiers have been using as a base. I thought all of you were inside one of the buildings there now, and I certainly didn't expect to find you in the back of a car.

"You don't have to talk to me now though. I understand that you have been through a traumatic experience, but we've got to get moving. I'm certain that you know one of my friends I have with me, because she and her husband were living out there in the camp with you. Her name is Cindy Delacroix."

"Cindy? Cindy is here with you?"

"Right over there," Eric nodded, pointing in the direction of the woods before calling out Cindy's name.

SIX

SAM NECAISE MOVED QUICKLY INTO THE ROOM AND CLOSED the door behind him after dropping the lone occupant with a single round from the 9mm Beretta. Once inside, he took in the layout of the room, noting the heavy steel plate lining the entire front wall below the level of the window. Sam ducked low to stay behind its protection as he approached the fallen soldier to retrieve his rifle. There was plenty of light to see by in this room, most of it coming through the shattered glass of the big window above the fortified part of the wall. The dead man's weapon was an Army-issue Colt M4, with the 3-round burst mode option. Sam checked the 30-round magazine that was in it and found it half empty. A half dozen more empty mags were scattered on the floor where they'd been discarded among the spent brass. Sam made a quick search but was disappointed to find no loaded mags on the man's body or elsewhere in the room, and he realized that was why the guy's shooting had slowed to the occasional single round. He'd probably panicked in the initial onslaught and sprayed bullets wildly, hitting nothing. Sam would have preferred to have more ammo of course, but a good rifle with a dozen or so high-velocity rounds was far more than he'd had when he'd entered the room. And in checking the soldier for mags, he'd found another fully loaded Beretta pistol that matched the one he'd taken from the other guy, so now Marcus and Charlie would be armed as well.

Sam tucked the extra pistol in his belt as he scanned the room for anything else that might be of use, but there was really nothing that would help him at the moment. After peeking out one of the shooting slots and seeing nothing moving outside, Sam switch the M4 to burst mode and adjusted the sling so that he could keep a finger on the trigger and point the muzzle forward using just one hand as he carefully opened the door to exit the room. He knew it was risky to do it, but before he went back to Charlie's room to get him and Marcus, he had to clear that other room adjacent this one across the breezeway, because he was almost certain he'd heard shots fired from in there as well since the initial exchange heated up. It made sense that it would contain a protected shooting station too, since both rooms faced out the front gate and the road leading in.

Once he saw that the corridor was clear, Sam scanned the open space out front where he'd seen the dead bodies and the gray SUV. The dead men were still there, but there was no SUV. He ducked and moved as quickly as he could to the wall on the opposite side and flattened himself against it, next to the door. Keeping the M4 in tight against his torso on the sling, Sam tried the knob and found it unlocked. He had no way of knowing what would greet him behind that door, but he cracked it open anyway, again leading with the muzzle of the M4 to make his entry, and as soon as he could see inside, he knew why he'd heard no shots fired from in there since he'd come to the front of the building. There was indeed a man with a rifle in this room too, but he was as dead as the one Sam had shot across the way. The bullet that had removed a portion of the back of his skull hadn't come from a mere handgun though, and Sam knew that one of those sharpshooters outside had either gotten very lucky or was simply quite the expert. The fatal round had come from the considerable distance it was to the woods, passing through a slot barely two-inches wide. Whatever the case, finding the soldier dead solved Sam's most pressing problem, and he was confident now there were no more defenders from the post inside the big lodge building.

Discovering that the second soldier had died before wasting most of his ammo was a bonus to Sam as well. He now had a second M4 to add to his armament, as well as four more full mags and a partial. This one had no handgun on him, but it didn't matter, because Sam had weapons for everyone now, including Darryl, if they could only locate him. He returned to the room where'd he'd found Charlie to get Marcus so they could commence the search. If they were going to do this, they had to do it fast, and then figure out how they were going to get out of the building and then down to the ground level and into the woods.

"This makes me feel like we at least have a fighting chance!" Marcus said when Sam handed him one of the M4s.

"We do, I reckon, but you can bet the 'fighting' part is going to be the biggest part of any chance we may have. I still don't know what we're up against out there." Sam told him about the SUV he'd seen pull up, and how it was gone when he looked back out a few minutes later. "Whoever it was, they must be in cahoots with the ones shooting up the place, since they pulled up out there in the open like that."

Sam left one of the Berettas with Charlie and then he and Marcus left the room again to do a quick check of all those other rooms he'd seen that didn't have hasps and padlocks on the outside of their doors. He'd dismissed them the first time around as unlikely places to find his missing companions, but now he was out of options. The search turned up nothing, however, other than to reveal that those other rooms had indeed been used as troop barracks, just as Sam had suspected. They found several cots set up in each of them, along with personal effects and numerous sets of the Multicam BDU uniforms the soldiers in the unit wore.

"Damn these things stink! They smell like they've been rinsed in the river once or twice, but without any soap," Marcus said.

"You know after I shot that interrogator, it occurred to me that putting on his uniform might make it easier to get by the other guards and get out of here. I was even gonna suggest it to the rest of you when I found you. But that was before I knew that whoever was attacking the place was gonna get the upper hand. Wearing these would only make us targets now I suppose. It seems to me those bastards running this operation have had their asses kicked for real. I don't imagine whoever did it will treat us any different though, and looking like the folks they came here to wipe out will guarantee they won't."

"I'm glad we won't need them," Marcus said, tossing the jacket he'd picked up back onto the cot where he'd found it. "But how are we going to get by whoever it is out there? And what about Darryl? We can't leave without Darryl."

"Well to answer your first question, I don't know. Maybe we can negotiate with them? Maybe just flat-out tell them we're prisoners here against our own will and have nothing to do with the operation here? Sort of like saying we may not be your friends, but we're the enemy of your enemy so that gives up something in common, right? And as for Darryl, I reckon the only other place he could be is in one of those other two buildings down there. And getting in either one won't be easy unless they let us."

Sam had barely finished his sentence when shooting erupted again, in the very direction of those buildings.

"Whatever's going on out there, it's not finished yet," Marcus said.

"No, and even if we weren't looking for Darryl, you know the two of us can't get Charlie out of here in a hurry in the shape he's in. If it was just you and me, we could take our chances and try to climb down from that back deck then maybe fight our way to the river, but not with him. No way."

Leaving Charlie hadn't crossed Sam's mind any more than leaving Darryl, of course. There was just no way he would do it, knowing he was laid up in that room, suffering the pain those evil bastards had inflicted upon him. Sam knew Marcus wouldn't consider it either, and that the two of them would go down fighting rather than abandon either of their friends. He just wished they'd found Darryl first so they could all fight together, but since he wasn't in the building, Sam had to think again that maybe the soldiers had already done away with him. There was the matter of all those pistol shots he'd heard, after all.

"We've gotta figure something else out," he told Marcus, "but before we can do that, we've got to try and get a better idea of the situation and what we're up against. I was just thinking about that observation deck up on the roof, where they've got that machine gun set up. The way the stairs go up to it from inside the building, it's possible to get up there without anyone outside seeing."

"You're not thinking of going up there and trying to use that machine gun, are you? Didn't you say they shot the soldier that was up there? You heard him hit the roof, right? You'll be an easy target like he was if you go up there, Sam."

"I'm not talking about using the gun, at least not yet. I'm just gonna climb up the steps until I'm high enough to crawl out on that deck on my belly and get a look around. There's a railing all the way around it and they've got sandbags around the gun. I don't think anyone'll notice as long as I stay low and don't hang around too long, especially since they already shot that gunner and no other soldiers in here tried to go up there to replace him. I think it's worth the risk to look, because that deck is the highest place around here, and you can see a full 360 degrees from up there."

"Do you want me to come with you, and help you look?"

"Nah, there's no sense in both of us going. Besides, Charlie's bound to be getting anxious, hearing more shooting out there and all, and not knowing where we are. Why don't you go back and check on him and make sure he knows we're not gonna leave him, no matter what!"

Marcus left and Sam made his way to the middle of the corridor to the foot of the narrow stairway that ascended to the small deck. It was a strenuous climb in his condition, because the steep roofline of the main building peaked 20 feet above the corridor. The observation deck had been built so that it essentially straddled the peak and was accessed through an opening at the top that was protected from the weather by the second roof over the upper deck itself. It was a unique and interesting design, like the rest of the big lodge building, but Sam figured the architect probably hadn't considered the defensive capabilities that were built into it by accident.

As he neared the opening at the top of the steps, Sam felt the pleasantly dry air of a late fall day, cool and refreshing for south Louisiana. But it was the blood dripping from one side of the framed opening that he noticed more than the weather. As soon as he was close enough to look over the rim onto the edge of the deck, Sam saw where it was coming from. There was another dead guy up there, and seeing the body, he realized there must have been two of them on the deck when the shooting started, because he was certain he'd heard one fall and hit the roof on the way down. He couldn't avoid the blood since he had to crawl through it to stay as flat as possible to the deck, and there was a lot of it since the soldier had been shot in the neck and had bled out where he fell. Sam didn't want to end up the same way, and he'd seen more than enough evidence that whoever it was that attacked this outpost had some superb sharpshooters among their ranks. He had no idea where they were hiding or if they were even still there, but Sam figured they were somewhere down there in that narrow strip of woods between the lodge and the river. With the dense undergrowth that was typical of the bottomland forests everywhere around here, picking them out would be nearly impossible unless they were moving. But Sam didn't plan to try anyway. He was up here to take in the big picture and figure out what was happening in the rest of the compound. He wanted to know if the attackers had begun to move in to seize control of the buildings, and whether or not there were any defending soldiers still alive and trying to stop them. He figured if he could just get a glimpse of some of them, he might be able to tell whether the attackers were soldiers or perhaps from some other kind of organization like a militia or band of hired mercenaries. It was even possible that they were the good guys, even though Sam hadn't seen any evidence of any good guys coming here to help the residents of the region since the hurricane had hit months before. And what he learned from talking to Eric Branson seemed to confirm his hunch that there seemed to be a lot more bad than good headed this way.

Sam was still curious about that gray SUV he'd seen pull up to the edge of the compound and he'd thought that maybe from this higher vantage point he would see it and perhaps some other vehicles the attackers may have arrived in. But even from up there, only a short stretch of the road leading in was visible through the woods, and there was nothing on the section that he could see. Using the magnified optic sight on the M4 he'd taken off of the soldier he'd killed, Sam studied the bodies he'd seen out there in front of the gate earlier. There were six of them in all—one farther out, apart from the others—and the other five relatively close together, as if they'd been cut down in a group. Sam noted that two of the dead men wore the same pattern of camo BDUs all the soldiers here wore, while the other four were in T-shirts, running shorts and boots. He figured they were the men he'd heard scrambling to leave the building before all the shooting started, and that there must have been some last-minute warning that trouble was coming that caused them to run out like that without fully dressing. The clean BDUs he and Marcus had found were left unused.

Sam had seen enough to convince himself that the defenders here had failed in a major way, and he was about to see what he could pick out among the other buildings with the riflescope when another exchange of gunfire rang out from out there in the direction of the road. He still didn't see a vehicle or anything else out there, but then sudden movement at the edge of the woods on the north side of the compound caught his eye. Sam was pretty sure the shooting hadn't come from there, but it seemed to have caused a lone man to run straight out into the open, heading in the direction of the dead bodies. He could see even without the help of the scope that this man wasn't wearing the uniform of the soldiers posted here. He had on a camouflage jacket, but it was more of a hunting pattern than military, and it didn't go with the brown work trousers he was wearing with it. The man was carrying an AR-type rifle though, and Sam had to assume he was probably one of the attackers, especially since he'd emerged from the woods out beyond the edge of the clearing. Sam brought his rifle in line with him to get a better look, and as he tracked the running man's face through the glass, his jaw dropped in disbelief. It was impossible, but it was none other than Elroy Roberts, a fellow Sam had known most all his life, and one of the men who'd been camped with them in their hideaway down on the Atchafalaya!

Elroy ran past the dead soldiers with barely a glance in their direction. He seemed to be focused on something else, but Sam couldn't tell what. Sam wanted to get his attention, but he didn't know how to do it without giving himself away to whoever else could be out there watching. It made no sense at all that Elroy Roberts would be here, of all places, but there he was, running in plain view. Sam was just about to go ahead and shout anyway, when a rifle rang out from someplace he couldn't pinpoint, and he feared he was about to see his friend bite the dust. But more shots followed the first, and now Sam could hear the bullet impacts to the front of the building below him. Elroy kept running until he disappeared from view into the woods on the southwest side of the gate, and then the shooting stopped. Someone was covering for Elroy, shooting at those barricaded positions in the front of the building where they'd already killed the one soldier in that southwest corner room before Sam killed the one in the room opposite. Sam knew that could only mean one thing, as crazy as the idea of it was: *Elroy Roberts was part of the attacking force that just decimated this outpost!*

SEVEN

"Brenda? Is that really you?" Cindy cried out, when Eric led the frightened woman back into the woods to the spot where he'd left Cindy and Diane to stand watch over the wounded man from the SUV. "Where did she come from?" Cindy asked Eric, the confusion written all over her face.

"They had her in the back of the vehicle! Tied up and gagged. I thought she looked familiar, and then she recognized me too. She saw me when I met all of you at your camp, but I don't remember meeting her personally. There were several people there I didn't really have a chance to talk to."

"Her name is Brenda. Brenda Benoit. She's Charlie's wife, Eric! She and Charlie and their two boys were definitely with Sam and the others on the river that night! But why would she be alone in a car with these guys?"

"I don't know, but I knew she would know you and was hoping she'd tell you. She's been through a lot; that's obvious."

Eric remembered the name now. Many of the folks in Sam's group had the French surnames that were so typical of the region, and he remembered Brenda and Charlie Benoit, because Debbie had spoken of them when she related her story. She had told him they had two young boys with them and that the boys were so annoying she was riding in the towed pirogue rather than in the john boat with them and her father. But like Cindy had asked, if they had all been taken together, then how did Brenda end up in the back of that SUV alone? And why were the two men bringing her here to this outpost today? Eric was afraid to ask for the details, but he could plainly see that Brenda was comfortable with Cindy the moment she saw her. But then she also saw the wounded man that Cindy and Diane were standing over at gunpoint and the sight caused her to recoil and turn away.

"It's okay," Cindy said, as she came over and put an arm around her. "You're safe now, and he can't hurt you. He's lucky to still be alive, but Eric has questions to ask him. We came here to get all of you out and take you back where you'll be safe. You just need to tell us where everyone else is. Do you know where Brian and Cameron are? What about Charlie?"

Brenda shook her head at first and then looked back at the vehicle and the dead man lying beside it, and then back to the wounded one Diane was still watching. "My poor boys are still back there at that awful place where we've been the whole time! I don't know what's going to happen to them! I was there with them and with Phyllis and Suzanne until they took Phyllis away yesterday and then came and got me today. They said I would see my husband soon, but I haven't seen him since the night they stopped us on the river! They wouldn't tell me where he was, but today those two men came and got me and took me out to that truck, saying they were taking me to see him," Brenda looked at the SUV again. "But then they tied me up and put that rag in my mouth. They picked me up and crammed me into the back and drove off. I was certain that they were lying and that they were just taking me somewhere to kill me, and when they finally stopped here and opened the doors, I figured it was about to happen then. I could hear them cocking their guns before they got out, and I knew any minute they were going to open the back and drag me out of there to shoot me! But then, I heard a lot of gunfire and I wondered why I didn't feel any pain, even after I kept hearing the shots. I thought they were shooting at me, but maybe they were missing! Now I see that they were the ones who got shot."

"You heard one of them trying to shoot my friend Diane first," Cindy said. "And that's why he's dead now. I shot him myself, and Diane shot the other one you see over there as he was trying to run away. We had no idea anyone else was in that vehicle though, or we would have already gotten you out."

Brenda was quiet for a moment, and clearly confused. "Where are we, Cindy? And how did you get here?"

"It's a long story, but Eric Branson is the reason we were able to find this place. He got information that the outpost right down there at the end of this road is where Sam and all of you were supposed to have been taken. We thought you were all still in there, but now you're saying you never were. Maybe they just brought your husbands here?"

"I don't know," Brenda said. "I haven't been anywhere but that one horrible place they called a 'refugee' camp since we were taken away that night. They had us locked up in wire cages that looked like big dog kennels or something. We were afraid they had already killed our husbands, since they didn't take them there with us. Yesterday, when they came and took Phyllis away, we didn't know where they were going with her, or why, but we knew it wasn't good. When they came and got me today, I knew that whatever happened to her was probably going to happen to me too.

"How many other people like you were detained there at this place?" Eric asked. "Were there any men at all or just more women and children?"

"I don't know how many... but there were a lot. I mostly saw other women and children—but there were some men there too—just not our men. I heard they were taking the men out somewhere every day and making them work, because the man that brought our food and water told me he'd been going with them when they first brought him there. He said the work was so hard it nearly killed him."

"So, he was being detained there as well?" Eric asked.

"Yes, but I don't know why. We were barely able to talk to him because the guards were always watching.

"I know you couldn't see anything on the way here, confined and tied up in the back of the vehicle the way you were, but do you have any sense of where this place was? Maybe how far away it was, and in which direction? Do you have a rough idea of how long you were in there while the vehicle was moving?" Brenda was still in shock and clearly disoriented, but Eric could tell she was doing her best to think about it before she answered.

"It seemed like we were moving a long time because I couldn't see anything. But then, when we stopped, I remember thinking how scared I was, because then it didn't seem very far at all and I was hoping it would be a longer ride, because I was sure that when the ride was over, it was all going to be over for me. So, I want to say it was at least an hour, but probably less than two hours. But we weren't going all that fast, like on a highway. It was all on backroads, I think, because there were lots of bumps and there were sharp curves that caused me to roll and slide around back there. And I knew the last part of the drive before we stopped was on gravel, because I could hear the small rocks popping and crunching under the tires."

Eric had heard enough from Brenda for now. He had a lot more to ask her about that camp she described, but it would have to wait until the mission here was complete. But the intel he got from here was useful indeed. He wasn't going to find Sam's entire party here and complete the rescue in one operation as he'd hoped, despite what Sergeant Davis had led him to believe about this place. That was a disappointment, and it presented a new set of problems, but once again Diane and Cindy had done a stellar job with no help from him. The two guys in that SUV were clearly bringing Brenda

Benoit here for some specific reason, but seeing the dead bodies and open gate out front, they had retreated to hide the vehicle and move in on foot with their weapons to investigate. Diane had bravely confronted them, and now one was dead, and the other in custody to be interrogated. Eric would get his answers now that he'd ensured the guy wouldn't bleed out before he could talk. But first he had to see that Keith and Willis were okay and find out whether or not they'd eliminated all the threats in those ground floor buildings. If they had, the only resistance remaining was the shooter or shooters that Bart had reported in the front rooms of the elevated lodge. Eric would get them out, whatever it took, and with any luck at all, find Sam and the other men that Brenda hadn't seen since the night of their capture.

"That's helpful information, Brenda. If anything else comes to mind, no matter how insignificant it may seem, please tell Cindy. I need you to wait here with her while I finish up what I have to do. You'll be safe here with her and Diane."

"You have to help me get my boys out of there! I'm not going anywhere without them!"

Eric promised her he would, and then he walked back over to where Diane was watching the wounded man and squatted down beside him. "If you want to live, you'd better start talking. This woman who already shot you once will be asking the questions until I get back, and believe me, if I hadn't already persuaded her not to, she would have killed both of you when you first got out of that vehicle. And that was before we knew about the woman you had in the back. Her husband was murdered by men like you. I know who you're working for, and I know what your organization is up to. You're going to tell Diane here where you brought the woman from today, and where they are holding her two sons and the other two women that were with her!"

Eric took Diane aside before he left, speaking to her in a low voice the wounded captive couldn't hear. "He's lost a lot of blood and he may pass out, but I can't spend any more time on him until I know that compound is secure. Just try to get details from him if you can... where that camp is... how many men they have guarding it... anything you can think of that will help us! I don't know how long he'll last, so get what you can out of him. He may be the only source we have, other than Brenda, and she's understandably traumatized and confused."

BART BRANSON HAD FOCUSED MOST OF HIS ATTENTION ON THE big lodge building since taking out the gate guard at the beginning of the assault. The reinforced shooting positions up there in those two front rooms were an unexpected complication, and not knowing whether or not there was still someone holed up in one of them made moving forward risky for the entire team. Bart thought he'd gotten one of them in the room on the southwest corner though. He'd already had his reticle fixed on one of the two shooting ports there when the muzzle of a rifle appeared, so he was able to squeeze off a round instantly, while the shooter's head was behind his own optic. The weapon in the slot seemed to fall away, rather than get yanked back deliberately, and there hadn't been another shot fired from that room since. But he hadn't had a similar opportunity to get the shooter in the other room, and so it had turned into a long stalemate, with the enemy effectively protected by whatever hard cover they had up there, and Bart so well camouflaged and hidden that anyone looking for him down there within the edge of the trees wouldn't have a chance in hell of spotting him unless he moved.

Bart's motivation to take out those shooters was enhanced by the fact that he knew his two sons, Eric and Keith would be the first ones going in to clear those buildings. It wasn't the first time he'd been put in that situation, covering for them though, and Bart knew they were the best men here for the job. He also trusted Eric's decision to take Willis with him. But though he was a patient man, Bart was getting anxious because of all the delays and new developments since Eric had told him what he planned to do and had left to get Willis and Keith. He'd heard gunfire around there on the back side of the compound where he knew they were going in first, and that was not unexpected. What was unexpected was what happened shortly after, when Bart noticed movement out of the corner of his eye and looked back to the road to see a gray SUV rolling to a stop out there where Sergeant Davis lay dead in the gravel.

Bart had immediately repositioned his rifle to try and see who was in that vehicle, but two things worked against him, the heavy tinting of the side windows and an impossible glare on the windshield because of the way the vehicle was facing into the midmorning sun. Frustrated by the impossibility of seeing who was inside, Bart had watched to see if the doors would open, but after a minute or so of sitting there motionless, the vehicle began moving in reverse back along the road from which it came. Bart noted that the driver hadn't panicked though, as a normal person probably would have, coming upon a scene like that. He had a strong suspicion that the occupants of that vehicle were unperturbed by the sight of death, and he was certain they must have had business here with the soldiers manning this outpost. Watching the SUV back away, Bart was torn as to whether he should let them escape. He knew he could shoot into the front passenger area and likely hit the driver, whether he could see him or not, but there was that very small chance that doing so would be a mistake, and he couldn't bring himself to fire at someone he couldn't see that hadn't proven to be an enemy. The thought of it reminded him of that night when he was keeping watch over his boatyard on the Caloosahatchee River. He'd already shot several looters he'd caught in the act there in the chaos after the hurricane. Some had come in kayaks, sneaking in late at night, and when he picked out the shadowy form of yet another one landing on the narrow beach in front of the property, Bart had watched the figure through his scope with his finger firmly on the trigger. Less than four pounds of pressure was all that determined the balance between life and death for his target, and the last second recognition of his son's face when the man turned his head was closer than Bart Branson ever wanted to come to making a mistake like that again.

Bart knew that Diane and Cindy were watching the road out there and that they would have seen the vehicle approaching well before he did. He knew they must be aware of it leaving too, but when they hurriedly put this rescue mission together, there had been no time to go back to their base at Sierra Zulu and get enough handhelds for every person on the team. Eric had asked Diane to call him on the VHF if they saw something, and he knew she would, but if Eric was already inside with Keith and Willis as Bart figured he was, there was little he could do. And if he was in close and suspected there were still tangos in there, he would have turned the radio volume all the way down or off and may not be aware of the vehicle's appearance at all.

Bart wished he could call Diane himself and see if it kept going or not, but a few minutes later, he didn't have to wonder. Several shots fired from that direction told him it was likely the women had an encounter with whoever was in the SUV. But Bart couldn't leave his hide and go see what had happened, because doing so would give whoever was up there in that building a chance to reposition or escape. He had to sit there waiting instead, the not knowing causing him to get more agitated by the minute. Bart was ready to kill that last soldier in the building, even if he had to go up there and do it up close and personal. He was just about to move his rifle back around and glass the shooting ports again when another movement from across the compound caught his eye. This time, it was a person running, and Bart didn't need his scope to see that it was Elroy, one of the volunteers from Sam's camp that he'd just recently met and knew almost nothing about. But whether he knew the man's background or not, Bart instantly pegged Elroy for a fool. Why in the hell would anyone run out across a wide-open killing field like that in the middle of a standoff? Bart knew he wouldn't have to wait long to find out, because Elroy was running straight towards him. The man knew exactly where to go because Bart hadn't left his spot since the beginning of the operation.

Bart turned and leveled his rifle at the room on the northwest corner. He didn't see any sign of a shooter in there, but he quickly put several rounds through each of the narrow slots to cover for Elroy, just in case. Moments later, Elroy dove into the bushes beside him, unscathed, despite his reckless and idiotic adventure.

"Eric wanted me to tell you he went out there by the road! He took Hal with him. He got a call from Diane about some guys out there and was going to check it out!"

"You're damned lucky you didn't get shot, running out across there like that! We haven't cleared that building yet!"

"Well, he said it was important, so I figured it was! I didn't think I had time to go all the way around."

Bart said nothing else about it, because what good would it do? But now he knew that only Keith and Willis were inside the compound. Hal was with Eric and with Elroy here with him, only Steven, Trey and Lenny were left to secure the perimeter and cover for Keith and Willis.

"Did Eric say what Dianne told him about those guys she saw?"

"Just that they got out of their vehicle with guns, and that she thought they might be some of those C.R.I. contractors."

Before Bart could reply, someone shouted from the direction of the lodge. Bart couldn't locate the source of the voice, even though he scanned the shooting ports again and the open entrance to the breezeway that bisected the center of the building. But it wasn't just the location of the voice that was a mystery; it was the question being shouted that was the real surprise:

"HEY ELROY! IS THAT REALLY YOU?"

Bart looked at Elroy in wonder. "How would anybody here know your name?" But before Elroy could reply, the author of the strange voice answered for him:

"ELROY, IT'S ME! SAM!"

Bart had never met Sam or any of the others taken captive that night on the river. But he could see by the look on Elroy's face that it really was Sam calling out to them. He'd thought all along that Sam and the others with him were in there somewhere, and the boarded-up windows of some of the rooms were a good indicator that they were confined in those, but if that were the case, then how did Sam see Elroy when he ran across from the other side? The answer came after Elroy shouted back to confirm that it really was him and to tell him why they'd come. Sam answered again, and this time Bart saw him wave from behind the rail of the observation deck atop the building.

"IT'S ALL CLEAR IN HERE!" Sam shouted.

EIGHT

The news Bart had for him when Eric made it back to where Sam was waiting changed everything. He no longer had to worry about securing the lodge or whether or not they would find any prisoners there or elsewhere in the compound.

"We finally figured out he was up there on top," Bart said, pointing to the upper deck where the machine gun still sat unused.

"He said that every last one of those soldiers that stayed in the building were dead, and that he'd killed two of them himself. Then he told us that two of his buddies were in there too, but that one of them was injured, and couldn't walk. He also said the fourth one that was brought here with them wasn't in there. When Hal got over here after you sent him, he and Elroy went on up to double check that it was really clear and to see about the one that was injured."

Bart said he'd gotten a second "all-clear" signal from Hal after the two of them reached the breezeway, but he had stayed in position anyway just in case there was some holdout Sam didn't know about that might try to slip out of the building. But that was highly unlikely now that Hal and Elroy had made a sweep as well, and

Eric knew that the rest of the compound was secure too when he saw Keith and Willis heading their way by way of the still open front gate. It was something they would never do unless they'd cleared the ground level buildings and had seen that the lodge was under control.

"That fourth man isn't with them," Bart said.

It was true. Eric had confirmed after Bart told him one prisoner was missing that he now expected to find just four men here. The new information he'd gotten from Brenda guaranteed they wouldn't be rescuing the entire missing party from this one location.

"I'll go see what they found," Eric said, after giving Bart a 20-second synopsis of what occurred out by the road with the SUV and how he'd found the wife of one of those men in the back of it.

"You hit that last guy in the building when you fired at him through the window," Keith told Eric, when they met just outside the front gate. "He was down and hurt bad when we finally got through the door where he was. He took a shot at me with a pistol, but he missed, and Willis finished him with one round."

"I told you he was legit," Eric said, giving Willis a friendly shove to the shoulder that forced him to take a step back.

"Yep. There was no one else in either building though. No prisoners. No more soldiers. I guess all the prisoners were in the lodge?"

Eric told him only one man was missing. Then he told him how he knew the women and children weren't here.

"There was a room they may have been holding someone in," Keith said. "It had a hasp on the outside of the door, but there was no lock on it, and no bunk or anything like that inside. Other than that, we did find lots of supplies we can use if we can get them out of here in time before those other troops get back."

"Provisions?"

"Yes, enough to supply all the men here for a couple of months; MREs as well as dried and freeze-dried goods. And coffee! Plenty of M4s, magazines and ammo too, and other goodies like some more M249s and a couple of crated M2s and boxes of 50-cal belts for them."

"Great! We'll take it all. We can't pass up a haul like that!"

"How though? It's not like we're getting a helo extraction out of here. And we've got to put some distance behind us before those Humvees come back this afternoon."

"That was the original plan," Eric said, "but everything has changed with what we've found here, and with what I got from the woman. I hope Cindy will have even more for us after spending some time talking to her. And if Diane got anything out of the C.R.I. guy, we may have our work cut out for us."

Eric didn't have time to get into the details of what he was thinking with Keith. The first thing he wanted to do was see Sam Necaise and get his version of what happened. He told Willis to wave in Trey and Lenny and go fetch the three women, and then to put the wounded C.R.I. guy in the vehicle and drive back to the compound. Eric figured they might need the SUV for what was taking shape in his mind, but even if they didn't, he didn't want to leave it out there where it would be the first thing someone approaching on that road would see.

"After you're done with that, I want Trey and Lenny to keep watch out there at the road. Make sure one of them has Diane's radio."

Eric would find out soon enough if Cindy had gleaned more information from Brenda, and if the surviving contractor had talked to Diane. But first, he wanted to speak to Sam and the other two men that had been imprisoned there with him in that lodge. Keith followed as he ascended the steps to the breezeway, where he found them all gathered outside one of the rooms. It appeared Hal and Elroy were getting the initial debriefing from Sam and his friends. One of the three was sitting on the floor with his back against the wall, and Eric could see that one leg was horribly swollen in the area of the knee. The man was one of those Eric hadn't met when he was at the camp, and he wondered if he could be Charlie, the husband of the woman he'd found in the back of the SUV.

But before Eric got over there to speak to him and have a look at that knee, Sam Necaise and Marcus Thibodeaux intercepted him with a firm handshakes and then grateful embraces.

"I don't know how you did it, finding us out here and pulling off that attack the way you did, but I had a good feeling about you the day I met you, and I should have known you'd come through," Sam said.

Sam looked like he'd aged ten years since the last time Eric had seen him. His face and head were bruised and battered, the cuts from what were surely vicious punches scabbed over with dried blood. Eric saw the exhaustion in his eyes and noted the weight Sam and his friends had lost due to being nearly starved while here. But Sam was a fighter, and slung across his chest was the M4 he'd taken off one of the soldiers he'd killed. And the filthy clothes he'd been wearing since he'd been taken captive were now heavily stained with blood—blood that Sam told Eric he'd crawled through up there on the deck from which he'd spotted Elroy and realized that it was his friends who'd launched this assault.

"Those two up there by that machine gun never knew what hit them," Sam said. "The one that bled so much took a round right in the side of the neck. Everything you guys did was as professional as it gets, and I know you're the reason for that, Eric Branson. You're every bit the badass that young buddy of yours said you were. Is he okay? Was he part of this operation today?"

"Jonathan is fine, but no, he's not here. He and Ronnie played a big part in getting us close enough to move in here undetected though."

"Makes sense to come by boat," Sam said, "unless you were unlucky like I was that night. I feel responsible for everyone that got swept up with me. I reckon we should have been more careful, but those fellows surprised us, I'll tell you that."

"It could happen to anybody," Eric said. "It's sure happened to me more than once since I got back here." Eric turned to Marcus. "We wouldn't have known about any of it if not for Debbie. Your daughter is a brave girl. She made her way alone back to where you all were camped, and when Jonathan and I came back looking for you, she told us what happened."

Marcus was overwhelmed with relief at this news of his daughter, especially after Eric assured him that she was safe at Sierra Zulu, their remote and secure base of operations.

"We've got to move fast, but it looks like your friend over there with the bum knee is going to need help. Charlie, right? How bad is it?" Eric nodded towards the injured man.

Sam confirmed that it was indeed Charlie, and that he couldn't walk at all. Eric went over and squatted down beside him, to have a look.

"I know you can't walk, but we're gonna get you out of here."

"That's the best news I've heard all day," Charlie said.

"Maybe so, but it's not the best you're gonna hear! What's even better is that your wife is here, and you'll have her to look after that leg for you while it heals up."

Charlie was speechless, but Eric assured him it was true.

"Brenda is here?" Charlie asked in disbelief. "What about Cameron and Brian? Are they here with her too?"

"Yes, she is here and you're going to see her in a moment. But your sons aren't with her. They are still in the refugee camp where Brenda was being held, along with Sam's wife, Suzanne." Eric was aware that Sam was standing behind him and had heard everything he told Charlie.

"And you know they are still alive?" Sam asked. "Did Brenda tell you that?"

"I know they were this morning. She was just taken away from there today." Eric said, as he stood and turned to catch Sam, who nearly collapsed with relief upon hearing that Suzanne wasn't dead. "From the intel I had, we expected to find all of you detained here together. Now I know you haven't seen your wives since the night you were captured."

"Did she say what they did to them there? Did anyone hurt them?" Charlie asked.

Eric knew Charlie must have feared the worst, considering what they'd done to him over the course of multiple interrogations.

"She didn't say they weren't, and I didn't have time to ask her a lot of details, but I left Cindy with her to get more answers, and you can get them from her yourself real soon."

"What about Darryl's wife, Phyllis?" Sam wanted to know. "We never found Darryl when we searched the building. I know he was brought here with us, because we were all on the same truck, but I never saw him again after they made us get out when we arrived here. I was hoping he was somewhere in one of those other buildings after we determined he wasn't in this one."

Eric told him what Brenda had said, about the men that had brought her here today coming and taking Phyllis away yesterday, and Keith confirmed that they had checked every part of the compound for any place in which a prisoner could be confined and had come up empty. Darryl wasn't on the premises.

"There were pistol shots fired out there in the direction of the river yesterday afternoon," Sam said. "I couldn't help but think the worst when I heard it, because that interrogator had already threatened us with execution for what we'd been accused of. I didn't know if they were shooting my friends or just doing some target practice, but it seemed odd, just a few shots out of the blue like that and then nothing else."

"I'll take one of the guys down there to the riverbank and have a look around," Keith said.

"I'd go with you," Sam replied, "but I'm sure you understand that I want to talk to Brenda and hear everything she can tell me about Suzanne."

Eric wanted to be there for that conversation too, but first, he had questions for the man Diane had shot in the leg. The clock was ticking, and decisions had to be made before that patrol returned to base. The only thing of which Eric was certain was that he and his team were not going to be returning directly to Sierra Zulu when they left this place. He followed Keith down the steps to the ground, meeting Brenda along the way, as she was being escorted by Cindy and Diane to the lodge. Willis was right behind them with news for Eric regarding the prisoner, and Eric saw the SUV parked over by the front gate of the compound.

"That son of a bitch told Diane why they brought Brenda here," Willis said. "He said they knew her husband was here and that he was one of the terrorists that had attacked their patrols on the river. He said they're hunting down the people behind it, mainly, a dude named Eric Branson!" Willis laughed. "Can you believe it? He said the interrogators here had been trying to get information out of the prisoners with no luck, but their patience had run out, so they'd asked for help from the bunch he's with; that same bunch we fought in St. Martinsville the day Joe got killed. He said they brought one of the women yesterday, and they came back with another today for the same reason; to make them pay if they didn't talk!"

"Did he say what they did with the one they brought yesterday? Brenda said her name is Phyllis. We've got one guy missing here now, and I just found out that it's Phyllis' husband, Darryl."

"I asked him what he meant when he said 'they were gonna pay for it' but he said he was just the driver, and he didn't know what they did after he left. He said just like today, they sent him with his buddy riding shotgun to deliver the package to this outpost. I told him he was gonna talk when you got through with him, but he swears that's all he knows."

"We'll see!" Eric said, when Willis told him the man was in the back of the SUV, just the way Brenda had been when he found her. "Let's get him out of there and move him over there under the lodge building. Sam is going to have some questions for him too, considering that was his friend's wife they had tied up and gagged like that and his wife is still wherever they brought her from. We'll get Diane down here too and compare notes with everything he told her. He knows he's screwed, and I doubt he'll hold back now if he thinks talking will save his skin."

"How long are we gonna hang around this place? You were already concerned about those soldiers coming back, even before we kicked off the attack."

"I was," Eric said, "but everything's changed now. After you help me get this guy over there to the building, I've got another job for you and Hal. Find Steven and get him to help you too. I hate to ask you to do it, but we need to get those dead guys out of sight. You'll need one of those trucks they've got parked inside the gate if you can find the keys. Get the sergeant and the others that went down out front first, and the guard that was by the gate. If there's still time after that you can grab the one that fell from the upper deck and bounced off the roof around back. You may as well climb up and push the other one that's still up there over the side so you can pick him up too. We'll need that machine gun emplacement, and it would be better if whoever's up there doesn't have to worry about tripping over a body."

"Are you talking about hanging around to wait for all those Humvees to come back?" Willis couldn't hide the excitement in his voice.

"I am, but I'll know more after I question the C.R.I. guy further. And, I'll have to run the details by Bart and Keith. Just get the bodies out of sight! Park the truck back where it was. You don't have to worry about dumping them out again, but we can't just leave them laying around where they're the first thing anyone coming down that road is going to see."

"I'm on it man!"

Willis took off and Eric went and got Sam and Diane to join him in his conversation with the man from the SUV. Sam was livid when he first saw the man, of course, and it was all Eric could do to keep him from killing the guy right then and there. Eric had to remind him that other than what Brenda could tell them, this man was the only source of info they had about the camp where Suzanne was being held. Any hope of getting her and the others out was contingent upon what they learned from him, because otherwise, there was no way of knowing what they would be up against there or even how to find the place.

In the face of the intense pressure the three brought to bear on him, the man did indeed talk. He confirmed that he was working for C.R.I., as Eric had accused, and that one of his assignments was getting any information he could find on the 'terrorist' named Eric Branson. Eric didn't tell him he was one and the same, of course, because Sanders was likely more useful if he didn't know. When pressed about his trip here today, he said that the camp from which he'd brought Brenda was one of the first that had been established in Louisiana by another security company working under contract for C.R.I. He said the really big refugee centers were all in Texas, and that most of the residents they were relocating were being moved to those, but that was going to change over time as they expanded their operations in the state. He told them that the detainees in all of those camps were mostly the civilians that had surrendered and gone along without resistance, and that most believed it was for their own safety and went gladly.

"Bullshit!" Sam glared at him. "My wife damned sure didn't go there because she wanted to!"

"I didn't say all of them did!" The man said. "But the ones taken there have it better than a lot of the others—like you and your friends who were brought here to be interrogated, tried, and punished!"

"Let's cut to the chase," Eric said. "The why of any of this isn't what's important to me. My friends Sam and Diane here have good reason to want you dead just like your partner. The only reason I did anything to stop you from bleeding out was to give you a chance to save yourself by telling me what I need to know. And the intel I really need from you boils down to the specifics of that detention camp. I need the best route and the alternate routes to get there. I need the number of security contractors or other guards assigned to it, and I need to know the schedule and the nature of their daily and nightly activities. If you can't provide all of that, then I'm fresh out of reasons not to tell Sam to go ahead and shoot you here and now."

"And if I tell you, he'll shoot me anyway, right?"

"No, because if he did, I would have no way of knowing whether or not you were lying to me. What I want you to do is answer the questions. After you do, we'll do what we can for that leg. Then, you're going with us for insurance to make sure I didn't misunderstand your directions. I can't make any promises about what'll happen when we get there, because that depends on how your buddies guarding that camp react to our arrival. But if we get our people out, my business with you will be done. That's the best offer you're going to get. Talk and take your chances, or take Sam's bullet and be done with it!"

He talked, and when Eric was done with the interview, he was convinced that most of the intel he got was legit. Sam and Diane, who were there for the duration, agreed. Like Sergeant Davis, this fellow, who said his name was Michael Sanders, was ultimately willing to sell out the subcontractors running the camp to save his own ass. It was what Eric expected, especially from someone who worked with an organization like C.R.I., where loyalty could always be bought by the highest bidder.

The detention camp wasn't all that far away, which matched Brenda's impression when she'd tried to guess how long she'd been on the road in the back of that vehicle. If they left quickly, they could get there by early afternoon, even taking the tedious backroad route that Sanders had described. But Eric wasn't convinced that was the best strategy, and Sam agreed, even though he was understandably anxious to get there and get his wife out as soon as possible. Keith had returned from scouring the riverbank and had found no sign of Darryl or Phyllis, and when asked again what had become of the other woman after they brought her here, Sanders swore he didn't know. He said he and his now-deceased partner had dropped her off and left, and then this very morning had gotten orders to bring the other one today. There was no one else to ask, at least not until the other soldiers returned to the outpost at the end of the day, and when they did, Eric doubted that talking to any of them was likely. When he told Keith what he had in mind, his brother was surprised, but open to the idea, and even Bart warmed up to it when Eric laid out his reasoning.

"Sure, if we'd found Sam and everyone taken with him all here in one place, then getting the hell out ASAP would be the smart thing to do. We'd have no reason to hang around and we'd want to put as much distance between this place and ourselves as possible before those other troops get back. But now we know we don't have everyone, so we're not going home yet anyway. This operation was practically flawless despite that most of the team had no training and we had so little time to plan. We pulled it off without casualties and with none of the enemy escaping to tell anyone what happened. It goes to show what a determined civilian militia with a cause can accomplish, just as we discussed when we moved everyone to Sierra Zulu. We've taken complete control of this entire outpost, along with the vehicles, provisions and equipment on the premises. There's no reason now to pull out and give the rest of those troops time to regroup, or more likely, call in reinforcements. We have the opportunity to wipe out this entire unit, just like they wiped out Sergeant Patterson's unit. Unless they return a lot earlier than expected, we have enough time to finish getting ready. If we do this right, they'll roll in here thinking they're returning to base like any other day, and we'll light them up before they know what hit them. But if we're going to do it, we've got to make our preparations now!"

NINE

A KEY PART OF ERIC'S PLAN FELL INTO PLACE WHEN SAM TOLD him of the idea he'd had earlier, when he still had no way of knowing who was attacking the outpost or who was going to win the battle.

"It crossed my mind that we might get out of the building by putting on the uniforms I found in those rooms the soldiers were using as barracks. But I knew that would only work if the guys here were winning. When it looked obvious that they weren't, I figured wearing that camo pattern would just make us targets. And after I saw how good some of your sharpshooters really were, I'm damned glad we didn't make that mistake." Sam was looking at Bart when he said the last.

"I'm glad you didn't either," Bart said. "I'd feel pretty bad knowing I'd shot the very folks I came here to get out!"

Eric immediately wanted to see the uniforms upon hearing Sam mention this. When Sam took him to the rooms of the lodge where he'd found them, Eric grinned. "This is perfect! We need to get everyone who will be visible outside into one of these ASAP! I want this place to look just like it did when the convoy left this morning; two guards posted at the front gate, two up there on the top deck standing by on that machine gun, and one or two moving about inside the fence close by those other buildings and looking busy! That'll be enough to keep them rolling in, at least until the first vehicle reaches the gate. Everyone else will be in position to make sure none of them get out alive before they have time to figure out something's wrong!"

"I'm glad I remembered to bring them to your attention then," Sam said. "Most of those duds were half-assed washed in dirty river water and hung up to dry, so I guess they're good to go, even if they do still stink. I'll put one on myself if you want me to."

"You're like me," Bart said to Sam. "Too damned old looking to pass for a grunt! They didn't seem to have any distinguished looking officers on duty, so maybe you and me oughta be part of the hidden ambush team!"

"He's right," Eric said. "I'll get Lenny and Trey up here first. They're the right age and build to pass for the guards assigned to that gate. It won't matter as much who is up on the top deck, due to the distance, but at least one of them needs to know how to run an M2."

"I'll do it," Keith volunteered, adding that he'd found helmets in the supply room and that Lenny and Trey should definitely wear them, since the guards posted out front this morning were both wearing lids while on duty. "I'll put one on too since they'll see me up there. If I can get Willis as my partner with his rifle, we can do our part to hurt them when the shooting starts."

Eric had no disagreements with any of it. The good thing about the plan was that it only required a few visible guys in uniform in order to look legit, since that's all that were left guarding the post while the patrol was gone. He ran through the list of the rest of his team members he had available to close the trap and initiate the ambush. Bart would play a key role as a shooter of course, and Eric would let him choose his own position. That left Hal, Elroy and

Steven, as well as the two women, Diane and Cindy. Then there were Sam and Marcus, both of whom were famished, bruised and beaten, but eager to help and more motivated to be a part of the action than anyone there, except maybe Charlie, who would definitely be sidelined for this one.

Sam considered one of the fortified shooting positions in the two front rooms of the lodge, but then said he'd rather be closer to the action so he could move around if he needed to. Eric suggested putting Hal and Elroy up there, because both could shoot but would likely do a better job of it from a protected position, since they had little experience under fire. Being behind a steel plate and shut inside a room would certainly improve Elroy's chances of survival, considering his display of enthusiasm that could have gotten his head shot off earlier. At least up there the two of them could pick their targets from relative safety, using skills they'd perfected shooting deer from tree stands. Their lack of military training wouldn't matter as much because they wouldn't have to worry about getting flanked or having to fall back unless things went so wrong that everyone else on the team was in the same situation. Charlie and his wife, Brenda, would ride it out in one of those rooms with them, safer there than anywhere else they could be until it was over, and Sanders, the wounded C.R.I. contractor, would be confined in one of the secure rooms where the men had been locked up.

This decided, Eric did some calculations in his head as he considered how best to use the remaining resources he had. More shooters would be better, of course, but if everybody present did their part and if the element of surprise was on their side, as he fully expected it to be, what they had was sufficient. The enemy casualty numbers so far came to exactly a dozen, excluding the sergeant they'd brought with them as a hostage. By Eric's count there were another 16 men in that patrol, since it appeared there were four in each of the four Humvees. All of the vehicles were the basic unarmored units with the doors removed for quick entry and exit, and only one was equipped with a mounted weapon; a Browning M2 like the one up on the observation deck. The armed Humvee had been in the lead when the patrol pulled out that morning, and Eric figured it would be up front again, but there'd be no reason for anyone to be up top behind the gun upon returning to base and he hoped they would be able to take that one undamaged, so as to have it available for the mission that would come next.

The returning patrol would be a formidable force in a fair fight, but the way Eric was building his trap, this fight was going to be anything but fair. The arriving soldiers wouldn't even have a chance to reach cover beyond the limited protection of their vehicles, and even if they did it would only delay the inevitable for those not hit with the first rounds of the incoming onslaught. Keith would have a sweeping view of the entire patrol with the Ma Deuce from up above the lodge, so there was really no place for them to hide. Eric also intended to make use of the additional firepower Keith had found in the supply room in the form of those M249 SAWs. With him hitting them from ground level with one of those and Keith up there with the sandbag protected M2, they could simultaneously hose those troops with a shitload of full auto lead. Grenades were available too, and he would use them if necessary, but he hoped to avoid putting any of the Humvees out of commission until he decided how many they needed. He knew already that the GMC Yukon the C.R.I. guys had arrived in would be essential too, and not wishing to get it shot up in the firefight, Eric personally drove it back out of the gate and around the outside of the perimeter fence to a narrow dirt lane that entered the woods by the river. The rough path was passable just far enough to hide the SUV from view of the compound entrance, and out there away from the impending action, it was unlikely to catch any stray bullets.

Eric then worked out the placement of each of his remaining shooters, positioning them where they could take advantage of the soldiers' own fortifications. Sam and Marcus would do well in close, and he knew they wouldn't flinch under the pressure of up-close heavy return fire, as they'd already proven during the capture of the gunboat and again in their resilience as prisoners of war here. But he also knew both men were at the limits of their endurance, so if they were going to be in the action, they needed to be in locations that wouldn't require them to move fast in order to be useful. Putting them behind the armored trucks that were parked on either side of the gate would provide them with good shooting angles and the opportunity to get the retribution they craved against men that had treated them worse than animals.

Diane and Cindy had already performed so well watching the road out front that Eric wanted them back there again, and in the same locations as before, but this time with Steven to help them out. With the radio, Diane would give Eric the first heads-up that their anticipated guests were arriving, and after the last Humvee drove past them, Steven and the two women would be set up to put it and the others ahead of it in a rear flanking crossfire that would prevent any attempt at a hasty retreat if the drivers realized what was going on before they were shot dead.

"This will help you stop them if any of the vehicles try to break through," Eric said, giving Steven one of the M249s. "It's what we call a SAW: short for squad automatic weapon. I know you don't have any training on it, but I'm going to set it up out there on its bipod for you in a good spot to cover the road and get it ready so all you've got to do is pull the trigger. You've got a 200-round belt inside this attached box magazine. It shoots the same 5.56 as your M4, so it's easy to control, but it's designed to operate on full auto, so you can keep firing in long, sustained bursts until you run through the belt. Two hundred rounds will go faster than you think though, and when it's gone, you'll have to switch back to your rifle, because we don't have time to go over everything you need to know to change the belts and clear jams. Besides, if you can't stop them with 200 rounds and whatever Diane and Cindy throw at them too, they'll probably already be out of sight before you could reload anyway."

Steven said he was happy to get it and assured Eric he would do his best to make sure no vehicles escaped once they were inside the kill zone. Eric knew a lot could happen to cause the three of them to fail in that mission, but Steven, Cindy and Diane were as well-equipped as they could be, given their lack of training in other options such as grenades and heavy machine guns. He hoped it would be a moot point anyway, and that all the vehicles would be far enough inside that he and his main shooters could eliminate any chance of retreat before it began.

His next step in getting ready was to ensure the convoy actually entered the gate, and that depended on the performance of Lenny and Trey. Of the entire team, it was those two young men who would expose themselves to the greatest risk, in much the same way as Diane and Cindy had in the first phase of this morning's operation. Eric wanted to make sure they understood the danger, and that they realized the ruse would likely be up as soon as the first vehicle reached the gate. After they selected uniforms that fit them and Eric made sure they were wearing them and the helmets properly, he gave them a five-minute lesson on how to stand, how to hold their weapons, and how to salute the returning members of the unit so that they would look the part at first glance.

"They seemed to be following standard protocol while I was observing them during our recon, so we'll go with that and hope for the best. But the unit is small, and everyone here is surely on a first-name basis, especially when off duty. If that first driver stops when he approaches the gate and looks directly at either one of you, then you can bet it's game on! We'll be ready if it happens, but it'll be so much better if they all just roll on through and we can hit them on the inside as they are unassing the vehicles. But either way, you guys are going to be in the thick of it, and up close and personal. We'll do our best to keep the heat off you with all the firepower we're gonna throw at them, but you've both got to be ready to bring your weapons into action and take out any face-to-face threats yourselves while you fall back to cover behind the berms as fast as you can. The main thing is you've got to create distance between yourselves and those soldiers to give us some clear targets! I don't want to see you guys get wasted by friendly fire! Got it?"

Lenny and Trey assured him they could handle it. "We owe it to Justin," Trey said. "The assholes on that bridge that fired on us and killed Justin may be in that patrol! I want to get as many of them as I can, and I'm glad you decided to stay here and finish what we started, instead of pulling out before the rest of them come back. I say we kill them all and burn this place to the ground!"

Eric had thought of that too. There was no sense leaving the lodge standing so that a replacement unit could be sent here to fall right into such nice accommodations, and it was too exposed and too accessible to serve as a future militia base, in the event the militia grew and expanded operations this far upriver. It would be worthwhile to destroy it if they could, along with everything else here they weren't taking with them, but that was for later. Right now, it all had to look normal for the plan to work, so after getting everyone else on the team ready and into position, Eric and Bart made the rounds for a final check. They stopped at each assigned station, finishing up out at the road with Diane, Cindy and Steven so that on the way back they could assess the compound and the perimeter to be sure it appeared intact and unchanged since the patrol's departure that morning.

"Looking good, guys!" Eric said as Lenny and Trey, who were now standing at attention in uniform at the gate, opened it to let them pass. "It shouldn't be long now, so stay alert!"

"Don't worry," Lenny said. "The hard part will be trying to avoid looking *too* alert when they pull up. It's kinda hard to look bored knowing what's coming!"

"You can do it," Bart said, "Just avoid direct eye contact as long as you can. If the two of you can just act like you're having a conversation with each other, it'll be easier to look natural. But you won't have to keep up the charade for long. Count on that!"

Bart was right, of course. Eric had no intention of letting this drag out one second longer than necessary, because it was essential they made the first move, rather than the enemy. He was going to let Bart have the first shot to kick it off this time though, because he knew that whichever unlucky soldier the old man put in his sights was as good as dead. Bart would be hidden, but Eric had donned one of the uniforms himself now and was going to be outside somewhere close by, pretending to be working at something. Because his brother was in the best position to observe the entire perimeter, Keith had the radio and would receive the first heads-up from Diane. Eric would keep him in sight so Keith could let him know with a hand signal and then he would tell Bart to get ready. Eric would have his M249 out of sight, but close at hand and ready to pour on the lead that would help overwhelm the soldiers before they could attempt a response. When the two of them finally settled in for the wait, the trap was complete. Bart was set up with his .308 back in the shadows behind an open window in the cinderblock office building. Eric had found a deep wheelbarrow and a shovel in the supply shed and had rolled it out by the corner adjacent that same window. He would be messing about in plain sight, pretending to work on the berms with the SAW concealed from view in the wheelbarrow until it was time to grab it. It was a little more dangerous than hiding in a fixed position, but Eric wanted freedom of movement once the action began.

With all preparations made and everyone in place, the only thing left was to wait. Eric used the time to ponder the new information he'd gleaned today from both Sanders, the surviving C.R.I. contractor and Charlie's wife, Brenda. What Sanders told him explained why they'd brought her here today and Phyllis yesterday. Apparently, Sam and the other men with him had held firm in their refusal to admit they had anything to do with the disappearance of that gunboat, or that they'd ever met this 'Eric Branson' that the

C.R.I. commander in Texas was so keen to find. Bringing their wives here was a way of applying more leverage in an attempt to break them. There was no way of knowing whether it had worked with Darryl yesterday, because Sanders swore he and his partner had left shortly after dropping the first woman off. Regardless of whether it had or not, the truth was that neither Darryl nor any of the other men here had much information that would be of use if they did talk. While it was true that Sam and Marcus had participated in taking the gunboat, neither they nor anyone else at Sam's camp knew where Eric took it when he headed downriver with it. And none knew it had been taken back from him and then recaptured yet again. Still, Eric knew how units like this one operated from having worked in collapsed countries torn by civil war in other parts of the globe. It was quite possible that Sam was correct when he said he feared Darryl had been executed, and since his wife was missing too, it was just as probable that she'd met the same fate. Keith hadn't found anything in his quick check of the riverbank where Sam had heard the shots yesterday, but the river itself would have taken away the evidence if the bodies were thrown in. Eric knew that if they killed every soldier in the patrol there would be no one left to question that knew the truth about the missing couple, but with that many heavily armed men returning in a group, there was really no reasonable way to take them alive. It would be too bad if they never found out, but at this point he couldn't worry about it any longer.

Time seemed to drag as the afternoon wore on, and when the sun dropped below the tops of the trees in the direction of the road, Eric had to consider the possibility that the patrol wouldn't return until after dark or perhaps even the following day. The longer they had to wait, the more the tension would wear on them all, and as he stood by outside the window, chatting with Bart about it, Eric hoped everyone was staying alert and maintaining readiness. Eric glanced around at all of them he could see as he mucked about with the wheelbarrow and shovel. But the next time he looked up at

Keith and Willis, his brother was standing at the rail, staring back at him, just waiting for him to make that next visual check. Keith was holding the VHF radio up in one hand where Eric could see it and pointing out in the direction of the road with the other. *The patrol was coming!*

TEN

Eric gave Bart a heads-up and then picked up the shovel he had leaned against the wall next to the wheelbarrow. The SAW was locked and loaded and ready to grab, and he would do so as soon as he heard Bart's first shot. In the meantime, he continued to rearrange dirt and gravel with the blade of the shovel, doing what he could to look at first glance like one of the grunts doing useful work. He couldn't watch the road from where he was as well as the guys at the gate, but he was relying on Keith to keep him apprised of the situation through the use of hand signals. That would cease, of course, once the convoy was close enough to see him, at which point Keith wouldn't be visible except in silhouette next to the M2, looking bored but in reality, ready to grab hold of the grips and rock and roll.

But as Eric waited for him to move into position, Keith remained focused on the road with the radio up to his ear. When he signaled Eric again, it was to let him know something wasn't right. The lead vehicle had stopped before driving into the clearing, and that meant the rest were even farther back, spaced out along the road adjacent to where Steven, Cindy and Diane were watching. Diane would be telling Keith what she was seeing, but would she understand what the soldiers were doing and why? It occurred to Eric that they may have had a check-in protocol by radio before proceeding into the compound, or even long before their arrival, but there was no tower here nor any base station unit that they had found. If one of the guards posted at the gate or on the observation deck had been carrying a handheld, Willis and the other guys that moved the bodies hadn't mentioned seeing it.

Eric told Bart what was going on and started towards the gate to see if he could get a first-hand look. But he'd just begun walking when he heard a sharp whistle from his brother and looked up there to see Keith signaling that they were moving again. Eric went back to where he'd left the wheelbarrow before glancing back up. This time Keith flicked up three fingers, one at a time to motion that three were coming. Next, he made the sign for "four" and shook his head to indicate that it was not. *So, three of the Humvees were coming on in, but the fourth was hanging back?* Eric didn't like it, but there was nothing he could do about it now. Keith was done and had to move back to the gun in order to present the right image. There would be no more updates from him, so Eric kept his focus on the front gate as he continued to fiddle with the shovel. It soon became apparent that he wouldn't need to pretend to be busy for long, though. The vehicles were coming faster than he'd expected, and Eric figured his theory of an unanswered radio call was correct. The NCO in charge of that patrol was in a hurry because he probably thought he was about to chew somebody out.

Eric saw Lenny swing open the gate while Trey stood at attention beside it, awaiting the first vehicle. Whatever happened next was going to happen fast, Eric knew, and he hoped it hadn't been one of the men assigned to the gate watch that was expected to answer. But the lead Humvee rolled on through without stopping and he noted that it wasn't the one with the mounted gun, as he'd expected, neither were the two that followed it. For whatever reason, Eric realized that one had to be the one Diane reported was holding back, and it could be a problem if the gunner opened up on them with it from a distance when the shooting started. But there was no way the ambush could be delayed now. The three Humvees were coming to a stop and time was up.

Eric knew Bart must have already picked his first target in the lead vehicle and was waiting on the opening shot until the other two had rolled past the gate as well. But it wasn't Bart's rifle that kicked off the action. Before the other two Humvees reached the gate, Eric was surprised to hear a sustained burst of machine gun fire from out there on the road. He knew immediately it was the M249 he'd left with Steven, rather than the M2 on the vehicle, and that if Steven had fired first, it could only mean one thing! *The men in that fourth Humvee were attempting to leave!* Eric grabbed his own SAW just as Bart's shot took out the driver of the first Humvee and unleashed a burst into the vehicle, not letting up until he was certain nothing inside could still be alive. When he finally let off the trigger, he heard the 50-cal bursts Keith was directing at the other vehicles outside the gate, while rifle shots and short M4 bursts from all sides told him the rest of the team was likewise engaged in giving those soldiers hell.

Eric didn't have to check for survivors as he worked his way forward past the first Humvee. His burst had ripped through the interior hitting all four passengers with multiple rounds and if that were not enough, they'd taken even more hits from the other shooters on both sides. The occupants of the other two Humvees hadn't fared any better. While some of the soldiers may have returned a few rounds of wild, reactive fire in their panic at the surprise attack, it had done them little good. The dead and dying were slumped over the seats and dashboards and hanging half in and half out of the open sides. The rest of the team had ceased fire now, having no more targets available, and Eric approached each of the two vehicles to be sure they were clear of active threats. The M2 had done a number on the last vehicle in line, and Eric doubted they would be using that one for anything.

Knowing the other shooters were covering for them, Lenny and Trey and then Sam and Marcus came out from behind the dirt berms to help Eric assess the results. But before they reached him, Eric had already determined there was only one survivor still barely breathing that was only minutes away from taking his last. Sam drew his pistol to shoot him when he saw that he was in no condition to tell them anything, and Eric didn't object. The ambush was a total success, but there was still the matter of that fourth Humvee, and even as Eric started that way, more gunfire rang out from somewhere in the vicinity of the road leading out.

Eric tried calling Diane on the radio but got no response, so he waved to Lenny and Trey to follow him as he started her way. He knew Sam and Marcus would want to come too, but in their condition, they weren't going to be able to keep up with Eric and the two younger men, and they couldn't wait for them to catch up. "She's probably in the thick of it, whatever's going on down there," Eric yelled. "We need to cut through the woods to get to her and stay out of the open until we know what's going on!"

The shooting was sporadic, and Eric couldn't tell if it was all coming from the positions of the three posted out there to watch the road, from the occupants of that fourth vehicle, or both. He hadn't heard the M249 again after that first long burst, but he hadn't heard the M2 aboard the Humvee either. The fact that there was still shooting going on at all though suggested to Eric that the soldiers in that vehicle hadn't simply driven away. Once he reached the edge of the woods, Eric threaded his way through the undergrowth to the spot where he'd left Diane, stopping to try the radio one more time to avoid surprising her in the fading light and risking getting the three of them shot. This time, he got a reply:

"I'm still in my position!" She said. "The Humvee has been stopped!"

When the three of them reached her side, Eric could see the vehicle jammed head-on into a big tree where it had left the road when the driver had tried to escape and turn back west. He was clearly dead, his head slumped against his chest behind the wheel. A second body was hanging from the roof hatch behind the M2. With no doors to block his view, Eric could see that the other seats were empty and didn't know if the two dead were the extent of the crew or not.

"What happened? Are Steven and Cindy okay? Do you know why he opened fire before we initiated the ambush?"

"As soon as the other three Humvees started moving towards you guys again, the driver of that one, the last one in line, began turning around in the road. You said not to let any of them get out, so I guess Steven thought he'd better use the machine gun to try and stop them. The driver had just started accelerating to go back the other way and they would have escaped if he hadn't opened fire when he did. I think he killed the driver right away with that burst, because the Humvee went off the road and straight into that tree almost immediately and I guess he was probably dead before he hit it. Steven may have killed the one that was up there behind the gun too, but it could have been any of us, because we were all shooting at them by then.

"I couldn't see the other side of the vehicle from over here, but Cindy yelled back at me that she'd seen two of the soldiers bail out and run into the woods. I don't know if they were hit or not, but Cindy said she and Steven were going after them. I heard shooting from somewhere over there a few minutes later, but I have no idea what happened. I stayed here where I could see the road because I was the one with the radio and those were the orders you gave me."

"Could you tell where those last shots you heard were coming from?"

Diane pointed across the road to the woods northwest of the stalled vehicle. It was a straight line almost directly between the positions where Steven and Cindy were each set up, and Eric figured they'd slipped through them only because of the growing darkness in the dense woods that would make running men clad in camo a difficult target. Sam and Marcus had caught up to them now, but they were winded and clearly not up to joining the pursuit, and Eric didn't want them to try.

"I'm taking Lenny and Trey with me," he told them. "We don't have much daylight left and if we don't get those guys before dark, we probably never will. If you two can pull those dead guys out of there and get that vehicle back to the compound and secure it, that would be great! I don't want those two that left it to try and circle back to take it and make their escape after it gets dark. And grab the M249 I set up for Steven before you head back too. Diane knows where it is. It's probably jammed, because I don't think he went through that entire 200-round belt. If he had, we probably wouldn't have to go hunting down survivors."

"We'll get it if he didn't take it with him," Sam said.

"He wouldn't have. He had his M4s and Cindy's got her AR. That SAW would be useless to him in a chase, and I didn't have time to give him a lesson on clearing it or changing the belts, so I didn't even leave him a spare. It served the purpose I brought it out here for, and that was to give him enough firepower to take on those Humvees if he had to. I'd say he did a hell of a job, especially since he's never touched one before. He stopped the Humvee and neutralized that Ma Deuce up top before they could use it on him or us!"

"What about me," Diane asked. "Don't you want me to go with you? I can catch up after I show Sam and Marcus where the gun is. I won't slow you down!"

"No. The three of us can handle it. I still need you to watch the road, because we have no way of knowing why the convoy stopped in the first place and why the guys bringing up the rear tried to turn back even before they knew there was an ambush. It's possible someone else will come down the road, but you're going to be alone out here now, so do not engage them! I'll have my radio off, but when I can, I'll give you a check-in call so you can update me."

Eric turned to Lenny and Trey: "You guys follow me! We'll spread out once we're on the other side of the road and make a sweep until we hear more shooting or get a visual. I know I don't have to tell you to stay alert and be quiet! Those guys could stop and set up an ambush most anywhere. They must know they're being pursued since Diane heard shooting in the direction they went."

Eric knew the soldiers may have already doubled back and used that tactic on Steven and Cindy, because there was no way of knowing who'd fired those last shots. But whether that was the case or not, there was no time to waste. If Steven and Cindy had failed to stop them, then it was going to be up to Eric and the two young hunters he was taking with him to track them down. The last rays of sunlight that filtered through the heavy timber would soon be replaced by twilight and then full darkness, and Eric knew if they didn't catch up to the surviving soldiers before that happened, it was unlikely they'd ever find them.

They fanned out with Eric in the middle and Lenny and Trey within visual contact to his left and right as they moved northwest into the woods across the road. Barely five minutes into the maneuver, two closely spaced rifle reports, followed by several more in rapid succession gave them a definitive heading to zero in on, and though the shooting had stopped after they moved another quarter of a mile, Eric saw Lenny signal to him that he could see something. Eric and Trey converged to his position and from there they saw Steven and Cindy, pinned down in the middle of a partially open area of storm damaged timber.

When Eric saw the situation, he knew they were in trouble and were now on the defensive as the men they'd pursued had stopped or turned back to set up an ambush or counterattack, just as he'd feared they might. The only thing protecting them now was the huge clay root mass of a toppled oak tree they were using as cover. Steven and Cindy could do little at this point but stay put behind it, as they had lost any advantage they had before. They were unaware reinforcements had arrived in the nick of time, and Eric couldn't call out to them for fear of alerting their adversaries as well.

Eric figured the soldiers had bailed out reactively in the face of that withering machine gun burst and ran just far enough to create some distance and figure out what they were dealing with. They'd probably gotten a glimpse of their pursuers and realizing there were only two of them, a man and a woman, decided to turn the tables and take them out. It was a wonder Steven and Cindy were alive at all, considering how they'd been led into that trap, and Eric knew they were fortunate to be near available cover when the encounter began. But cover from one direction wouldn't be enough to save them if even now, the enemy was attempting to flank and kill them. Eric was all but certain that Steven and Cindy didn't understand the strategy the two soldiers would use against them. The militia training he planned with Keith and Bart hadn't yet begun at Sierra Zulu, and there'd been little time to work with the hastily-assembled team that came with him for a rescue mission that couldn't be delayed. Eric and his two companions were just in time to save the young couple from being slaughtered, but there was no room for error.

"I need one of you to make your way up there closer to them, so you can let them know what's going on," he told Lenny and Trey. "Whoever does it will have to be careful, but quick; and stay low to the ground and take advantage of all the fallen trees! Don't get close enough to let the enemy see you; just far enough in so you can get Steven and Cindy's attention without having to shout."

"I'll do it," Trey said.

"Good. Go ahead and get moving then! Lenny, you and I will split up and circle wide. You go west and to the left of their position by at least a couple hundred yards, and I'll do the same from the other side. Then, we'll move in from both directions out past Steven and Cindy until we spot the shooters. They're leap-frogging in on them, one providing cover fire while the other moves a little closer. It's a classic tactic and it'll work if we don't intercept them first.

"I know you're a bowhunter, so you know the importance of stealth. You're gonna need to put it to use, but we've got to get there quickly at the same time. Those men are focused on Steven and Cindy right now, and probably can't imagine that they're the last survivors of their entire unit. But I want to make sure there are *no* survivors so none will have a chance of getting somewhere to tell anyone what happened before we can get to that detention camp. So, let's go hunting, but be damned sure you identify your target before you pull the trigger, and I'll do the same! These uniforms we're wearing make us both look like the bad guys."

"Yeah, and to Steven and Cindy too, as dark as it's getting out here now!"

"That's exactly why Trey has to let them know we're here. Hopefully, they'll just hold their fire and let us do our thing."

When Lenny was on his way, Eric swung wide the other way, taking advantage of the thickets and shadows that would keep him out of sight of both Steven and Cindy and the two soldiers. The suppressive fire the two men were delivering was sporadic, and Eric knew they were conserving their ammo because they had bailed out fast with just the mags they had on them and in their weapons. The long intervals in between shots created a bit of guesswork for him as he attempted to home in on them, but he knew he was getting close when at the sound of the next report, he spotted a faint muzzle flash low to the ground somewhere ahead out there in the dark.

Eric regretted leaving behind the small night vision monocular he normally carried, but he'd given it to Keith when they were setting up the ambush since he had the best view and there was a possibility they would be waiting after dark for the approach of the convoy. He shouldered his rifle and scanned the area of the flash with the 1x6 variable optic zoomed out to the widest angle, looking for any part of a human form he could pick out of the shadows. But the shooter wasn't moving, and it was too dark to spot him unless he did so or fired his weapon again. Eric was frustrated. He wanted to get this guy and quickly find the other one and finish the job, because it was far from ideal, having to rely on untrained civilians in a situation like this. Eric hated exposing them to risks they had no comprehension of, but they'd volunteered for it and if they survived this battle, the larger war for their homeland would require countless more risks and sacrifices.

Keeping his focus on the area where he expected to see another flash soon, Eric slowly eased closer, hoping that by decreasing the range he'd have a better chance of finding a target. But the next shot he heard didn't come from where he'd spotted that flash at all. It was considerably farther away, from the approximate area where he knew Lenny should have been by then, and there was no follow-up or return fire in answer. Eric waited to see how the one he'd been searching for would react to that shot. It seemed to take a lot longer than he knew it really did, but finally, Eric heard something unmistakable. The soldier had stepped on a dry branch in the dark, so he was on the move. Eric kept his focus in the direction of the sound until finally, he saw movement among the shadows, yards to the left of where he'd expected the man to be.

When he shouldered the rifle and looked again with the scope, the back of the man's head and shoulders materialized, and he could see that he was stalking quietly in the direction of that last gunshot. Eric's finger was on the trigger, and he could have taken him out then and there, but then he suddenly changed his mind about doing it. He was willing to bet on Lenny's success in getting the other guy in the absence of more shots after all those long minutes, and if he was right, it meant this one was now alone.

Eric had neither the time or the patience to deal with another prisoner, but there was still the question of what happened to Darryl and Phyllis, and this soldier was possibly the last man alive that could answer it. He lowered his rifle and began following the man, gradually closing the gap until he was close enough to be certain of a kill if the man failed to comply:

"FREEZE RIGHT THERE AND DROP YOUR WEAPON! NOW!"

ELEVEN

Eric disarmed his prisoner and ordered him to remove his boots and socks, warning him that any attempt to escape would get him shot in the back. The man was sullen and slow to comply at first, pretending not to understand his instructions and mumbling something under his breath in Spanish until Eric gestured with the barrel of his rifle at the boots and told him again to get rid of them. Eric could see that the man was Hispanic, so it was believable that English wasn't his first language, but since he was part of a unit run by former American soldiers, he had to understand a lot more than he let on. He squatted down to unlace the boots, and as soon as he was barefoot, Eric pointed the rifle at him again and told him to get moving.

He and Lenny had been in such a hurry to head out to find those guys that they hadn't established a rendezvous point or made a plan on how they'd check in with each other or with Trey, Steven and Cindy. At this point, Eric figured the odds of getting shot by one of them in the poor light was greater than the odds that it hadn't been Lenny who'd fired that single last shot he'd heard, so he took his chances and called Lenny by name, telling him that he had one tango secured.

"ONE DEAD OVER HERE!" Lenny shouted back.

"So, you are officially the sole survivor of your entire unit now!" Eric prodded the prisoner to start walking again, urging him in the direction of the road. "What are the odds of that, amigo? I'll bet it means you still have a little unfinished business in this life, no? Like maybe explaining to some friends of mine why all of you gave them such a hard time while they were your guests here, and why you and your compadres ever brought them here at all!"

The captured soldier said nothing as he walked, but Eric figured he would talk later when he saw the outcome of the raid and understood that he *really was* the only survivor. Sam and Marcus would want to ask their own questions about Darryl and Phyllis, and Eric knew that bringing the guy in alive was the right choice, even if it was a little extra trouble. When he reached the spot where Steven and Cindy had been pinned down, Lenny and Trey were already talking to them. Eric called Diane on the radio and gave her the scoop.

"Everything is quiet on the road," she answered.

"Good, we'll be right out. You can go back and tell Sam and the others that every man from that patrol is accounted for and that I've got one prisoner to be questioned."

They had much more to do than just interrogate this soldier though. Eric knew Keith and Bart were probably already on it, but those Humvees had to be cleared of their dead occupants and checked for damage and drivability. Eric would go get the C.R.I. vehicle he'd hidden in the woods, and they would load it down with the supplies and hardware they were going to take from the post. Then, there was the matter of what they were going to do with Charlie and Brenda. Charlie was in no condition to fight or do much of anything else, but since it was their boys that were still in the detention camp with Suzanne, he doubted he'd be able to talk them out of going. Besides, other than leaving them somewhere in hiding, there wasn't much else they could do with them. Eric couldn't spare the two or three men it would take to get them back to real safety. He would discuss the options with them, but he didn't want to stay at this outpost any longer than necessary, even if it was unlikely anyone would arrive there after dark.

"All but one of the Humvees are good to go, even if they did get perforated pretty good," Bart said, after Eric secured the prisoner and handed him over to Keith for questioning. "Keith tore up the third one in line with the Ma Deuce though. Couldn't be helped, I guess."

"That's good enough. Three will be perfect, along with the Yukon." Eric counted to himself in his head. "There are 13 of us now, including Charlie and Brenda, plus two more if we take that C.R.I. guy and the soldier as hostages."

"Do we really need 'em?" Bart asked.

"It's debatable. I haven't made up my mind yet about the soldier. The only reason I didn't shoot him out there in the woods is because I knew Sam and Marcus would want to question him about Darryl and Phyllis."

"You still thinking about just rolling up to that camp in broad daylight tomorrow, acting like we belong there?"

"It's the only thing I can think of that'll give us a chance," Eric said. "From what I gathered from our man, Sanders—and from Brenda—the place is out in the wide open, like in the middle of a big field or pasture. There's no way to get in close like we did here for a covert attack. We're gonna have to rely on trickery again, and I feel pretty good about the tactic, considering how well it worked here. We'll definitely need these uniforms for this—all of us this time, including you. Sanders said that no one was expecting him and his buddy to come back to the camp yesterday or any other particular time, so when they see the Yukon turning in with three Humvees in line behind it, it won't necessarily raise an alarm. But we have to look the part of those North American Interior Defense forces, and that means wearing their uniforms and brain buckets. I doubt that the shot-to-shit condition of our rigs will raise any eyebrows. The guards there are bound to know these units are running in to some resistance out there on their patrols."

"The uniforms will help, but most of the dead men from that patrol don't look anything like us," Bart said.

It was true. Like the one Eric took alive, many of the other soldiers looked like recent immigrants or foreign recruits. The prisoner had refused to speak on the walk back, but it was already clear that Spanish, rather than English was his first language. He was from somewhere south of what had once been the country's southern border, and Eric intended to find out from exactly where in the course of his further questioning. Among the dead there were others that also appeared Latin American, as well as a couple that were certainly Middle Eastern. From what he'd seen, Eric estimated that Sergeant Davis and only perhaps half of the others were former American soldiers from the original national guard units that had merged into this new North American Interior Defense force. Like the paid mercenaries of C.R.I., these foreign recruits would have no qualms about displacing local residents and killing those who resisted, because there was no telling what they'd been led to believe about them before they were sent here. If the truth was known, they'd probably expected little organized resistance anyway, but this particular unit had found out the hard way how wrong that thinking was. Eric was proud of the victory he and his team had accomplished here. It would be a significant setback for the invaders and as word got out, a rallying cry for more residents to join his militia. After they liberated that camp they were going to pay a visit to tomorrow; the news would spread that it was possible to fight back and win.

After inspecting the three Humvees they would be taking on the mission and moving them into line outside the perimeter fencing, Eric and Bart went down by the river to get the Yukon and pulled it into the compound next to the building where Keith had found all the supplies. Inside under the glow of a dim LED bulb powered by the solar electric system on the roof, several of the group had gathered around where Keith, Sam and Marcus were attempting to interrogate the new prisoner, whom they'd secured with rope to a folding metal chair. Eric could tell that it was all his brother could do to keep Sam and Marcus from killing the man, and their sentiment was understandable after what the soldiers here had done to them and their friends.

"Have you gotten anything out of him?"

"Not really. He's trying to pretend he doesn't understand our questions, and you know my Spanish is limited."

Eric's was too, and there was no one on the team who was fluent. He wished now that Vicky were here, as she'd done an excellent job of translating during his interrogation of Enrique Valverde aboard the *Miss Anita*. Even Shauna and Megan were far more conversant in the language than Eric, but Eric wasn't buying that this guy's English was that deficient anyway. He'd been taking orders from Sergeant Davis and working with others here that likely didn't speak a word of Spanish, so it was just a matter of letting him know that he wasn't doing himself any favors by keeping up that game. Eric drew his pistol and leveled it on the man's face from three feet away.

"Okay amigo, the time for games is over, *comprende?* You see my friends here," Eric pointed at Sam and Marcus. "You know that they were brought here because they were accused terrorists. Maybe you were even one of the men who brought them here from the river? You also know that there were two more men with them. One of them is still over there," Eric pointed in the direction of the lodge building. "He can no longer walk because one of the men asking him questions kicked him in the knee so hard that it shattered. You also know that there was another man with them, a fourth amigo, no? But we cannot find him here, or his wife, the woman that the men in that GMC brought here yesterday. You will either tell me what happened to them, or I will shoot you right now. I have no more time to wait."

The soldier stared back at Eric and glanced at the other men surrounding him. Looking at him now face-to-face, Eric guessed he was in his mid-thirties. His face was scarred from above the right eye all the way down over the bridge of his nose and across his left cheek; the result of what must have been a wicked knife slash received in some fight years prior. The tattoos that extended up his neck from out of the collar of his uniform suggested he was a member of one of the old Mexican cartels from back in the days before the collapse. This man was no stranger to death, and looking into his eyes now, Eric was surprised he'd surrendered at all out there in the woods. The only reason a man like him would was that maybe he hadn't really believed he was the last of his unit and still thought there was some way to reverse his misfortune. But there under the glare of that light and of four angry men, he decided to give in and talk.

"You want to know what happened?" He finally asked, in excellent, if heavily accented English. "What happened is what always happens in war. People die. Those men were killers, and they were brought here so that they could tell us where to find all of the other killers they are associated with—killers like you and your friends who have come here today. Today, it was your time to do the killing. Yesterday it was different, and tomorrow, it will be different yet again. You cannot stop what is coming to this place, and to all of what you mistakenly claim to be your country. There are more than you can imagine and fighting against what cannot be stopped will only get you killed. Just like your friends."

"So, you're saying they *were* killed?" Sam asked. "The other man that was with us and his wife that they brought here?"

The soldier turned his gaze to Sam and gave him a slight smile. "At least they were together when they died, amigo. Neither one of them will have to be sad because of the other passing first. Could there be a better way for lovers to go?"

Sam exploded with rage and lunged into him, grabbing him by the neck with both hands and slamming the chair to the floor with the man still lashed to it. Eric had to intervene to keep Sam from choking him to death before he could ask the prisoner another question.

"What else do we need to know? The son of a bitch probably killed them himself! He seems delighted that it happened!"

"Where?" Eric demanded, as he helped Sam back to his feet and glared down at the bound man. "Where were they killed and how?"

"Down beside the river! Where else? The crocodiles you have here—how do you call them—*alligators?* They are always hungry, are they not? It is a perfect solution!"

Before Eric could say another word, Sam stepped back quickly so that neither Eric nor Keith could stop him as he drew the pistol he had tucked in his belt. Eric saw instantly that it was the Beretta M9 that Sam had taken from the interrogator he'd killed, but he wasn't quick enough to grab it before Sam pulled the trigger. It was an instinctive shot that Sam had little time to set up, but Eric saw that his aim was true anyway, because after all, he was at practically point-blank range. The 9mm full metal jacketed bullet made a neat hole in the soldier's forehead just above his right eye, exactly where the old knife scar started. Sam was practically trembling with rage and the pistol shook in his hand as he followed up with another half dozen, totally unnecessary rounds to the man's face and torso.

"That settles that," Eric said, "when Sam finally stopped shooting and lowered the weapon.

"I couldn't take it! I'm sorry, but Darryl and Phyllis were good people! I've known Darryl since he was a kid; knew his folks all my life too. I know you might have had more questions to ask him, but you said finding out if he knew about them was the main reason you brought him in. I was afraid if I didn't take care of this business now, it wouldn't ever happen. I knew you wouldn't just kill him yourself because they weren't your friends, and I knew we weren't going to have a trial or anything to decide on it, so I did it myself, because I've got good reason!"

"I'm glad you did, Sam," Marcus said. "I would have done it if you hadn't beaten me to it. Darryl and Phyllis *were* good people. They shouldn't have had to die like that."

"It's okay fellows," Eric said. "You're right, this guy needed to be dealt with and we damned sure didn't need another prisoner to keep up with. There may have been a few more questions I could have asked him, but just looking at him told me plenty, and not just about him, but about what we're up against in this fight. This new army they've assembled seems to be made up of as many foreigners as American traitors. I guess that's how they built their numbers up so fast. They are every bit the mercenaries those C.R.I. guys are, they're just wearing uniforms and following a more structured chain of command. I guess it's part of the strategy to ensure mass compliance in the areas they are trying to control. Regular folks assume they're the good guys and go along with them thinking it's in their best interest.

"That dude definitely looked like a former cartel assassin," Keith agreed. "I would be surprised if he wasn't the one that actually pulled the trigger; either him or that interrogator you told us about. You did the world a favor, Sam. Don't give it another thought!"

"Okay, that's settled, but we've still got work to do!" Eric said. "I want to get out of here and move to a staging area somewhere off one of these backroads until we roll out again at daylight. It's too risky to hang around here any longer than it takes to get everything loaded and moved out."

"Are you still thinking of burning down the lodge like we talked about before?" Keith asked.

"No, that was before we found out what we know now. A big fire like that is way too risky now. It may attract attention, from some other patrol on the river or who knows where? It'll burn for too long and put out too much light in the dark and too much smoke in the daytime. What we're doing tomorrow will work far better if no one knows this outpost has been attacked."

It took another half hour to finish clearing out the supplies and equipment they wanted to take and pack it all into the vehicles. When they were done there was barely enough room for everyone to ride, so it was decided that some of the extra supplies and gear would be dropped off and stashed at the staging area, either to be picked up on the way back or at some other time when it was more convenient. The proximity to the Red River would make it easy to return in the boats now that the enemy unit at this outpost had been destroyed. They hadn't used that waterway for the rescue team's insertion before the operation, because Eric deemed it too risky after interrogating Sergeant Davis. Because the distance overland from the head of the Atchafalaya at Simmesport was only about ten miles, they'd instead disembarked from the *Gulf Traveler* and the gunboat near that juncture and gone the rest of the way on foot at night. The plan had been to exfiltrate in much the same way. Jonathan and Ronnie would be standing by with the boats until Eric or someone from the team was close enough to get word to him over the handheld VHF that they either needed a pickup farther upriver or at the original drop-off point. Because of the second mission they would now undertake tomorrow, they would be making that call a full day later than expected, but Eric had already discussed the probability of delays with Jonathan, so unless there was an extremely good reason for him and Ronnie to leave, the kid would sit tight until he heard from Eric.

When they finally pulled out onto the road and were leaving the outpost behind for good, Eric was driving the lead Humvee with the mounted M2, with Sanders, the C.R.I. guy in the front passenger's seat and Willis and Lenny in the back. Sanders was in no condition to try anything stupid, but it appeared that he might survive his wound despite the loss of blood. With little choice but to comply, Sanders gave Eric turn-by-turn directions that retraced the route he and his partner had used to get there. He insisted it was the best of several options, as it avoided the highways where there were checkpoints and bypassed contested areas where they might run into trouble. There were lots of forks and turnoffs on a series of rural blacktop roads after they left the gravel roads of the wildlife management area, and soon the landscape changed from heavy river bottom forest to wide open expanses of agricultural land; the fields abandoned and neglected after months of disruption. When they had put the outpost sufficiently far enough behind them that Eric felt comfortable stopping, he turned off into an overgrown soybean field and led the convoy to a spot behind a narrow strip of trees along one edge that would conceal the vehicles from the road.

It was time to organize weapons and gear and make a plan for their arrival at the detention camp. The first step was to offload everything they didn't need, so that the Humvees would appear to be taking part in a military operation, rather than shuttling a bunch of random supplies. Eric had brought a notebook and a pen he'd found back at the outpost in one of the offices, and giving them to Sanders, had him sketch the layout of the facility as well as he could remember it. His drawing included the location of the front gate, the staff buildings that housed the guards, and the lockup facilities that were scattered over several acres contained within the perimeter fencing.

"There's only one entrance, and you will see it as soon as you turn off the main road. It's set back about a half mile off the pavement. The guards will be able to see us coming as soon as we turn off that road, but you already know they're familiar with this vehicle and like I said, they won't be alarmed about the Humvees following behind."

When they approached, Eric would be driving the Yukon, but would still be wearing the Multicam BDUs of the NAID unit from the outpost. Sanders said none of the guards there would have met any of those soldiers before anyway, and Eric would look the part well enough to get waved through, especially with Sanders in the front seat beside him. The story they would present would be one of an attack along the road somewhere; an attack that had killed Sander's partner and that he'd survived only because he was rescued by this patrol. The condition of the Humvees would lend plenty of credence to the narrative, as would Sanders' serious wound. Their purpose in coming here was to get the remaining woman and the two boys that were associated with the two women Sanders and his partner had already taken away for questioning. It would be quite plausible that information they'd obtained was related to the resistance groups the military units had been trying to hunt down and destroy, and this recent attack was all the more reason to question anyone even remotely associated with them. Eric was convinced it was a workable plan that would get them in the gate and hopefully enable them to secure Suzanne and the two boys as they assessed the overall situation before deciding whether or not it was feasible to liberate the entire camp.

It was a long wait for dawn, but soon as the sky began to lighten, they were on the road again headed west. Eric was leading the way in the Yukon, with Sanders in the front passenger's seat beside him. Cindy and Diane were in the back behind them in the third row, ready for action with their rifles and concealed from view behind the dark-tinted glass where they were safe from discovery unless the vehicle was searched. The rest of the team was dispersed among the bullet-riddled Humvees, all of them wearing the uniforms and carrying their weapons at ready, looking every bit the part of battle-weary soldiers expecting more trouble. Lenny drove the one with the mounted M2 that followed directly behind the SUV, and Keith was riding shotgun with him so he could quickly get to the machine gun if necessary, while Willis and Steven were in the rear seats behind them. Elroy drove the next one in line, with Hal, Marcus and Trey on board, while Bart and Sam brought up the rear, since they were the oldest of the bunch and most likely to attract attention under close scrutiny. In the back seats behind them, Charlie and Brenda lay still and hidden beneath canvas tarps; tarps that covered the bodies of their dead, if anyone saw them and asked the men what was under there.

The distance to the camp from where they'd pulled over to wait was only about 30 miles. By the time the sun was fully above the horizon behind them, the convoy reached the turn-off and Eric saw that the camp was just as Sanders described it. The metal roofs on long rows of what could only be described as cages gleamed in the sunlight as he turned onto the lane leading to them. Eric scanned the perimeter fencing as he drove, counting the guards he could see as he slowly closed the gap at 10 miles per hour. Everything was riding on what Sanders had told him, and if it wasn't true, Eric knew the shooting could begin before they even reached the gate. Sanders had the most to lose if that happened though, because Cindy and Diane were sitting right back there behind him, ready to make sure he was among the first to die the second anything went wrong.

TWELVE

Daniel Hartfield's day started pretty much the same as they all had in recent weeks. The guard came and unlocked the gate that was the door to his new 'cell', which in reality was nothing more than a wire pen more suitable for housing animals than human beings. The eight-foot wide by ten-foot-long enclosure was at least sheltered by a galvanized metal roof that kept off the rain and the worst of the sun though. Even as far into fall as it already was, the afternoon sun most days in South Louisiana was brutal, and having a roof of any kind was a luxury compared to the larger, communal pen into which he'd been thrown when he first arrived here with his hands cuffed behind his back. In that situation, he'd had no privacy, and no protection from the elements or his fellow detainees. Most of the other men were tolerable at first, but beginning the next day, when he'd been forced to join them on the work detail that involved sunup to sundown manual labor, Daniel had borne the brunt of their disdain when he couldn't come close to keeping up with his more hardened fellow inmates. Excavating foundations with a sharpshooter shovel left his hands a mess of open blisters before the morning was half over. Daniel had struggled with the heavy wheelbarrows they used to move the hand-mixed cement they were pouring, and he'd been yelled at and ordered to move faster despite that he was doing the best he could to keep up.

The guards overseeing the work detail seemed to take sadistic delight in Daniel's suffering, and of course wouldn't listen when he told them at every opportunity it was a huge mistake that he was even here. No one posted there had listened to him the day he'd been dropped off by those men from the I-10 roadblock. Daniel had tried telling anyone who walked by the big holding pen that first day that he wasn't supposed to be there. But his demands to see someone in charge so he could explain his situation were ignored. The two that arrested him had lied to him outright, after confiscating his vehicle and weapon and conning him out of the gold coins he'd found aboard the schooner. They'd put him in handcuffs on the side of the road and told him they would get him a face-to-face meeting with Commander Reyes if he would just shut up about those coins that they clearly intended to keep for themselves. But instead of taking him to the outpost across the state line in Texas, they'd brought him here, to this new detention facility they were building out in the middle of nowhere in Louisiana. At the end of that first day, when the other men sharing the enclosure with him returned from their long hours of hard labor, Daniel had tried to tell them what happened too. Some of the men listened to his story but had little sympathy when it came down to it. They were tired, filthy and constantly hungry, and they did little more than assure Daniel that he would be too, from that moment on.

Daniel didn't believe them of course, and still expected special treatment and profuse apologies from the men running the encampment just as soon as someone realized it was all a mix-up, and that he had valuable information to share with them. But it didn't happen that first day, or the next. Daniel had been there almost a week before a vehicle pulled out to the site where the labor gang was working on the newest expansion of the camp, and a man got out and asked the guards for him by name. Somehow, word had finally gotten to someone in authority in the organization, and Daniel had his opportunity to speak. He was delighted to learn that it was Reyes himself that came to see him, and Daniel knew it was only because the name Eric Branson had somehow gotten to the commander after all.

Reyes wanted to know everything Daniel could tell him about Eric Branson, and Daniel spoke freely when they were situated in one of the new staff buildings at the entrance to the camp. Daniel already knew that Reyes had personally met Shauna and Megan, and even Keith, Bart and Jonathan. But Reyes wasn't aware that Shauna was divorced from Eric and now married to Daniel. That detail made him a little suspicious of Daniel's motivation at first, but Daniel did a good job of reassuring him he'd had valid reasons for wanting to get his family away from Eric Branson that had nothing to do with jealousy.

"The man is a lunatic!" Daniel said. "No, he's worse than that; he's a homicidal maniac! I don't know if it's PTSD or what, but he cannot function in normal society. As long as Shauna knew him, he was always signing up for new contracting jobs so he could go and kill more people all over the world. Apparently, he didn't get enough of that when he was on the SEAL teams, and apparently, he still hasn't gotten enough."

Daniel told Reyes that Eric bragged about wiping out that C.R.I. team in the operation he'd been a part of in New Mexico. He knew this was what Reyes wanted to hear, but more than that, he knew Reyes wanted to know where Eric was now. Daniel wasn't particularly good at navigation, especially off-grid navigation of the kind required in a place like the Atchafalaya Basin, but he had a general idea of where that trawler, the Miss Anita was anchored in relation to the bayou where Keith's property was located. Looking at the river basin map that Reyes spread out on the table before him, he did his best to pinpoint the little hidden dead lake, even though it wasn't shown on the map. As Reyes took in all the information he gave him, Daniel was adamant about getting his reassurance that only Eric would be a target, and that the men he sent there to find him would bring his son Andrew back with them so that the two of them could be reunited at one of those safe refugee centers in Texas. Reyes said that of course they would, and then the interview was abruptly over. But instead of asking Daniel to come with him, the commander just nodded to the guard before leaving the room to return to his vehicle and his waiting driver.

"Hey!" Daniel had yelled at him as the guard grabbed him by the arm and led him outside. "What about me? You're taking me back to Texas with you, aren't you? I told you what you wanted to know!"

But Reyes didn't seem to hear him at all, even though he was less than 50 feet away when he got back to the truck.

"I've got more information you'd be interested in too! Information about a couple of your men and what they took from me!"

Reyes opened the door and got in without looking back, even when Daniel yelled that it was gold those men had taken and surely failed to report to their superiors.

"You can't take me back there!" Daniel protested, when the guard grabbed him by the arm and urged him to move along as the truck pulled away. "I'm not supposed to be here at all, and I'm sure not supposed to be penned up with a bunch of prisoners, working like a slave every day!"

"You're not going back there," the guard said. "It's obvious you can't keep up with the other workers, so we've got a new job for you. Commander Reyes recommended it even before your interview. The good thing about it is that you'll have your own space in the new facilities, so you won't have to live 'with a bunch of prisoners' as you say. Think of it as a promotion!"

The so-called 'promotion' did provide Daniel with a modicum of privacy and freedom from the constant ribbing he got from the other men in that work crew, most of whom had adapted well to the forced hard labor. But Daniel was hardly 'free' or free from working to earn his keep. His new job, now that the additions to the refugee camp were rapidly expanding, was cleaning up after and carrying water and food to the new influx of detainees that now included rows of separate holding areas for women and children, as well as sick, injured or old men that were unable to do hard labor.

Unlike how it was in the pen where he'd first been confined, these new facilities were built on rough slabs of concrete instead of directly onto the ground and were covered with simple metal shed roofs. The individual enclosures were separated by partitions of the same galvanized sheet metal used on the roofs, making it impossible for those inside to see other detainees in the same row. When he first saw the way they were built and laid out, the enclosures made him think of dog kennels more than anything else, though he knew that even dogs would be unhappy locked up in such abysmal conditions. One of the guards had told him they were only temporary holding areas until the people in them could be transferred elsewhere, but after his experiences here so far, Daniel doubted this was the case. The days turned into weeks, and the only thing that changed was that the work crews built more enclosures to house the ever-growing population of detainees that were brought there.

One small improvement compared to where he'd first been confined was that each enclosure was furnished with a plain 3-gallon bucket that served as a toilet. It was hardly a private arrangement, especially since many of the enclosures were shared by more than one occupant, but it was a step above having to use the bare ground. Daniel's first job of the day was making the rounds to collect the buckets after the occupants set them outside through the dugout openings under the wire designed to be just large enough to allow them to do so. Daniel carried them two at a time down to a small creek that ran through the back of the camp to empty and rinse out before taking them back. It wasn't a pleasant task, but it was far less physically demanding than digging footings and mixing cement with a shovel, and Daniel had the freedom to work mostly at his own pace without a guard standing over him at all times.

Watching him closely was unnecessary, because Daniel understood perfectly well that he wasn't getting out of here until they let him out. There were always a couple of guards manning the front gate and at least two or three patrolling the main perimeter fence, and since all of them were armed with rifles, they could easily pick off anyone trying to escape across all that flat, open ground. But as long as he appeared busy and didn't go anywhere near the perimeter, Daniel noticed that the guards paid him little attention. Since the job necessarily placed him in close proximity to the detainees on the inside, Daniel took advantage of that fact to strike up hurried conversations with some of them as he worked. He knew he'd been observed doing this, but no one had stopped him because he took care not to linger too long at any one enclosure.

What he learned from most of the folks he talked to was that they were mostly from the nearby towns and surrounding rural countryside. The story he heard over and over was one of trucks arriving without warning, and armed men getting out and going house to house, rounding people up. Those that were here were for the most part, the ones that went peacefully. But some told of friends and family members that tried to resist and were either killed or wounded and taken elsewhere. The majority of those Daniel talked to were women, because there were so many here, and there were two in particular that caught his attention, because they mentioned that they had been arrested while traveling down the Atchafalaya River at night. Daniel told them he'd been on that river too, before he tried going to Texas, and he was very interested in hearing more of their story, but then he saw the guard staring at him, and he had to move on and take care of more buckets.

It wasn't until a couple of days later that Daniel had the opportunity to talk to the two women again, and this time he learned that the woman and the two young boys confined together in the next cell adjacent had been brought there with them. The partition between them prevented them from all seeing each other, but not from conversation. As they continued to talk, one of the women, who looked a bit older than Daniel, maybe in her mid-to-late forties, told him her name was Phyllis. She said that the men that took them captive were in uniform, and that she and her friends were certain they were U.S. military. She said that the soldiers treated her group like they were terrorists though, even though they weren't doing anything but traveling down the river at night because it wasn't safe to be on the roads or the river in the daytime. Daniel didn't know why it would have been soldiers that arrested them rather than C.R.I. contractors, but when she told him they were serious about the terrorists accusations and that all the men in the group, including her husband had been taken away someplace else, he became more curious.

"Why would they think that? Was anyone out there causing problems for them, the way terrorists would?"

"They said so, yes. They seemed to think our husbands were involved in stealing a gunboat from them," Phyllis whispered. "Stealing it and killing the crew. But Eric said it wasn't theirs to begin with. He said they had taken it from an Army unit up at the Simmesport lock and dam that had been wiped out just before he found us."

"Eric? Who is Eric?"

"I've probably already said too much," she whispered again, after glancing out towards the nearest guard standing by the fence less than 50 feet away. "I don't really know who he is. None of us did, except what he told us. But he said he was going to help us, and Sam and my husband, Darryl, and most of the other men believed him. That's why we were going down the river to meet him. He talked about fighting back against the people taking over the parish, and all of south Louisiana. He said he and his brother, who was a sheriff, I think, were building a militia!"

Daniel had heard enough! *A man named 'Eric' who had a brother in a sheriff's department on the Atchafalaya River?* It was mind-blowing if it were true, and he knew this 'Eric' Phyllis spoke of had to be the one and the same Eric that had caused him so much grief recently. He wondered how the man could still be out there, planning and scheming to kill yet more people with this so-called 'militia' of his, when he'd already told Commander Reyes where to find him. Because of the limited privileges that went along with his reassignment, Daniel had recently begun speaking with a couple of the camp guards on an occasional basis now and then. There was one in particular he felt comfortable enough with to relate what he'd heard, insisting when he did so that it was information that he knew Commander Reyes would find of interest. The man listened but didn't commit one way or the other as to whether he would relay the message up the chain of command. Daniel doubted he would ever know if he did or not, and he knew too there was little else he could do unless sometime in the future he got another opportunity to speak to Reyes in person; something which seemed unlikely after the first meeting.

But a couple of days later, after he had finished making his rounds to pick up and service the buckets, Daniel was carrying fresh drinking water to all the various enclosures when he came back to the row where the women were and saw that Phyllis wasn't there, even though he'd just seen her earlier that morning. Her cellmate, whose name he now knew was Suzanne, was clinging to the wire, clearly upset as she talked to the mother, whose name was Brenda, and her two sons on the other side of the partition that separated them. Phyllis was nowhere in sight, and when Daniel asked them what was going on, Suzanne pointed to a gray SUV out by the gate, telling him that two men they'd never seen before, accompanied by one of the guards, had come and taken Phyllis out of the enclosure. Daniel couldn't see inside through the vehicle's dark tinted windows, but the guard Daniel had spoken to before was standing there by the gate through which it would have to exit when it left the premises.

"They didn't say where they were taking her or why, and they wouldn't even look at us when we asked," Suzanne said.

But Daniel knew it was that same guard who'd singled her out from among the other three, and he knew exactly why. He'd begun to doubt it was ever going to happen, but now he knew someone wanted to follow-up on what he had reported and ask the woman more questions. Suzanne said the men tied and gagged her before putting her in the back, so he figured they were taking her elsewhere for the interview. He wished he had a way to find out more, but he didn't dare ask the guards too many questions. He'd said enough to get results of some sort. Whether it would finally lead to the demise of Eric Branson, Daniel had no idea, but he certainly hoped so!

Eric Branson was to blame for every bad thing that had befallen him, as far as Daniel Hartfield was concerned. He should have long since been back in south Florida with his family by now, or better yet, should have never left at all. If Eric hadn't come back and messed everything up, they wouldn't have. Yeah, Daniel got that Shauna was worried about Megan, but he didn't think she would go to the extreme of abandoning him to go halfway across the country with her ex-husband to find her. They'd had a good marriage as far as he was concerned before all this happened, so he knew it was much more Eric's fault than hers. Eric had manipulated her using her worries over their daughter, and then he'd turned her against Daniel and stolen her away from him because of it. The only solution Daniel had seen was getting Eric out of the picture, and that wasn't something he could do himself. He'd thought that sinking the boat to prevent Eric from carrying out his ludicrous plan to sail away with them would at least enable him to get his son out of a dangerous and damaging situation. But after his arrest, Daniel realized the very reason the authorities were forced to act so heavy-handed with the population was because of people like Eric Branson. People like him were malcontents who could never accept that the greater good of society would be better served by going along with those who were in charge of managing such things. Branson was the kind who always thought he knew better, and now, he was apparently stirring up discontent among the few other stubborn holdouts remaining in the Atchafalaya Basin, and it would only result in more suffering for all of them. Daniel hoped that by reporting what he'd heard, he had prevented some of that. It was time for Eric Branson to be stopped, and he felt certain that as soon as the last of those remaining residents were rounded up, he and all the rest of them would be removed to the real refugee centers in Texas, where they would have some semblance of a civilized life while waiting on the authorities to complete the restoration of the power and transportation grids and implement a peaceful transition back to the world of law and order.

Daniel was in good spirits that evening thinking he may have helped nudge things in the right direction and he knew something else was happening when he saw the same SUV parked inside the gate at about the same time the following morning. It only took a moment for him to understand why it was back. This time, he watched from a distance as they took the mother of the two boys out of the other enclosure adjacent to the one in which Phyllis had been, and Daniel heard her screaming and the boys crying as they tied her arms behind her back and led her away. The one remaining woman was clinging to the wire fence as close to the partition as she could while trying to calm the kids down by talking to them. Daniel was curious as to what exactly was going on as he watched them bind the woman's ankles and gag her before putting her into the back of the vehicle. Yesterday, he'd figured they were taking Phyllis somewhere for serious questioning, probably to Commander Reyes himself, if he had to guess. For some reason, they must have concluded this other woman named Brenda had useful information too, but why had they singled her out instead of taking both of them? Daniel didn't know, but he was almost certain it had something to do with what Phyllis had told them about Eric Branson.

The next morning at dawn, as he redistributed the rinsed buckets among the enclosures, he saw that Suzanne, the last remaining woman of the three had been moved into the same space with the boys whose mother had been taken away, and he wondered if they would come for the three of them next. It seemed he had his answer when shortly after sunrise, he saw a gray SUV approaching the front gate. Daniel knew it was the same vehicle that had taken away the others, but this time it was accompanied by three larger military vehicles that followed in a line behind it. This was interesting, because it had to mean that useful information had been gleaned from the women already questioned. *Maybe the soldiers that followed along now knew exactly where Eric Branson was, and were on their way to deal with him....* Daniel smiled to himself and kept moving, making sure to look busy, while keeping a watchful eye on the approaching vehicles so as not to miss whatever happened next.

THIRTEEN

"Just ease up a few more feet and stop," Sanders said, as Eric slowed the Yukon to a crawl when he neared the gate. "One of those guards always comes out to the driver's side to meet us. I see that both of them are the same two that were posted there the last couple of times I was here. They'll recognize me."

Eric only half-trusted Sanders, of course, and he had studied the perimeter of the place to the extent he could during his slow approach, noting that the staff buildings and the rest of the layout looked close enough to the sketch Sanders had drawn. He felt he had a sufficient force to take out all the security guards here if something went wrong and the shooting started when they pulled up, but that was the last thing he wanted to happen upon initial contact. The goal, of course, was to get Suzanne and those two boys out unhurt, and if they could accomplish that without a fight, so much the better. Any exchange of gunfire in such close proximity to all those caged detainees would put them at risk, so reducing the likelihood of it happening was the top priority.

When one of the two guards manning the gate came out and approached the vehicle, just as Sanders said he would, Eric pressed the button to roll down his window and sat there waiting with an indifferent expression. Sanders had told him that while all the men here were private contractors, they weren't working directly for C.R.I. The corporation had subbed out a lot of the work of setting up and running the refugee centers and the detention camps like this one to smaller outfits, so that they could keep their more experienced combat operators in the field manning checkpoints and conducting the round-up raids. Eric didn't underestimate the approaching guard or the others that were here based on that information alone though. They may have been getting paid less than the C.R.I. guys, but they still had training and good equipment and considering the situation in recent months, probably lots of experience in getting their hands dirty too. The one coming out to his window was carrying his rifle at low ready as he looked inside at Eric and Sanders.

"What's up with all this?" He asked, glancing at Eric but then directing his question to the man he knew instead. The guard was referring to all the extra vehicles and men of course.

"Ran into trouble!" Sanders answered. "I'm lucky to be alive, and wouldn't be if it weren't for these guys. Unfortunately, my partner, Robert didn't make it."

"Are you and your men from that Red River Wildlife Management Outpost?" The guard asked Eric.

"Yes sir! We had just rolled out for our morning patrol yesterday when we saw this vehicle boxed in at a roadblock set up by the insurgents. They had them spread out on the ground while they were searching the car, and as soon as they saw us, they opened fire. Sanders here and his partner were caught up in the middle of it. He took a round in the leg and lost a lot of blood, and like he said, his partner was KIA. Some of those bastards took off into the woods and my troops spent half the day hunting them down, but they got all of them. We took Sanders back to the post to look after his wound, and make sure he was going to survive. He said he was up for the trip back here today and asked for our help."

"I've got unfinished business," Sanders said, when the guard asked what he'd come back for. "That other woman that was with the two we took away for questioning... I need her to come with us too... her and the two boys that were with them. All of them have direct ties to the same bunch that attacked us. We got that much from interrogating the first two. We need all of them now though for leverage in bringing down the whole organization. Just like we thought, they're tied to that group operating on the Atchafalaya River."

"The one run by that Eric Branson guy?" The guard asked.

Eric was staring right at him when he asked that, but gave away nothing by way of reaction to hearing his own name. "Yeah, that's the one," Eric said. "Word of him has gotten all the way out here, huh?"

"Well, of course! Didn't Sanders tell you? He works for Commander Reyes out of Texas, so he knows Reyes has been trying to track down that Branson guy for weeks.

"He told me. He said one of the guards here overheard those women mention the guy. That's why they brought two of them to our post where we were holding the men. We knew those men we took in that night on the river were involved with the resistance operating out there, it was just a matter of getting them to talk. Are you the one they said something about Branson to?"

"No, that was Dyson, not me." He's working the perimeter patrol. I can get him over here if you want to talk to him though," he said, tapping the handheld radio clipped to his belt.

"That would be good," Eric said, glancing back to Sanders as if to confirm before turning back to the man with a question: "Are you gonna open that gate, or what?"

"Yes sir, sorry about that!" The guard stepped back and waved to his companion on the inside to swing it open.

"Thank you. The rest of my troops will wait out here," Eric looked into the side mirror at the three Humvees in line behind him. There was no good reason for all of the vehicles to go inside. If a fight broke out and they needed them in there, it would be a simple matter to breach the light-duty chain link gate by driving the relatively heavy vehicles right through it. But having them hang back made it far less likely that the guards would notice that any of the occupants looked out of place in those uniforms they wore, especially Bart and Sam. When his conversation with the first guard began, Eric still had some concern that he or his partner would look closer into the SUV and discover the two women in the back even though Sanders said they wouldn't since they would recognize him as the one who'd come here twice before in the same vehicle. As it turned out, the extra-dark tint of the back and side glass did its job, and Eric drove right in with no further scrutiny. With Diane and Cindy both well-armed and sitting there on ready inside the perimeter, Eric knew he'd already gained considerable advantage if the transfer of the three detainees they'd come for went sideways.

He left the vehicle running and got out to continue his conversation with the guards while Sanders remained in his seat, under Diane's watchful eye, lest he attempt some covert signal that all wasn't well. His wound was a valid reason for him to stay put where he was, and the two guards didn't question it. The one Eric had first talked to had already made the call to the fellow named Dyson that he had expressed interest in seeing. Eric didn't really want to talk to him, of course, but pretending like he did made the entire ruse seem more authentic and couldn't hurt. The *real* reason it was a good idea to let the other guy call him over was to draw him in where Eric and the rest of his team could keep an eye on him. The more of the guards they could concentrate up front by the gate and within easy shooting range the better. Eric had noted that the perimeter of the camp was big, and guards with rifles on the far side presented a real threat if they weren't neutralized quickly.

"I had no idea this place was so big," Eric said, as they waited on Dyson to get there. "Sanders tells me that most of these people inside here are from the smaller towns and rural areas between Lafayette and the river?"

"They are. That and a few that were trying to travel through that got picked up at the roadblocks and checkpoints."

"It looks like you guys have got them under control here. No real issues, I take it?"

"No, we've got it easy compared to y'all. Too easy, if you ask me. It's boring as hell out here. I'd rather be out there hunting down terrorists in the swamps to tell you the truth. We never even get to fire our weapons anymore. Haven't had an escape attempt in weeks!"

"Sanders said you've got most of the able-bodied males working construction, right? Hard work is always a good way to keep men too busy and too worn out to try anything stupid."

"Yeah, it's worked that way so far. Only about twenty percent of the detainees are healthy men anyway. It's mostly women and children we've got here, but they keep bringing more and we have to have somewhere to put them, so there's always new construction to keep the crews busy, including a new camp that's being built to handle the overflow. We've been making improvements ever since we got here. All those new enclosures you see there are a big step up from how we started. They're built on concrete to keep the detainees out of the mud, and as you can see, all the new ones have a roof overhead. None of the individual cells have more than two-to-four people, depending on whether or not they are family units and on the age of the occupants."

"Looks like really first-class accommodations." Eric said.

"Yep, like I said, it's a big step up. These folks in here are luckier than a lot of people that have been resettled, I'll tell you that."

Eric was seething with anger at what he saw, but neither his words nor his expression betrayed his disgust. Like Brenda had said, the people detained here were being treated like animals or worse. The wire cages were de facto kennels, upsized just enough to house human beings. The unfortunate people locked inside them had little protection from the elements, despite the overhead sheet metal roofing. It appeared from what he could see that each person had been issued a small blanket, and he saw the water jugs and toilet buckets Brenda had also mentioned but nothing else. Eric knew as he took it all in that he couldn't simply drive away from this, even if they *did* manage to secure Suzanne and the two boys without a fight. He was lost in his thoughts of his possible options to rectify it all when the guard named Dyson arrived after his long walk from the other side of the camp.

"Just follow me," Dyson said, after meeting Eric and saying hello to Sanders and learning what happened to him. "The woman you're looking for was moved into the same enclosure with those boys after they took their mother out the other day. I'll take you down there right now. They'll probably put up a struggle if you plan to bring them with you though. Have you got something to secure them with?"

Eric showed Dyson the coil of heavy cord he had stuffed in his pocket before the convoy rolled out that morning, and then asked what else he'd heard when he had gotten the name, Eric Branson from the captive women.

"Oh, they didn't talk to me directly. It was another detainee here on the premises. A trustee, I guess you'd call him. He's one of the men that was brought here that couldn't hang with the work crew. We've had the occasional fellow like him. I don't know what guys like him did in their prior lives, but they damned sure never did an honest day's work with their hands, that's for sure. Anyway, this guy got assigned to the shit bucket detail, which as you can see, gives him enough work to keep him busy in the mornings. He wasn't supposed to be talking to the detainees, but most of us let it slide, figuring it couldn't hurt anything, and as it turned out, I guess he learned something useful from one of those conversations that benefited us all."

"Funny how that works out, isn't it?" Eric smiled. As he walked a few paces behind the man, Eric visualized possible scenarios in his mind. He'd left his rifle in the vehicle, as it would have appeared strange to bring it with him in a place so obviously secure under the watch of armed guards. He *was* wearing his pistol in plain view in a combat holster though, as that was expected and wouldn't raise eyebrows anywhere in the field these days. And besides, after sizing up Dyson and the casual way he carried his M4, Eric knew he could take it from the man before he ever knew what was happening if he needed a rifle in a hurry.

It was hard to look at the pathetic faces of all the miserable people they walked by, and Eric was glad he didn't really have to and that to play his part he was required to look indifferent and uncaring. There would be time to make it up to those folks later, he hoped, but right now, he had to focus on the primary objective. When Dyson finally stopped as they walked along one of the long rows, Eric recognized Sam's wife, Suzanne, even though she was deliberately looking away from the two of them and focusing her attention on distracting the two boys, who were seated across from her with their backs against the wire.

"On your feet!" Dyson yelled. "You and those two punks need to come with us!"

Eric saw the fear in Suzanne's eyes as she looked up at the guard, and he knew she must have already seen the SUV parked out there and realized it meant they were about to take her away just as they had taken her friends. He was sure that she probably hadn't singled him out in particular from the guards, because as far as she was concerned, all the men here, whether in uniform or not were a threat and were not to be trusted. But now as she was getting up, she looked directly at him, and Eric saw the recognition change her expression a couple of seconds later. He was slightly behind Dyson at that moment, so he raised a finger to his lips and gave her a subtle wink. Suzanne was visibly shaken and confused, but she seemed to understand what she needed to do. Turning to the boys and taking each of them by the hand, she spoke to them in a soothing voice and told them they were all going somewhere and that it was okay, and then she led them through the open door that Dyson had just unlocked.

"I need you to put your hands behind your backs! All three of you!" Dyson ordered, as he grabbed Suzanne by one arm and pulled her away from the boys.

"Where are you taking me? Where are my friends those other men took away?"

"It's okay," Eric told her. "You're going to see your friends, but we have to secure your hands first." Eric gave her a slight smile that Dyson didn't see and then inserted himself between the guard and Suzanne. "I've got this," he told Dyson, taking one end of the roll of cord he'd pulled from his pocket before turning to the boys. "You're going to see your mother soon, but you've got to stay calm and put your hands behind your backs. It's just our standard Army procedure."

"I thought you Army people were the good guys!" The youngest of the two retorted. "But you took our daddy away and stole our boats and everything!"

"You'll understand why soon enough, and you'll see your mom and your dad. Just do as I say, and you won't have to come back here to this place ever again. I promise."

Eric saw the smirk on Dyson's face as he finished securing the boy's wrists. The guard no doubt thought Eric was telling the kid a bald-face lie, and that what he really meant was that both of them would see their parents in the next life, because he surely believed they were no longer still in this one. But Suzanne was cooperating in helping to keep the boys calm. Eric had no idea what she was thinking, but he was certain that she was in shock at seeing him there. Things were going as perfectly as could be expected, and Eric indicated to Dyson that he was ready to escort the detainees out to the vehicle as soon as he'd finished the last of his purposefully loose wraps and false knots.

But they had just started walking back when a sudden shout

from down by the far side of the perimeter stopped Dyson short. Eric turned to see what was the matter and spotted another security guard he hadn't seen before running towards them and shouting for them to stop. Behind the guard was an unkempt, bearded man dressed in clothes that were little more than rags, Eric had noticed him earlier, carrying buckets between the enclosures two rows over, and wondered if he was the trustee Dyson had spoken of that had talked to the women. Eric was aware of him stopping to stare as the two of them approached the cell holding Suzanne and the boys, but it had seemed inconsequential at the time, since after watching them for a few more moments, he seemed to be more interested in getting back to the task at hand. But it was apparent now that he'd slipped off to the opposite side of the perimeter unnoticed by either Eric or Dyson. And now Eric heard him screaming frantically at Dyson, while the other guard was running right behind stopped and took a stance to raise his rifle and point it their way.

"THAT'S HIM!" The man screamed. "THAT'S ERIC BRANSON, THE MAN YOU'VE BEEN LOOKING FOR! SHOOT HIM! SHOOT HIM NOW, DON'T LET HIM GET AWAY!"

FOURTEEN

Eric had no idea how the ragged looking man who was screaming at the guards could have recognized him, but it didn't matter. He had gotten their attention and there was no time to waste trying to figure it out. Before Dyson could react to what the man had just told him, Eric grabbed the two boys who were standing beside him and pulled them and Suzanne with him as he took them all down to the ground. His pistol was in his hand as soon as he rolled off them and out of reach of Dyson. The confused guard was still fumbling with his rifle that had been hanging loose in its sling when Eric fired two rounds that caught him center of mass and dropped him in his tracks. The distant guard with the rifle opened fire in his direction but didn't have a clear shot at him from where he'd stopped now that he was on the ground. Eric knew that would change in a moment though, and that the other guards by the gate and elsewhere in the camp would all respond to the sudden gunfire.

"Get back inside there! All of you!" Eric yelled at Suzanne, pointing to the still open door of the wire cage. "Stay down as flat on the floor as you can get!"

Eric was still on his belly as he crawled over and grabbed Dyson's rifle. When he saw the other guard that had fired at him come into view again, he dropped him with a double tap from the prone position. The trustee prisoner that had outed him went to the ground nearby too, probably fearing he would be next, but Eric was more concerned with the remaining guards that had weapons, especially those that could still be inside the buildings and in other parts of the camp that he couldn't see. He knew that Keith and the rest of the team were taking care of the two out at the gate, because multiple rounds of rapid rifle fire erupted from that direction almost immediately after the first shots were fired at him.

"I need you to stay here and keep down with those boys!" Eric yelled at Suzanne. "I'm coming back to get you, but we have to take care of all the guards first!"

"But there are a lot of them!" Suzanne warned.

"I'm not alone; don't worry! I've got plenty of help right outside the gate, including your husband, Sam, so hang tight!"

"Sam? *Sam is alive?*"

Eric assured her he was, as were the boys' parents, but he didn't have time to elaborate. He took off in the direction of the staff buildings, taking cover in the rear of the first one even as he saw Willis, Lenny, Trey, Hal and Elroy all following Bart through the front gate. He couldn't see how many guards were coming out of the front entrance of the buildings, but he knew Keith was waiting to greet them with the M2 when he heard a burst of 50 cal coming from the lead Humvee. Eric pressed in close against the side of the nearest structure and moved up to the front corner where he could see Bart and the other guys flattened against the walls on either side of the door in preparation to go in. When Bart saw Eric there ready to lead the way, he tossed an M67 grenade through the shattered glass of the front window that Keith had destroyed with the M2. Immediately after they heard the blast, Eric signaled to Willis and Lenny to follow him and then charged through the door to finish what the big machine gun and grenade shrapnel started. At least one survivor was still in the building though. Eric saw him dash from behind a solid wood counter and through an open door adjacent, slamming it shut behind him. The room in which he'd locked himself had no exit other than one small window on the back, and if the man attempted to climb out of it, Hal and the others still outside would have an easy job of picking him off. But Eric wasn't in the mood to wait for that to happen or to kick in the door and risk getting shot.

"Go tell Bart to go around to the side and toss one of those grenades through that window! We're clear in here except for that one room! You guys can check that other building, but it seems to be unoccupied. I'm going back to get Suzanne and those kids!"

Eric slipped out the front door to retrace his way back around the building to the rows of enclosures. He was anxious to get back to Suzanne and the two boys, knowing they had to be terrified after being caught right in the middle of what had just happened. Eric didn't ask for any help, but glancing over his shoulder, he saw Elroy following along, probably because he felt left out and didn't know what else to do. Eric didn't really need him but didn't want to hurt Elroy's feelings by sending him back, so he told him he could wait there by the corner of the staff buildings and cover him. As he made his way down the pathway between two rows of the enclosures, Eric saw the terror on the faces of all the occupants. He spoke to them as he went by, telling them he was not with the forces that were occupying the region, despite the uniform he wore, and informing them that they were about to be set free just as soon as the camp was deemed secure and in control.

When he came into view of Suzanne and the boys, he saw that she was watching hopefully for him, and the relief at seeing him return alive was written all over her face. The poor woman must have been petrified with fear after hearing all the shooting and explosions from the building and not knowing whether it was the guards or Eric and those who came with him who'd emerged victorious. Eric entered the enclosure and took her by the hand to help her up. The boys were already on their feet and raring to go, of course, after so many days of confinement there. Eric knew Suzanne must have told them while the firefight was raging that Eric really was one of the good guys and that he was there to help. He hadn't met the two of them directly when he and Jonathan were at Sam's camp, and even if they'd seen him there, he knew they were surely so traumatized by this experience of being brought here and caged that they wouldn't remember. And on top of that, as the younger one had already said, Eric looked like one of the bad soldiers who did all this to them. His return now and the promise of freedom that went with it had changed everything, but just when it seemed the worst was over, a burst of full auto fire sent bullets punching through the metal partition beside him and ricocheting wildly off the steel support poles in all directions. Eric dove through the enclosure doorway to grab the boys and slam them to the ground again. Suzanne knew what to do this time and was already prone on the concrete floor when Eric glanced back at her, but he heard the scream of another woman farther up the row that told him she must have been hit. The boys cried out in terror as Eric dragged them back inside just in time to avoid another stream of bullets that ripped into the gravel and dirt where they'd fallen. Before he could shift his focus to search for the shooter, Eric heard three quick shots from a semi-auto in the direction of the staff building, and knew they'd come from Elroy, who'd hung back to cover him as he asked. There was quiet again as the echoes of the gunfire died away, and Eric raised into a low crouch to scan for threats in the direction from which the full auto had come. But by then he heard Elroy reassure him:

"I got the son of a bitch!" He yelled. "Right down there!"

Eric saw Elroy jogging confidently in his direction and pointing beyond, towards the far end of the row of enclosures. When he stepped outside, after warning Suzanne to sit tight and wait, Eric saw the form of a man squirming and rolling about on the ground near the end of the row of enclosures. He could hear moaning and muffled cries of agony from the man now, and knew he was in bad shape. And he also saw that the wounded man wasn't one of the guards. But Elroy hadn't made a mistake. The weapon that had been used to fire those two bursts was laying on the ground a few feet away from the fallen man, and seeing how he was dressed, Eric knew he was the trustee that had shouted his name earlier, urging the guard that was with him to shoot and kill him. As Elroy reached him and the two of them moved in on the fallen man, Eric was pissed at himself for once again making a stupid mistake. He should have shot the deranged looking man as soon as he shot the guard next to him, just for calling him out, but he hadn't because he'd written him off as crazy but not much of a threat. But apparently, the guy had grabbed the dead guard's rifle and tried to kill him with it, and Eric still didn't know why. How did some stranger detained in this camp recognize him upon first sight, and why did he want that guard to kill him? Eric didn't know, but he aimed to find out.

"I had to stop him," Elroy said, as they neared the fallen man, who was curled up in a fetal position facing away from them and moaning. "I knew he wasn't one of those guards, but he was trying to shoot you!"

"You did the right thing, Elroy, and I appreciate it. That was good shooting!"

"Not good enough, I reckon, or he wouldn't still be alive!"

"Don't worry, from the looks of it, he won't be for long."

Eric circled around the fallen man with his weapon leveled. He wouldn't make another stupid mistake, and the first sign of a pistol, knife or other weapon would result in an immediate point blank response. Eric knew the man was mortally wounded when he saw the two exit wounds in the back of his blood-soaked shirt. He had every reason to finish him then and there with an anchoring shot to the back of the head, but he wanted to know who the guy was before he died, if at all possible.

"Secure that weapon and go check all those folks back in those enclosures for wounded. I heard at least one woman scream like she was hit!" Eric told Elroy, nodding at the fallen M4 as he dropped to a crouch to get a better look at the dying man. The scraggly beard, longer hair and dark tan all fooled him at first, as did the extreme weight loss since the last time he'd seen him. But as Eric stared closer and looked into the man's eyes, the recognition suddenly hit him like a punch in the face: *Daniel Hartfield!* This was Shauna's husband, Daniel Hartfield; the man who'd sank Eric's schooner, *Dreamtime* and left Shauna and his only son to flee to Texas! Eric hadn't expected to ever see the man again, let alone encounter him here, but there he was, bleeding out on the ground in front of him after trying to kill him by spraying rounds indiscriminately amid dozens of innocent detainees trapped in exposed wire pens. Daniel wanted Eric dead, just as he'd been screaming when he urged the guard to shoot him, and when that didn't work, he'd grabbed the fallen man's weapon and sneaked closer to try and do it himself! Eric knew Daniel's plan when he left was to get to one of the refugee camps in Texas, because that's all he'd been talking about for days prior. After discovering that he'd taken his stash of gold and fled in Keith's patrol truck, Eric figured Daniel would be stopped and shaken down by C.R.I. contractors somewhere along the way, but now it was apparent he'd never reached the state line at all, and that he must have been here all along!

Lots of things suddenly made sense to Eric now in light of what both Sanders and Brenda had told him yesterday. Daniel was the one Phyllis had been talking to, and whatever she'd told him, Daniel must have relayed it to the guard named Dyson, whom he'd recently become conversant with on some limited basis. Eric knew that had to be how his own name came up, and that whatever Daniel repeated had led to the execution of Phyllis and Darryl, with Brenda and Charlie slated to be next in line. On top of all that, Eric was already certain that Daniel had told someone working for C.R.I. where to look for him on the boat anchored in that remote dead lake off the Atchafalaya. The damage this man had done was really incalculable, but Eric hadn't had the time or resources to go hunting him down and had figured it virtually impossible to find him anyway. Yet here he was, lying right there on the ground in front of him. Daniel's time was running out now, regardless of what Eric might do, and knowing the man was Andrew's father and still technically Shauna's husband, Eric was glad he hadn't been the one that fired those fatal shots. Elroy had saved him from having to tell the two of them that he killed the guy, regardless of how much he deserved to meet his fate. Daniel was aware of Eric's presence now as he fought to breathe and tried to speak while he lay there coughing up blood.

"You didn't have to do any of this, Daniel," Eric said. "All I wanted to do was get my family to safety. I know you thought I was making the wrong choices, but I tried to warn you about what I'd learned was going on over in Texas. I told you it wasn't going to be what you were expecting, but I couldn't stop you from finding out the hard way."

"Try... just... trying to get my son to a better place..." Daniel said. "Where is he? Is he... okay?"

Eric could see the terror in Daniel's eyes as he asked this. The man wanted to know, but it was obvious he was afraid of the answer too. But Eric did his best to reassure him by telling him the truth.

"Andrew is fine, Daniel. He *is* in a better place and he's perfectly safe for now. We are going to do everything in our power to make sure he stays that way. He has a stepmother and stepsister that love him very much."

"Tell him... I... Tell him... I...do...too... I'm sorry. Sorry man.... I just couldn't... Couldn't do this... I couldn't live this kind of life... I just... couldn't...." Daniel tried to take in another breath, but then his body relaxed as the last of the air in his lungs was expelled.

"I'll tell him," Eric said, as he stood and then turned to go back to check on Suzanne and the two boys.

When he got back to the enclosure, they were all gone, but Hal, Lenny and Willis were going up and down the rows unlocking the gates to let the other detainees out, and they told him Elroy had taken Suzanne out to see her husband and to reunite the boys with their mother and father. Hal said there was another woman who went with them that had been shot in the arm and was in pain, but wasn't in life-threatening danger. The staff buildings were clear and all the guards on the premises were dead. They'd found padlock keys on a couple of them and so far, were having no trouble unlocking the dozens of enclosures in this part of the compound.

Now that the fight was over and Eric could assess the other problems unrelated to securing the premises, he was struck by the sheer number of people they were freeing here and the resulting problems of what to do with them and how to move them to safety. The truth was that it was beyond the capability and resources of the small team he had at the moment, and most of them were going to have to seek refuge and fend for themselves to a large degree until he could figure out something better. Eric shook his head as he looked at all the people coming out of those cages the guys unlocked. It was an overwhelming problem, but at least they were free of that barbaric confinement. He made his way out to the front gate to find Bart and Keith, both to tell them about Daniel Hartfield and to get their take on the situation and make a plan for what would come next.

"What an idiot!" Keith said. "And now he's dead just because he wouldn't listen to any of us and had to do things his way."

"Didn't know how good he had it!" Bart said. "I reckon he found out when he landed in here. Well, I hate we're gonna have to tell Andrew when we get back, but you know I always told both of you boys that there's just some folks you can't help. You can try 'til you're blue in the face and they just won't listen to common sense. I hate it for the boy, but that fellow pretty much got what he was asking for, especially still trying to gun you down when we showed up to liberate everybody here."

"I'd hate to think we liberated him," Keith said. "And I'd really hate it if we had to take him back with us and listen to his shit again."

They all knew damned well that wouldn't have happened even if Daniel had begged them to let him come. Not after the way he sabotaged Eric's plan by sinking the schooner, and then nearly got them all killed by giving away their hideout.

"Daniel couldn't be helped," Eric said, "but what about all these other folks? What are we going to do about them?"

"I've been wondering the same thing," Keith said. "We found enough food on hand in the supply room to feed all of them for a while, but they won't be safe here, of course. Marcus and Trey are collecting all the weapons off the guards we killed and any they find in the buildings and vehicles. I was thinking we could distribute some around if there's a few folks in the bunch that know how to handle them."

"That's a start," Eric said, as he looked beyond the building to the parking area on the other side. "It looks like we've got five full-sized pickups with open beds. A lot of people can fit in those, but it'll still take a few trips."

"But to where?" Keith asked. "We can't take all these people to Sierra Zulu, and even if we could, we couldn't feed them long term, and most of them are women and children and won't be joining our militia."

"No, I know we can't take them there, but we can't exactly just wish them luck and drive away either. That guard I spoke to, you know, the one that took me down there to where Suzanne and the boys were locked up, and as it turned out, the same one Daniel had snitched to after talking to Phyllis, also told me something else. I didn't know it was Daniel at the time, of course, but he said the man who talked to her and told him what she said had been on a work crew and had been pulled off to do bucket duty because he couldn't keep up in construction. That crew is the reason there are so few men here, if I had to guess. If we can find out where they take them every day, it should be a simple matter to set them free too. If we do that and arm them, then they can take care of their own and we can go."

"I understand what you're saying, son," Bart said, "and everything's gone smooth so far, but we're getting in pretty deep out here, so far from the river. You never know what we could run into if we go any farther or hang around any longer. I'm not saying we shouldn't do it; I'm just saying there's a lot of risk."

"I agree that we need to try, but my question is how do we find out where the work crew is, now that the guards are all dead?" Keith asked.

"I'm going to see if Sanders knows anything first. Of course, Daniel probably knew, but it's too late to ask him. Maybe there are others here like him that went out with them but couldn't cut the mustard and got locked up with the women and children instead? I noticed one or two wimpy-looking dudes when I was walking through. Maybe get some of our guys to ask around, see if anyone they've let out of those cages can tell us something? We know that wherever they're working, they'll probably bring them in before night, but we can't wait that long and besides, there's no way to hide what happened here today like we did at the outpost before the patrol came back. We've got to go to them. Whatever guard detail they have watching over them out there, when they see us rolling up in the Humvees, they'll probably assume we're on their side, just like here. It'll go just as smooth—we've just got to know where to look for them!"

FIFTEEN

"Where's Diane?" Eric asked, when he returned to where he'd parked the Yukon inside the gate and found Cindy alone inside it keeping watch over Sanders.

"She went to look for her Aunt Lucy. She said she saw someone over there among all the people that were released that was from her aunt's neighborhood. She said that since everyone that lived there was rounded up by the C.R.I. men, she thought her aunt may be here too."

Eric nodded. He didn't like that Diane had left her assigned post, but he understood her motivation, and remembered her worries about her Aunt Lucy the day he met her after the contractors swept through that community. Besides, Sanders was hardly a threat or an escape risk in his condition, reclined and in pain. as he was in the front passenger seat. Cindy had him under control just fine.

"What you've told me so far has proven to be true," Eric said to Sanders. "Our deal was that my business with you would be finished after we got what we came for, and I intend to keep my end of the bargain. But you can see the problem we have now: all of these people suddenly released but with nowhere to go and no one to provide protection and help them. My understanding is that most of the men brought here are being used for forced labor, and that's why there are hardly any around. What I need to know is where I can find them. If you know of any new construction projects the company in charge of this camp has underway, I need you to tell me where they are so I can get those men out and let them watch out for these women and children. It'll probably go better for you too if that happens, because if the guards in charge of that work crew return here and find you here alive after all this, you're going to have a lot of explaining to do."

"I'm going to have a lot of explaining to do no matter what happens," Sanders said.

"Yeah, but it'll go a lot better for you if it's some of your own guys that are asking the questions, won't it?"

Sanders nodded, but asserted that he really didn't know the details of the new projects underway in the area. He worked under Reyes, in Texas, and most of his business here in Louisiana had been coordinating C.R.I operations with what the North American Interior Defense forces were planning. "They're probably building more detainee facilities somewhere nearby, but I couldn't tell you where. If I had to guess though, it would be somewhere north of here, because the resettlement program is mostly complete farther north."

Eric believed he was telling the truth, as he knew Sanders could care less whether or not Eric and his team killed a few more contractors from a company he didn't work for. And the fact that they were liberating scores of civilians C.R.I. had already rounded up only meant more job security for him when he recovered from his wound and was sent out to try and get them back. Eric still didn't know where the funding was coming from, but this entire operation was a gold mine for a company like C.R.I., which had no doubt expanded its profits exponentially in recent months.

Eric left him there with Cindy and headed for the crowd of

detainees, hoping to find someone that had an idea of where the work crew had been going in recent days. He spotted Diane walking with her arm around an older woman and knew she had found her Aunt Lucy. Before he could go over and meet the woman though, Trey intercepted him, saying he had located someone with information about the work crew. It was a man who was fit enough and at the right age to be among the laborers but was sidelined by a fall that had him limping with a badly swollen foot and ankle. Eric followed Trey back to where the man was sitting in the shade of the staff building and squatted down beside him to hear what he had to say. When he rose again to go talk to Bart and Keith, Eric had his mind made up. Rescuing that work crew was the only solution to the problem of what to do with all these newly released people.

"That's nearly two dozen able-bodied men we're talking about," Eric said, as he related the information to them. "From what that guy just told me, anyone capable of keeping up out there is already a survivor. I could tell by looking at him that he was fit and strong too, he just had a nasty fall, probably because they were pushed and in a hurry all the time. If we set those men loose and arm them, that's a decent little force right there. They can take care of the others that need protection for now, but they'll owe us a favor in return later. There's nothing to lose by going there right now and doing it."

"And this new camp they're building is only a few miles away?" Keith asked.

"Yep. Best he could guess, he figured less than ten. They drive them up there in the back of the trucks every day, so he had a good view of everything along the way and memorized the route. He said he'd been there with them every day for a couple of weeks before he had the accident. Four pickups with the drivers and usually a couple extra guards, so figure half a dozen total. And the place is out in the open like this one. They're digging footings and mixing concrete by hand, just like they did here."

"Planning on penning up a lot more folks, it sounds like," Bart said. "They are some sick bastards!"

"We can put a stop to it. But we need to get going."

"What about security here?" Keith asked. "More guys from that company may show up anytime, or even a C.R.I. patrol."

"Of course. We'll leave most of the team here, and that includes you, Dad."

Bart grumbled but understood. It would be better if the small team Eric took all appeared to be military-aged men. It would be hard to hide anyone approaching a site out in the open like that.

"I'd like you to go with us though," Eric told Keith. "Let's take Willis and Lenny. They've both proven they're up to it. Four of us should be plenty, and we can all go in just one Humvee. That'll leave enough here to defend the camp while we're gone, which hopefully won't be long. Does that sound okay to you?" Eric looked at Bart. "We'll leave the Humvee with the M2 here. You can back it up inside that front gate and have the gun ready to light up anything coming down that road that doesn't look like us. Just make damned sure to confirm though, because we will be bringing those four trucks with us if the intel I got is correct!"

Willis and Lenny were eager to go of course, and after a quick weapons check the four of them rolled out, all in uniform and helmets and looking like legitimate NAID soldiers. Sanders told Eric to expect the appearance of the Humvee to be a bit of a surprise to the work crew's guards, but not the sort that would put them in immediate danger. Like the guards here at the main camp, by the time they figured out something was off about the arriving soldiers, it would be too late.

Sanders' guess that the new encampment would be somewhere to the north was correct too. Eric was behind the wheel of the Humvee as he followed the route the injured man from the work crew had described. The scenery on both sides of the rural parish road was more of the same that they'd seen this morning on the way to the main camp; broad expanses of untended soybean and rice fields, broken up by narrow strips of woodlands and the occasional cluster of abandoned rural houses here and there. None of the local inhabitants that had lived in these easily accessible locations remained in their homes now, but it was impossible to know how many had left before the raids and how many had been swept up in them and removed for resettlement. This was going to keep happening and spreading unless a serious resistance could be built and sustained, Eric knew, but for folks in this part of the state, it was already too late. If any of the survivors they'd liberated today were from around these parts, there was no way they could simply return home. They were going to have to move east to the river basin or beyond, but whether they could make it there or not was another matter and a question that could only be answered in time.

Eric spotted the parked pickup trucks out across an empty field on the east side of the road long before they reached the turnoff that led to the construction site. There were three of them instead of the four he'd expected, but it wasn't a real cause for alarm, because he knew that maybe only three came out here today. If there was another one somewhere else, it meant they wouldn't get all those guards in one go, the way he intended, but they couldn't wait and see, because the Humvee's approach had already gotten the attention of everyone out there. When they turned off onto the dirt road leading to the site, they spotted the group of workers they'd come to get out, busy under the watch of two guards standing over them. But to get to them, they first had to deal with the one who was standing in the road waiting to greet them, and his two companions leaning against the side of one of the pickups behind him.

"So, what do you want to tell them?" Keith asked. "That we're here to check out the future facilities?"

"We ain't gotta tell them shit!" Willis said, as he leaned forward between Eric and Keith from the back seat, trying to get a better look.

"I agree," Eric said. "It's not like we're trying to do this in a subtle way or anything. "I count five of them. Anybody see something I missed?"

"Looks right to me," Keith said.

"If there *is* a fourth truck that came out here today, it may be somewhere nearby, so keep that in mind. But those five shouldn't be a problem. I'll pull up to the nearest one like we do want to talk and take him out first with my Glock, so he won't see it coming. Willis, you and Lenny have your rifles ready so you can focus on the two out there by the crew. Keith and I will bail out and get the other two standing by that truck. Just be careful and don't hit any of our future recruits!"

Eric studied the guards and the workers as he made his slow approach. The men glanced at the Humvee but didn't stop what they were doing. Both guards standing out there with them were armed with rifles they carried on slings, while the other three close by only had their sidearms on them, as they had been hanging around the vehicles rather than directly supervising the work. Eric trusted Willis and Lenny to take the longer shots and neutralize the two with the rifles. Since they were in the back, their weapons would be less obvious when he pulled up and stopped near the three pickups.

The nearest guard that had been waiting began walking straight towards them to see what this unexpected visit was all about, just as Eric figured he would. He was looking directly at Eric and his companions with a serious expression, but the helmets and uniforms the four of them wore seemed to have the desired effect of diffusing any doubts he may have had about their right to be there. His hands were relaxed at his sides as he walked up to the Humvee, and a glance at the other two still standing next to the truck told Eric none of them felt threatened. But Eric didn't give him a chance to even ask the first question. He already had the Glock in hand, holding it down between his right thigh and the shifter. As soon as the guard was adjacent to the wide-open side of the doorless vehicle, Eric brought it to bear and shot him twice in the face.

The man had barely hit the ground before he and Keith stepped out simultaneously on either side to engage the other two that were some 20 feet away. Both men attempted to draw and move at the same time, but they had the huge disadvantage of being on the reactive side of a gunfight that Eric and Keith had already visualized in advance. Eric's guy did manage to sidestep fast enough that he caught the first bullet in his left shoulder, rather than center of mass however, while the one Keith engaged took one in the throat and a quick follow-up to the chest. Eric lunged low on a diagonal line to stabilize and present a smaller target just as his opponent got off a wild shot that hit the already bullet-riddled Humvee. His next two shots put an end to the fight, and he turned to check on Willis and Lenny to see how they'd fared with their two, more distant targets.

"They're running off!" Lenny yelled, as Willis pushed a couple more rounds into the side loading gate of his .30-30, cussing about botching his first shot too and needing a second.

Eric looked where Lenny was pointing and saw it wasn't the guards he was talking about, because both were down and either dead or dying, but sure enough, every man on the work crew had taken off at a dead run across the broad expanse of that empty field. Eric quickly surmised that the captives must have seen this as their one and only chance of escape and were going for it. The back side of the field was more than half a mile away but was bordered by heavy woods and Eric knew if they made it to those trees, they'd never round them all up. He and all three of his companions tried shouting after them to tell them they were here to get them out, but it was to no avail. As far as those men were concerned, the four soldiers that had killed their guards were every bit as much their enemy as the men that enslaved them.

"Go after them!" Eric yelled at Willis. You and Lenny are faster than us. We'll follow this road in the Humvee and see if it goes around to the back side of that field. It's way too wet to cut straight across."

Willis and Lenny took off without another word, but the men

they were chasing had a good 200-yard head start on them now. Eric and Keith were just about to jump in the Humvee and try to find their way around there when Keith looked out towards the main road and stopped Eric short.

"We've got company coming! Look!"

It was the missing truck! Eric saw it coming down the paved road from the opposite direction they'd arrived. He could see that there were two men in the front seats, and was sure they'd noticed the Humvee, even if they were still too far away to spot the five dead guards or see the foot race that was taking place out in that huge field.

"Go!" Eric said to Keith. "Go ahead and try and cut those guys off! I've got this."

Keith nodded and got into the driver's seat while Eric took up a position behind one of the parked trucks. As Keith drove past the work site down the two-track dirt road that appeared to lead to those distant woods, the arriving pickup turned off the pavement and sped in Eric's direction. He didn't know how much they had seen yet, but he figured they were on alert for trouble by now, and he was about to give it to them. Eric watched as they took in the scene and knew they must be in disbelief. Finding all their companions dead and the work crew gone had come as a shock, and he was sure they must be having second thoughts about pursuing that Humvee after seeing the fate of the other five men. Eric waited until they pulled up and stopped a few feet from the body of the first man he'd shot from inside the vehicle. This fourth truck was a nice, late-model Ford F250, and there was no sense messing it up with bullet holes and shattered glass, so he held off until the two men inside got out with their weapons and approached their fallen comrade. Eric had intended to waste them then and there and be done with it, but then a sudden thought changed his mind. These men had put a lot of innocent people through immeasurable pain and suffering, treating them worse than animals both in the way they caged them in the camp and then worked them half to death on their projects. He decided they needed a taste of that suffering as well, while serving as a warning to the others they worked with that it could happen to them too. Eric had the drop on them, and when he shouted out to them from where he was partially concealed behind the other truck just 20 feet away, both men chose wisely to comply. They knew after looking into their dead coworker's glassy eyes that the man pointing an M4 at them wouldn't hesitate to pull the trigger if they didn't.

Eric ordered the two men to remove their boots and socks after collecting their weapons and tossing them into the cab of the truck. Like the other five that lay dead nearby, these two weren't fighters on the level of the better trained and better paid C.R.I. contractors. What they were good at was bullying unarmed and helpless people, and with the tables turned their cowardice in the face of death was readily apparent. Eric had noted the rows of handcuffs locked to pad eyes in the bed of the trucks that were already parked there, and the Ford these two arrived in had them too. Their purpose was to keep the workers riding in the back from jumping out to escape en route to and from the job sites. He ordered the two men to climb in and cuff themselves to the bed of the Ford, and then got in it and drove it down the rough path Keith had taken to see if his brother had any luck heading off the running men.

Dodging mud holes and the deepest of the ruts, Eric followed the tracks of the Humvee until he caught up where Keith had stopped at the edge of the woods. Willis and Lenny were sitting in the grass catching their breath from their all-out sprint, as were the men they'd succeeded in stopping just before they disappeared into the tangled undergrowth behind them. When Eric pulled up and the men saw the two unarmed guards he had secured in the back, they got to their feet at once and converged like an angry mob. It was all Eric and Keith could do to keep them from climbing up there and tearing those two apart, and no one could blame them for wanting to.

"I know exactly how you feel," Eric told them. "And they'll get what's coming to them. They're only alive now because I decided they would be a good way to send a message to the others who would come here and do what these men did to you and your families. They'll find them in the cages they made you build, and if they're still alive when they do, these men can warn them that the people that live out here will not submit to what they have planned. There are more of us willing to fight and die than they think, and we are only just beginning to organize the resistance that will drive them out of Louisiana and beyond. But what we need to do now is get all of you and the others that were being held in that camp to safety. We'll use the trucks they brought you here in, and then you can keep them or do whatever you want with them. We will collect their weapons and we have plenty more weapons and ammunition back at the camp, as well as supplies to last you a while. But we need to go now, before someone else comes and finds out what happened, because the time to fight isn't today, but later, when you are better prepared and better organized and set up in a secure location."

Eric's logic defused the situation, and the grumbling men backed off. Keith drove three of them back to the work site to get the other trucks, and when they returned, the entire crew loaded up and followed Eric back to the liberated detention camp. After sorting through the weapons they'd picked up but didn't need, Eric and the rest of his team distributed them among the freed men and told them to take all the food and other useful supplies and equipment they wanted from the staff buildings. He then gave them the keys to all the trucks belonging to the contractors, as well as the GMC Yukon that Sanders had been waiting in.

"I told you I would let you live if you cooperated, and I intend to keep my word," Eric told Sanders. "It was all I could do to save those two guards from being beaten to death by that work crew, and I'm sure they'd be happy to do the same to you too. I have to secure the three of you in one of those enclosures to ensure that all the civilians here can evacuate the premises unchallenged. I'll leave you with enough food and water for a few days, because I'm sure someone from your company or theirs will be along before it runs out. If not, then there's really nothing I can do about it. You knew the risks when you signed up for the job. But if they *do* come and let you out before it's too late, you can tell Commander Reyes that Eric Branson has a message for him: Tell him the price to take south Louisiana is a price too high for him to pay. Tell him Texas may be in control for now, but the people here know what is happening and won't give up another inch. And every attempt to do what was done here in this place will end the same as it did here today."

"You're Eric Branson?" Sanders was staring at him dumbfounded, until Eric turned away to go get a couple of the guys to carry him from the vehicle, ignoring the barrage of questions Sanders shouted after him.

SIXTEEN

"It's about time!" Jonathan said to Ronnie, as he jumped up from the small table in the cabin of the *Gulf Traveler* to grab the VHF microphone off its hanger and answer the long-awaited radio call. The speaker hailing them on the preselected channel Jonathan and Ronnie had been monitoring was Willis, and he was calling for an upriver extraction!

Jonathan and Ronnie had been passing the time with card games and conversation as the wait dragged on and on. Both knew the longer they went without word from Eric and his team, the greater the odds that something had gone wrong. Jonathan had been working with Eric long enough now to doubt he would fail, but the uncertainty was still nerve wracking. They were tucked away in a dead-end canal at the head of the Atchafalaya near the Simmesport lock and dam where Sergeant Patterson's Army post had been wiped out. They had both the *Gulf Traveler* and the gunboat tied up there, as they had used both vessels to transport the team here and hoped to have the boats even more loaded on the way back if the rescue went as planned. It was risky to hang around on this remote part of the river, especially since it was just the two of them, but there was no other reasonable way to get everyone out. They had no radio that could reach as far as Sierra Zulu, so Jonathan and Ronnie couldn't go back there to wait in the meantime. They needed to be on standby, because if Eric and the team succeeded in getting Sam and those taken with him, they were going to need a ride downriver as soon as possible. Vicky didn't like it when Jonathan told her he would be gone as long as it took, and neither did Ronnie's wife, Becca, but the men weren't willing to put their women at risk by bringing them along either.

As far as they knew that traitorous North American Interior Defense forces unit that Sergeant Davis was in command of had no further capability to conduct river patrols, now that the gunboat and the *Gulf Traveler* were back in the hands of the new militia Eric and Keith were building. But there was still the uncertainty of not knowing whether some other vessel might come from downriver or attempt to enter the Atchafalaya from the Mississippi by way of the nearby locks. It made the waiting stressful, and it was a huge relief to both men to finally hear that voice over the radio, calling for a pickup.

"I'm at the drop-off point," Willis said, referring to a small sandbar on the west bank of the Red River, where Eric's team had inserted for the overland trek to their objective.

"Roger that!" Jonathan answered. "We're on the way. ETA fifteen minutes!"

They scrambled to start the engines and untie the lines they'd secured to trees at the edge of the canal. Ronnie would pilot the gunboat, while Jonathan followed in the *Gulf Traveler*. While Jonathan was supposed to be Ronnie's gunner, they didn't have anyone else that could run the other boat, so the M2 on the bow would be unmanned until they picked up Willis. They saw him when he emerged from the undergrowth as soon as the two boats pulled up to the sandbar.

"We wiped that outpost up there off the map!" Willis said. "Not a single man got out alive! We got Sam and his wife out, a guy named Marcus, and one other guy with his wife and two sons. But those sons of bitches had already shot two of the prisoners before we got there!"

Willis went on to tell them that they'd taken three good Humvees and several pickups, as well as another big stash of weapons, ammo and food supplies. "And we're probably going to have a lot of new volunteers. We took down an entire detention camp those contractors had built to 'resettle' local people they'd forced out of their homes. There's about 20 pissed off dudes I know of that have been forced to do hard labor ever since they were taken in. They're loose now, thanks to Eric, and they'll be ready to join us to fight back just as soon as they get what's left of their families back together and moved somewhere they can hide out. They're using those trucks to do that now, and Sam told them about an old abandoned farm not far from the river where they could go for the time being. Eric sent me to call you guys to come pick up him and the rest of the team up there near that outpost we took down, because some of those we rescued couldn't walk all the way here. I know right where they're waiting though, and I'll show you where to stop when we get there."

They reached the extraction point without incident and Eric and the team boarded the boats for the downriver run. Sam's friend, Charlie, was the only one that had to be carried aboard, and they put him in one of the bunks down below in the *Gulf Traveler* before loading on the supplies they'd taken from the outpost and stashed in the field where they'd staged their assault on the detention camp.

"There was a lot more food and other stuff at that camp, but we gave it to the folks we freed there," Eric said. "Some of them are about half-starved and need it a lot more than we do. I want to get Sam and his friends down to Sierra Zulu so they can recover. We'll be running back upriver soon to meet up with the refugees again and make a plan for bringing them into the militia."

"I'd like to see the look on those contractors' faces whenever more of them show up at that camp and see it emptied out and their own guys locked up." Jonathan said, when Eric told him about the two guards he'd taken back alive, locking them in one of the same pens they'd been keeping the innocent detainees in.

"We certainly sent them a message. I don't expect it to change much, but it's a start. Sanders will tell them we mean business, because he saw what happened at the outpost too. It won't change their plans in the big scheme of things, but I think it will cause them to focus their efforts elsewhere for a little while and avoid the Atchafalaya Basin. If so, it will buy us more time to prepare, and to see what other help we can get."

When Jonathan questioned Eric about the nature of that other help, Eric told him that he had talked quite a lot more with Sergeant Davis between the serious interrogation of the man and the implementation of the deceptive ploy that ultimately resulted in his death. Davis had told Eric much more of what he knew of the big picture of all that was going on, and with that information, Eric started thinking in much bigger terms himself. He told Jonathan that while they may have won these smaller battles they couldn't avoid; they weren't going to win the larger war for the region without lots of organized and coordinated help. And when Eric told him where he thought he might find such help, Jonathan begged him to let him go too.

"You're gonna need me, man. You know you need me to cover for you, like I always do."

"Yeah, but Vicky may need you more. You're going to have to beg her for permission to go on a trip like that. I may be gone a while."

"Vicky will be cool with it! If you can convince Shauna it's a good idea, I can handle Vicky!"

"Maybe, but don't get too excited yet. I've got a lot to talk about with Keith and Bart first, because they'll be in charge while I'm gone, if I do go."

Jonathan already knew it would happen, no matter how noncommittal Eric was about it now. It made a lot of sense in almost every way, and if Eric didn't think so, Jonathan knew he wouldn't have even mentioned it. The only question now was how much time he would have to spend with Vicky before he was saying goodbye to her again.

"I'M SORRY IT WENT DOWN THAT WAY," ERIC SAID, AS SHAUNA turned and stared out into space over the bayou at the news he brought her. She was silent for a long moment, and Eric didn't know what to say or do while she was lost in her thoughts. He'd just given her the news that her husband was dead, and no matter what she may have thought of the man due to his actions in recent weeks and months, Eric knew she'd once cared about him enough to marry him and take his name.

"At least now we know," she finally said. "I really thought something had already happened to him, but figured I'd never find out for sure."

"Me too," Eric said. "It was a surprise finding him there."

"I'm just glad he didn't succeed in what he tried to do. I'm shocked that he went so far off the deep end that he would do something like that. It's a wonder he didn't kill you and several others, firing into those enclosures like that. But I'm also glad it wasn't you who killed him."

"Yeah, I thought of that. I don't know how I'd ever face Andrew if I had. Do you want me to be there with you when you tell him?"

"I don't think we *should* tell him, Eric. He's been through enough already, just knowing his dad left without him the way he did. He doesn't talk about it anymore, so why bring all that back on him now, and make it worse by telling him he no longer has a father? Maybe I'll find a way to tell him later, but there's too much uncertainty right now anyway. Andrew may not show it, but he has to be afraid, just like all us adults are. We don't know how this is going to end for any of us, or if we'll ever escape this nightmare we seem to be stuck in."

Eric didn't try to change her mind about telling Andrew and it was a relief to him to hear her say that. Shauna was probably right. The kid had been through enough without having to hear that his father had died too. Everyone in their group had family members and friends that were unaccounted for and unreachable in a world where modern communications systems were down, and travel was nearly impossible. Sometimes not knowing was better than knowing, and a little glimmer of hope could provide a reason to keep driving on when otherwise there was little. Andrew was young and resilient. He was surrounded by good people now, and Eric would do his best to make sure it stayed that way. But as for the nightmare Shauna said they were stuck in, Eric had to disagree. 'Stuck' was a temporary situation. He'd just scored a significant victory against two different organizations that were aligned against them. Eric had no intention of slacking up now that the momentum was starting, but he did recognize the need for outside help if he could get it. Shauna had heard none of the intel Eric got from Sergeant Davis until now, so he filled her in from the beginning, and laid out his reasoning for the next course of action he planned to take.

"A large area east of the Mississippi is still in control of real national guard units and militias," he told her. "Davis talked about it like it was their biggest problem, and one they hadn't even begun to address. From what I gathered, things over there are surely better than here."

"Then why don't we all go?" Shauna asked. "I told you before that we should take the boats we have and head east along the coast to some of the other bays or coastal rivers. There are lots of isolated areas along the Gulf that are probably safer than here."

"Maybe, but we don't know which specific areas are, and it's too risky to move everyone even if we did know. Besides, it's unlikely that we'd be welcome. Places that are maintaining law and order are only doing so by keeping their security tight and keeping outsiders out. It's not like we can show up and expect them to welcome us with open arms."

"But you said those areas are in the control of legitimate soldiers! If that's the case, then we have every right. We *are* American citizens, after all!"

"Don't assume we have any rights anywhere now, Shauna. You've seen enough to know that already. Those forces over there may or may not be as helpful or welcoming as those who helped you and Jonathan get to Colorado. It would be a huge mistake to show up there as desperate refugees seeking asylum, especially the way our numbers here have grown. We'd have to have something to offer in return, otherwise, we'd just be more mouths to feed in a time when everyone's resources are stressed to the limit.

"Besides, I can't even be sure that the intel I got from Davis is accurate. Everything else he told me was, but he hasn't been east of the river personally, so it's not verified firsthand. The only way to find out is to go, and that's what I intend to do, just so you know."

"You want to go off on your own again? When is this ever going to stop, Eric? Every time you go, there's always something else that happens that delays your return, just like this mission you just got back from."

"You know it couldn't be helped. I just told you everything that happened. The mission was a success, and achieving the objective is all that counts, not the timetable. Look, I'd rather not leave you and Megan again at all, and I wouldn't if I didn't have to. If I had my way, you know where we'd all be right now; anchored off some island in the middle of nowhere with no need to carry weapons all day and sleep with them at night. But that dream is still on the bottom of the bayou, and there's no way in hell I can resurrect it right now knowing the magnitude of the threat this entire region is facing. Now, if there is a sizable force of soldiers and civilian militia over there in Mississippi and Alabama like Davis said, it could be that they're not aware of the full extent of the threat that will eventually come for them too. That's what I have to offer them; firsthand intel from on the ground here, and the volunteers and resources we've managed to gather. If I can convince them that I know what is being planned and carried out here, maybe they'll be willing to send forces here to help prevent our mutual enemies from crossing the river into their territory. And if they won't do that, maybe they *will* invite us to come over there and take refuge or fight with them. There's too much at stake to simply ignore the possibility and not go and find out! We've dealt the enemy a setback with what we just accomplished, but it won't slow them down long, and we have nowhere near the number of fighters we'd need to hold them off indefinitely. So that's why, Shauna. That's why I have to go."

Shauna wasn't happy, but Eric knew he'd laid out his case for the expedition and she would accept it. She asked him who he was taking with him, and Eric told her he'd already spoken with Jonathan, Willis and Lenny about it. The three young men were all fit to travel hard in any conditions, and all had proven their competence and bravery in the face of extreme danger in battle. Eric told her he couldn't ask for better men, especially since Keith and Bart were needed here to work with the new recruits and maintain security patrols on the nearby sections of the river south of I-10.

"We'll go upriver to Simmesport in the gunboat with Ronnie and Bart. We'll have to operate the locks ourselves to get the boat to the Mississippi, and then they can run us across to the east bank. We'll go on foot from there until we can find and contact militia or military forces on the ground."

"And there's no telling how long that will take, is there, Eric Branson?"

"No. But I've got a damned good reason to get it done and get back as fast as possible! He pulled her close and lifted her fully off the ground as he kissed her. "And a good reason for needing a couple of days to rest up and get ready before we head out...."

FERAL NATION
OPPOSITION

SCOTT B. WILLIAMS

ONE

Eric Branson hopped off the bow with a mooring line as Ronnie Ferguson slowed and brought the gunboat alongside the heavily wooded riverbank. This drop-off point about a half mile below the lock and dam at Simmesport put Eric and his small team within easy reach of the Mississippi River. As soon as he had a line around a nearby tree, Eric was back aboard to grab weapons, ammo and the rucksacks containing the rest of their gear and supplies as Jonathan and the other three guys untied the three aluminum canoes from where they were lashed to the decks and the pilot-house roof. Now, as they slid the narrow boats into the shadows of the trees on the adjacent bank, the sounds of their movement and quiet conversation were muffled by the steady pattering of cold rain on the foliage and the surface of the river. The weather was far from pleasant that evening, but it made for perfect conditions for this sort of stealth operation. If things went as planned, the team would paddle upstream, portage around the lock and dam and cross the broad expanse of the big river well before the rain let up and daylight returned.

"You couldn't ask for a better night to sneak across that river," Bart Branson said.

Eric's father, Bart, was serving as Ronnie's crewman and gunner, and the two of them would return downriver in the gunboat to Sierra Zulu, their hidden base of operations, as soon as Eric and his guys had disembarked and were ready to go.

"I don't mind the wet, but the rain could be a little warmer!" Eric said, as he pulled the hood of his parka lower over his forehead and shook his father's hand. "I guess we can't have everything though."

"Well, you can take comfort in the fact that anybody you run into that's foolish enough to be out there tonight will be just as miserable as you are!"

"Yeah, but not as miserable as they'll be if they try to interfere with us!" Jonathan said. We won't be in the mood to play nice on a night like tonight!"

"I'm betting we'll have the river to ourselves," Eric said. "It's what we may find on the other side that we have to worry about."

"You got that right!" Bart said. "I've still got my doubts as to whether this little expedition of yours is worth the time and trouble. I know you've got your mind made up to cross that river though. It's just ironic as hell when you think about it though, isn't it?"

"What's that, Dad?"

"I just mean who would have ever figured it—the Mighty Mississippi—playing such a key role in all this conflict going on right now, just the way it did back in the first civil war!"

"Not me, but then, I wouldn't have figured anything like this would ever happen here in my lifetime anyway."

"But you always knew in the back of your mind there was no reason it couldn't...."

"Only because you were always telling me and Keith that stuff when we were kids. I'm not saying we believed it, but you talked about it enough that I guess I couldn't forget it! I doubt Keith did either."

"Well, I couldn't exactly go back to thinking the way I did before the 'Nam! Most of us that went over there couldn't. I didn't know what to believe or who to trust and it turns out that was a good thing. It kept me from getting complacent! And it gave me a reason to raise you boys the way I did, so you'd be ready for whatever was to come one day."

"Well, I guess *one day* has indeed come, hasn't it, Dad?"

"Yep, it sure has! Look, I don't mean to cast doubt on what you're trying to do, and I sure hope it works out for you, but be careful over there, son! We're all gonna be anxious as hell, waiting to know."

Eric knew that Bart understood it might be a long wait before they *did* know if he and his team succeeded. But the old man was well aware of Eric's capabilities, as well as those of the four young men he'd chosen to accompany him. Most of the others back at Sierra Zulu were on board with the idea too, now that they understood what they were up against. Shauna, of course, was less than enthusiastic about it, and Eric couldn't blame her, because he knew that to her it seemed like every time they were back together it was only for long enough to explain to her why he had to leave yet again. It kept happening, just as it had for years—wrecking their marriage early on—but Eric didn't know what to do about it, because it seemed he was always needed elsewhere. Now Jonathan was having the same conversations with Vicky. Both women had, of course, said they'd rather go too than stay behind wondering when their men would come back, but Eric wouldn't hear of it. It was a given this would be a hard and dangerous journey, and he'd chosen Willis, Lenny and Trey for the rest of his five-man team precisely because they were young, fearless and willing to follow orders without question.

Eric had originally planned on taking only Jonathan, Willis and Lenny, but Trey had been added in the end, as he and Lenny were cousins and virtually inseparable since things fell apart in their prior lives. They were even more so since the two of them had lost their best friend, Justin, to a bullet fired from that I-10 bridge, and they were highly motivated to do all they could to avenge his death and stop the invasion of their state by the ruthless forces that were responsible. Like Jonathan, all three of these young men had proven themselves in the face of death on multiple occasions. What they lacked in formal military and combat training, they made up for with adaptability and a willingness to learn. All-in-all, the three of them were solid choices for this mission and taking Jonathan as his right-hand man was a no-brainer for Eric, considering all that the two of them had been through together. The kid had made a few mistakes along the way, but he learned from them and could keep his cool under pressure. Now that he and Willis had finally seen eye-to-eye and put aside their differences, Eric was confident that all four of these guys would work together with him as a smooth-operating unit.

This wasn't a combat mission per se, but all of them knew that going anywhere these days entailed the risk of getting into a sudden life or death firefight, and they had to be armed and ready. Eric had no idea what they would find on the east side of that river, but he knew they were crossing over to what had once been a sparsely populated part of the mostly rural state of Mississippi. Whether it was still that way was uncertain, but he figured that like everywhere else he had been since his return to his homeland in collapse, there'd probably been some shifting of the local populations as people did what they had to do to survive. Working off the intel gathered through his interrogation of Sergeant Larry Davis, Eric had reason to believe that there were military forces and organized, law-abiding militia on that side of the river that were making an attempt to maintain order. He couldn't be sure the now-dead sergeant had been telling the truth, but a collaborating story from one of the refugees of the C.R.I. camps who claimed to have been in that state a few weeks prior lent credence to his claims.

Still, they wouldn't know for sure until they were on the ground east of the river and likely much farther beyond. He was counting on having to travel a considerable distance to find what they were looking for, as it seemed doubtful any security forces were in control of the territory directly bordering the watercourse, considering how inaccessible most of it was. Naturally, Eric wanted to get in and get out as quickly as possible, as time was of the essence. The survivors holding out in the Atchafalaya Basin needed reinforcements if they were to succeed in stopping the invasion that was still coming from the west, and if Eric couldn't find help, he was going to have to quickly come up with a Plan B. But he wasn't thinking about other options right now. He intended to succeed because a lot of folks were counting on the success of this mission and Eric had no desire to let them down. He and his guys would cross the river in the three canoes and then stash them somewhere in the woods so that they could continue on foot, traveling as light and fast as possible. With any luck at all they would find and make contact with the military forces Sergeant Davis seemed to think were still holding out over there. Whether Eric could convince them to help out with the situation on this side of the river was another matter altogether and a bridge to be crossed once they came to it. But Eric had lots of intel to give them, specifically intel regarding the forces that were aligned against them, including that North American Interior Defense business that Sergeant Davis was a part of.

They had to travel as light as possible, but the five of them still required weapons and plenty of ammo for them, as well as adequate supplies to sustain them for several days of unsupported cross-country travel. Fortunately, supplies were a non-issue due to the stash they'd recovered from the captured Red River outpost. The original plan had been to cross the river in the gunboat, with Ronnie and Bart dropping them off over there, but that involved operating the lock and dam and increased the risk of being seen or heard by anyone else that happened to be in the vicinity. Keith had suggested canoes when Eric lamented the fact that he no longer had his Klepper folding kayak he'd used to sneak ashore in Florida.

They'd gotten the canoes from some of the local volunteers who had moved to Sierra Zulu, and Eric thought them perfect for the task of getting his team across the river. Each boat could carry two men and a large amount of gear, but Eric would paddle the third one alone, with the bulk of their ammo and other heavier items stashed in the bow.

The lightweight boats would be easy to portage around the dam but of course were slower than other options, limited to a paddling speed of around three miles per hour. But crossing the big river in them was a simple matter of adjusting for the strong current. Eric intended to take advantage of the eddies near the shore to travel a few miles upstream so as to land in the most remote area in the nearby vicinity. Once they were ashore on the Mississippi side of the river, the canoes could be easily carried into the woods and concealed, which was a critical advantage, as they were going to need a way to get back to Louisiana if the mission failed or was aborted.

"You two better get out of here," Eric told Bart and Ronnie, as soon as everything was offloaded. "There's no telling who may have heard the sound of our approach. Don't give them time to set up an ambush!"

"Don't worry about us, son. I'll be up here behind the old Ma Deuce if we see any sign of trouble, but I don't expect we will tonight; not in this slop!"

Eric hopped to the bank again and tossed the mooring line back to his dad. Bart coiled it and without another word took up his station at the bow mounted machine gun as Ronnie turned the boat in a tight circle and pointed it back downriver. The sound of the gunboat's engine had faded away completely by the time the team slid the canoes into the dark water and began paddling upstream. It was a short paddle to the lock and dam and with the five of them working quickly to haul the canoes and their gear up over the seawall and carry them to the upstream side, they were past that obstacle a half hour later. Another short paddle took them to the

Mississippi River itself, and after a short stop to reconnoiter and make sure there was no vessel traffic in evidence, Eric led the way as they paddled out onto the dark waters of the mile-wide river that seemed even wider than it really was with the opposite shore obscured by the darkness and the falling rain.

"The current will set us downstream a good bit, but we'll make up for it once we get near the other side. The way the river bends hard to the north of here, there should be a good eddy current close to the shore over there that'll make it easy to paddle a few miles upstream before we land."

With no visible lights from riverboat traffic or shoreside buildings, the Mississippi felt almost pristine that night. Being out there on wide open water reminded Eric that all he'd really wanted to do when he came here was to find his family and sail away on the ocean to some unspoiled island. That idea seemed far from reach right now though, and he didn't know if it would ever happen, but out there on big water again, he felt the connection to who he really was for the first time in weeks. Eric was weary of war and weary of planning mission after mission against an enemy he still didn't fully understand. With no knowledge of the big picture, he didn't know if it was a war that was even winnable, or if his country could be restored even if it was. But he'd gotten involved with a lot of good people he had never planned to meet and many of them had sacrificed much to help him attain his goal of uniting his family. Eric felt he owed it to them to return the favor, and right now, that meant fighting for them and finding help to do so if there was any help to be found.

"Can't see land behind us, and can't see a damned thing ahead," Willis said, as he and Jonathan paddled hard to stay alongside Eric's canoe.

"Which means no one can see us either," Eric said, pausing to check the bearing on the compass that was built into his dive watch.

"Willis is just feeling out of his element," Jonathan said.

"Hey, I don't have a problem with big water, Florida boy! You forget that I was working on Joe Lambert's shrimp trawler before I hooked up with you guys. We'd stay out of sight of land for days out in the Gulf," Willis said. "I'm just saying this is a big damned river and it feels even bigger when you can't see shit out here because of the dark and the rain!"

"Don't worry," Eric said. "If we stay on this course we'll be in Mississippi in no time." Trey and Lenny were alongside now in the third canoe, and as they paused it was easy to perceive the strong current that was already sweeping them downriver below the point where they'd entered the channel. "But don't stop paddling, or we'll end up in Baton Rouge!"

When they were at last able to make out the tops of trees on the opposite bank through the gloom, Eric was relieved to see that the land on that side of the river appeared to be as dark and deserted as the shore they'd left, just as he'd hoped. But as he led the small flotilla nearer, closing in on a wide sandbar that stood out in contrast against the background of the woods, Eric spotted movement that caused him to stop paddling and grab the night vision monocular he wore on a cord around his neck.

"What is it?" Jonathan whispered.

"Looks like coyotes!" Eric said. "Several of them...big ones!"

"What are they doing?"

"Some of them are looking this way, trying to figure us out. Some are slinking off into the woods."

"It's hard to get close to a damned coyote," Willis said. "They either saw us, heard us, or smelled us! Probably all three."

"I'm not interested in getting close to them," Eric said. "But I *am* interested in what they were doing on that sandbar. Take a look!"

Eric handed the monocular off to Jonathan, so he too, could see the dead bodies that were strewn about there—bodies upon which the scavengers had no doubt been feeding.

TWO

"Is that what I think it is up there at the top of that sandbar?" Jonathan asked. "Is that a freakin' *helicopter?*"

"Yep, it *was* one, but from what I could make out, it's not one that'll ever fly again."

"What do you think happened? Do you think it crashed there?"

"Hard to tell for sure, but I'd like to check it out. Let's paddle down to the lower end of the bar where we can hide the canoes at the edge of the woods and slip up there to take a closer look. This could be an indicator of something going on over here that we need to know about!"

Eric stopped to check the sandbar again with the night vision from time to time as they paddled quietly downstream to the place he wanted to land. All of the coyotes had disappeared into the woods now, and it appeared there was nothing else moving that presented a threat. He paddled his canoe to the edge of the river and tied it off to some bushes ashore. When the other two boats were alongside, Eric took point with his M4 at ready and slowly approached the scene of what was clearly a battle or an ambush of some kind. From where they stood now, Eric and all of his team could see what he'd first made out with the aid of his night vision optic. Seven dead soldiers were scattered across the sloping sandbar and situated on the level area at the top near the edge of the woods, was the twisted and charred wreckage of a large military helicopter.

"Dude! I wonder whose side those guys were on?" Jonathan whispered.

"That's what I'd like to try and find out...."

Eric made his way up to the wreckage of the destroyed helicopter. It was obvious there had been an explosion, but Eric didn't think the aircraft had crashed.

"It looks like they hit it while it was on the ground," he said, as he walked around it, telling Jonathan that it was a UH-60 Black Hawk, just as he had thought when he'd first spotted it. The burned remains of the pilot and copilot were still inside what was left of the cockpit, but the seven dead men scattered about on the sandbar appeared to have been cut down by enemy fire while out in the open, away from the aircraft. "Someone was waiting for them and probably opened fire on that squad as soon as they bailed out. Or maybe the pilot was coming into extract them and they were ambushed before they could get back on board. It's hard to tell."

"Well, it's not surprising," Jonathan said, "considering everything else we've seen."

"No, but the main reason it's concerning to me is that it looks like it just happened! Those coyotes haven't been at those bodies for long. It looks like they just found them tonight."

"So, what do you think? Did it happen yesterday?"

"No, probably the day or night before," Willis said. Ever the hunter and tracker, he'd stopped to examine a couple of the dead men on the way to the helicopter. "They've been dead at least twenty-four hours, I'd say. Looks like the vultures had time to get to them first." Willis pointed out the large bird tracks in the sand, with three toes pointed forward and one back.

Eric agreed. "I'd say it happened the day before yesterday, or sometime that night." In addition to the vulture and coyote tracks, there were many boot prints in the sand as well, far more than the seven dead soldiers would have likely made. The bodies were stripped of weapons and gear, and one was even missing his boots. It suggested that the killers had taken the time to gather up everything else of use after the slaughter.

"So, whoever did this probably isn't that far away, unless they had a helicopter of their own or left in a boat..." Jonathan said.

"There's a road leading back into the woods over here," Trey called out, from a short distance north of the helicopter. Eric and the others walked over there to see, and sure enough, there was a dirt two-track there, and more evidence in the form of boot prints that someone had recently used it.

"Maybe they had vehicles of some kind hidden back in the woods," Trey said. "That road's bound to lead in here from somewhere. Should we check it out?"

"No, it doesn't really matter at this point. Like Willis said, this didn't happen tonight or even yesterday, so whoever did it is long gone, whether they left by way of this road or some other way. We need to get moving and focus on finding a better place to land before the rain lets up and we need to do a damned good job of hiding the canoes when we do. We know now there's some major trouble over here, so we don't want whoever's involved finding our boats and looking for us!"

Before they left the scene, Eric stopped to examine the uniforms of a couple of the dead soldiers. They appeared to be legit military issue, but after his experience with Sergeant Davis and the men under his command, Eric knew that meant little. The fact that they'd arrived in a Black Hawk helicopter didn't either. Neither the aircraft nor the uniforms bore any official markings or insignia, so he couldn't reliably judge whether they were friendlies or hostiles from the evidence to be found there on the scene. But it mattered little. The true significance of this discovery was that it told him more of what he already knew; that there was ongoing fighting in the region along this important river corridor, not only in Louisiana, but on this side as well. How far east it extended in the direction he intended to travel was the main question that remained unanswered. Until he made contact with someone who could tell him, it was crucial to avoid being seen and best to assume anyone they met was an enemy out to kill them.

The five of them returned to the canoes and paddled upriver for several miles to put some distance between them and the scene of the one-sided battle. By the time they finally found a suitable spot to land it was only about an hour before dawn, but it was exactly the kind of place that Eric was looking for. No one would expect anyone to come ashore there, because just to get out of the canoes, they had to pull themselves up a slippery, 15-foot vertical clay bluff using the exposed roots of riverside trees growing precariously close to the edge of the bank.

"Careful!" Eric whispered, as Willis went first, ignoring his warning and scampering to the top with the agility of a monkey. Willis prided himself in his tree climbing ability and claimed he had practiced his skills at every opportunity while growing up in the bayou country, clambering into the branches to ambush deer and wild hogs without the aid of mechanical climbing tree stands or other safety equipment. Lenny was nearly as adept and fearless, and followed close behind him with a coil of rope over his shoulder. When the two young men were in position, they used the rope to haul up all the gear and then the lightweight canoes, one by one as Eric and the others secured them in turn to the other end. When all five of the men were atop the bluff with their equipment, they carried the canoes another hundred yards into the dense undergrowth of the heavy woods and turned them upside down, where they carefully hid them under piles of fallen branches and leaves.

At the first hint of daylight, Eric looked around the vicinity to get his bearings and soon found a muddy dirt road that seemed to run roughly parallel to the river just a short distance east of where they'd hidden the boats. "This road looks like it goes both ways up and down the river. I'll bet it connects to the one we found leading to that sandbar."

"If it does, those guys that pulled off the ambush didn't come this way," Willis said, after quickly scanning the rutted lanes for recent tire tracks and footprints. "Maybe they went south instead...."

"Maybe. That's good if they did, because we'll go north until we find a way to turn east. But first, all of you need to etch this location in your memory, in case we all don't come back here together. This ridge we're on seems hard to miss. Just remember to follow it west from here to get back to the top of that bluff where we landed. We may not need the canoes again at all, but it's a good idea to know how to find them, just in case."

"I've never been anywhere that I couldn't find my way back to," Willis said. "Especially not anywhere in the woods."

"And that's one of the main reasons you got a spot on the team. We're going to be in the woods for a while from the looks of it." Eric turned to the others. "I hope you guys are ready for a hike!"

They all knew they had many long miles ahead of them, every one of which they would travel on foot while carrying their weapons and loaded rucksacks. But Eric knew that the young men of his team were ready. Even if they grumbled a bit, like all men did on a forced march, his guys were eager and willing and itching to see where this new adventure would lead. Their youthful, come what may attitude was as important as their endurance and strength, and all four had their minds in the right place as far as Eric could tell.

The assault packs they'd liberated from that Red River outpost would prove invaluable now, as they provided a way to carry enough MREs to keep them fed for several days, as well as all the other gear each man needed for the trek. With those packs, their load-bearing vests full of spare magazines, and their modern weapons they almost resembled a military patrol. That wasn't the impression Eric wanted his team to make, because he didn't want them to be mistaken for private contractors or members of that North American Interior Defense Force, if anyone over here knew of it, but it was hard to carry what they needed without looking somewhat like a squad of soldiers. The only real difference was that they were wearing camo hunting clothing, rather than BDU uniforms, and Willis, especially, looked like a local hunter, because as he had ever since Eric had met him, he still insisted on carrying that Marlin lever-action .30-30 he was so damned good with. Eric didn't argue with him as long as Willis brought his M4 too, strapped to one side of his rucksack.

The plan was to avoid being seen at all, but Eric fully expected to encounter civilian residents and possibly organized militia groups before making contact with any regular military forces. He knew that whatever command structure there might be here, it was unlikely that military authorities could control a territory as vast and remote as that entire rural state unless they had civilian cooperation and outright help. For now, the most important thing Eric and his team could do was to avoid being seen by the wrong people, and that meant avoiding being seen at all if possible. As with any reconnaissance mission, the idea was to observe first and assess the situation. Only then could they determine when to reveal themselves and to whom.

"We'll go ahead and follow this road north now, "Eric said. "As long as it's still raining and we're in these heavy woods, we can make a few miles in the daylight without much worry. Hopefully, we'll find a way to turn east before long."

Eric knew from studying Keith's maps, that the area near the river was crisscrossed with a network of gravel hunting club and wildlife management area roads. He didn't want to leave evidence of their passage in the form of footprints in the mud, so they did their best to avoid the soft spots by spreading out and sticking to the leaf-covered ground along the edges. After they found a route heading east Eric planned to find a place to hole up and get some rest from the full night of being on the move. They would head out again at dusk, making most of their miles after dark to avoid detection.

"Willis, you're more at home in these woods than any of us," Eric said. "I want you to take point for now and stay about 50 yards out front. You know what to do. We'll be moving slow now that it's daylight but keep your eyes and ears open and be ready for anything."

Willis readily agreed. He was in his element out here in the deep woods and swamps along the river bottom, and Eric knew that if there was anyone or anything moving out there, Willis would be the first to know it. The deeply rutted road wound its way through some surprisingly steep hills and bluffs east of the river and seemed to go on and on to nowhere. But just as the rain finally stopped, they came at last to an intersection where a slightly larger road turned off and ran directly to the east, exactly the way they needed to go. Eric wanted to closely examine this new route for tire tracks and footprints before they set out that way, and Willis was already on it.

"Right here," he said. "Someone just came through here, probably late yesterday afternoon before dark or even during the night ahead of us. One guy, wearing combat boots from the look of it!"

Eric squatted beside him to examine the tracks Willis pointed to. He was right that the person appeared to be wearing combat boots but that didn't really mean anything. The boots could have belonged to any random hunter or civilian survivor, but then again it could also be someone connected to what had happened on that sandbar downriver. They hadn't noticed any tracks along the road they followed north, but that didn't mean there weren't any, because the light was poor, and it was still raining. Whoever made these boot prints they were studying now probably wasn't very far away, according to Willis. While one person was unlikely to present a serious threat to the five-man team, there was always the possibility of being ambushed by a lone wolf using sniper tactics and if they weren't careful, any one of them could be taken out before they realized they were a target.

But since this was the first road they'd come to that was leading in the direction Eric wanted to go, it didn't make sense to pass it by just because of one person that might present a potential threat. He decided they needed to proceed anyway, taking into account the unknown stranger's presence as they did so. It was foolish to put the entire team at risk at once though, so he told Jonathan, Lenny and Trey that he was going on ahead with Willis and for them to spread out and follow a good quarter mile behind until he gave them an indication to do otherwise.

"We'll work our way carefully down the road for at least a few miles until we find some place to hole up. If we don't come across whoever made these tracks before then, we may never, but I don't want to stop for the day with the possibility that he's still nearby. It may be that he's just some refugee living off the land out here in the river bottom, and he may be harmless, but he could be most anywhere, and he may turn around and come back this way at any time too."

"Well, like you said, we're going to have to talk to somebody around here eventually. Maybe we won't have to wait as long as we thought..." Jonathan said.

"True, but it would be ideal if we could find someone who can actually tell us what we need to know. I'm not counting on it, but I'm still hopeful."

Eric followed closely behind Willis, watching him work. While Willis wasn't the tracker that Wolf and some of the other men from the Jicarilla reservation he'd met out West were, he was still quite competent and Eric found it easier to let him concentrate on the tracking while he focused on watching out for movement or any other signs of danger. As they continued on in silence through the heavy woods, Eric pondered the scene of that slaughter that they'd come upon on the sandbar. It was hard to piece together exactly what had happened with just the evidence they could see in the dark, but he knew it had to be a pretty substantial force to take out a Black Hawk helicopter and all those soldiers in such an effective ambush. *The real question was who were they—both the unknown killers and the soldiers they'd massacred? If those soldiers were legit military still in service to the nation Eric had once served, their involvement meant there was as much trouble on this side of the river as they'd left behind in Louisiana. But their presence could also mean there was an active, official resistance to what was happening, and that was exactly what Eric came here hoping to find. If it were true, the question was whether that resistance was enough to make a difference....*

The tracks Willis was following continued to lead them down the muddy road, and the road was still running east, in the right direction, so they kept to their slow, methodical pace for another hour. Eric was beginning to doubt they would ever catch up to the unknown person they were trailing until at last, Willis suddenly stopped and signaled to him to freeze. Eric followed his gaze to the bottom of a deep ravine off to the south side of the road, and there he saw a camo-clad man moving around on the ground down there, crawling about on his hands and knees. What he was doing made no sense at first, but then as Eric watched, he could see that the man was turning over rotten logs and digging into them with a big knife he clenched with both hands, obviously looking for something. Whatever it was he was searching for; he was so focused on finding it that he was completely unaware that he was being observed. Eric signaled to Willis that they should split up and circle around to either side of the guy before making their approach. Eric didn't intend to detain or hurt him, but he certainly hoped to find out who he was and what he was doing out there. And since it appeared the man was unarmed, he thought the danger of he and Willis revealing themselves to him was low. The biggest risk was that he would take off running and get away without answering their questions. That was why Eric thought it best that they go ahead an approach him now, before Jonathan and the others caught up. The sudden appearance of all five of them would probably scare the hell out of the unsuspecting guy.

Splitting up and approaching from either side decreased the chances of him bolting and getting away, but as they closed in to within a few yards, Eric realized he needn't have worried. The stranger was so focused on tearing apart the rotten wood and picking through it with his knife blade and his fingers that he was totally oblivious to all else. When Eric saw that he was putting what he was picking out of there into his mouth, he realized that it was probably edible grubs the man was searching for. This fellow was clearly desperate, and it appeared he had no gear or equipment of any kind other than that knife and the clothing and boots he was wearing. Eric spoke softly to him from where he stood, doing his best to sound calm and non-threatening.

"You must be hungry, going to all that trouble for a few worms... how about some real food?"

THREE

At the sound of Eric's voice, the stranger spun around and got to his feet, gripping the knife like a dagger and backing away instinctively upon seeing Eric standing there, barely 15 feet behind him. But in his panic and haste to create distance, the man stumbled over the very log he'd been digging in and fell hard to the forest floor on the other side.

"I didn't mean to startle you..." Eric said. "I just want to talk...."

Eric's rifle was on its sling in front of him, but he had both hands off the weapon and out to either side, with his fingers outstretched to show that he was empty-handed. This apparently did little to make the stranger feel better though. He had no interest in what Eric had to say. All he was thinking about was getting out of there, and he was back on his feet again as quickly as he fell, turning to run the other way when he saw Willis blocking his path from that side too. When he then attempted to cut between them at a hard right angle, Eric moved to intercept him and asked him to please stop:

"Hold up! We're not your enemy! We were just passing

through! We were following the road up there and couldn't help seeing your footprints. When we finally caught up and saw you down here, I couldn't help wondering what you were doing."

It was obvious that the man wanted nothing to do with them and was severely unhinged by their sudden appearance from seemingly out of nowhere. It was also clear that he was alone, unarmed and hungry. As he looked furtively about for another possible escape route Eric saw a new look of dismay on his face and realized the fellow had just spotted Jonathan and the other two guys from the team now approaching along the road.

"They're with us," Eric said, "but everything's cool! Please, just relax...."

"I don't know who you are or what you want, but you can see that I'm unarmed, so if you're going to shoot me, just go ahead and get it over with right now!"

Eric glanced at the large blade the man still clenched in his right hand in a white-knuckle grip and smiled. "I wouldn't say you're *completely* unarmed, but like I told you, you can relax. We're not going to shoot you or do anything else to hurt you. It's all good!" Eric knew the man wasn't convinced and who could blame him? Five heavily armed men had suddenly appeared on his trail, demanding he talk to them. It wasn't the ideal way to meet, but it was the way it happened and that was that. Eric looked him up and down as he lowered his knife hand and began to relax, noting that the BDUs he wore were of the same digital camouflage pattern as the dead soldiers on the sandbar.

"Are you military? Are you in the Army, or the Army National Guard?"

The stranger was hesitant to answer that question, and Eric couldn't blame him because it was possible he thought they were part of some rogue militia or whatever other enemy the military here was contending with, if he were indeed a soldier in active duty. He probably even thought they were associated with whoever wiped out the rest of his squad down there if he was one of them and that's the next thing Eric asked him, because it seemed likely he was.

"We came upon the scene of a massacre on a sandbar about ten or twelve miles downriver. It looked to me like an army squad got wiped out in an ambush of some kind. There was a Black Hawk helicopter there that was destroyed on the ground. Do you know anything about that?"

The man stared back at him in silence. Now that Eric told him he knew about the helicopter and the dead soldiers, it was plain to see that he thought they had tracked him down and that they had done so on purpose. It was clear too that he indeed thought they were his enemies, and that he was done for now, with nowhere to run and no real weapon with which to fight back. Eric wasn't sure how he could convince him otherwise, but since there was little the guy could do to them now, no matter who he was, he saw no reason to withhold information from him or tell him anything other than the truth.

"Look, we're not from around here, and we had nothing to do with that firefight or anything else that's going on over here in Mississippi. We crossed the river last night from Louisiana because we are dealing with an ongoing occupation and invasion over there that you may or may not be aware of. But if you *are* with the Army or some other still-functioning branch of the actual U.S. military, then you can probably help us find what we're looking for. We are here because we heard that the Army is still in control of things over here and still maintaining a semblance of law and order. I can see that you're obviously hungry, unarmed, cut-off and alone. We have supplies and gear we can share with you if you'll just give us some information that will help us on our way."

By this time Jonathan, Lenny and Trey had moved down the hill from the road and joined them. The lone man looked at all five of them, still unsure what to believe and what to make of them, but after a moment, he spoke again: "I hope you don't expect me to believe that you just randomly happened upon the scene where my squad was ambushed and wiped out. You obviously tracked me down, so I know you're with the insurgents who did it and you followed my trail because you were hunting for survivors."

"No," Willis said. "We didn't set out to track you down. We crossed the river last night, like Eric here said. We didn't expect to find anything like what we found on that sandbar, but when we did, we paddled on upriver a few miles before we landed again, just to be safe. We were following the dirt road that runs north along the river, looking for a place to turn east. When we came to this road where we found your tracks, we knew someone was around, so we were just being careful, like anyone would. That's the only reason we were so quiet when we approached and the reason you didn't hear us coming. If we'd been hunting you and wanted to kill you, we could have done it without you ever knowing what hit you, so you can believe whatever you want, but that's the damned truth if I ever told it!"

"That's exactly right," Eric said. "We couldn't miss your tracks because they were so obvious in the middle of that muddy road. We figured we'd catch up to whoever made them, but we were being extra cautious because we didn't know who we'd run into. When Willis spotted you digging in that rotten log, and I saw that uniform you're wearing, I figured you were probably a survivor from whatever happened by the river down there. So, was I right?"

"There's five of you guys moving through the woods with weapons like you're looking for a fight. Why would I believe you're anything *but* one of the outlaw militia groups?"

"Because like I told you, we're not with *any* group here in Mississippi. This is the first time we've crossed the river. We're based in Louisiana for now, and yes you could say we're a militia of sorts, but only if you consider that a militia is a group of civilians forced to band together to fight for their own survival. None of my team here is military or former military. I'm the only one with a military background, and I was U.S. Navy, but that was years ago. Now, do you want to tell me who shot up your squad? Do you really think it was some kind of militia force? Was that what your mission was about? Hunting down insurgents?"

"I'm not at liberty to discuss the details. If you really *are* former military, then you know why; although I'm not sure how you swabbies did things back in the day."

"Eric was a freakin' *SEAL*, dude! It's not like he was some kind of deck hand on a boat or some shit! Show the man some respect!"

The stranger looked at Jonathan and then back at Eric, as if to size him up. If he believed what the kid was telling him, he didn't seem impressed, and Eric didn't expect him to be. Eric wasn't here to tell of his own exploits. He was looking for intel, and it seemed he'd gotten lucky and found a potential source right off the bat, if he could just get the guy to loosen up and talk.

"Look, I understand military protocol and I'm not asking for explicit operational details. I don't care how your officers are running things over here or why they're doing whatever it is they're doing. What I'm looking to do is make contact with someone up the chain of command who may be able to assist us or at lease advise us as to the scope of the broader situation. We've been operating in the dark for quite some time, and holding our own if I may add, but the situation to the west of here is worse than you or your superiors can possibly understand unless you've been there and seen it firsthand. I've got intel from that area that I doubt your commanders are privy to, so it could be a win-win for both parties if we can get together. If you don't want to talk to us though, we're not going to force you to. But it looks like you could use something to eat and whether you help us or not I'm going to give you a few of the MREs we have on us."

Eric removed his backpack and set it on the ground, opening it up to retrieve a couple of the packaged meals. He handed one to the man and told him he was welcome to go ahead and eat it right then if he wanted. Jonathan and all the rest of the team were tired and hungry too, as everyone was ready for a much-needed break after the long night on the move. "Look, we were getting ready to stop for a bit anyway. So, we'll just join you for breakfast if you don't mind."

After Eric made this gesture, the stranger began to relax a little more, and finally, he gave Eric his name, Private First Class Robert Beckman, as he put his knife back in the sheath on his belt.

"Pleased to meet you PFC Beckman. I'm Eric Branson. This is Willis," Eric nodded, "and that's Jonathan, Lenny, and Trey."

"Thank you," Beckman said. "I *am* pretty hungry, to be honest. I haven't had a thing to eat since the day before yesterday, and I've got a lot of walking ahead of me."

"Figured you were, when I realized what you were doing down here. Putting that Army survival training you had to use, huh? Are you Special Forces?"

"Army National Guard, 26th Special Forces Group, yes sir! Is it true what your buddy here says? Were you a Navy SEAL?"

Eric nodded, but made light of it, telling Beckman it was something like a lifetime ago, if it was even real, but then Jonathan chimed in with firsthand accounts of what he'd seen Eric do until Eric asked him to shut up.

"We're here to get intel, Jonathan, not swap war stories!" Eric turned to Beckman. "Grubs will keep you alive all right, but I'll bet even a crappy old MRE will taste good to you now."

"You bet it will! I appreciate it!"

The six of them found places to sit where they could talk and eat, and Eric asked the soldier more questions.

"So, you were saying you can't discuss the details of your mission here, but you *were* with that squad that got wiped out down there. I understood that the Army had things under control on this side of the river, but apparently that isn't the case. Who's causing all the trouble over here? Is it an organized military force?

Private contractors? Gangs or militant groups exploiting the situation?"

"As far as we're concerned, they are simply classified as insurgents. I don't know the extent of how organized they are. I'm not sure anyone does, but we were on assignment to patrol the river for signs of their boats and their activities both on the water and ashore in the surrounding area. There have been multiple incidents of attacks on vessel traffic to the point that almost all movement up and down the river has been shut down for months. It's been worse to the south, below Baton Rouge, but our unit was assigned to this sector from the southwest corner of the state up to Vicksburg. We've been handicapped by lack of air support, communications and satellite surveillance, of course, so we're having to do everything the hard way. Even the use of assets like that Black Hawk we just lost has been limited because the few we have are spread so thin and our fuel reserves are running low. Losing another one puts a real dent in our ability to operate this far from our base, which is nearly 180 miles to the southeast. But we've been using them to insert and extract small squads like mine near the hotspots; I'm sure you know the drill. We were going in blind most of the time, and apparently, that was the case for sure this last time.

"Late in the afternoon, the day before yesterday, we were flying south and getting ready to turn back to base when we spotted smoke from a large fire about three miles east of the river. Having already seen how many gravel roads there are everywhere out here in these woods, we were almost certain it was a farmhouse or hunting camp occupied by local civilians and figured it was the target of another raid. A lot of that had been going on here recently now that there were almost no barges or other vessels to attack.

"Our pilot circled wide and came in low over the river west of the smoke, and sure enough, there was about a 30-foot open center-console sportfishing boat pulled up to that big sandbar down there, the only good landing place for several miles in either direction. When we buzzed over it just clearing the treetops, two guys aboard the boat opened fire on us with rifles, so we circled back around and strafed them with one of the .50-cals to take them out. There was no sign of anyone else with them, so we figured those two were waiting there with the boat for the main raiding party to come back, probably from over there where we'd seen the smoke. Our sergeant wanted to secure the boat and set up an ambush to be ready for the rest of them when they returned, so the pilot set it down on the top of the sandbar and we bailed out to secure a perimeter and get into position to wait. We thought *we* were the ones pulling off the perfect ambush, because we were going to be ready for them when they came back to make their getaway on the boat.

"The crew was just getting ready to take off while most of the men in the squad were checking their gear and preparing to set up in the woods. Four of us were heading down to the river to move those two bodies out of sight and collect their weapons when it happened. There was an explosion in the direction of the helo and then automatic weapons fire coming from everywhere out of the woods back behind the top of that sandbar. I think the helo was hit with a high-explosive grenade fired from a launcher, but whatever it was, it was bad enough to take it out, along with our pilot and copilot. The rest of the squad was caught out there in the open and didn't have a chance. They were cut down before they could even think about getting to cover, if there'd been any cover to be had."

Eric was listening intently, studying the man's face as he talked. It was a plausible story, he supposed, but there was a question begging to be asked. Hearing PFC Beckman describe it, it seemed unlikely anyone could have survived that assault unless they turned tail and ran off into the woods, so he came right out and asked:

"If that's how it happened, then how did *you* manage to survive when no one else in your squad did? You obviously lost your weapon, yet still managed to make it all the way here alone. How?" Eric knew his question came across almost as an accusation, but he didn't care. He wanted an answer that would help him determine whether this man was telling the truth.

"Well, it was mostly dumb luck that I wasn't on the sandbar when the shooting started, I guess. You see, the boat had begun drifting away from the edge of it and out into the river, maybe because one of those guys we strafed from the air managed to cast off the anchor line before he died. When my buddies were picking up the weapons and getting ready to start dragging those bodies into the water, the sergeant yelled at me to go out into the river to catch it. I knew I was going to have to wade out waist deep and maybe even more, so I took off my vest and handed my rifle to my buddy, Jacobs. As it happened, I had just reached the boat and was neck deep in the river when that explosion went off and the shooting started. It happened so fast and our guys were taken out so quickly there was nothing I could do to help them, especially with no weapon in hand. I swam under the boat and hung onto the opposite side to stay out of sight as it began drifting downriver. When I saw that the helicopter was destroyed and my entire squad was down, I knew there was nothing I could do for any of them. My only hope was to somehow survive and make it back to report what happened. I considered trying to get aboard the boat to try and escape in it, but I knew it was too late, because the shooters that sprung that ambush were already moving out of the woods to finish off the wounded, and three of them were heading straight towards the water, surely intent on trying to retrieve the boat. If I had climbed aboard, I would have been seen and shot on sight, so I kicked off my boots and swam underwater as fast as I could, going downstream with the river current and not coming up for air until I absolutely had to. When I did come up, it was just enough to grab a deep breath and go under again. No one saw me, and eventually I was far enough away from all the commotion that it felt safe enough to work my way back to the bank. I crawled into the bushes and hid there until well after dark. Finally, I heard the boat pull away and head upriver. I guess our machine gun didn't put it out of commission, even though we killed the two guys aboard it. I couldn't see it leaving from where I was hidden, and it was too dark anyway by then, so I never got a good look at any of the bunch that attacked us. I waited where I was for at least another hour, just listening to make sure none of them had stayed behind. When I heard nothing after all that time, I slipped back up there to where it all happened."

FOUR

ERIC DIGESTED THIS INFORMATION AS HE KEPT HIS GAZE locked on PFC Beckman's face. He could see how such a scenario could play out, and if it happened the way Beckman said it did, then he was damned lucky to be alive.

"It doesn't sound to me like that ambush was just the coincidence of those guys returning to their boat at just the right time to catch your helo on the ground. It almost sounds like it was a fairly sophisticated plan to lure you all into a kill zone," Eric said. "You mentioned that your unit had been assigned to patrol that river. I assume you'd already had prior encounters with some of those raiders that gave them reason to want to take out that Black Hawk?"

"Oh yeah, taking out any aircraft—not to mention a Black Hawk—is a big win for them, because the few helicopters we have left are one of our only advantages, especially when operating far from our bases and in unsecured areas like this region along the river. It wasn't the first time we'd strafed one of their boats from the air either. It's possible they set us up, for sure. The thought already occurred to me."

"Dude, you're lucky to be alive, I'll tell you that," Jonathan said. "If you hadn't been in the water..."

"For sure! If I hadn't been in the water *and* next to that boat when the attack happened, I wouldn't be here talking to all of you right now. Swimming downriver is the only thing that saved my life, but man, I feel like crap being the only survivor, and I can't help thinking I cheated somehow, hiding like that while all my buddies were dead. I've been working with those guys for months; some of them even longer. Most of them were close friends after all we'd been through together. I'm having a hard time dealing with it, I'll tell you that. It just doesn't seem right for me to be here while they're all gone. Hell, I couldn't even give them a proper burial or anything! I was afraid to hang around there long enough to attempt it, and besides, there were so many—seven soldiers and the pilot and copilot still strapped in that helicopter where they burned alive. It was all I could do just to face that scene, but like I said, after I felt sure none of the attackers were hanging around, I slipped back out there looking for any weapons or supplies they may have left behind. There was nothing though, not even a loaded rifle or pistol magazine. They had taken everything that was useful. All I had were the clothes I was wearing and what was in my pockets and on my belt, like this knife. I had ditched my boots in the river so I could swim, and I knew I couldn't walk out of there and cover all the miles I had ahead of me barefoot, so I had to replace them. I knew my buddy, Henderson, wore my size. Man, it sucked doing it, but I had to take his boots and socks. If I hadn't, I wouldn't have even made it this far."

"It sounds like you did all you could do, and you have nothing to blame yourself for," Eric said. "It's normal to feel survivor's remorse. Believe me, I've been there too. Your squad simply got waxed by someone who apparently knew what they were doing. You said you saw the boat go upriver. Do you think they're based up there somewhere?"

"I don't know. If we knew where to find them, I'm sure

Colonel Rencher would plan a major operation to take them all out. But the problem is that as far as we know, there's not much organization among these insurgent groups. They're like gangs of criminals or pirates, launching random attacks all over the place at unexpected times. It makes it hard to fight them, let me tell you."

"We've encountered the same thing everywhere we've been," Eric said, "especially me and Jonathan here. We've traveled from south Florida to as far west as the Colorado Rockies, and I even made a little side trip down into Mexico since all this started. It's chaos everywhere, some of it completely random, and some of it more organized than you can imagine. I've met with other Army units to the north and west that are still holding out, but there are also many that seem to be going in a different direction, becoming part of the problem, rather than the solution. Do you know anything about that?"

"You mean the breaking up of the high command, those that are still loyal to the constitution they swore to defend, versus those who are trying to tear it all down? We've heard rumors but can't confirm it. Can you?"

"Yes," Eric said. "We all can. We've just had several run-ins with one of those splinter groups over on the other side of the river, and I've got the feeling they weren't just an anomaly we'll never see again either. There's a lot of misguided and misplaced loyalty out there in many parts of the country, and it's hard to tell any more who's on this side or the other. I'm not talking about just unorganized gangs either. I mean entire battalions, maybe even brigades or divisions, of regular National Guard and Army. Probably the other branches as well. The NCOs and enlisted men are just following the orders of their commanders, most of whom are in the dark about what's really going on. But apparently, the highest levels of command have been subverted in many cases by traitors and foreign entities determined to destroy everything this country once stood for. They are using their subordinates to do the dirty work for them, pitting them against innocent civilians they have made out to be terrorists.

"They are using manpower and equipment from both National Guard and active-duty bases, but they are also subbing out a lot of their dirty work to professional private military contractors. There's one outfit in particular that we've been dealing with that seems to be in control of most of the state of Texas and much of the Mexican border even farther west. To top it off, they've also created some sort of alliance with one of the most powerful Mexican drug cartels in existence in the interest of gaining control of the entire coastline of the Gulf of Mexico. That cartel is already operating with impunity on the U.S. side of the border and along the Texas Gulf Coast. They aim to take it all the way to south Florida, based on the intel I got when I was south of the border myself."

"Well, I can tell you that they don't have control of the Mississippi coast – or Alabama and north Florida," Beckman said, "because we still do."

"I suppose that's because the infrastructure is still in place there for the most part, right?" Eric asked. "I mean, that area must have escaped the hurricane that tore up so much of the Louisiana coast...."

"Yeah, we got wind damage and power outages all across the state, but nothing like I heard happened to the parts of Florida and Louisiana the eye passed through. I know that made the problem worse considering all that was already going on before it hit."

"South Florida is a total disaster," Eric said. "And in Louisiana everything from Morgan City south was pretty much completely destroyed. Power is more or less permanently out everywhere south of I-10 and in many places above it too. But what we found out since is that the grid is down in most other places too, hurricane or no hurricane. I guess it's that way in most of the country. Sabotage and deliberate attacks put it all out of commission."

"Yeah, there's certainly no power in Mississippi aside from generators, if you've got the gas or diesel to run them. But at least things aren't torn up from the storm. It'll be possible to get the grid back up again once we get all the power plants back online, but we can't do that until we get this insurgency and lawlessness under control. And now with what you're telling me, it sounds like we're going to be dealing with a lot worse in the near future."

"You absolutely are," Eric said. "That's exactly why were over here, to try to get in touch with legitimate forces that may be interested in doing something about the problem before it can cross the river. Do you have any idea whether or not that colonel you mentioned will be willing to listen if I can get to him?"

"Colonel Rencher? That's above my pay grade, Branson. You know that already though. The first problem would be getting to him. It's a hell of a long walk from here back to my base."

"Well, regardless of the distance, it seems to me that if the situation in this part of the state is as unstable as you say it is, you'd be better off traveling in the company of armed men."

"My plan was to travel mostly at night and hide out during the daytime, avoiding people completely until I was sure I was among law-abiding civilians I could trust, or until I made contact with some other army unit closer by."

"That's about the same plan we had as well," Eric said. "We didn't expect to be talking to anyone the first day we were on the ground on this side of the river but when I saw you this morning and I saw you had that uniform on it got my attention, because I knew it was the same uniform those guys we found on the sandbar were wearing. Finding you may have changed everything for our mission. Maybe it can change everything for you too? What do you say we team up? We've got food and weapons and you've got the connections we're looking for. It's a win-win for both of us. You won't have to live off grubs and we won't be stumbling around for weeks not knowing where to go to find a functioning military base. With your help we can go straight to yours with you and then you can make the introductions for us. Does that sound like something you'd be interested in?"

"Well, you can see I don't have a lot of options, but I'm still leery of bringing unknown operators to one of our bases. If you're not who you say you are and your intentions are not what you say they are, then things won't go well for any of you or for me. It's not just a matter of going to the brig for a few days anymore! I'm talking court-martial and execution!"

"I understand," Eric said. "And I don't blame you for being cautious, because I would too. But what are five guys going to do? You know if you take us there, we'll be disarmed at the gate and questioned, probably even interrogated and treated as prisoners until we prove who we are. Do you think we would agree to that and go there willingly if we had bad intent?"

"I suppose it wouldn't make sense, but you understand I still don't know what I should do. If I get caught collaborating with the enemy, then I'm no better than they are."

"But on the other hand, you'll be a hero if you provide intel that no one on this side of the river is privy to. I'm telling you, PFC Beckman, what is coming from the west is something that your commanders aren't ready for! If they get caught unprepared, it's going to be the same here as it was in Texas and is now in Louisiana. So, tell me, you said you thought you might find another unit closer by than your base. Do you know where one might be?"

"I don't know the status of it, but there used to be a small base of the local armored brigade about 50 miles to the northeast of here. It's called Camp McCall. If I knew I had to walk the whole way, that's where I'd go, but I was hoping to find some trustworthy civilians or civilian militia members somewhere along the way that would give me a ride back to Camp Hurley. We've got reports of some sizeable militia groups that have formed in several parts of the state. It's possible some are in this area too, but what they're up to, I couldn't tell you. Probably not much, other than keeping watch over their local communities."

"Well, if we have to walk, 50 miles isn't so bad," Eric said. "We figured we might have to walk halfway across the state or better when we got here. It's probably worth going there first, if you're up to it. But it's your call whether you want to go together."

Eric could tell that Beckman was giving it serious consideration. And why wouldn't he? He was alone and unarmed and had nothing to eat and nothing to defend himself or procure food with but that knife. Eric could understand his reluctance to get into trouble with his superiors, though. It was hard to know who to trust these days, and he didn't know if it was a good idea for him and his team to put their trust in Beckman, either. The only difference from Eric's point of view was that they had all the advantage over him, at least until they reached an active military unit. It was a bigger leap of faith for Beckman to trust five strangers that emerged out of nowhere in the woods, claiming to be his ally. But Eric had the feeling the soldier was going to give in and agree to do it, and he did.

"Okay, I suppose you're right," Beckman said. "We're both going in the same general direction so we may as well go together. I'd feel a lot better though, if you guys would trust me enough to let me carry one of those weapons." Beckman turned to Willis: "I couldn't help noticing that you have two rifles. I don't know why you're toting that old lever action, but if that M4 you've got strapped to your ruck is a burden, I'll be glad to carry it for you."

"It ain't no trouble at all for me to carry it!" Willis said. "I'm toting my Marlin 336 because I'm good with it, and Eric can vouch for it, just ask him!"

"I don't have any problem with you carrying a weapon," Eric told Beckman. "If Willis doesn't want to give you that M4, then we've all got handguns and you can have one of those if it makes you feel better. Even if I'm making a mistake to trust you, I don't think you're stupid enough to try something with the five of us around."

"Hell, he can carry the M4, I don't give a shit! You know I ain't planning on using it anyway unless I run out of .30-30 ammo."

With that settled, the six of them finished their MREs, and

Willis told Beckman he'd give him the rifle when they were ready to get moving again. But they all needed a few hours rest first, including Beckman. Eric set up a rotating watch system among his team and they moved farther off the road where they could safely get some sleep. When they were all awake and anxious to get moving again by late afternoon, Eric asked Beckman for more details of what he knew of the area.

"I know you've seen it from the air if you've been making all those patrols in the helicopter, so how far can we stay on this road, and how far is it to the end of these heavy woodlands?"

This road will probably take us at least another ten miles or so before it crosses any pavement," Beckman said. "As far as the woods go, hell just about the whole state is nothing but woods these days. We're in wildlife management area and hunting club land right now, but east of here even on the private land, it's almost all grown up in timber plantations. Pine timber is about the only cash crop that was worth anything in recent years and it's what everybody went to planting. Other than that, what little open land you still see around here is used for cattle pasture."

"So, it won't be hard to avoid people, especially traveling at night?" Eric asked.

"Not all that hard, but you never know who's going to be out and about, even after dark; people up to no good, for the most part, and there's a lot of those around now. Even if they're not affiliated with any of the terrorist or insurgent groups, there's still random individuals and small gangs going around robbing, raping and killing. It's what happens when you have no law and order. But you know that already from what you've told me."

Eric did and he didn't doubt that the conditions were as bad here as Beckman claimed. But knowing now that there was a real effort going on here on this side of the river to quell the violence and restore that law and order was ample justification to continue this mission no matter what dangers they may encounter. It meant one obstacle was already overcome, especially now that they had with them an insider that could make the introductions that would enable Eric to present his case to the officers in authority. With Beckman's help, Eric could get his answer quickly, and whether it was the answer he wanted or not, it meant getting back to Sierra Zulu quickly as well.

Once they were on the move again, they found relatively easy going on the little muddy road, covering another dozen or so miles that night in the direction of their destination. They crossed some intersecting roads along the way, most of them also gravel, but there were two small paved ones as well. When daylight came again, Eric wanted to keep moving a bit longer before stopping, and it was because of that decision that they ended up in a situation that would have best been avoided. It happened shortly after sunrise, when they came to a place where the trees on the north side of the road gave way to the first expanse of open pasture they'd seen, with a barbed wire fence running along its perimeter. Eric was about to lead the team into the woods to the south of the road in order to skirt around it, since it seemed likely there was a farmhouse somewhere nearby. But just as he made a move to do so, gunfire erupting from the near distance brought them all to a sudden halt.

FIVE

Eric wouldn't normally have given a few gunshots from the direction of a rural homestead a second thought, in present times or in the world as it was before the country collapsed into chaos. But this was more than a few rounds fired, and it was obvious the reports were coming from more than one or two weapons.

"What do you make of that, Beckman?"

"It doesn't sound like someone just hunting or doing a little target practice, does it?"

"It's a gunfight for sure if you ask me," Willis said. "Ain't nobody dumb enough to waste that much ammunition for no good reason, and no hunters I've ever seen are bad enough to miss that many times!"

"I think you're right, Willis. It sounds like a two-way exchange to me." Even as he said it, the sporadic shots continued. Sometimes there was a long pause, followed by a single bang or a double or triple, then several fired in rapid semi-auto succession. But then, a sustained burst of full-auto ripped through one of those short periods of silence in between and Eric knew someone was in a battle to the death over beyond the far side of that big pasture.

"Well, whatever it's about, it's none of our business, is it?" Jonathan asked.

"Nope!" Willis agreed. "Our mission is clear! Avoid civilian contact and get to that base Beckman told us about. Isn't that right?" Willis looked at Eric and Beckman in turn.

"I can't exactly ignore this," Beckman said. "What we're hearing could be a firefight between law-abiding civilians and members of the same insurgency my squad was ordered to interdict."

"Yeah, but you don't have a squad anymore!" Willis reminded him. "You don't even have a weapon of your own, so this isn't your call. Eric's our team leader, and whatever he says goes if you're hanging with us!"

"I'm not talking about intervening directly, but that shooting is really close! There's no reason why we can't move in near enough to get a look at what's happening. Then, I can report it to the commander of that Camp McCall outpost if there's anyone there when we get there. Every bit of intel we can gather is vital to bringing an end to this conflict and restoring order over here. If I ignore this, what was the point of even being here? What did all the guys in my squad die for? Was it all for nothing?"

Eric started to answer, but Willis cut him off.

"You coulda died with them and no one would ever know what happened, so just be glad you survived to report back at all! And be glad we came along when we did to help you *get* back, or else you'd still be digging under rotten logs trying to find something to eat! But we've got our own mission here, and it's not the one your unit had!"

"You've never served, Willis! So, what do you know about missions, much less honor and duty?"

"All right," Eric cut in. "Let's avoid an argument, shall we? Look, I agree we probably ought to see what this is all about, but if we do, we're going to do it my way!" He turned to Beckman. "That means staying out of sight, keeping our distance, and *observing*, not getting involved, no matter what we see over there. Am I clear?"

Willis and Jonathan were far from enthusiastic about it, but reluctantly nodded in agreement. As usual, Lenny and Trey had little input. Both were ready and willing to do what was asked of them, and Eric was grateful he didn't have to convince them as well. Moving towards the sound of gunfire was a lot to ask of anyone, particularly when that gunfire was being exchanged between unknown strangers and for unknown reasons. But still, Eric agreed with PFC Beckman. It *was* in their best interest to see what was going on there, particularly since it was so close to their path of travel anyway. Eric knew if he and his team did their part to help this sole survivor return to his base not only alive, but with useful intel that would help them in their campaign to purge this district of insurgents, it would give him an advantage. And Eric needed every advantage possible to get the attention of that colonel and the other officers he would eventually have to make his case to. At least that's what he thought when he made the decision to go have a closer look.

"I don't know why some of these folks are so stubborn," Beckman said. "People in rural Mississippi are just like that for some reason! They think they're safe out here because they're in the middle of nowhere, but nothing could be farther from the truth. These isolated farms are nothing but targets. Sure, some of them may have escaped notice for a while just because they *are* isolated, but they all get discovered eventually—there are just too many gangs of desperate people roaming about. The idea that they're safer way out here is a delusion. A single family can't maintain proper security watches or fight off a coordinated attack. It takes organized defensive efforts, because believe me, even aside from the real insurgent groups, some of these looter gangs have learned how to plan and coordinate their attacks. It's not just random opportunists we're dealing with at this stage."

Eric had to agree. Even out West in the Rockies where he'd

recently been, remote ranches like the one owned by Vicky Singleton's grandparents were not immune to such violent raids. Most parts of the East were far more densely populated, but there were still plenty of isolated hideaways to be found in the woods and swamps of the Deep South. It was likely many of them, like this one, *had* gone unnoticed until now, but like Beckman said, it was inevitable that trouble would eventually come knocking, even way out here. The ranches and farms most likely to survive it were the ones on which neighbors had banded together for mutual support and increased firepower. From the sounds of all that shooting, Eric wondered if this one was just such a place as the six of them circled around the edge of the pasture to try and get close enough to have a look.

"There's really no telling what this is about," Beckman said. "We've mostly been patrolling the river itself, because it's a natural corridor for all manner of traffic coming from either direction. We don't have the manpower or sufficient aircraft and fuel for them to fly all of this rural territory away from the river course. I don't think the other units in the state have the armored vehicles and soldiers to patrol the countless little paved and gravel roads that run through it either. The folks that are still holding out around here are mostly on their own, and I honestly don't see how they've done it this long."

Eric, Beckman, and the rest of the team were now hunkered down in a narrow strip of woods between that first pasture they'd come to and a bigger one of about double the acreage stretching between them and a distant house on the other side of it. Because of a low rise midway across the pasture, nothing was visible of the house other than part of the roof. But the shooting was definitely coming from that direction, either from the house itself or some road or whatever was beyond it on the other side. To the west of them, at the opposite end of the pasture, crowded up against the back fence, was a small herd of cattle that had retreated from the noise of the gunfight.

"Somebody must have been living here all along, to still have those cows on the place," Jonathan said.

"Yeah, but who's to say the folks in that house are even the rightful owners?" Willis argued. "Maybe it's a gang of looters or a group of those insurgents that have already taken over the place and the folks shooting at them are the good guys? We don't know who the other shooters are or where they came from. Just because this looks like an ordinary farm doesn't mean it's not an insurgent camp."

Of course, Willis was right. There was no way of knowing, but Eric *wanted* to know. There was something about this situation that intrigued him, even though he couldn't quite put his finger on it. He knew it wasn't just because of Beckman's desire to gather intel though. Maybe it was just the likelihood that the occupants of that house really were honest, simple folk trying to hang on and weather the storms of adversity that surrounded them. If so, it was nothing he hadn't seen a hundred times already since his return, but Eric admired anyone willing to take a stand and fight. Whatever it was though, his thoughts were soon interrupted by the roar of the automatic weapon they'd all heard before, and this time, it came in the form of several long, sustained bursts.

"Someone's got some serious firepower in there!" Trey said.

"I'm pretty sure that was the sound signature of an M249," Eric said.

"I agree," Beckman said. "Some of those were more than 30-rounds. That really makes me curious."

"I still say it's none of our business!" Willis said.

"Maybe not," Eric said, "but a firefight of that scale is hard to ignore! It's worth getting a closer look just to see who's involved. Hell, it may even be people connected with the outfits we've already run up against—contractors, or cartel enforcers— who knows? If it is, I want to know about it, and so will Beckman's superiors!"

"They sure will," Beckman agreed. "You know, it looks to me

like this strip of woods runs all the way around the edge of this pasture. If it does, we can work our way around there and get into a position where we can see all of the house without being seen."

"That's what I'm thinking too," Eric said. He turned to Jonathan and Willis. "Look, I know both of you would have preferred to stay away from this whole business and keep going east, and that's fine. You two can hang back here and keep an eye out for trouble in this direction while we go take a closer look. Trey can stay here with you too." Eric turned to Lenny. "Are you up for going with us?"

Lenny said he was, of course, and then Willis jumped back in.

"Look, I don't have a problem going with you, if you want me to go. Hell, I don't even have a problem going in there with guns blazing and taking care of business if that's what you decide you want to do. You know damned well I ain't scared of a fight!"

"No one is accusing you of being scared, Willis; you or Jonathan! But somebody needs to hang back, so we don't run the risk of exposing the whole team. It may as well be you two and Trey. The other three of us can sneak up there with less chance of being seen than all six."

"Do you mind if I still take your rifle?" Beckman asked Willis. "I know you may be reluctant to let your weapon out of your sight, and I wouldn't blame you if you are, but I'd feel better having it if you're okay with it."

"That damned thing? Hell, Eric'll tell you what I think about plastic guns! Be my guest, but don't even think about putting your hands on my .30-30, because *nobody* touches it but me!" Willis turned around so Beckman could remove the M4 from where it was strapped to the outside of his ruck.

"Thanks Willis," Eric said. "We won't be doing any shooting anyway, but it's better if we're all armed, just in case. Hang tight here and keep your eyes and ears open, because someone from either side of that fight could come out this way too."

With that settled, Eric led the way, with Beckman following

close behind and Lenny bringing up the rear. There were no more full auto bursts after the last one they'd heard a few minutes before, and almost all of the shooting had stopped but for an occasional round now and then. The three of them were well aware that some of the defenders could have retreated into this same strip of woods or that the attackers could use it to move around in order to hit the house from a different angle, so they stopped often as they advanced to look and listen for indications of movement. But it wasn't until they reached the point where they had a clear view of the side of the house that they saw anyone at all. From there, they could see several disabled vehicles parked out front, most of them with tires and glass shot out and the sheet metal riddled with bullet holes. There was one dead guy visible on the ground just outside the open driver's side door of a pickup truck, but it seemed all the shooting had ceased for now.

Eric could see movement out among the trees beyond the driveway momentarily though, and then several men dressed in matching olive drab green BDUs materialized from the concealment of the undergrowth and began advancing towards the house. And as he watched them move closer, Eric saw that most of them were wearing helmets and appeared to be soldiers, though the solid-colored uniforms in which they were clad didn't match the digital-pattern Beckman wore. Eric turned to glance back at the PFC for his reaction, and saw relief written on his face at the sight of these men in uniform.

"Are they part of your battalion?" He whispered.

"No, but I'm thinking maybe they *are* state National Guard. They may be from that small outpost I was telling you about—Camp McCall—if they are operating this far west. It's the only one I know of that's close enough to this area to make it logistically feasible. I'm still not sure why they'd be way out here, but I told you it was worth coming to see what all that shooting was about. We may have just saved ourselves a long walk!"

Eric considered what Beckman said as he watched the men

approach the house. *Maybe Jonathan's idea that the occupants of this property were some of the insurgents or other troublemakers was correct?* If so, these soldiers must have gotten wind of the fact that they were using the place and mounted an assault to shut them down. That seemed to be the obvious explanation when three men dressed the same as those approaching the house stepped out of the front door to greet them in the yard.

"It looks like this fight has already been decided," Eric said. "It looks like an entry team has already gone in and cleared the house while those that were out in the woods covered for them."

When two more of the men emerged from the back door of the house, Eric was convinced that was the case, especially when he saw that one of them was carrying a SAW, indicating that it was the assault team, rather than the defenders that were wielding all that firepower they'd heard. Beckman made a comment about going to talk to them, as Eric had expected him to, but Eric urged him to be cautious before making a rash move.

"You go stepping out of these woods right now after they just cleared that house and you're liable to get shot!"

"Not if they see me in this uniform!" Beckman said. "They'll recognize me as a member of the 26th Special Forces Group."

"I wouldn't be so sure. It appears they've launched this assault directly from the front. Anyone making an appearance from a different quadrant will likely be considered the enemy! I'd hold off a few more minutes and see what happens next. We don't know for sure if this fight is over even though it looks like it probably is. I agree it's a good idea to talk to them, because it may save us a lot of time and trouble, but those guys are amped up from battle and still have their fingers on the trigger! Let's give them time for the adrenalin to settle."

It was understandable that Beckman was impatient. The man was desperate to meet up with other men in the Guard after the devastating loss of his entire squad. But the PFC listened to what Eric said and agreed to wait a bit for the right moment. So, along with Lenny, they crouched there in the thick undergrowth of the little strip of woods and watched as the rest of the assault team converged in the front yard of the house. Eric guessed it was a platoon-strength unit, as he counted fifteen guys that he could see and figured there must be several more standing watch wherever they'd dismounted their vehicles.

Some of the men that had cleared the house were now bringing out weapons they no doubt collected from the hapless defenders, and were piling them onto the hood of one of the pickup trucks parked out front. Eric knew they probably had orders to collect every weapon and magazine along with any other ammunition or materials they found on site, and he assumed this was a fairly high-value target to warrant this kind of assault force. The various AR and AK-style rifles in the pile seemed to suggest the occupants of the house were likely with one of the organized gangs or insurgent groups Beckman had spoken of.

As he watched the soldiers sort and unload the rifles and handguns they collected, it appeared they were getting ready to hump everything out of there on foot. If they had vehicles nearby as he had assumed, they weren't waiting for them to arrive, and Beckman was growing more impatient by the minute. Eric knew he wouldn't be able to restrain him much longer.

"I know you guys will cover for me when I show myself," he told Eric. "I mean, I sure don't want you shooting any of our own guys, but if worse comes to worse and I have to run back into the woods you can at least fire some rounds over their heads to let them know that I'm not alone and discourage them from coming after me! Of course, I don't expect that'll be necessary. I'll walk out there unarmed and I won't give them a reason to shoot, but like you said, they're probably still jumpy so soon after all that action."

"We've got your back," Eric said. But if it goes sideways, we are all in trouble, because by my count, there's fifteen men right here that we know of, and probably a few more wherever they left their rides. The two of us can't do a hell of a lot to help you against those odds, and they may shoot you on sight anyway!"

Eric considered sending Lenny back to tell Jonathan and the rest of the team what was going on, but there wasn't enough time for him to get there and come back with them before the soldiers left, as it looked like they were about to move out any minute. If they were going to make contact, they needed to do it now, and Beckman was their best bet, since he was in a uniform he insisted they'd recognize. Eric went ahead and gave him the go-ahead, while he and Lenny remained in concealment to watch and see what sort of reception he'd get.

Beckman left Willis's rifle with Eric and slowly walked out of the woods into the open, waving both hands over his head as he shouted his name, rank and unit name to the soldiers. Just as Eric expected, every man within earshot pivoted instantly at the sound of his voice, raising their rifles and dropping to a knee or behind the vehicles and other available cover as they assessed this new and unexpected potential threat. Eric and Beckman both knew full well that was the moment the soldiers might simply shoot first without bothering to I.D. their target, but it was a risk the PFC was willing to take.

But no gunshots rang out. Instead, Beckman was ordered to freeze in place where he stood less than a dozen yards away from the edge of the woods. The PFC had his hands thrust high into the air as a detachment of six men fanned out and rushed towards him with their weapons leveled and ready to cut him down at the slightest provocation. Before they were in contact distance, one of them shouted at him to drop to the ground, face-down with his arms out to his sides. Beckman did as he was told, while repeating again his name and the name of the Special Forces group and battalion he was assigned to.

As two of the soldiers circled behind him to prevent his escape, the one in front that had ordered Beckman to the ground was pointing his weapon at his head from point blank range, demanding to know why he was alone, why he had no weapon, and why he was approaching the scene of an active operation without authorization. Eric figured he was one of the NCOs from the way he was taking charge, but there was no rank insignia on his uniform to distinguish it from those of his companions. Meanwhile, most of the others in the unit that had at first remained near the house were now coming out there to see who this stranger was that had the nerve to interrupt what they were doing.

Eric was watching all of this intently, sizing up the six men closest to the woods while keeping tabs on the others as much as possible. If he had any second thoughts about the wisdom of approaching these men, it was already too late to change his mind, because Beckman blew his cover.

"I'm not alone!" Beckman replied to the fellow asking all the questions. "I have friends right here with me! Friends who helped me after my squad was wiped out and are still helping me return to the nearest Army outpost. And they have critical intel from west of the river!" Beckman turned as much as he dared while lying there surrounded at gunpoint and shouted: "HEY ERIC! LENNY! COME ON OUT HERE AND TELL THESE MEN WHAT YOU TOLD ME!"

SIX

"IDIOT!" ERIC MUTTERED UNDER HIS BREATH TO LENNY, when Beckman called out to the two of them to come on out of hiding. Eric would have preferred Beckman keep his mouth shut about their presence until he knew for sure how he was going to be received. At this point it wasn't looking great, as he was still face down on the ground with several rifles pointed at his head. Now, he'd put Eric and Lenny in a tough spot as well. Several of the soldiers had already diverted their attention to the woods in the direction Beckman indicated, and Eric had only a split second to make a decision. He and Lenny had to either show themselves momentarily or attempt to evade now. Eric knew if he chose the latter, the two of them would have a difficult time extricating themselves from the area without a firefight, something he didn't want to initiate as long as he had reason to believe these men were on the side of the good guys. Besides, if any shooting started for any reason, Beckman would probably be the first to die at the hands of one of the nervous soldiers guarding him. And if that weren't reason enough, Jonathan, Willis and Trey were completely in the dark as to what was going on here. If Eric and Lenny tried to run back and rendezvous with them on the way out, they would simply bring the fight to them too. And even if they bugged out in the opposite direction, the three of them would still be in danger simply due to their proximity to the farmhouse, not to mention the fact that a new exchange of gunfire now would certainly draw them in to find out what was going on. Even if the three of them figured it out in time to avoid detection, a successful escape would still result in the separation of the team. So, whether he liked it or not, Eric was left facing the first option, which meant trusting these uniformed strangers with the same faith Beckman had.

He'd been watching the way the men moved, and his first impression was that they were organized and were carrying out tasks with military precision. Even now, on edge as they were from the assault and then the sudden appearance of a stranger from out of the woods adjacent their objective, they still exhibited discipline and were acting together as a cohesive unit.

But now that he'd seen some of them up close when they came out to meet Beckman, it was apparent their appearance was on the scruffy side by military standards. That sort of raised a red flag to Eric after all his recent dealings with unscrupulous private contractors, but then he knew too that formal standards meant little in guerrilla warfare conditions such as what these men were likely involved in. It was the way Eric had often operated when he was a member of the SEAL team, so it didn't necessarily mean the soldiers weren't professionals. Eric decided the only thing to do was to go all in like Beckman and take a chance with them. But first, he slipped the extra rifle Willis had loaned Beckman around to the other side of a big pine tree and made sure that Lenny saw him do it. Eric knew the two of them would be disarmed, and the extra weapon left behind was an ace in the hole in case the meeting fell apart and they had to make a run for it. But that was the worst-case scenario, and Eric was hoping for the best. "Let me do all the talking," he whispered to Lenny, before turning towards the men to shout:

"WE'RE COMING OUT! There are two of us, and our hands will be empty and over our heads!"

At the sound of his voice, the men that were already focused on the woods in his direction shouldered their weapons, pointing them in the direction from which he spoke. Eric and Lenny didn't keep them waiting. They slowly rose from where they'd been crouching and took a couple of steps out of the concealing foliage. "Take it easy guys! We have no weapons in hand!"

Both men still had their weapons on them, but they'd positioned their rifles behind their backs on the slings before they made a move. They'd left their rucksacks behind where Jonathan and the others were waiting, but they both wore handguns and knives on their belts. Eric hated to submit to being disarmed, even temporarily, but he hoped it wouldn't take long to sort things out so they could get their gear back. So far, Beckman hadn't made a mention of the other three members of the team, and Eric had his fingers crossed that he wouldn't. It was Eric's place to decide when and if to reveal that he and Lenny and Beckman were not alone.

Eric and Lenny kept their hands high as the soldiers encircled them, and with several rifle muzzles in their faces, there was little they could do but stand quietly as their weapons were stripped from them. By this time, another man who was apparently the commander in charge of the assault was storming up to them with several of the other men from the unit, demanding to know who had dared approach the scene of his active operation. Like the other men who'd first detained Beckman, his uniform bore no rank insignia, but Eric had taken part in many special ops in which non-standard uniforms were worn, so that minor detail didn't immediately raise an alarm either.

"The name's Eric Branson, sir! Former Chief Petty Officer, U.S. Navy Special Warfare Group Two. This is my nephew, Lenny Polk," Eric lied regarding his relationship to Lenny. He hadn't preplanned it or told Lenny, but he knew the young man wouldn't deny it or show surprise. It simply came out because the same story had worked to Eric's advantage before when he passed Jonathan off as a nephew to provide a plausible reason why he was traveling with a much younger man who was obviously a civilian. Eric then nodded at the man on the ground: "PFC Robert Beckman there is a member of the Army National Guard Special Forces Group. He's trying to make his way back to his base or the nearest outpost en route after his squad and the Black Hawk helicopter carrying them were wiped out in an ambush! We knew nothing of your operation here, sir. We were passing through and heard the sounds of an intense gun battle, so we thought we'd better see what was going on, considering the situation."

"I ought to have you shot right now or do it myself!" The assault leader replied. Why am I supposed to believe that you're not part of that same gang of outlaws that was barricaded in that house?"

"They're not with any of the groups over here!" Beckman shouted. "They crossed over the river from Louisiana. They are looking to meet with the military high command over here because they have valuable intel to share."

"Did I give you permission to speak, Private?"

"No sir! Sorry sir!"

"Just who the hell are you, and what outfit are you with?"

"Private First Class Robert Beckman, sir! 26th Special Forces Group, 3rd Battalion, Camp Hurley, Mississippi!"

"Then what in the hell are you doing way over here then? And why are you alone?"

"My unit was assigned to patrol the adjacent sector of the Mississippi River. I'm alone because my squad was ambushed, sir, exactly like my friend, Branson here just said. Every man but me was KIA, including our pilot and copilot in the Black Hawk we were flying the river in."

"Where? Are you telling me your helicopter was shot down and you survived the crash? You don't look any worse for the wear to me!"

"No sir! Our aircraft was destroyed on the ground, sir. We were ambushed shortly after we set down on a sandbar on the Mississippi River about 20 miles to the southwest of here. I don't know where your unit is based, sir, but if you're operating in this region, I assume you're aware of the ongoing raids happening along the river. Surely you knew that SF has been running helicopter patrols up and down the Mississippi and over the coastal waters. Are you from that armored brigade post I've heard about to the northwest of here, the one called Camp McCall?"

"I'm asking the questions around here Private! What my mission is about is no concern of yours! But I can tell you that anyone caught running around this region armed the way your friends are is generally considered an enemy and subject to being shot on sight! If it weren't for that uniform you're wearing, you'd have been dead as soon as you stepped out of those woods. The only reason all three of you are not already is because I'm curious about anyone dumb enough to show themselves here in a situation like this."

"Sir, if I may, Eric Branson here is a former Navy SEAL with combat deployments all over the world. I think you're going to want to listen to what he has to say regarding what he's seen on the west side of that river. That's why he's here, to bring a warning to the high command over here about the invasion that's sweeping through Louisiana and coming this way!"

"I'm going to hear what he has to say all right, but not now!" He turned to the men clustered around Eric, Lenny and Beckman and told them to get Beckman to his feet and bring all three of them with them, because it was time to move out. Eric glanced at Lenny as they were forced to walk at gunpoint towards the house with their hands on top of their heads. Beckman was behind them, under the guard of two more of the soldiers, still trying to get them to listen to why the three of them were here. So far, he still hadn't mentioned Jonathan, Willis or Trey, and Eric could only hope he would continue to omit that particular detail. Eric knew Lenny would keep quiet about it, but he figured Beckman wouldn't if he were pressed by further, persistent questioning. And Eric had no reason to think they weren't all facing actual interrogation, considering they were in fact, being detained at gunpoint and taken away against their will.

∽

"I wonder what the heck is taking them so long?" Willis grumbled. "They've been gone nearly an hour now, and we haven't heard another gunshot in at least thirty minutes!"

"I'm not worried about it yet," Jonathan said. "I know how careful Eric is. He would've taken his time moving around there even if Beckman was being impatient. It probably took them twenty minutes just to get close enough to see what was going on. If that shootout is really over, Eric and Beckman are probably watching whoever's left standing and trying to figure out who they are. That's what'll determine what they do next."

"I still think it's kind of stupid for us to take a chance on getting this close to a firefight when we have no idea who's involved or what it's about. Before we came over here to this side of the river, Eric said we were going to avoid all contact until we reached our objective, especially contact with civilians!"

"I know," Jonathan said. "But how do you know they're civilians anyway? You heard that machine-gun!"

"Hearing a machine-gun don't mean shit these days! You know anybody can get them and you know we've already run into plenty of crazy folks that have them."

"Well, whatever's going on over there, you can be sure that Eric's in control. He won't show himself unless he's got a damn good reason to believe there's a benefit to it. It doesn't matter what that Private Beckman dude thinks."

"It'll suit me just fine if Beckman finds himself some new friends and joins up with them! He's talking a big talk about his

Special Forces unit and all, and telling Eric he can help us, but how do we know we can trust him? He may be making it all up!"

"He can't be making it all up, Willis. You saw the dead guys from his squad, and you saw the Black Hawk helicopter! How would he know about all that if he hadn't been there? Besides, he *is* wearing the same uniform as the men on that sandbar."

Jonathan knew that Willis didn't think too much of the stranded soldier whether his story was true or not. If he *was* telling the truth, then it sounded to him and to Jonathan too, if he were being honest, that the man was probably a deserter, considering how he'd managed to survive that ambush when every other man in his unit was cut down on the spot. The elaborate details of that part about going out into the river to retrieve that boat and then escaping by ducking behind it and swimming underwater seemed a little sketch. For all they knew, the truth could be far simpler: like maybe Beckman just took off running into the woods at the first shots fired, leaving all his squad mates behind!

But if Eric thought that at first, he didn't seem to believe it now, and what did Jonathan and Willis know of military operations anyway? He could understand why Eric agreed to take him along with them, because being in the National Guard, Beckman had the connections they needed. He could be the key to getting through the gate, whether it was to his own base or to some other military installation they might come upon first. Without that insider edge, Eric said it was far more likely they would be turned away before he could share his intel and present his case for the forces on this side of the river to take an interest in what was happening in Louisiana. Even with Beckman's introduction, Eric would still have to do some slick talking to convince anyone to listen to him. He didn't really look the part of a military man these days with his heavy beard and untrimmed hair, but if he could just get that first meeting with someone higher up, Jonathan figured Eric's expertise and knowledge would quickly become apparent.

Jonathan kept telling himself as they waited there that Eric and the others would be back any moment, but as the time dragged on, he began to share some of the same concerns Willis had. There was always the possibility the three of them had run into trouble over there, but since there hadn't been any more shooting, as Willis pointed out, Jonathan kept finding reasons to dismiss the thought. Eric was too careful to walk blindly into a trap, and no enemy was likely to get close to him unless gunfire was involved. The most plausible scenario was that he and Beckman and Lenny were simply too near the scene of the gunfight to extricate themselves while the victors were still in the area. It was either that, or they were already talking with them now if they deemed them trustworthy enough to approach.

Another half hour later, however, and Jonathan couldn't stand the not knowing any longer, much less Willis' persistent grumbling about how they ought to go and see what was going on. But he knew he was breaking a direct order from Eric if they didn't remain here and wait. It hadn't turned out well the last time he did that, when he was ordered to remain aboard the gunboat on the Atchafalaya and keep watch over it with Ronnie. It had cost them the boat for a time and had nearly cost Ronnie his life, and the intensity of Eric's anger that was directed at him was something Jonathan never wanted to experience again. But despite that memory, he couldn't shake the feeling that something was up, especially after this much time had passed. If everything was really cool, Eric probably would have sent Lenny back to get the rest of them so they wouldn't have to wait and wonder. He could have done the same if there was a problem and he needed their help—unless the problem was so bad he was *unable* to send for help. Considering all this, Jonathan made up his mind then and there that it was time to find out what was really going on, and Willis and Trey didn't need convincing that it was a good idea. In fact, Jonathan let Willis lead the way as they moved quietly through the narrow strip of woods following the same path Eric and the others had taken.

But even when they were near enough to have a clear view of

one side of the house, there was still no sign of Eric, Beckman, or Lenny either out in the open or within the woods nearby. There was no sign of whoever had been doing all that shooting either, which indicated the fight *really was* over. But if that were the case, then where in the hell was Eric?

Jonathan tried to signal him with the subtle bird whistle the two of them had used before but got no response after several minutes. He and Willis and Lenny moved on around through the edge of the woods until they could see most of the front side of the house too, along with all the vehicles that were parked there. There was no indication anyone was still around, but there *was* a single dead guy sprawled on the ground next to the open door of one of the trucks. It looked as if he'd been trying to get in it to leave but didn't make it.

"I don't know what to make of this," Jonathan whispered. "Unless they're inside the house I don't know where else they could be."

"I guess one of us'll have to go in there and find out, right? I know it's a good way to get shot, but I'll do it if you'll both cover me."

"Maybe we ought to circle all the way around, and check those woods around the driveway out front," Trey said. "They may have gone around there to get a better view."

"It's possible," Jonathan said, "but that was a *lot* of shooting! It's hard to imagine everyone involved in it disappeared that fast. And if they did, then why wouldn't Eric have come back to get us before he went looking any further?"

"Maybe because he saw them leaving and didn't have time?" Willis said. "It looks to me like whoever attacked this place won the fight, otherwise there'd be somebody here besides that one dead guy over there by that truck. I'll bet there's more dead ones inside the house."

"Maybe so. But all that really matters to me is finding out where Eric, Lenny and Beckman are. Let's do what Trey suggested and circle around front first. If we don't find them out there, then we'll have to go in that house and try and figure out what happened here."

"Whatever it was, I don't like it," Willis said. "I tried to talk Eric out of coming around here."

"Eric does what he sets his mind to. I can't blame him for wanting to know what this was about, but I've got a bad feeling you're right, Willis. We probably should have gone the other way when we first heard the gunfire."

"Hey, look!" Trey had taken a few steps ahead of them, moving farther along in the direction of the driveway. Now, he was just within the tree line at the edge of the front yard, and he was pointing at the base of one of the tall pine trees that stood there amid the thick undergrowth of bushes that surrounded it. *Leaning against its massive trunk was a rifle—the same M4 rifle that Beckman had borrowed from Willis!*

SEVEN

"I'll be damned!" Jonathan whispered. "Eric wouldn't have let Beckman leave that rifle there unless he had a good reason!"

"But what would that reason be?" Trey asked"

"Maybe Eric was leaving us a sign," Willis said.

"Maybe, but a sign of what? He and Lenny are nowhere in sight. Beckman's nowhere in sight. They came here to see what the shooting was about, and now whoever was involved in it is nowhere in sight either. It makes me think even more that they went wherever the ones that attacked this place went."

"Like maybe they followed them?" Trey asked.

"Maybe. Or maybe they made contact with them," Willis said.

"Eric would have probably sent Lenny back to tell us if he was going to do something like that."

"Unless he couldn't, for some reason."

Jonathan had to admit Willis had a point. The only thing he was certain of was that Eric or Beckman left that rifle there deliberately. It wasn't dropped or misplaced. It was leaning against the side of the tree opposite the yard surrounding the house, so that it would be hidden from anyone peering into the woods from that direction. They were either thinking they'd need it later, or like Willis said, leaving it as a sign that he knew the three of them would find when they eventually came looking for him. Jonathan was certain they saw something significant here, or they never would have left without coming back to get the three of them. The nagging question in the back of his mind though, was whether they'd left voluntarily or otherwise. It was a mystery, because there'd been no more gunfire, as he would have expected if Eric and the others ran into trouble.

"So, what do we do now?" Trey wanted to know."

"We have to figure out where they went!" Willis said. "That's about all we *can* do."

Jonathan checked the M4 and saw that it had a full mag, and that a round was chambered. It seemed to him Eric or Beckman left it in Condition 1 because they thought they might need to grab it in a hurry. Otherwise, there was no reason to do so if they were simply leaving it for Willis to collect when they got here. He put it back against the tree exactly as he found it, since there was a possibility Eric or Beckman might still need it for some reason unknown to them. Willis wasn't interested in carrying it anyway, as they had left their rucks back where they'd been waiting in the same place Eric and Lenny left theirs. Jonathan glanced back at the house, trying to imagine what Eric had seen there to make him leave like this. Willis was probably right. *Surely Eric or Beckman must have observed someone there that they thought they could talk to. But if they did, then where did they all go?*

"I guess we need to go into that house and see if we can determine who those people are that were killed," Jonathan said to Willis. "If we can tell whether they were the family that owned the place or a bunch of armed men that took it over, it may give us a clue as to why someone attacked them and who the attackers might be. You heard me tell Eric before we split up that I thought it could be a gang or some other group of outlaws holed up here. If we can figure that out, maybe we can figure out whether whoever attacked them were good guys or just more bad guys."

"Maybe, but we've gotta be careful, because this could be a trap too. I ain't scared to go in there, but it makes more sense to circle on around through the woods to that driveway and check things out from that angle first. We'll have a better idea whether they all really left or not, and we may find another sign of Eric and them along the way."

That sounded reasonable to Jonathan, so he told Willis to lead the way, knowing he was the most skilled woodsman among them and the one most likely to see something they may otherwise miss. But several minutes later, after the three of them reached the gravel lane leading into the property, it appeared the place was truly deserted. They were still far enough within the edge of the woods to be out of sight of anyone that might still be hiding out inside the house. But from the angle at which they could view it now, it was obvious that the dwelling had been the target of a major attack, just as all that shooting they'd heard suggested. Aside from the one dead guy out by the truck, they could now see another body slumped against the wall to one side of the door. The door itself was broken off the hinges and most of the windows were shot out, as was most of the glass in the pickups, SUVs and cars that were parked there. It was hard to make out any details, but it looked like there were bodies on the floor inside too, just as he'd expected, and seeing the extent of the aftermath, it seemed really ominous that whoever did this was already gone, along with Eric, Lenny and Beckman. At this point it seemed a waste of time to go looking around inside that house. They needed to figure out where everyone went, and the best way to do that was to follow them by the most likely route they'd taken when they left.

"There's a lot of boot prints on that road," Willis said. "And it looks like about all of them are headed away from the house."

Like Jonathan and Trey, Willis was still standing within the edge of the woods when he said this, staring at the tracks he could see there from several feet away.

"I need to get out there where I can get a better look at those prints. I need to see if I can find any made by those boots Eric wears. They've got a sole pattern you don't see every day."

"It's probably not a good idea to do it right here, Willis. We ought to move out a little farther from the house, so we won't be seen when we step out into the open just in case there's still someone alive in there."

Willis agreed. They followed the road out another 50 yards or so away from the house, staying within the trees until they were at a point where the front yard was barely visible. There were still no sounds to indicate anyone was in the area, but the tracks showed that a sizable group of men wearing boots had just walked that way, following the road.

When Willis went out there to examine them with Jonathan and Trey following, crouching low to the ground, Willis pointed out a variety of distinct sole patterns, some that he said were combat boots and others that were more generic hunting or hiking boot patterns. He knew Lenny's boots were of the latter type, but that Eric's were a bit unique, since they were a pair of minimalist patrol boots with no heel rise that he'd gotten from his brother, Keith. It took him several minutes to find what he was looking for, because it appeared that more than a dozen different people had walked out there on that road, and there were prints on top of prints. To make matters worse, they were mostly a muddy, confused mess because of all the recent rain. But when he at last found a smooth patch of wet sand that held the shape of the impressions in place, the sole pattern he was looking for was there, and the size was right too by his judgment.

"Is that one of Eric's?" Jonathan asked.

"Yes. Eric definitely went this way. It's hard to tell about Lenny and Beckman, but I haven't seen soles like that one anywhere other than on those boots of Eric's. The thing is though, if he came this way, the same as the others that made the rest of these tracks, I don't think he was following them. I think he came *with* them!"

"How can you tell?"

"By the other tracks that are on top of some of the ones Eric made," Trey answered for him, pointing to several more that were now obvious in the mud beyond the first one Willis found.

"Exactly," Willis said. "Not just one type either. Look at this..." he led them along, pointing to the ground. "See, there are several different patterns of boot prints overlapping some of Eric's. That tells me that it wasn't just Beckman and Lenny walking behind him. It looks to me like he was right in there in the middle of that big group when they left, and Lenny and Beckman probably were too."

Jonathan stood there thinking about the implications of all this. If Eric went *with* these men instead of just following after them, then it had to mean that he was talking to them. And there were only two reasons he would have done that. One was that he and Beckman must have determined they were legitimate authorities, perhaps a law enforcement or military unit, or two, they'd been forced to go along with them against their will.

Beckman had said that he didn't expect to find any other army units patrolling in this area because it was so remote and so far from the nearest post that it wasn't really feasible. But maybe he was wrong about that; at least Jonathan could hope, because he didn't see how the three of them could have been taken captive with no shots fired, if that other possibility was in fact, the truth. Eric was just too careful for that. But the footprints indicated that the group continued on away from the property, walking along that muddy road, so there was little else they could do at the moment but follow them and try and figure out what happened.

"Shouldn't we go back and get our gear first? Trey asked.

"There's no time for that!" Willis said. "If they're already out of sight and sound now and they're still moving, there's no telling how far away they'd be by the time we went back there to get our packs and came all the way back out here. I say we go after them now!"

"He's right," Jonathan said. "Besides, we don't know that they aren't in trouble! They may need our help and the best thing we can do is try and catch up as fast as we possibly can and see what in the hell's going on here."

They were still leery about walking down the middle of the road though, because it was easy to see how that could set them up for an ambush. Having no idea who these people were or where they went made for an uneasy feeling, especially since Eric went with them without sending Lenny back to let them know. *Could this be some kind of a trap? Was that why the M4 was left there, not by Eric, but by someone else, to purposefully lure them in?*

Jonathan's mind was racing with possibilities, but most of them were unrealistic. There was probably a more reasonable explanation for all this, and it was likely they would soon come upon Eric and the rest of this unknown group and learn what it was. *Maybe it was as simple as Eric, Beckman and Lenny going this way with them because the strangers wanted to show them something?* It was quite possible that there was no ill intent or danger at all.

To minimize the chances of being seen, the three of them stuck to the edges of the road, walking mostly just inside the shallow ditches bordering it so that they could quickly duck for cover if there was a need. Willis was leading the way of course, with his .30-30 in hand, as he examined the footprints to make sure that he still picked up one of Eric's from time to time. The little road continued on much farther than Jonathan would have expected. If it were indeed a private driveway, then the property encompassed by this one farm was probably several hundred acres, maybe more than a thousand. Beckman had said there were some large private holdings out here like that, some of them timber plantations used by the hunting clubs and some of them open cattle pasture. Now, of course, it was likely most such properties were either abandoned or used as refuges for the landowners that were trying to avoid the chaos of cities and towns. If it were possible to defend it, the landowners around here were lucky to have property in such a remote location. Jonathan figured it wouldn't be hard to hide out and live off the land here if one had to. It was just that like everywhere else, others that didn't have such resources were sweeping through the countryside, taking what they needed from those who did.

Wherever this road they were following led, it was obvious that the group had been walking it at a good pace because there was still no indication they were catching up. It now appeared that the road was more than just a private drive, and Jonathan figured they had transitioned to a different piece of property when they came to an area where there were barbed wire fences along the edge of the woods on both sides. It went on like that for about another quarter mile, until finally, they came to a T-intersection with a bigger gravel road. There was a large pull out in a clearing on the other side of that road, and Willis zeroed straight in on it, following the boot prints until he came to what Jonathan feared he would find there: *Tire tracks!*

"It looks like there was a bunch of trucks or other vehicles parked here," Willis said. "This is where the trail ends, at least the part they walked!"

Jonathan and Trey caught up to him and looked around at all the evidence. Sure enough, there were large tire tread marks everywhere, tearing up the muddy ground and obliterating most of the footprints that seemed to end there.

"What do you make of it, Willis? Were these regular trucks or do you think they were military vehicles?"

Willis was still walking bent over around the entire area, studying the tire marks when he answered Jonathan's question.

"A little bit of both I think." Some of these sets are too wide to be made by a regular truck or SUV. Looks like it was Humvees to me; just like those we took from that post over there at the Red River Wildlife Management Area."

"Well, if those men were in vehicles," Trey wondered, "why in the world would Eric, Beckman and Lenny get in them and go with them?"

It was a good question. Jonathan agreed it didn't make any sense that they would have gone anywhere without coming back for the three of them. It was even more baffling than the fact they found evidence that Eric had walked all that way with them to begin with.

"Maybe they didn't get in them," Jonathan said. "Willis, we need to check everywhere around this clearing in a big radius and see if there's any possibility that Eric and Lenny went somewhere else instead of getting into those vehicles. Maybe they went in a different direction and we just interpreted the sign wrong?"

"I wish I could believe that," Willis said. "But I don't think so. The evidence is pretty compelling. It looks like the trail ends here. You can see which way they went when they drove out of here though; back up to the north the same way they came in. They must have parked their vehicles here and then slipped through the woods on foot before they attacked that house this morning. Probably got here during the night and went in around daybreak to get into position. I didn't see any evidence that a big crowd like that went marching down that road on the way in, so I bet they cut through the woods going down there and then after they killed all those folks in that house, they probably didn't give a damn whether they left tracks or not. That tells me they didn't know about the three of us being with Eric and them. Eric and Lenny would've kept their mouths shut if there was any chance it would bring trouble to us. I don't know about that Beckman fellow, but I do know that it looks like all three of them must have gotten into the vehicles that were parked here."

Willis took the time to examine the surrounding area thoroughly anyway, and Jonathan and Trey followed along behind him ever hopeful they would find just a single footprint to indicate Eric didn't get into one of those vehicles. But though they scoured at least a 50-yard radius all the way around the parking area, they found no more footprints leading in a different direction. Nor were any of Eric's distinctive tracks pointing back in the direction of the farmhouse. The picture was clear now. *Eric, Lenny and Beckman were gone!*

EIGHT

"What are we going to do now?" Trey asked. "It's not like we can track vehicles! There's no telling how far they'll go now that they're driving."

Trey was right of course, but Jonathan didn't have the answer as to what they were going to do next. "About all we can do is go back and get our rucks," he said.

"We could follow the tire tracks on out to the north for a ways if you wanted to," Willis said. "But like you say, if we don't have our rucksacks, we're not going to have any supplies. And it's true there's no telling how far they went. They could have stopped a couple miles down the road or they may be going a hundred. But I'm betting it's pretty far, otherwise they wouldn't bother driving at all considering how far they walked through the woods just to get to that house before they hit it."

"I'm thinking you're right," Jonathan said. "We don't have any reason to believe they're close by. What we need to do is get our gear and find someone else that can give us some answers."

"Someone else?" Trey asked.

"Yes. Someone local; like some of the people that are still

holding out on some of these properties around here. Maybe they'll know what's going on in the area, and whether it's the military or law enforcement, or if it's some other group that's operating out here. Hell, for all we know, it could be more of those sleazy contractors like the C.R.I. guys we've been dealing with for so long! We don't know what Eric has gotten himself into this time, and it may not be easy to find out. I think we need to do our own intel gathering though, and the only way I see to do that is to talk to somebody local... somebody that knows the area and can maybe help us out. Other than that, all I know to do is try to find a way to get to that Camp McCall outpost that Beckman was talking about. There's a chance that the military vehicles that were here are going there now, but I don't know why they would, unless it was the actual Army that arrested Eric and Lenny and Beckman. If they *are* in control here like that Sergeant Davis guy told Eric, they may be enforcing strict martial law and arresting everybody. I don't see why they would take them in if Beckman is really who he says he is though."

"Just having guns on them would be reason enough in that case," Willis said. "It probably wouldn't matter if Beckman was with them or not. But Beckman didn't have a firearm since he left that M4 out there in the woods."

Willis was right of course, but none of this really made a lot of sense. It was hard to know what to think and everything they came up with was just speculation, for the most part. But Jonathan did think that finding somebody from around the area to talk to was probably the most logical thing they could do. He didn't know how they could figure this out on their own, unless they could actually follow those vehicles to wherever they went, and that would be impossible once the gravel turned to pavement. Of course, once they got their rucksacks, they would return here anyway, because it was a place to start, even though Jonathan doubted there was much to gain by walking down a dirt road staring at tire tracks. He knew the road would take them somewhere though, and eventually, they would find someone they could talk to.

The three of them were dejected and worried as they made their way back to the farmhouse, but by now Jonathan was used to plans falling apart just when it seemed things were going well. Running into PFC Beckman the first day they were on the ground here seemed too fortuitous to be true when it happened, and now it had backfired. The four of them may have been able to talk Eric out of investigating that early morning shootout had it not been for Beckman, but having him along clouded Eric's thinking. Jonathan knew Eric saw helping the stranded soldier as a fast track to making contact with the military commanders he sought, but now the team was divided, and Jonathan and his two companions were alone in the middle of nowhere. The mission was on hold until they found Eric and Lenny, regardless of what happened to Beckman, and Jonathan knew they could be facing a long, drawn-out ordeal before he ever returned to Sierra Zulu where Vicky awaited him. His thoughts of her were interrupted though when they reached the other end of the road and he had a view of the farmhouse again. This time, he knew they had to go inside to take a look around.

"Like you said, we have to try and figure out if the dead people in that house in there were regular folks, or some kind of bad guys. That'll at least give us some idea whether they were killed by the authorities or not. I'll do it if none of you want to go."

"I'll go with you," Jonathan said. "But I don't think we need to all go. Trey, if you'll hang back here and cover the two of us, that'd be great. If we need you, I'll wave you in."

Jonathan was well aware that they were taking a risk going into the house. But he felt they really needed to do it, because Willis was right. They needed to get an idea whether the men Eric and the others left with were the legitimate authorities or something else. Although he knew there was no guarantee they'd be able to tell simply by looking at the bodies left behind, Jonathan figured they'd get a pretty good indication if they proved to be all men, or if instead there were women and children among them as well.

Willis went first, moving quickly from the edge of the woods to the cover of one of the nearest SUVs parked in the yard. As he worked his way among them towards the front of the house, slipping quietly from vehicle to vehicle, Jonathan followed. Once the two of them had reached the last pickup truck that was only about twenty feet from the front entrance, Jonathan braced his rifle over the hood while Willis went through the doorway with his .30-30 ready to shoot from the hip if there was a threat. But Jonathan saw him wave momentarily and give the all-clear sign, so he followed him in, making his way around the remnants of the battered down front door.

What he saw when he looked around inside from up close was absolute carnage. There were bodies strewn everywhere, and the amount of blood was more than he'd seen in the aftermath of any of the situations he'd been involved in since he'd first hooked up with Eric. That machine gun had done more damage than he could have imagined when used against soft targets with no available hard cover, and the damage was multiplied by the close range and the sheer number of rounds fired into the dwelling. Jonathan held his breath as much as possible as he stepped over bodies after Willis. And although Willis was a lifelong hunter accustomed to blood and gore and killing things, even he was having a hard time with this scene. It took little more than a glance to determine that not all of the dead inside were likely combatants, even though the two adult men they'd already seen outside and four more on the floor under the front windowsills may have been.

In the small kitchen and dining room, they found three dead women, as well as a man far too old to be a threat to anyone. And if that weren't convincing enough, they also discovered the bodies of three older teens in the corner of one of the back bedrooms, two of them boys, and one a girl. Jonathan knew from the sounds that drew them here in the first place that the shooting had been a two-way exchange, so he was sure some of these folks that died here had tried to defend themselves. But whatever arms they may have had were gone now, probably because the attackers that killed them came in afterwards and took them.

"Well now we know it probably wasn't the military or law enforcement that did this!" Willis said. "These people don't look like terrorists or looters to me. It looks to me like they were the family that lived here—at least some of them were. Maybe some of the extra folks were neighbors, or in-laws or cousins, but whatever they were, they were murdered, plain and simple, and I don't know what for. It doesn't look like the killers that did it took anything."

"No," Jonathan said, "nothing but whatever weapons or ammo they had. I've seen all I can stand of this. Let's get out of here!"

Jonathan was just about to step back outside to warn Trey that there was no need for him to come any closer to the house when he was stopped in his tracks by the sound of Trey's shout:

"HEY YOU! DROP THAT GUN! DROP IT NOW AND STAY WHERE YOU ARE!"

Jonathan moved as close to the front entrance as he dared to see what was going on. He was surprised to see that Trey had stepped out of the woods completely and was standing in the open with his rifle pointed towards the other side of the house. Trey shouted again yelling to someone over there: "I SAID PUT THAT GUN DOWN RIGHT NOW! PUT IT DOWN OR I'LL HAVE TO SHOOT!" A few seconds of silence followed, and then Jonathan saw Trey point his rifle up into the air and fire two rounds in rapid succession.

"Who in the hell is he shooting at?" Willis asked, as he joined Trey at the doorway.

"I don't know but I'm going to slip out there behind that truck and see if I can get a better view."

"NOW, GET DOWN ON THE GROUND AND STAY WHERE YOU ARE!" Jonathan heard Trey yell again. As he stepped just outside the door, Trey turned to face him. "He put the gun down, Jonathan! It's just a kid, but he had a rifle. It's okay now, I've got him covered!"

By this time Willis had made his way out the back door and he and Jonathan converged on the side yard from either end of the house. Trey was coming in closer now too and Jonathan saw a small boy crouching with one knee on the ground and his hands in the air. There was a rifle in the grass in front of him, and the kid looked terrified. As three of them moved closer to him, he suddenly jumped to his feet and took off running across the open pasture, leaving his gun behind.

"I'll get him!" Willis yelled as he put down his own rifle and took off after him in an all-out sprint. The kid was fast, but he was no match for Willis and within 50 yards, the young man ran him down and tackled him to the ground.

Jonathan quickly scanned the woods around them, to make sure the boy was alone before he went out there after them to see what this was all about. As he walked by the spot where the kid had first stopped, he stooped to pick up the rifle that he left on the ground there. It was a youth-sized .22-caliber bolt action hunting rifle with a scope mounted to the top rail. Trey caught up with him as he was looking at it and explained what had happened.

"I was just watching the house, and all of a sudden I saw someone come out of the woods over there. I was getting ready to shoot him until I saw that he was just a kid, but still, he had that rifle in his hands, and he was sneaking up to the house. I don't think he knew that you and Willis were in there. He sure didn't see me until I yelled at him. If he hadn't been out in the open when I told him to put the gun down, he probably would've gotten away. But it startled him so much when I got the drop on him that he didn't know what to do, at least not until you and Willis got close, then I guess he panicked. I'm glad Willis was able to catch him, and I'm sure glad I didn't have to shoot a little kid like that. But I would have if he'd pointed that rifle at you or Willis!"

"You did the right thing, Trey. Let's go see what he has to say.

Maybe he's part of the family that lived here and can tell us what happened."

"You mean it was a family?"

"Yes, there were men, women and older children in there, all dead."

Willis had gotten up off of the kid by the time Jonathan and Trey reached them, but he still had a grip on one of his wrists to keep him from taking off again. The boy looked to be about nine or ten years old to Jonathan.

"I told him we weren't going to hurt him," Willis said.

"That's right," Jonathan said to the kid. "My friend here just wanted you to put that gun down, because he was afraid you might try to shoot somebody."

"I was going to shoot somebody!" The boy replied. "I was going to shoot anybody I saw in my house because I know they were trying to kill my aunt and uncle and my cousins!"

"This is your house?" Jonathan asked.

"Yeah. It don't seem like it anymore though. Not since my uncles and aunts and cousins moved in and especially not since my momma and daddy were killed. I've still had to live there though because I had no place else to go."

Jonathan hated to hear that the kid's parents were dead, but he was greatly relieved that it already happened before today, and that they were not among the dead men and women inside that house now. But those slaughtered in there were surely the relatives he spoke of.

"I'm sorry to hear about your mom and dad. I really am," Jonathan said. "Have you got a name? Mine's Jonathan."

The kid stared down at the ground as if he wasn't sure whether he wanted to say or not, and then he finally looked back up at Jonathan. "It's Michael."

"Well, Michael, that's Willis that's got ahold of you there, and this is Trey that hollered at you to put your gun down back there."

"Are you going to give it back to me now, or what?" The boy demanded.

"I don't intend to keep it," Jonathan said. "I just don't want anyone else to get hurt, so we need to talk about it. It looks like enough people have been hurt here already. Do you know who did this? Where were you when all that shooting was going on?"

"I wasn't here at the house, but I saw who did it. I was way down there on the other end of that pasture," the boy pointed to the back end of the big pasture where the small herd of cattle was still clustered near the edge of the trees.

"Who were they then? Were they bad guys, like robbers or looters? Did you know any of them or were they all strangers?"

"No! I don't know any of them. All I know is that they looked like they were soldiers!"

"Soldiers?" Willis asked. "Are you serious?"

The boy nodded.

"You're sure they were soldiers? Jonathan asked again. "What made you think that? Were they wearing Army uniforms or something? Did they come here in green trucks or Army jeeps?"

"I didn't see any trucks or jeeps, but they were wearing green Army uniforms. I could see them plain as day through my scope when they came out of the woods. I could have shot some of them if I'd had my daddy's deer rifle, but they were too far away for me to shoot with a .22. I didn't see any trucks or anything like Army jeeps or tanks. They just came out of the woods and started shooting. I heard machine guns and all kinds of shooting. My uncles and my cousins were shooting back too; I know they were, but I don't know if they killed some of them or not. I don't know where everybody is that was in the house. Did you find any of them still in there?"

Jonathan wasn't sure how to answer that. What he and Willis saw in that house was something no small boy like Michael should ever have to see. Of course, Jonathan had no clue as to how much death the boy had already seen, because he'd said that he'd lost his mom and dad, and Jonathan had to assume it was to the violence so many others had lost their lives to. He told Willis to let go of Michael and then suggested that they all go sit down at the edge of the woods and talk.

"There is nobody in there that is still alive," Jonathan said, once they were sitting down over there by the fence. "I don't know if they were your aunts and uncles or not, but we saw two men out front that were killed, and five more inside, including one really old man. There were three women in there where we found the men and two teenaged-looking boys and one teen-aged girl in the back. They may be your cousins, I guess. I'm sorry Michael."

The boy took in this information with a stoic expression on his face, and Jonathan could tell it was what he expected to hear anyway.

"I guess they never really had a chance," Michael finally said. "There were so many of those soldiers, and they had machine guns too."

"Yes," Jonathan said. "We heard the machine guns. We heard all the shooting and that's why we came over here from where we were on the road just to the south of here. We didn't know what it was about, so we came around those two pastures and through the woods to see what was going on. But it was already over before we got here."

"So, tell me, Michael," Trey asked, "How is it that you were out of the house so early in the morning and were able to avoid getting caught in there when this happened?"

"That's easy," Michael said. "I was down there in those woods behind the end of the pasture, squirrel hunting. I go every morning, even though there's not a whole lot of squirrels left down there now. We've been eating them for so long now there's hardly any squirrels, rabbits or deer left in the woods close to the house anymore. But I still go hunting every day and I usually go just before daylight so I'm sitting under a good tree, ready when it gets light enough to shoot. I got out of the house even earlier than normal this morning, before anybody else was up, because I couldn't sleep. Sometimes my cousins go with me, but they weren't awake when I left today. I guess that's too bad for them."

"I'm sorry," Jonathan said.

"We're looking for three more of our friends that were with us before we came up here to the house," Willis said. "They were here about an hour before us. Did you see anybody else you didn't know besides those soldiers?"

Michael looked at Willis as if he was thinking really hard about whether he should keep talking or not. Then he finally said, "Yeah, there *were* three other men! It was a little bit after the soldiers had finally quit shooting when I saw some of them run over to the side yard over there," Michael pointed to the exact area of the yard that was adjacent to the pine tree where Trey had found Willis' M4 rifle.

"That's where you saw the other three men? What could you tell about them?" Jonathan asked. "Did they come out of the woods to talk to the soldiers?"

"They came out of the woods with their hands up like they were surrendering! First it was just one guy and I thought he was one of the soldiers too, because he was wearing green camouflage that looked like an Army uniform too, just not the same as theirs. But he had his hands up, and he didn't have a gun at all, that I could see, and I was watching everything through my scope. They made him lay down on the ground and I thought they were going to shoot him, so I kept watching to see what was going to happen next. That's when two more men came out of the woods from right over there behind where he was, and they had their hands up too. They both had guns on straps behind their backs, but the soldiers took them away from them. Then they made them go with them!"

NINE

"We need to get away from this place," Jonathan said, after Michael told them what he'd seen. "There's nothing we can accomplish by hanging around here any longer. Let's go back to where we left our rucksacks and try and sort this out."

Before they left though, Jonathan went into the edge of the woods and grabbed the M4 from behind the big pine tree. It wasn't likely Eric or Beckman would need it now, but it made sense why they'd left it there, because according to Michael, Beckman had approached the soldiers first and Jonathan figured he probably didn't want to be carrying a weapon when he did. Then when Eric and Lenny followed him out of the woods, there was no reason for them to bring the extra rifle. Eric would have expected to be disarmed, and he'd probably left it there as a backup option thinking he could grab it if something went wrong. But now that Michael had told them he'd seen the soldiers lead the three of them away and the tracks they'd followed to where the vehicles had been parked confirmed it, there was no reason to leave a good rifle behind whether Willis wanted to carry it or not.

They weren't leaving Michael behind either, after what just

happened to his relatives. A kid that age didn't need to see what was inside that house, and he didn't seem to want to anyway, which was a relief. Jonathan didn't know exactly what they would do with him, but until they figured it out, he planned to question the boy further and see what else they could glean from him. For now, Michael would just have to go with them until they found a neighbor or someone else they could leave him with. When they got back to where they'd left their rucksacks, Jonathan offered him something to eat while they talked a bit more.

"You must like squirrel hunting a lot if you get up before daylight every morning to go," he said.

"My Uncle Randy said if I wanted to eat every day, then I had to hunt every day, but I didn't mind, because hunting's my favorite thing to do anyway. I've been going with my daddy ever since I was old enough that he'd let me."

"You said your mom and dad both died. What happened to them, Michael?"

"They got shot by some robbers that tried to steal their truck and trailer when they were going to town to try and trade a couple of head of cattle for some other things we needed. Uncle Randy and my cousin, Brad, were in the truck with them. They got in a big shootout and killed all the robbers, but my mom and dad both got hit too. Uncle Randy and Brad tried to get help for them in town, but they couldn't find a doctor in time before they died."

"I'm sorry to hear that, Michael. Where were you when that happened? Were you over there at your house?"

"Yeah, I was there with my Aunt Molly and my Aunt Connie and Great Uncle Fred and some of my other cousins. They all came up here from Hammond after the hurricane, because things were so bad down there in Louisiana they couldn't stay. They said they needed to move in with us for a while because we had plenty of land, and we were far enough out from the cities that it was safer here. They also said we had plenty of cattle and chickens for food and that we oughta share because they didn't have anything. My momma didn't like having all those people crammed up together in our house, but Aunt Molly was my daddy's oldest sister, and Aunt Connie was his youngest, so he said he couldn't just tell them no. Aunt Molly's husband, Uncle Randy and their son Brad were kinda mean though, and ever since my mom and dad got killed, they've been making me do whatever they tell me to, mainly a lot of hard work! They said everybody's got to work hard now because times are hard and I had to learn to be hard too, if I was gonna survive. I didn't like living there with them all taking over my own house like that, but I didn't have nowhere else to go, so I did what they said."

"Wow, it sounds like you've had a pretty rough time!" Trey said.

"Yeah, but I guess I'm better off than Uncle Randy and Brad and the rest of them right now. At least I wasn't in my house when it got all shot up!"

"Where can we find the nearest neighbors?" Willis asked Michael. "Are there any other farms around here that you know of where people are still living there? We followed the tracks those soldiers made when they left here, and we came to a road way out there at the end of the lane leading in here. If you turn left on it, it goes north, and that's the way they went, according to the tire tracks we found there. Do you know if anyone else lives nearby up that way? What about the other way, if you turn right along that road and go south?"

"If you go right instead of left when you come out to the road, there's a house about two miles away down there. It belongs to Mr. Claude Busby and his wife, Annabel Busby. You can also get to that same road by cutting across this big pasture behind us and crossing the little road that goes behind it. But I know a better way to get to Mr. Busby's place too, following a little creek."

"That's the road we were on before we came over here," Willis said to Jonathan. "The one that we were on ever since we met Beckman."

"I think we ought to go check that Busby place out," Trey said.

"The tire tracks we saw were all north of the spot where the vehicles had been parked. I'd say there's a better chance of finding somebody at home if we go south. Two miles isn't all that far out of the way, and if we can find that guy that Michael knows there, maybe we can get more information about what's going on around here and figure out who attacked this place and why."

"Sounds like a plan to me," Willis said.

Jonathan had to agree, because he couldn't think of a better one, but before they left, a decision had to be made about what to do with Eric's and Lenny's gear. "I say we leave their rucksacks here. Anybody got a reason why we shouldn't?" Jonathan asked.

"Not me. We can't really carry anything else besides our own rucks anyway," Trey said. "And there's always a chance they'll figure out a way to escape and come back here. It's the first place they'd go, looking for a sign of us, and if that were to happen, they'd probably need their stuff, especially the food."

With that settled, they stashed the packs amongst some nearby bushes where they wouldn't be obvious to anyone that happened by. Eric and Lenny were sure to find them if they did a sweep of the area to figure out which way Jonathan and the rest of them went though. While they were doing this and Michael was out of earshot, finishing his meal with Trey, Willis pulled Jonathan aside to express his concerns about what the kid had told them.

"The men that hit that place couldn't have been legit soldiers," Willis said, "not unless they were part of some turncoat outfit like the one Sergeant Davis and his men were involved with. I'm thinking they were probably contractors instead. It'd be hard for a little kid like that to tell the difference, watching from a distance, even with that scope of his."

"That's true," Jonathan said. "But what about Eric and Lenny? And especially Beckman? They'd be able to tell the difference, don't you think? The kid said Beckman went out there first. Wouldn't that mean he thought they were the real deal?"

"Maybe, but anyone can be fooled, Jonathan, even Eric."

"I'm just thinking if they were contractors or something like that, they would have just shot Beckman, Eric and Lenny instead of taking them away. I mean, they'd just killed all those people in that house, what difference would three more have made?"

"So, you're thinking they may be legit?"

"I'm not saying that. All I'm saying is that there's a lot here that doesn't add up. That kid is messed up if you ask me, and not just from what happened here today. In fact, it didn't even seem to bother him as much as you'd expect it would. You heard him say there was a lot of friction between that one uncle and cousin of his and his parents. Then, his parents end up dead when they go off alone with them. You never know what the truth is in a situation like that. There's no telling what those relatives of his did, seeing how they had to leave their homes and everything they had behind and come up here just to survive. It sounds to me like they just kind of barged in on Michael's folks without an invitation."

Jonathan had to admit it sounded that way. Considering all the desperation and lawlessness he'd seen everywhere else, it was possible too that some of Michael's relatives had done something to make themselves a target for the authorities. But if they did, it had to be something super serious to merit that kind of response. Still, no matter what they may have done, Jonathan was certain that not all of the folks killed inside that house were involved, especially not the old man that had to be in his late eighties. And while he knew it was possible the women could have been accomplices, as well as the three teens, Jonathan kind of doubted it.

There was no denying that when they first heard the shooting, it sounded like a two-way exchange. If those soldiers or whoever they were had come here to specifically arrest certain individuals from among the group, then things had likely changed when those first shots were fired. But they'd apparently come in sufficient numbers and with sufficient firepower to overwhelm any possible defense the inhabitants of that house could muster, and the result was the indiscriminate massacre of everyone inside. And Jonathan had no doubt Michael would have been among the victims too had he not gone hunting that morning when he did.

But whatever the truth was, they weren't going to figure it out by hanging around talking about it. The important thing was to get that kid somewhere safe and then find someone who might know who those men were that took Eric, Lenny and Beckman, and where they could find them. Jonathan knew the latter task wouldn't be easy though. And he knew too, that even if they succeeded, they might be too late to save their friends.

When it was time to move out again, Jonathan let Michael lead the way with Willis right behind him as he took them on a shortcut through the woods east of the pasture and then across the road and down into a deep hollow on the other side. Down there in the bottom of the ravine, was the small creek the boy had told them about, its shallow water running fast and clear over a sand and gravel bottom. Michael assured them it was the best and safest way to get to Claude Busby's place without being seen.

"If we follow this creek upstream," he said, "it'll take us all the way back over to the backside of Mr. Busby's land. That way we don't have to get on the road at all to get there. Besides that, I think it's the way we need to go anyway because Mr. Busby's got a deer camp down in the back of his place on this same creek. It's hidden way back in the woods where nobody would be able to find it except by accident. He said his sons built it back before I was born. It ain't nothing but a little cypress board cabin, but I'll bet they're using it for sure now. It's a lot safer down in there because their regular house is right on the road. There's not even a road going to the cabin, just a 4-wheeler trail, and this creek that goes right behind it. That's why it's quicker to get there just following the creek."

"Lead on, my man," Jonathan said. "You know where you're going. We're just tourists over here on this side of the river."

"You never did say what you were doing here or why you came. Y'all don't look like tourists to me, and neither did your three friends that got taken off by those soldiers! Y'all look like you're on some kind of mission, the way you're carrying all those rifles and pistols and ammunition, and those Army packs with all those Army meals in them! When Trey pointed that rifle at me and told me to put mine down, I thought he was gonna shoot me for sure. I never would've believed y'all weren't with those soldiers if I hadn't seen them take away the guns from those other guys when they came out of the woods."

"We *are* on a mission," Trey said. "But it's only to find help for our friends back home. We're looking for the good guys so we can ask for their help, because we've got a lot of really bad guys back where we came from that are doing the same kinds of things to people that the bad guys are doing here."

"It seems to me like there's bad guys everywhere nowadays," Michael said. "Mr. Claude Busby ain't one of them though. He's a good guy, for sure, but I doubt he can help you, because he's pretty old now and so is his wife. I imagine he just wants to be left alone."

"I hope he'll talk to us."

"He will when I tell him you're with me. If you went down there by yourselves though, he'd probably shoot you on sight, thinking you'd shoot him if he didn't."

"How do you know he won't shoot us anyway?" Jonathan asked.

"Because he'll recognize me. I ain't been down there since my daddy died, but they knew each other pretty well and I used to go with him sometimes when he went to visit. As long as he sees I'm carrying my own rifle, he'll know y'all didn't take me prisoner or anything like that, so he won't shoot."

Jonathan figured the kid had a point. There'd been no reason not to give him back his .22 rifle when they set out from the farm, and Jonathan really felt sorry for him, thinking that rifle was about the only possession the boy was leaving there with other than the clothes he was wearing. He said his father had given him the Remington .22 for his ninth birthday, almost a year ago, back before things got really bad and long before all his Louisiana relatives moved in on them and changed their lives completely. All-in-all though, the kid was handling this remarkably well, and right now he seemed as at home in the woods as Willis as he led the three of them into the heavy timber through which the little creek ran. They were moving quietly and taking their time, so it was nearly an hour before Michael finally said he was pretty sure they were on Mr. Busby's land.

"I think his cabin is pretty close to here, he said. "Y'all need to stay close behind me when we go up there and see though."

They followed as Michael led them along a slightly worn path that he said was a four-wheeler trail that probably hadn't been used in a long time. "Mr. Busby's like everybody else around here," Michael said. "He probably don't have much gas, and what little bit he's got, he ain't wasting just riding back-and-forth for nothing."

Finally, they emerged at the edge of a small clearing and Jonathan saw that there indeed was a cabin there just as Michael had told them. It appeared to be inhabited too, because there was fresh-split firewood stacked on the small porch to one side of the front door, and clothing hanging out on a line to dry.

"MR. BUSBY! IT'S ME, MICHAEL SEARCY! I need to talk to you! There's been a lot of trouble over at our farm this morning. They came and shot everybody dead but me! But I've got friends here with me that are looking to find out who did it and where they went."

If there was anyone in the cabin, they didn't reply, and they weren't coming out. Jonathan, Willis and Trey were still standing back in the woods a few feet from the edge of the clearing. Naturally, they were leery of the prospect of approaching a stranger's property like this despite the fact that Michael said he knew the man pretty well. Considering how remote this place was and all that was apparently going on around here, Jonathan didn't think it was a good idea for any of them to go any closer to the cabin, much less knock on the door. The boy didn't argue with him when Jonathan conveyed that concern to him.

"I don't reckon he's here anyway," Michael said. "Maybe he and his wife went up there to their main house to check on things after all that shooting stopped. I know he probably heard it even from all the way down here."

"We'll follow you," Jonathan said. "You said the house is right up there by the road, right?"

"Yeah, it's pretty far from here though, because he's got a big piece of land and these four-wheeler trails don't go straight. But we can probably walk up there in about fifteen or twenty minutes."

As it turned out, they didn't get a chance to walk very far at all. They had just crossed the clearing on the other side of the cabin and started up the four-wheeler trail Michael had pointed out when they were stopped short by a sound that none of the four could misinterpret. It wasn't a woods sound though. It was the unmistakable mechanical sound of a shotgun slide slamming home, and it came from within a dense thicket of young hardwood saplings just a short distance off the trail to their left.

"ANY ONE OF YOU MAKES A MOVE WITH ONE OF THOSE RIFLES I'M GONNA BLOW YOUR HEAD OFF! I want to see those hands up in the air! All of you! And I want to see you keep them up there!"

TEN

AT THE SOUND OF THE MAN'S VOICE, JONATHAN DID EXACTLY as he was told, letting his M4 hang freely from its sling in front of him as he watched Michael drop his .22 to the ground and raise his own hands high. He was already wondering if this man with the shotgun was Claude Busby, when Michael called back to him.

"It's just me Mr. Busby! You know, *Michael Searcy!* I came down here because I was looking for you, and I figured you and Mrs. Busby may be staying in the cabin now."

"You oughta know better than to bring three gun toting strangers down here to my property, boy! What in the heck were you thinking? Who are these fellows? They sure ain't from around here, because I've never seen any of them in my life!"

Michael turned to face in the direction of the man's voice and Jonathan and his companions did the same as they saw him making his way out of the thicket. When he emerged into the open, Jonathan saw that he was wearing green and gray hunting coveralls with a pattern that blended perfectly with tree bark. He looked to be in his late 70's or early 80's, judging by his white beard and weathered face, but he moved easily and cradled the shotgun that was leveled in their direction like it was a natural extension of his body. The size of the gaping muzzle told Jonathan it was a 12-gauge, and he'd recently seen first-hand what buckshot and slugs from one of those could do to a man at such face-to-face distances.

"I apologize for disturbing you sir," Jonathan said. "I don't know if you heard all the gunfire this morning or not, but there was a terrible attack on the farm up there where Michael lives. He's the only one that survived, and he suggested that we come here and find you."

"Well, who the hell are you and what were you doing on that Searcy farm anyway?" The old man asked.

"His name is Jonathan!" Michael said. "And that's Trey and Willis he's got with him. They gave me food and said they'd take me with them, and I know they're good guys, because they gave me back my gun even after I was sneaking up there planning on shooting anybody I saw close to my house."

"I did hear a bunch of shooting up that way," Busby said. "Hell, I believe I even heard a machine gun a couple times!"

"That's exactly what you heard," Willis said. "We didn't see the men who did it, but Michael here did, and he said they were soldiers! He said there were a bunch of them, and the tracks we found out on the dirt road confirmed it. They killed all of Michael's relatives that were in that house, including the women and the teenagers. They also took three of our friends away at gunpoint, and we're trying to figure out where they may have taken them and why. We only went there in the first place because we heard the same gunfire you did and wanted to see what was going on. We didn't want to get involved in whatever's happening around here, but now three of our friends are missing and we need to find them and get out of here!"

"Well, it doesn't matter why you came. If you're here, you are involved in it. I don't know where you're from, but I reckon you're from somewhere down in Louisiana like all the other troublemakers that have taken over these parts." Claude Busby said.

"We came across the Mississippi River from the Atchafalaya River Basin area, where our friend is a deputy sheriff," Jonathan said. "But I'm not from over there, I'm from Florida. And so is my friend Eric Branson, who we're looking for. One of the other guys that was taken away with him is an Army National Guard Special Forces soldier from Camp Hurley, Mississippi. I don't know if you've ever heard of it or not; he said it's a base about 180 miles to the southeast of here."

"Camp Hurley? That's way the hell over there on the Alabama line not too far up from the coast! I can't imagine any National Guard soldiers coming here from way over there. I imagine they've got their hands full closer to home!"

"He came by helicopter." Jonathan said. "He and the rest of his squad were ambushed when their Black Hawk landed on a sand bar down on the Mississippi River just south of here. We came upon the scene when we first crossed the river from over near Simmesport. His entire squad was killed except for him, and the helicopter was destroyed. He doesn't know who did it, but he was trying to make his way to the nearest National Guard post when we found him. He said there's one about 50 miles away called Camp McCall. Since we came over here to Mississippi looking to meet with military officials too, we decided it would be a good idea to go there together with him. We figured we'd have to walk the whole way, and that's just what we were doing, heading east on that gravel road that runs by Michael's family farm. We were just at the place where their pasture borders the road this morning when all of a sudden, we heard that gunfire break out.

"Private Beckman wanted to see what it was all about, because it was obvious to all of us that it was a gunfight and not just a bunch of random shooting. He said that it was his unit's duty to interdict the vessel piracy and other raids going on along this stretch of the river, and if he could get any intel to take with him when he got to that National Guard base, he had to do it.

"Well, I know where that Camp McCall is that you're talking

about, but I can tell you there are no National Guard troops from over there operating in these parts. There's no legitimate military or law enforcement this side of Interstate 55! Most of the good folks that used to live here are either dead or gone someplace else, or they're hiding out like me and my wife, hoping to get by until things settle down again. Most of us don't expect that they ever will though."

"But Michael here saw the men that attacked his house, and he's pretty sure they were soldiers." Willis said.

"They were!" Michael said. "They had green Army uniforms and some of them had Army helmets too. And they had machine guns!"

"They may have looked like soldiers," Claude Busby said, "but they were more than likely one of Sheriff Farley's posses, which is the same thing as an organized criminal gang if you ask me! But just about everybody that's still alive in these parts is part of a gang or a militia or some such. You'd best stay clear of all of them, but some are a lot worse than others, especially that crooked sheriff's little private army!"

"So, you're saying he's put together his own private militia to enforce the law?" Jonathan asked.

"They're enforcers, all right," Claude said, "and while they may be enforcing *some* laws that were on the books, they're making up new ones as they go along too, and there's not a damned thing anybody can do about it! Ever since things started falling apart around here, Sheriff Farley started acting like he was the judge, jury and executioner. He's exerting his authority with the barrel of a gun, and he's got a lot of guns on his side, let me tell you. They don't have a problem using them either, and everybody knows they're doing away with anybody that crosses them, wherever and whenever they please.

"Me and my wife Annabel, we're still hanging on out here on our land, because both of us made up our mind when all this started that if we couldn't make it here, we'd just as soon die here.

We don't wanna leave and we're too damned old to go someplace else anyway! It ain't easy though, let me tell you. I just went up there to our real house this morning after I heard that shootout to see if anybody was gonna try and burn it down this time. They didn't come around there today, but the gangs of looters already have, too many times to count. That's why we're staying way down here on the back side of the place, laying low to stay alive. It's just not safe at all that close to a road anymore, even the little gravel roads out here in the middle of nowhere that hardly anybody knew about before."

After a few more minutes of conversation, when Claude Busby was satisfied that Jonathan and his two friends weren't a threat, he led them back across the clearing to his cabin. His wife Annabel had been hiding inside the whole time, and Jonathan was glad they didn't frighten her by knocking on the door or letting Michael do it. She was armed too, with a lever-action rifle similar to Willis' and considering the situation in these parts now, she likely would have started shooting right through the door if she felt threatened.

While Annabel was fussing over Michael and trying to offer him something to eat and drink after hearing about the traumatic experience he just went through, Mr. Busby called Jonathan and the others outside in the yard to have a chat about Michael's situation. "There's a lot I could tell you about those folks that were staying up there at Michael's place, but it's enough to say I never did trust them from the moment they first got here.

"They didn't do anything but cause trouble as far as I'm concerned, and they barged in on Tom and Linda with no consideration and just took over their home."

"How long have they been staying there?" Jonathan asked. "Michael told me that his mom and dad were killed by robbers when they went with his uncle Randy and his cousin, Brad, to go try and sell or trade a couple of cows."

"Yeah, that's the story they told everybody, but I don't think I believe it. I know they were having trouble because Tom told me he was trying to get rid of them but couldn't get them to leave. That Randy, especially, was a troublemaker, and Tom was afraid it was going to come to a fight or a killing before it was over, and sure enough, I guess it did."

"So, you think Michael's own Uncle Randy killed his father?" Jonathan asked.

"I think that's about the size of it. I sure wouldn't put it past him. That whole elaborate story they told when they got back never did make a lot of sense to me."

"Did the law get involved with this? That Sheriff Farley you were talking about before, did he investigate it or do anything?"

"Not really, but he just recently put out word that everybody living in the county had to turn in their guns unless they had special permission from him to keep them. Mostly that meant they had to join up with his organization to qualify, but not just anyone could join, especially out-of-staters. He was picking men he thought he could trust, and anybody that didn't make the cut had to submit to being disarmed. If they wanted protection, he said they could move into town with their families and join the workforce there."

"Workforce?"

"Yeah, working for him basically. But not for pay, just protection and a couple of crappy meals every day. One step up from jail if you ask me."

"Wow! That sounds almost as bad as what they're doing to folks over in parts of Louisiana—locking them up and making them work!"

"I'm not surprised to hear it. But anyway, that Randy and the rest of those relatives of Michael's sure weren't planning to turn in their guns or go to work. Of course, I wouldn't turn mine in either. But I didn't have any problems with Sheriff Farley, because like I said, me and Annabel are laying low down here in the woods. We're not running around causing trouble, robbing and looting, and besides, all I've got is my shotgun and my hunting rifles and a couple of revolvers. We don't have any of those fancy semiautomatic rifles or machine guns like you fellows are toting.

"I'll tell you something else about those relatives of Michael's; I believe some of them broke into my house too. It was just too close and too much of a temptation for them to pass it up. It got broken into several times after we left it to move down here in the woods. There ain't no way to keep them out, but there's hardly anything there worth taking anymore anyway. The looters had long since taken all our food that was stored up there, but I had a good stockpile down here too because I knew what was coming before it ever happened. I always like to be prepared for things like this and Annabel didn't mind helping. She doesn't mind roughing it to live down here either if it means we don't have to worry as much. We're doing pretty good compared to most folks, so I can thank the Lord for that!"

"So, what you're telling me is that what happened back there at that farm today is not exactly a clear-cut issue is it?" Jonathan asked. "I guess Michael is the only one that's truly innocent in all this. He's too young to know any better or really know what was going on, wouldn't you think?"

"Absolutely! Michael wouldn't have anything to do with it. Annabel was telling me before that we ought to try and get that boy out of there, but we were scared to go around that place with all those thugs living there. We had strong suspicions about what they were up to and what they were involved in, and I knew they were dangerous and best left alone. I can't really say I'm sad to hear they all got killed, but it *is* sad for Michael, because they were his relatives and they were all he had left, even if they weren't good folks. Now he ain't got nobody around here that I know of."

"We didn't know what to do with him," Jonathan said. We couldn't just leave him there, but I still don't know what we'll do. The boy's only ten years old!"

"You ain't gotta worry about that anymore. You saw how Annabel took him in there and tried to feed him as soon as she saw he was out here. He can stay with us, it's no problem at all. We'll look after him until we can figure out something better or he decides that he wants to do something different."

Hearing Claude Busby say that he and his wife would let Michael stay there with them was a huge relief for Jonathan. He wasn't going to just leave the boy somewhere on his own, but this took care of the problem in the best possible way. Michael already knew Claude and his wife, and their place was familiar to him as well, so it was the perfect solution. After that was settled, they spent more time talking out there in the yard and Claude told Jonathan, Willis and Trey even more about the situation in the area and about Sheriff Farley and the formidable force he'd assembled from his deputies.

"Farley always was a bit of a hard ass even before all this breakdown of the country got started." Claude said. "He was power-hungry and liked to throw his weight around and come down hard on people, not just the criminals but most anyone he didn't like."

"So, I guess he was originally from around here and knew a lot of folks in the county?" Willis asked.

"Yeah, typical good-old-boy stuff. He got himself elected and then the county couldn't get rid of him. Hell, he's been sheriff here for nearly fifteen years! He grew up here and he's about the same age as my son, who went to school with him. He was always a bully and a blowhard since grade school."

"How did somebody like that ever get elected in the first place?" Trey asked.

"Money, plain and simple! His folks owned land all over this county and the next two counties over. When they started drilling natural gas wells around here back in the '70s and '80s, they had some that hit on one of their properties, and that's all it took. They used that money to get into all kinds of things, and they needed protection for some of their enterprises, including protection from the law. There was no better way to get it than to get a family member into the sheriff's office, and law enforcement was a perfect job for Lee Farley when he got out of the Marines.

"So, he served in the military... I guess that's where he got his ideas to organize his force the way he did?"

"Yep. He always claimed he was in a lot of combat over in Iraq. I don't know how much of it is true, but he ran his sheriff's department like a military outfit, and even more so now. A few of his main deputies were military men too, and the ones that weren't had to go through the boot camp training facility he set up on his own property and at his own expense."

"I guess that explains the automatic weapons we heard," Trey said. "Those long bursts were the main reason Private Beckman wanted to go up there in the first place to investigate that farmhouse. It sounded like the military could be involved in whatever was going on up there. Where did they get that kind of equipment?"

"Oh, they had all that stuff long before all this started! If these small-town police departments and rural Sheriff's offices had enough money or could get the money somehow, they could buy anything they want. The federal government was selling them surplus hardware, and Sheriff Farley more than had the means to get his hands on whatever he wanted. I know he's got Humvees and some Army trucks. He may even have a tank for all I know! Aside from buying that stuff though, his men could have also raided a National Guard Armory. A couple of the little towns east of here have armories like that with equipment on hand. So, there's no telling what they've got, to tell you the truth."

"Beckman said he thought whoever attacked them used a grenade launcher to take out that Black Hawk on the ground," Jonathan said. "Whoever did it knew what they were doing, and he thought they purposefully lured them into landing there where they had an ambush waiting."

"I wouldn't put it past Farley to think of something like that. Like I said, he hates the federal government! He's been that way ever since he got out of the Marines. He got into all kinds of conspiracy theories and stuff like that. He thought they were out to get him, and nothing would change his mind. He damned sure didn't want them sending troops into his jurisdiction, and there's no telling what he'd do to stop them. From what I hear, he's using some of the terrorist tactics he learned from the enemy when he was fighting overseas."

"It sounds like we're going to have a tough time getting our friends back if they're in the custody of a bunch like that," Willis said. "You got any ideas, Mr. Busby? Do you know if that National Guard post called Camp McCall would be worth going to? If it's manned by real soldiers, then that Sheriff Farley wouldn't have gone there, would he?"

"He wouldn't try to pull off anything that far to the east of here, I don't believe, unless he's managed to get some of the other county sheriffs on board with his ideas. I kind of doubt that though. Things are so chaotic there's not much cooperation of any kind going on. To answer your question though, I don't think I'd count on any help from Camp McCall. That place may or may not even be manned at this point. And even if it was, you wouldn't have time to get there and back with help, even if they were willing to send it, which they wouldn't be, because you'd have no way in hell of proving who you are or why you're even here. I imagine you're on your own, and it's going to be up to you fellows to figure out how to get your friends out of the pickle they've gotten themselves into."

"What do you think they'll do with them?" Jonathan asked. "I know they probably wanted to question them. But do you think they'll be accused of being terrorists or something else that sheriff just makes up? What will they do to them if they are? Will they just shoot them?"

"I wish I could tell you, son. All I know is that Sheriff Farley is one mean son of a bitch and so are all of his main henchmen he surrounds himself with. But I don't have to tell you that, because you saw it yourself firsthand this morning! Whatever those uncles and cousins of Michael's may have done, it didn't warrant the kind of raid you described. Besides that, like you said, there were women in there too, as well as those teenagers and that old man. That man was Michael's great uncle. Tom told me about him. I never met him, but Tom said he was 86 years old."

"It looks to me like they went there determined to get whoever they were after," Willis said. "They probably met some resistance when some of those guys shot back, and after that they just went all out."

"Yeah, they gave them no quarter at all," Trey said. They just laid down the fire until everybody inside there was dead. It looked like they made a sweep afterwards and took all the weapons, so they know exactly what they did. They know they killed women and an old man and some teenagers, but I guess they didn't care."

What Claude told them created a huge dilemma for Jonathan and the rest of the team. He thought the man was correct when he said it didn't make sense to go all the way to that National Guard post to try and get help. It was doubtful anyone there would listen to them, and the whole point of coming over here was for Eric to use his military background to try and get the attention of some officer. Jonathan, Willis and Trey wouldn't have a chance of even getting through the gate, looking like they did. It was dangerous to be seen at all carrying the weapons and gear they had on them, but it was too dangerous not to have them as well.

"If we're going to have to figure out how to do something ourselves to get Eric and Lenny and Beckman out of there, where will we even start?" Trey asked.

Jonathan turned to Claude to ask him if he had any ideas. As it turned out, the old man did have a suggestion that gave him a glimmer of hope. But if they were going to act on it and do anything to intervene before the worst happened, they had to get moving immediately!

ELEVEN

Eric, Lenny and Beckman were escorted at gunpoint from the edge of the woods to the driveway in front of the house, passing close to the dead guy that had fallen next to one of the pickup trucks parked out there. It appeared to Eric that the rest of the assault team had completed their task of gathering what they were taking from the scene and were ready to move out. From where he and his companions stood now, Eric could see another dead man slumped against the wall by the front entrance, and a quick glance through the broken-down door confirmed there were more bodies inside the structure as well. He couldn't see them well enough to make out any details of the casualties, but the two dead outside appeared to be civilian locals. There was nothing special about the house or the vehicles parked there to indicate the occupants were members of some kind of organized insurgency, such as Beckman had spoken of, so the size of this assault operation seemed far out of proportion to the target. Eric hoped he would learn more of what really happened here eventually, but for now he had far more pressing concerns, since he'd foolishly allowed himself to be talked into approaching these men. Now, he and Lenny found themselves detained against their will, as did Beckman, who'd thought he'd be welcomed by these troops as one of their own.

But were these men even National Guard troops at all, as the PFC had so confidently asserted? Eric was beginning to have his doubts now that he was close in amongst them and could observe their actions and overhear some of their conversations. Perhaps some of them were in the reserves or had served in the past, but at the moment they were acting more like a rogue militia than professional soldiers. Particularly disgusting was the joking he overheard about the effects of the M249 on the occupants of the house, and how dumb they'd been to think they could try and fight back.

And now the unit commander, whose rank Eric was still unsure of, seemed completely uninterested in the three of them after his initial brief questioning. He kept his distance and barely glanced their way as the men prepared to move out, though Eric was certain more questions would come later. He figured it would happen shortly after they reached whatever place they were being taken to, but whether from this man or someone higher up the chain that he answered to remained to be seen. As he pondered the potential ramifications of that questioning, Eric briefly considered his options.

He was glad Jonathan and the rest of his little team we're still free, but it was too bad they hadn't been observing from somewhere near enough to see what had happened. If he could rely on the three of them to provide a diversion of some kind, then extricating themselves from this situation might be more feasible for him and Lenny and Beckman. As it was, Eric's only alternative to going along with these men was one that entailed great risk. He would have to physically disarm one of the guards standing nearest him and then use that man's weapon to deter any who stood in his way. Eric was sure he could do it if he only had himself to worry about, but he couldn't be sure if he could count on Lenny and especially

Beckman to realize what was happening and to react quickly enough to save themselves. It was even possible Beckman would work against him and Lenny if he was still convinced he was among friendly forces and that this was all just a misunderstanding. Eric didn't know if Beckman had it in him to grab one of those rifles himself and turn it against men he thought were fellow Guardsmen. And even if he did and Lenny and Beckman both knew exactly what Eric was thinking and were on board with it, the odds of the three of them escaping unscathed from fifteen armed captors were stacked high against them. Considering all that and realizing there was no way to even communicate such a plan to either of his companions, Eric dismissed the whole thing as impractical. He resigned himself to just go along for now and see where it took them. He knew he might regret it, but on the other hand, there could be a better opportunity to escape later if it came to that. Besides, there was still some possibility that these men *were* acting within the bounds of their rules of engagement when they carried out their operation here. And it was possible he might learn later that they'd had a good reason to do things the way that they did.

They were marched east along the dirt and gravel entrance lane for a good half a mile before they came to an intersection with a larger gravel road and Eric saw vehicles parked near the edge of the woods on the other side. But he saw right away that all but two of the vehicles there weren't military units at all but were instead a mix of civilian and law enforcement SUVs, pickup trucks and squad cars. Some of them had remnants of sheriff's department star emblems still visible on the doors, but he saw no county names or other identifying information to go with them. The closest thing in the small fleet to a National Guard or Army vehicle was a single Desert Tan Humvee that looked like surplus from the Gulf War and probably hadn't seen military service in decades. Eric's suspicion that something was off about all this ramped up another notch. *Were these men part of a legitimate law enforcement agency that had become militarized, or were they some mix of National Guard troops and local law enforcement and civilian militia?* Eric had no idea, but the one thing he felt certain of was that this was no normal military operation working solely under a centralized command. And that confirmed his earlier suspicions regarding the ruthless nature of the attack on the occupants of that farmhouse.

He and Lenny were led to one of the police SUVs that had a prisoner barrier between the driver's compartment and the passenger area, while Beckman was forced into the back of one of the four-door squad cars. When they pulled out onto the road, Eric noted that the convoy of vehicles headed north. This bigger unpaved road wound through heavily wooded hills for a few miles until they came to an intersection with another gravel road onto which they turned east. That road eventually changed to pavement and led into a semi-open countryside that was a mix of empty pastures and unplanted, overgrown fields. Eric saw nothing along the way to indicate that any of the farms they passed were still inhabited, much less operational.

They arrived at what was apparently their destination some twenty minutes later, but it was neither a military post nor the small town or county law enforcement facility he'd expected. Instead, it looked to Eric like the entrance to some wealthy person's private property, but it was way out in the middle of nowhere, surrounded by more of the same rural countryside through which they'd just passed. The entrance was by way of a heavy wrought-iron gate guarded by two armed men who wore the same olive-drab BDUs as those on the assault team.

Once the vehicles cleared the gate, a paved access road wound through hundreds of acres of woods and pastures bordered by well-constructed and perfectly maintained barbed wire fencing. Eric spotted scattered clusters of cattle here and there along the way, and then finally, they came to a central area or complex where there were multiple barns and horse corrals and even a small arena with bleachers that looked like it was built to host rodeo events. Atop the landscaped hill on the far side and overlooking it all, was an extravagant two-story ranch house that was more mansion than single-family dwelling. In the corral nearest the arena, Eric saw several expensive-looking horses, and a young woman leading a saddled solid black one by the reins was closing the gate behind her as she brought it in from a workout.

Eric thought it odd that the men in this outfit would bring them here, until the convoy continued on around the base of the hill beyond the massive house and he spotted the dirt berms of a rifle range, and beyond it, a fenced-in compound. Two new-looking metal buildings within the perimeter suggested he may have arrived at the headquarters and barracks that housed this outfit. Whatever this place was, it was an elaborate setup, and a far cry from a typical military outpost or rural county sheriff's department headquarters. The possibility that he was again dealing with private contractors came to mind, but something told Eric that wasn't the case.

When the vehicles rolled up to a stop outside the wire fencing, Eric and Lenny were ordered out and then they were joined by Beckman as the three of them were escorted through the gate and into the compound. Once inside, they were led into the larger building near the rear perimeter and taken through an office area and down a hallway where there were several solid metal doors. When three of the doors were unlocked from the outside, Eric was shoved into the first one alone and the door was locked behind him, and he was sure that Beckman and Lenny were likewise confined in the other two. But the guards hadn't bothered to handcuff or restrain them in any way. They'd simply urged them along at gunpoint as if they were confident they wouldn't attempt to resist.

The room he was in didn't look like a holding cell, but instead appeared to be purpose-built for interrogating prisoners, as the only furnishing inside was a heavy table with benches on either side. Eric saw that as a relatively good sign, because it still left the possibility that the extent of their detainment here would be to answer a few questions from the unit commander. The assault leader obviously didn't think they were affiliated with the targets of their raid on that house, or they would have probably been shot then and there. But it was clear he didn't accept Beckman's explanation without question and was bumping the problem up to whoever he answered to. With any luck at all, Eric thought that person might be more open to listening. He was anxious to find out who it could be though, as this entire setup was quite bizarre and unorthodox.

Eric sat on one of the benches and waited for what seemed like a couple of hours before the door finally opened again. When it did, two of the men he recognized from the assault team entered the room with their rifles in hand and positioned themselves in the two corners adjacent the doorway, where they could cover the entire room. The next man that entered was the assault team leader that had questioned Eric before, and behind him was another man probably in his early fifties who projected the image of a fit and combat-ready career soldier but wasn't wearing the olive drab BDUs the others wore. He was instead dressed in a khaki sheriff's department uniform and wore a brown cowboy hat. Eric couldn't miss the large brass star pinned to his uniform shirt that seemed to confirm that he was indeed a sheriff. *So, he'd been right to conclude this operation was some sort of local law enforcement organization using military tactics....* Eric pushed the bench back to stand, but the other officer he'd met before ordered him to remain seated where he was.

"This is the 'Navy SEAL' we told you about, Sheriff Farley. He claims he just crossed the river from Louisiana and says he's never seen Private Beckman before he and his friend stumbled across him in the woods yesterday."

"Is that right?" The man in the cowboy hat pulled out the bench on the opposite side of the table from Eric and sat down. The other man joined him as they turned their full attention to

Eric. "Is that Navy SEAL stuff true? Are the SEALs conducting operations here now too?"

"I was in the Navy a long time ago," Eric said. "I'm not associated with any military organization at present. I'm officially retired."

"Retired? You look a little young to be retired to me, especially considering all that's going on now. Lieutenant Pickett here doesn't believe you and that other fellow with him just happened to run into Beckman out there in the woods. He showed me the weapons you two were carrying. They look like government-issue to me. You were both on that Black Hawk that Beckman came here on, weren't you?"

"Those rifles are battlefield pickups," Eric said. "My brother is a deputy sheriff in St. Martin Parish, and we've been helping him fight off the private contractors that are being sent into his jurisdiction to relocate civilians from their homes and send them to labor camps. Like I told your lieutenant here, the young man that's with me is my nephew. He is in no way affiliated with Beckman or any military outfit. We came here because we heard that the Army was still in control of things on this side of the river. I was looking to make contact with the first unit I could find and tell them about our predicament over in Louisiana, and request help if they were able to provide it. We didn't expect to find a downed Black Hawk as soon as we crossed the river, but I take it you knew about the incident as well?"

"I know about *every* incident that happens in my county," the sheriff replied.

"Then who took out that helicopter and killed Beckman's squad? It seems to me like it was someone who knew what they were doing, and that it was a planned ambush. Beckman said they were dealing with vessel piracy on the river, but this was something different."

"The details of that are none of your concern, and besides, I'm the one asking the questions here. I want to know what your mission was. And don't tell me it's about patrolling that river. Whoever sent you didn't send a squad of Special Forces operators to do a job a couple of door gunners on that Black Hawk could have done without getting their boots muddy! That helicopter crew put you fellows down on that sandbar for a reason, and I want to know what it was!"

Eric doubted it would do any good, but he reiterated again that he and Lenny had nothing to do with Beckman and his squad that had arrived aboard the Black Hawk.

"PFC Beckman told me they were headed back to base late that afternoon, but the reason they circled back was because they saw smoke from a big fire not far east of the river. He said they spotted a boat down there pulled up to that sandbar and that two men aboard it opened fire on them. After they took them out with the machine gun, they landed to secure the boat and try and catch the rest of the crew when they came back from whatever they'd attacked when they set that fire. But apparently, the whole thing was a set-up, because as soon as they were on the ground and had deassed the helo, they were hit hard by some unseen forces waiting there in the woods. Beckman was the only survivor because he was already in the river, trying to retrieve the boat."

"We'll see how your story compares to Beckman's," Sheriff Farley said, "not to mention whatever that other fellow you're calling your nephew has to say. My bet is that I'm going to hear a different story or two. And no matter what the reason, the fact that you and your *nephew* were caught with unauthorized firearms means you've committed a capital offense!"

"Is anyone dumb enough to go around unarmed these days, Sheriff?"

"Unless they're working for me or have my special permission, the residents here know better than to be caught out in public with a weapon! The rules have changed, but those rifles you two were carrying were illegal even before all this started. Getting caught with one of those would have gotten you 15 years in federal prison, and you know it!"

Eric didn't argue the point. It was clear that this Sheriff Farley was doing things his way around here and he figured the death threats were mostly a bluff anyway, in an attempt to get information. From the way it sounded, Farley had a grudge against the National Guard, and probably all the other branches of the military too. And considering that he knew so much about that Black Hawk on the sandbar, Eric wondered if he and his men were even behind the attack on it. After seeing what he'd seen today, both at the farmhouse and here on this isolated property that seemed to be the center of Farley's operation, Eric was certain that his men had the capability to pull off that ambush. Realizing that answered a lot of questions that had been nagging at him ever since that night he'd first spotted the wreckage and the bodies of those soldiers. He'd known when he saw it that it took more than just some random gang of outlaws to take on a whole squad of soldiers like that and disable the helicopter at the moment when it was most vulnerable. If Farley was behind it, then it made sense that he would think Eric and Lenny were associated with Beckman and his squad somehow. Most anyone would make that conclusion, seeing how they were traveling together and considering the weapons and gear Eric and Lenny both carried.

Eric had no idea how Beckman would respond to the sheriff's questioning, but since Eric had told mostly the truth, there wasn't a lot of damage the PFC could do, other than mentioning that Eric and Lenny hadn't been alone. He didn't like that his team had been separated, but it was far better that Jonathan, Willis and Trey had been left there not knowing what happened than the alternative. At least they were free to go back across the river, though Eric doubted they would. He knew Jonathan would do everything in his power to try and find out what happened, and Willis and Trey would be willing helpers, but they had no idea of the situation here, and the risks of running into some of the sheriff's men were great even if those men weren't actively looking for them. If Beckman told the sheriff about them, the risks would be much greater. If the three of them were captured and brought here too and Sheriff Farley carried out his threats, then no one at Sierra Zulu would ever know what happened. Keith and some of the others would come looking eventually, and then they too would encounter this power-hungry and narcissistic sheriff that had somehow managed to put himself into a position of absolute authority.

TWELVE

"ALL OF THIS TROUBLE, JUST BECAUSE OF PRIVATE BECKMAN!" Willis said. "I tried to tell Eric that the gunfight we heard wasn't any of our business. Now look where it got him, and us too!"

"Eric probably would have wanted to check it out even if not for Beckman," Jonathan said. "You know how he is."

"Well, it's hard to believe that a sheriff's department acting like a military unit could fool Eric like that." Trey said.

"Not really. You heard what Claude said, about how most of those men, including the Sheriff were in the military before. And I don't know about you, but I remember seeing plenty of militarized police forces back in the day, even before all the shit hit the fan! It wouldn't be very hard for guys like that to organize things and operate with the same tactics they learned in their training. Especially the ones that were already in real combat before, like he said the sheriff claimed to have been. And you heard how easy it is for them to get the equipment, but we already knew that."

"Maybe," Willis said. "But I've kind of got my doubts about this Eddie fellow that Claude told us about. It's hard to know who to trust these days, but I reckon if it's true what Claude said about the sheriff and his men killing the guy's brother, then he's probably got a grudge against him."

"If he's willing to help us, it'll be great," Jonathan said. "Trying to do this on our own without a local from the area who knows where to go and what to look out for would be a whole lot harder. If the guy is even halfway competent, like Claude says he is, and we can talk him into it, I think that's what we ought to try to do."

Jonathan, Willis and Trey were discussing the last part of the conversation they'd had with Claude Busby before he went inside the house to have a talk with his wife about what he was going to help them do. He had told Jonathan and the others about a man who lived not that far away from his place that had been personally affected by the atrocities of Sheriff Farley and his men. Eddie Poole was his name, and Claude said that the sheriff had personally ordered the execution of his brother, Kirby. Eddie was biding his time, dreaming about an opportunity to get his revenge, and he had talked to Claude about it more than once. But there was little one man could do against a force such as the one Sheriff Farley had assembled. Claude thought that if he introduced Eddie to Jonathan, Willis and Trey and told him what had happened over there at the Searcy place, then Eddie might be interested in helping them look for their friends if it meant he might get a chance to exact some retribution. Claude also said that if they were going to do anything for Eric and their other friends, they had better do it quickly, because there was no way they would last long in the custody of Sheriff Farley. Once he got the information he wanted from them, that would be it.

"He's conducting routine executions in his jurisdiction. I'm not talking about legally sanctioned executions as a result of a fair trial. I'm talking about expedient, old-style military ones carried out with a firing squad right on the spot!"

Jonathan didn't doubt that what Claude told him in regard to that was true. Sergeant Patterson's unit had been doing the same thing over in Louisiana, and after seeing the results of the raid on

Michael's house, he wouldn't put anything past whoever was in charge of that. It was highly likely that Eric, Lenny and Beckman were running out of time whether they talked or not, and Jonathan knew for sure that Eric wouldn't give up more, even if he had the intel they wanted. Jonathan knew if they were going to do anything to help them, they were going to have to do it now. But it would surely involve high risk and they would have to strike with the same sort of indifference that Sheriff Farley had shown to his own adversaries.

There was simply no more delicate way to handle it. They couldn't go and appeal to the man or any of his men because none of them would care and if they got caught, they would be in the same dire straits as Eric and the others. Claude told Jonathan that he would take him over to Eddie's place to introduce them so they could talk and see if they wanted to help each other. Willis and Trey would stay behind at Claude's cabin to look out for his wife, Annabel, and Michael while they were gone. Otherwise, Claude wouldn't go because there was no way he was going to leave his wife alone there after what happened such a short distance away that very morning.

Willis and Trey agreed to stay, and Jonathan left with Claude to walk to where he had hidden his four-wheeler ATV about halfway between the house and the cabin. They would ride it to Eddie Poole's place, which was a double-wide trailer hidden well off the road about four miles to the south of Claude's property. Claude thought it was safe to ride there because he figured it was unlikely that the sheriff's men would be back down here again this soon after the attack. The tracks that Jonathan and the others had found indicated that they hadn't gone south of the lane leading to the Searcy place, so it was doubtful they'd double back now.

"There's hardly anybody using the roads anymore," Claude said. "It's not just because of the danger of being robbed or running afoul of Sheriff Farley and his men, it's also because hardly anybody has any gas. I've managed to keep just enough on hand for emergencies, but the only thing I ever drive anymore is this Suzuki quad. It's easy on gas and besides, I'm never going farther than a few miles from home anyway these days."

"Is this Eddie guy gonna freak out when he hears us coming and start shooting?" Jonathan asked.

"Nah, he'll know it's me. He knows the sound of the engine and he's pretty level-headed most of the time."

Jonathan didn't like approaching anyone's house in times like these, but he felt he could trust Claude on the matter, as the man seemed to be a straight shooter. Eddie's place was at the end of another long turn-off from the main gravel road, so it wasn't visible until they had rounded a couple of bends and crossed a hollow to the next ridge. When they pulled up into the small, overgrown yard, Claude beeped the horn a couple of times and a few seconds later, Jonathan saw a window shade at the front of the trailer move to one side.

"Looks like Eddie's home!" Claud said as he waved. "Just leave your rifle here when we talk to him."

"That's a hell of a thing!" Eddie Poole said after Claude and Jonathan finished describing the events of that morning at the Searcy place. "That son of a bitch isn't going to stop until he's gotten rid of everybody in the county he doesn't like! It's just a matter of time before he sends some guys like that down here to get me too, just because he knows that *I know* they killed my brother!"

"Well, he probably figures there's nothing you can do about it," Claude said, "and he'd be right too. But if you're looking for an opportunity to prove him wrong, this may be your chance. These fellows here have told me a hell of a story about the things they've been doing over in Louisiana. And that friend of theirs, the guy they followed over here, was a Navy SEAL! They been fighting assholes like Sheriff Farley all the way from Florida to Colorado and back! I think if you want to pull off something against that sheriff, Jonathan and his boys back at my cabin can help you do it, but they need a little help from you too. That's why I brought him here to have a chat with you."

They were standing out there in the yard now by the Suzuki four-wheeler and Eddie was looking over the M4 rifle that Jonathan had handed him. It was the one Willis had carried at Eric's insistence, and it was available and ready to use if Eddie wanted it."

"So, this is the real deal? The actual military version with the select fire and everything?"

"It sure is," Jonathan said. "That's a Colt M4. It's got the semi-automatic mode and the 3-round burst mode right there on the selector switch. We've got plenty of magazines for it too, but we have to use our ammo sparingly, of course, because all we have is what we could carry on us and in our backpacks. But it's enough to pull off a rescue operation at least, and maybe we can pick up more if we succeed. My only goal is to get Eric and Lenny out at all cost! But if we can get that Private Beckman out of there too, we certainly will, because I do believe he had good intentions to try and help us reach a real military base like we need to do. I know he pretty much talked Eric into getting into all this trouble, but that's done now and it's just the way things worked out."

"After what you've told me, I can totally understand why your friend would've been fooled by Sheriff Farley's men. It wouldn't be easy to tell them apart from a military unit, and that's the image they're trying to project. They want people to be afraid of them and they're showing as much force as they possibly can for the purpose of intimidation. Gone are the days of pulling people over with blue lights and that sort of thing. They've effectively declared martial law in this entire county and beyond, and they're enforcing it like they're in a war zone, which I suppose we really are. The thing about it though is that their enemies are the good folks, and they've made themselves the enemy of everything good that ever was around here. Somebody's got to stand up to them sometime, or it'll only get worse. There wasn't a whole lot I could do by myself, but four of us working together may have a chance if we catch them off guard where they think they're safe. But if we're gonna do it, we're gonna have to do it now. It may already be too late to help your friends, but it will be for sure if we wait."

"How far away is this old county landfill you're talking about?" Jonathan asked.

Eddie had explained to Jonathan that the sheriff was using one of his family properties as his headquarters and training facility for his new recruits. He said it was the first place they would have taken any prisoners they thought worthy of interrogation. It was far from the nearest town, out in the countryside, and it was also where Sheriff Farley lived and pursued his interests in horseback riding and competition roping. He said the sheriff had built barracks and a rifle range on the property, and that they had lock-up facilities for enemies they were holding for questioning. The main jail in town was relegated to punishing the people he still considered citizens when they sometimes got out of line. These were the folks that had already submitted to his orders to turn in their firearms and go to work. But if anyone questioned the tasks required of them or committed any minor offenses, they were locked in the jail for varying amounts of time.

But since Beckman was a soldier in the service of the government and Eric and Lenny were carrying the same sort of automatic weapons as the one Jonathan was offering to let Eddie use, they would be considered enemy combatants. Any useful intel that could be extracted from them would be gotten quickly through interrogation, and then they would be disposed of like all the others that came before them. There would be no trial and no appeal. They would be taken to an isolated, abandoned landfill a few miles away and placed against a clay embankment to be shot. Eddie knew, because it was what had happened to his brother, Kirby. Eddie had gone there later, when he found out, to retrieve the body for burial. He told Jonathan that no one was ever around there other than when the sheriff and his firing squad brought out the condemned, and rumor was they always timed it so that the executions took place at sunrise.

"We can get there before daylight tomorrow morning, even being as careful as we'll have to be to do it. The biggest risk is going to be driving the first part of the way in my truck. We'll have to do that though, to cover enough distance, but when we get closer, we can ditch it in a place I know and go the rest of the way crosscountry on foot. I know those woods and pastures out that way like the back of my hand. Sheriff Farley doesn't know it, but I worked for the county maintenance crew for a while many years ago, when he was off in the Marines. I know a good way that we can slip in from the backside where we can get an overview of that dump and get set up in rifle range. After that, it'll just be a waiting game."

"And you're sure that's our best option? You don't think we can get them out by slipping up on that property where they're holding them now the same way?"

"Not a chance in hell! There'll be too many people around, and especially too many of his armed thugs. Security will be tight as long as they have them there, but I doubt they'll bring more than a few extra guys besides the firing squad when they take them out there to the landfill. Most of the time, day and night, he's got his guys out running the roads or engaging in operations like the one they pulled off this morning at the Searcy place. However many they bring, they'll still outnumber the four of us, but if we do it right, we can pull this off and take them by surprise.

"I take it you and your guys don't have any problem with the 'shoot them all first approach,' right?" Eddie asked. "I mean we're going to have to shoot men that are actual law-enforcement officers in cold blood if we're gonna win this thing. But I'll tell you one damn thing; they'd sure do the same to us if they had an opportunity or had the slightest inkling we were coming!"

"Of course I don't have a problem with it!" Jonathan said. "We've dealt with crooked law enforcement and traitorous military units so many times I've lost count! I don't have any problem pointing a gun at anybody these days, and in fact, I consider almost everybody I meet to be the enemy until they prove otherwise. I learned that from Eric, and he was right!"

Jonathan could tell that Eddie was pleased with what he was hearing. The man was thirsting for revenge after what Sheriff Farley did to his brother and their arrival here today came as an unexpected gift that he was more than ready to receive.

"Well, I've got nothing keeping me here, so I'll come back with you and Claude and meet the other two fellows on your team. We'll talk it over and make a plan and we'll get moving as soon as it gets dark. Like I said, we'll go as far as we can in my truck and after that we'll have to go on foot, and we'll be walking the rest of the night. But if we don't let up, and if we don't run into trouble that causes us to have to detour, we should be able to get there just before daylight. We'll have just enough time to get set up in case they come first thing tomorrow, and if they don't, we'll wait until the next day, or the next."

Eddie went inside to change into his camouflage hunting clothing and boots and to grab his own personal rifle that he said he was going to bring in addition to the M4 Jonathan had for him. When he came back out, Jonathan saw that it was a bolt-action hunting rifle with a large, expensive-looking scope attached.

"It's a .243. I can hit a gnat's ass at 600 yards with this thing if he's sitting still! I may need the precision for my first shot when we kick this party off, and it's always a good idea to have a rifle that can do it! If I can get that damned Sheriff Farley in my crosshairs, he's gonna be the first man to die out there! Y'all can have as many of the rest as you want."

Eddie followed Claude's four-wheeler in his truck, with Jonathan riding shotgun, and parked it as far down in the woods as he could drive it when they got back to Claude's place. After they walked back to the cabin, Eddie was introduced to Willis and Trey and the four of them sat down on the front porch of the cabin to make a plan.

"What does the lay of the land look like around there?" Willis asked. "Is there good cover and concealment close enough in to do us any good?"

"It's like everywhere else around here; there's plenty of woods all around, but since it was a landfill, there's a good bit of cleared area and overgrown cutover too. The good thing about it though is that there's manmade hills all around that they pushed up years ago, so there's lots of good elevated places to set up an ambush with a good view overlooking it all. But I can't promise you it'll be exactly like it was last time I was there. There's always a chance there'll be some surprises, but from what Jonathan says about some of the stuff you guys have seen before, you know that already.

"I think with the four of us and the weapons we have and a flexible plan, we've got a good chance of pulling this off. But I want you guys to know going in that I'm good with whatever happens. I just want to get payback for what they did to my brother and get rid of that Sheriff Farley. If I have to die doing it, I'm about to the point where I don't give a damn! It's just like I've heard Claude say: If things are gonna continue to be this bad around here, what's the point of living anyway?"

"I understand where you're coming from," Jonathan said. "We don't mind taking risks either. We always know when we're going into it that we may not come out. Eric has driven that point home time and time again. But we've got a lot of other people back in Louisiana that are depending on us, so we're going to do everything we can to make it back. The main thing is getting Eric and Lenny out but that's not where our mission ends. Eric's not going to let one sheriff gone bad stop him from doing what we came over here to Mississippi to do. If we can get Beckman out of there at the same time, that'll be all the better, because I do think Beckman can help us as long as we don't let him sidetrack us again. If we do get him out, I'd imagine we're going to be making a beeline straight for that base and not investigating anymore firefights out in the middle of nowhere!"

The hardest part of the plan for Jonathan was that they had to wait until dark to get started. He was restless and worried, of course, wondering what was happening to Eric and Lenny and hoping they were making the right decision in trusting Eddie Poole. There wasn't a good alternative that he could think of though, so he and Willis and Trey did their best to get some sleep and rest up for the long night they knew they had ahead of them. They said goodbye to Michael and to Claude Busby and his wife shortly after sundown, before walking back to where Eddie had parked his 1989 GMC pickup in the woods behind Claude's house.

"Well, all I can do is wish you fellows luck," Claude said. "I know you're going to need it, but you're doing a good thing. I'd like nothing better than to see this county rid of Sheriff Lee Farley for good!"

"If it's up to me," Eddie said, "you won't be hearing much of anything about him again after this week. But yeah, we're going to need all the luck we can get, especially just getting there without being seen so that we get our chance!"

Jonathan, Willis and Trey, were all nervous about the idea of traveling the roads at all, but Eddie assured them he was going to stick to the smallest backroads and then pull off and hide the truck in a spot he knew of miles before they got to the area of the landfill. It was the only way they could get there before daylight, so even though he acknowledged it was risky, Eddie said it was what they had to do.

When they pulled out of Claude Busby's property and began heading north, Jonathan was riding shotgun in the cab with Eddie while Willis and Trey were back in the open bed with their rifles in hand, keeping a sharp lookout for any signs of other road users either in vehicles or afoot.

Eddie was driving slowly, keeping it to around fifteen miles an hour since he was running dark with the lights turned off on his old GMC truck. There was enough moonlight reflecting off the lighter-colored gravel to see the deserted road as long as he maintained those slower speeds, and to avoid having the brake lights give them away at an inopportune time, he'd flipped off the interrupter switch he'd installed under the dash as well.

"We used to run like this all the time back when I was a teenager growing up around here," Eddie said. "It's how we avoided the law when we were making our beer runs and partying on Friday and Saturday nights!"

It sounded like a good strategy to Jonathan, and he thought it must have been an interesting place to grow up, out in the middle of all these woods in south Mississippi. It was different than Florida for sure, but Jonathan could see how he would have fit in had he been raised here instead of on the bays and salt marshes of his home state.

They continued north on the same road for several miles until they were approaching an intersection with another one, also gravel, onto which Eddie said they would turn right. He said that one would take them east to a small county blacktop road where he said they'd find the drop-off point he had in mind to hide the truck. From there, they'd have to go the rest of the way on foot. But before they were within a hundred feet of the turn, the shimmer of headlights through the tall trees around the next bend in that other road brought Eddie to a sudden stop in the middle of the one they were on. As they watched the lights grow brighter, it became apparent that the approaching vehicle was slowing down to make a turn onto that very road.

"What the hell are we going to do now?" Jonathan asked. He knew there was nowhere to turn off because dense woods bordered either side of the road and even if they didn't, the ditches on both sides were too deep for the truck to cross. If they'd continued the way they were going they would have already met the oncoming vehicle and if they stayed where they were, they would anyway when it turned. Even if Eddie had room to make a U-turn, which he didn't, it was doubtful they would have time to get out of sight before it was on top of them. It was just bad luck that they were in the worst spot on their entire route to have such a chance encounter. Eddie knew all this of course, even as he was already in the process of executing a three-point turn to try and get the GMC heading in the opposite direction.

"Tell Willis and Trey to hang on and be ready to shoot!"

THIRTEEN

When Jonathan glanced back through the glass at the headlights of the vehicle coming up behind them, he could see that Willis and Trey were both low in the bed of the truck, looking out over the tailgate with their rifles braced on their rucksacks that were shoved up against it in front of them. By this time, it was obvious that the occupants of the other vehicle could see the GMC on the road ahead of them, so there was no longer any point in Eddie keeping his own lights off. He flipped them on bright and floored the accelerator, throwing gravel everywhere as the truck fishtailed on the loose surface before gaining traction.

"Who do you think they are?" Jonathan asked.

"There's no telling, but if they stay behind us it won't be looking good. Anybody minding their own business out here would stop as soon as they saw another vehicle ahead of them, especially one turning around and going the other way. Nobody would approach an unknown vehicle in the dark like that unless they were up to something or it was some of those damned deputies of Sheriff Farley's!"

"Well, they're still back there," Jonathan said, "do you think you can shake them if they follow?"

"Not really. Not in this truck and not on these roads! You saw it on the way out, there's no turnoffs until you get all the way back there to the Searcy place. Unless they back off, we're probably about to be in a gunfight. I hope you and your boys in the back are ready!"

Jonathan was, of course, but a sudden firefight in a situation like this was never anything to look forward to. They had no idea how many adversaries might be inside the vehicle behind them, or what kinds of weapons they might have. Nor did they know there weren't more vehicles following from farther back, out of sight. But still, if they took action quickly and decisively, they had more advantages than most would in that situation. Whoever was following them probably thought there were just one or two local folks in that old truck with at best, a shotgun or deer rifle and a pistol or two. If so, they were making a grave miscalculation, and would soon learn they were attempting to pull over a vehicle occupied by four men armed with select-fire M4s and a good supply of full mags. As it turned out, the pursuers didn't take long to make that miscalculation either. Jonathan had glanced back to the road ahead just in time to feel the truck swerve hard as Eddie zig-zagged back and forth across the road and yelled as he glanced at the rearview mirror. "They're firing at us now! It's on, buddy!"

Jonathan twisted in his seat so that he could get his rifle out of the window on the passenger side door. He could see the muzzle flashes now, just off to one side of the headlights. Someone was hanging out the passenger window of what looked like another pickup truck and firing at them! It was impossible to tell what kind of weapon it was, but he could see that Willis and Trey were already returning fire from over the tailgate. Jonathan joined in, opening up on the vehicle with three-round bursts until his bolt locked open on an empty chamber. The pursuing vehicle came to a stop in the face of all that oncoming automatic fire, but now

Jonathan's worst fears were realized when he saw another set of headlights closing in quickly behind it.

He was already reaching for a fresh magazine as soon as he dropped the empty one onto the floorboards. But as he tried to slam the new one home, Eddie's truck went into a sideways slide in the gravel, and the next thing he knew, it was off the road and bouncing hard into the deep ditch. He heard the impact as Jonathan and Trey were slammed forward into the back of the cab by the sudden deceleration, but both managed to catch themselves before they were thrown out completely. Eddie threw the truck in reverse as soon as it came to a stop, but his back wheels were spinning, and the GMC didn't budge. They were stuck fast with no possibility of getting it out!

Jonathan didn't know if the first vehicle was disabled or not, but the other one had pulled up close behind it as he and Eddie exited the cab and took cover behind the front of the pickup to assess the situation. They could see that the first one was stopped in the middle of the road a good hundred yards back from where they'd run into the ditch, and he figured their return fire had struck the occupants, or at least the driver. One of the headlights was out, probably from a bullet impact, but the other one was still burning, and in its glare, and the high beams of the second vehicle it was impossible to see anything of what was behind it.

"Are you guys okay? Jonathan yelled to Willis and Trey. He got his answer when he heard the two of them call back from over in the ditch, where they'd crawled after they bailed out of the truck bed when it was clear that the GMC wasn't going anywhere. By this time, they were receiving incoming fire again, and Jonathan figured it was from the occupants of the second vehicle.

"I'm gonna circle around through the woods and come up on them from the side!" Willis told them.

"Good idea!" Eddie said, "Maybe we ought to all go?"

"No!" Jonathan shouted. "We want whoever's doing that shooting to think they've got us pinned down. That way they won't be expecting it when Willis gets into position to open fire on their flank. One of us should take the other side of the road too though."

"I'll do it!" Trey said. "We'll cut them down from both sides!"

As soon as the two of them disappeared into the woods, Eddie and Jonathan fired answering shots towards the muzzle flashes coming from behind the other vehicle. It looked like there were at least two, maybe three weapons due to the spacing of the flashes, and from the sound of the reports, there was no doubt those weapons were semiautomatic rifles. If Eddie's truck hadn't been down in that ditch below the grade of the road, it would in no way have provided enough cover to protect them from the incoming fire they were taking. Eddie cursed as he heard the bullets shatter the glass and pierce the sheet metal of his old truck. Both rear tires were quickly flattened as well by the incoming rounds so the truck was going nowhere even if they survived the gunfight.

"I over-corrected in that last curve! That's why I lost control and went in the ditch!"

Jonathan thought Eddie had done as well as could be expected, considering how quickly the situation unfolded. It was simply a matter of bad luck that they'd been traveling this section of road at the same time as their unknown attackers. He now had his selector switch on semi-auto and was firing just frequently enough to keep their adversaries from advancing to where they could get a clear line of fire into the ditch. But he hoped Willis and Trey were moving fast, because once they closed in with their flanking maneuver, those guys would never know what hit them, because it would be coming at them from out of those dark woods on either side of the road.

But the incoming fire stopped completely a moment later, and Jonathan wondered if perhaps the shooters suddenly got the same idea. If so, they might attempt to circle around and come at the ditch from another angle. That seemed the most likely explanation for the cease fire, as the second vehicle remained where it was with the lights still on high beam. But then there were shots fired again, not at Jonathan and Eddie, but from somewhere else out in the dark. Jonathan heard a scream and then more firing and saw the muzzle flashes out to the north side of the road. Then he heard Willis call out and a few seconds after, Trey's answer. It sounded like all was clear, but Jonathan and Eddie waited until Willis and Trey secured the scene and called out to confirm it.

"We got all those sons of bitches!" Willis yelled.

"Are you sure?"

"Yep!" There were three more of them, plus the two in the first truck!"

Jonathan and Eddie made their way up the road to where Willis and Trey were standing over the three dead men behind the stopped vehicles. From there they could now see that the first one was a late-model Ford pickup, and the second was an older Jeep Grand Cherokee.

Jonathan saw as he walked by the truck that the driver and the man riding shotgun were slumped over in the cab behind the shattered windshield, probably taken out during the first exchange of gunfire before Eddie's truck went off the road. As he walked back to the second vehicle, he saw the other three sprawled in the road where they'd fallen to Willis' and Trey's deadly crossfire. The dead men had been armed with various AR-15s and shotguns, but the thing that Jonathan noticed first was that all of them were wearing matching solid green BDUs, like the 'soldiers' Michael said he saw after the attack on his house.

"Are those some of the sheriff's men?" Jonathan asked Eddie.

"Yeah, that's exactly who they are! The bastards were probably cruising back down this way looking for anybody they didn't get in the Searcy's house this morning. You never know where they're going to be, day or night though. I'd hoped we'd be able to slip out of here without running into any of them but at least that's five of the sons of bitches we won't ever have to worry about again! This is just the beginning, but it's a good beginning as far as I'm concerned, even though they messed up my truck and I'll have to leave it here."

"Well, we can use this Jeep to get where we were going," Jonathan said. "It doesn't look like it was damaged other than a few bullet holes."

"Yeah, we can do that," Eddie said, "but once we do, I'll be committed to seeing this thing through to the end even if I get Sheriff Farley first thing. I'll be their number one priority once they find my truck out here with the tires shot out, along with this Ford we shot all to hell and those five dead guys besides. They'll probably burn my place down and search this county from top to bottom. I'll have to totally get the hell out of here after this!"

"It looks like their pickup isn't really out of commission," Willis said, as he walked around to the front of the Jeep and inspected the truck. "Most of the glass is shot out but I don't think we hit anything important, and all the tires are still holding air, so we don't have to leave it here. We should be able to run it and the Jeep to that place you were talking about hiding your truck."

"If we do that, why don't we toss those dead guys in the back real quick?" Jonathan suggested. "Eric and I did that in another situation like this and it wasn't any trouble. At least that way if some more of them come along on this road tonight, they won't find hard evidence you killed some of their men. It may buy us some time, and we can just ditch this truck right there where we're leaving the Jeep and leave the bodies back there in the bed."

"That works for me!" Eddie said. "Help me drag this son of a bitch out from behind the wheel of the Ford and I'll drive it! But we need to hurry; not only because some more of them might come along any time, but also because we'll still have a lot of walking to do after we ditch these rides."

With that decided, the four of them made short work of loading the bodies into the back of the Ford. Then, they grabbed the rest of their gear out of Eddie's truck and threw it into the back of the Jeep and set out, with Trey driving it as he and Willis followed Eddie and Jonathan in the pickup.

"Do you think they were looking for us in particular?" Jonathan asked Eddie, "or were they just up here patrolling the road? Do they do that on a regular basis?"

"You never know when they're gonna come through, but it's not every night, at least not way out here. Considering what happened today, I wouldn't be at all surprised to find out they were here looking for you three."

Jonathan wondered what Eric, Lenny and Beckman had told the men who detained them. He knew Eric and Lenny wouldn't say anything about having more friends waiting back at the edge of that far pasture, but he didn't know about Beckman. And considering what he knew of these men now, he didn't know what they may have done to get him to talk.

The only thing that made him think the encounter was simply a coincidence instead was that there were just five men in two vehicles. It seemed to him that if they were looking for three more of Eric's team, it would have made sense to send more people, since Eddie said they had plenty. *But maybe they did? Perhaps they had split up and were driving all these roads near the Searcy farm?* Thinking of that made Jonathan quite nervous as Eddie drove east on the gravel road. He knew that at any moment now they could run into a replay of the same situation but maybe one far worse this time if there were more assailants involved.

But Eddie continued on until the gravel turned to pavement and then he turned north onto a paved road that ran past several houses and farms that Jonathan could tell even by moonlight were likely abandoned. When Eddie finally turned off again, it was onto a dirt lane that ended at a closed barbed wire gap. Willis hopped out to open it and then Eddie drove to a dead-end turnabout at the backside of what he told Jonathan had once been a soybean field. There was a tall stand of river cane growing at the back edge of the old field and just beyond it, Eddie said there was a small creek. Eddie drove the truck far enough into the canebrake that it was completely hidden from view, and then Willis pulled the Jeep in behind it.

"It's not likely anyone will find them here before tomorrow," Eddie said. "Anybody pulling down to the end of that road won't be able to see it, and unless they're looking close, they're not likely to notice the tire tracks coming in here either. But once Sheriff Farley's men start looking for their missing comrades, they'll check every pig trail in the county. They'll find these vehicles, and what's in the back of this truck!"

Eddie said that they could cut straight through the woods behind the canebrake and follow that creek for a while and then make their way around the backside of several more big fields that he said would be in the same abandoned and neglected condition.

It would take most of the night to work their way north to where they were heading, but by sticking to the backside of the fields and farms far from the road, their main obstacles would be just the numerous barbed wire fences they would have to cross. The chances of running into anybody out there at night were slim to none according to Eddie. But it turned out that wasn't the case, when after another hour of walking they spotted the light of a campfire down in the woods behind the field they were just about to cross.

"It's probably the landowners," Eddie said. "This is the Patterson place. I've known the family all my life; they're good folks. Just like Claude and Annabel Busby, the people that stayed on their farms around here have been getting out of their houses and taking to the woods for security purposes. Not many people would take the risk of sleeping in a house that can be seen from the road these days."

It made total sense to Jonathan after seeing what had happened to those people at the Searcy farm. That house wasn't visible from the main road, of course, but in that case, it was the target of a planned raid. The occupants hadn't had a chance against a force like the one Sheriff Farley's men brought down on them. By the time they realized anyone was even on the property it was already too late. Jonathan imagined that some of Michael's relatives in there had fired back at the green clad assailants, but they probably had no idea how many of them they were up against or the kind of firepower they were bringing to bear in order to prevail. And there was really nowhere to go even if they wanted to try and escape, because going out the back door to try and run for the woods was suicide with that many men firing on them. Michael had escaped certain death only because he happened to be hunting.

As they skirted around the distant campfire, Jonathan thought about the desperate family that was likely huddled around it. He understood the fear they must be feeling living under the oppression Sheriff Farley had brought to his so-called jurisdiction. If the four of them could accomplish what they hoped to do in the coming morning or the next, maybe things would change. They would not only be rescuing their friends but ending the tyranny and oppression that these innocent country folks were up against through no fault of their own.

Seeing all he'd seen tonight, Jonathan was glad to be walking now, rather than riding the roads. Eddie led the way with total confidence, and Jonathan could tell he hadn't exaggerated when he spoke of how well he knew the land around here. Eddie not only knew where to go, but how to get there without being seen now that they were on foot. He called the name of every family that lived or had once lived in the various abandoned houses they passed along the way. And he said he had hunted on most of those properties and spent time playing and exploring there as a kid. As such, he knew the trails and the backroads and the creeks and was able to lead them unerringly to the old abandoned landfill, which they reached just as the first hint of pale light appeared in the east.

There was something unsettling about the place from the moment he laid eyes on it, and Jonathan figured it was because of what Eddie said was taking place there on a regular basis. If he had any doubts as to whether or not that was true, they were erased when Eddie led them around to the other side of the large, graded clearing and pointed out the open pit not far from the near vertical embankment that separated the area from the surrounding woods. There were four large wooden posts set into the ground there in front of the 10-foot-high clay bluff and Jonathan didn't have to guess what they were used for.

"That's where they tie them up so they can't move when the firing squad takes aim. And into that pit over there is where they go after they're cut loose. Depending on who it was, they sometimes leave the bodies on the ground over there by the edge of it for a few days, both to serve as a warning and to give any family members a chance to come get them. That's how I was able to bury my brother, Kirby, back at my place."

"That Sheriff Farley is one sick dude!" Willis said.

"Yep, and I've been waiting for this day ever since I scooped the last shovelful of dirt onto Kirby's grave! I just hope they show up. I know where I'm gonna set up, right over there," Eddie pointed out the position he had in mind on the opposite side of the dumping area, about 120 yards away. "Y'all can pick your own spots, wherever you think best, now that you see where your targets will be. All I ask is that you let me have the first shot to kick it off. Besides, I'm the only one here that'll recognize Sheriff Farley when I see him, and that son of a bitch is mine!"

FOURTEEN

PFC Robert Beckman knew he had screwed up big time. Just when he thought he was about to make contact with fellow National Guard soldiers that would help him return to his base, he had been seriously fooled by first impressions. Now it was clear these men weren't actively serving in the National Guard nor any other branch of the US military, even if many of them had previously. But they were wearing the same type of combat uniforms that some regular Guard soldiers in the state were currently using. And watching them with Eric and Lenny from the edge of the woods, it appeared they were carrying out their assault operation on that farmhouse with military precision. Beckman had assumed that the occupants of the dwelling were dangerous insurgents that had given someone a reason to send such a large and well-equipped unit to take them out. But then once he had stepped out there and soon found himself being led away at gunpoint along with his two new acquaintances, it didn't take him long to figure out something was off about this entire outfit. His doubts were further confirmed when they reached the cluster of vehicles parked at the far end of the long gravel drive leading into the place and he saw that there was only a single military Humvee among a mix of various law enforcement vehicles.

Beckman was put into the back of an unmarked police cruiser like a common criminal under arrest, while Eric and Lenny were taken to a different SUV with a sheriff's department emblem on its doors. The driver and the other guy riding shotgun in the car wouldn't answer any of Beckman's questions as the small group of vehicles pulled out of there and headed north. And when they finally got to their destination, it made no sense at all to Beckman, as it was a far cry from a military post or even a rural law enforcement complex. It looked to Beckman more like a privately owned family farm or ranch, if one were to assume those private owners were also quite wealthy.

Beckman was stunned at the sprawling size of the place and the over-the-top extravagant mansion, as well as the barns and other outbuildings. There was even a large riding arena with stadium bleachers that looked like it was built to host small private rodeos and other events. Then the convoy proceeded past that area and he saw a rifle range and then more buildings inside a gated compound, one of which was obviously a barracks building. Looking at all this, it became obvious to Beckman that he'd fallen into the hands of some law enforcement organization that was likely operating by a different set of rules than any ordinary sheriff's department. And he was soon to find out how very different indeed.

Beckman began to get a clearer picture of the operation after he and Eric and Lenny were taken inside the larger of the two buildings and locked into separate rooms. After what seemed like most of the afternoon, he was finally questioned by the man in charge of the operation, a powerfully built middle-aged man who claimed to be a Marine Lieutenant Colonel but was now the sheriff presiding over this and two adjacent counties. But it was obvious that it was no ordinary sheriff's department that he was running since the collapse of regular law and order. What Sheriff Farley had created was in fact a small, independent army that answered to no higher authority than himself, and he had no problem telling Beckman that straight up. Having expanded his realm of control across those three counties, Sheriff Farley had created what he said was essentially a free state in this little out of the way corner of Mississippi. And the move was not without precedent, as Beckman recalled from his study of state history during the era of the Civil War.

The interrogation that Beckman was subjected to by the sheriff and two of his deputies was both skillful and deceptive. They wanted to know everything about the two men he was traveling with, and in particular, why they were posing as civilians. It was obvious that Sheriff Farley didn't believe Eric and Lenny *were* civilians, and it was true that Eric had told the assault team commander himself that he was a former Navy chief that had been assigned to one of the SEAL teams. As far as Beckman knew, they knew next to nothing about Lenny, other than that Eric had claimed the younger man as his nephew. But Sheriff Farley tricked up Beckman by saying that Eric had told him far more just an hour earlier when he interviewed him in the next room. It was believable to the point that Beckman slipped up and accidentally admitted to him that Lenny wasn't the only companion Eric had with him. He made that mistake before he understood the severity of the situation he and Eric and Lenny were in, but it was too late to reverse course once he set that line of questioning in motion. Now the sheriff wanted to know all about the three of them and where exactly they had been left to wait. Beckman knew that whether he gave the man the details or not, he would likely send a team of men out to hunt them down. There was little he could tell them, of course, because he'd only met Eric and his friends the day before. But Sheriff Farley had him in a real bind now, because he was threatening to have both Eric and Lenny shot in front of a firing squad, if Beckman didn't give him the information that he wanted. It was obvious that the sheriff was intent on shutting down any and all military and other government operations in this area that he was now calling a free and independent state. And he wanted not only the information about those other men that had been with Eric and Lenny, but also every detail of the operations Beckman's unit was conducting out of Camp Hurly.

"There's nothing else I can tell you," Beckman said in regard to the latter. "I don't have any information above the level of my squad and platoon. Our sergeant was killed in the attack on the sandbar, along with our pilot and crew. No one else outside of Camp Hurly has anymore intel than they did. I'm just an E3, and you know what that means! I'm not privy to all the operational details. I was just doing my job."

"Well, the problem I have with what you're telling me is that I don't buy it that this former Navy SEAL just shows up out in the middle of nowhere in the woods so soon after your squad landed in the area. I know damned well he was on board the helicopter with you, or he was dropped off by another one before or after. But since I now know that he's got three other guys with him, I have to believe it must have been the latter. So whatever joint operations your unit was conducting out here with the Navy, it's a lot bigger than you're telling me!"

"No sir. I can assure you that I've never seen any of those guys before in my life. They came up to me in the woods and nearly scared the hell out of me when they did. But after we got to talking and I found out what they wanted, we agreed to travel together and try to get to the nearest Guard post."

"So, you're telling me you believe they came across the Mississippi River from Louisiana in canoes? And that they've been fighting some unknown force consisting of private contractors and National Guard and Army units that are working against the same military that you're enlisted in? The same military that I served? Do you really expect me to believe all that horse shit, Beckman?"

"I can't tell you what to believe regarding Eric Branson's story. All I know is what he told me, and it sounded plausible to me. But I haven't been west of the Mississippi River other than what we've seen making our turns when we were doing our flyovers. I have no idea what's going on over there, but he said it was coming this way, whatever it is, and that he was here to bring us intel about it and try and muster some forces to stop it."

What Beckman gathered from the conversation, was that Sheriff Farley was purely interested in maintaining control of his own little corner of the world and didn't give a damn about what was going on beyond the borders he claimed. It was also clear that he didn't want anyone coming inside those borders and interfering with his illicit business, which was all about what he and those closest to him could personally gain from all this. It was apparent that by taking control of those three counties he was confiscating farm and timber land and all sorts of other real property from the residents that were unable to retain it. Most of the people in his jurisdiction and beyond were desperate, and more than willing to trade whatever they had for the promise of security the sheriff's little army could offer.

Sheriff Farley claimed, and Beckman knew it to be true, that there'd been massive hordes of refugees pouring north from New Orleans, Baton Rouge and the rest of south Louisiana after the hurricane. And many of them, like those people he said they had hunted down to the Searcy place, had been raiding and looting other people's property and stealing food and doing whatever they could to get by. Sheriff Farley claimed he had every right to take out those people with any amount of force necessary.

"The only way to keep that kind of lawlessness from spreading is to make an example of those who engage in it," he said. "Now that we're doing that, a lot of those people have moved on to find other places to ply their trade."

Beckman didn't know what else to tell the man regarding Eric and his companions. He wished now that he hadn't mentioned Jonathan, Willis, and Trey, and he hoped that it wouldn't get them captured or killed, but he had no idea what the three of them had done after he and Eric and Lenny didn't return. Surely, they went to the house where all the shooting took place to look for them, but what they may have done beyond that, he had no clue. He figured they would make some attempt to try and find out what happened to Eric and Lenny. But he didn't know where they'd even begin such a daunting undertaking without local knowledge of the area or anyone that lived there that they could risk making contact with. Beckman assumed that if they had no leads, it was likely they would return to where they'd left their canoes and try to get help from their friends across the river in Louisiana.

In either case it was a long shot that anything they might try could be accomplished in time to help him and Eric and Lenny, and Beckman didn't know who else would. There was a chance the 3rd Battalion might send another aircraft out looking for the missing Black Hawk. If they spotted that wreckage on the sandbar, it was possible Colonel Rencher would mount a search and rescue operation if he could. And if he did that, there would surely be an encounter with the sheriff and his men, considering the apparent size of his outfit here. That meeting might come too late to help Beckman, Eric and Lenny, though, because from what he could gather from this conversation, Sheriff Farley didn't use his resources to house and feed long-term prisoners. The matter-of-fact way he described it left no doubt in Beckman's mind that his implementation of a firing squad was real.

ERIC BRANSON'S SECOND INTERROGATION CAME MUCH LATER that evening. The sheriff and his three men returned to the room where they'd left him all day, ready for another round. This time Sheriff Farley told Eric that he knew exactly who he was and why he was here.

"Private Beckman spilled his guts about your mission," the sheriff said. "He said that you and all of your team were here for the purpose of assassinating me and undoing everything I've worked for in this county and the people that live here. I know that what he said is true, because the men I sent out earlier have already found those other three fellows that were with you."

Eric studied the sheriff's face for a moment before he replied. What he suggested about having Jonathan, Willis and Trey in custody already was hard to believe. They would be too careful for that after discovering that Eric and Lenny were missing and seeing the aftermath of the assault on that house. Still, he answered as if he accepted it without question. And now he knew Beckman had at least told the man about his companions, otherwise he wouldn't have guessed the correct number on the first try.

"Is that right?" Eric asked. "Because if it is, then you already know that none of those three have ever spent a day at a military facility much less served. I'm the only one other than Beckman that ever served, but I never met him before the other day, and I wasn't working with him."

What the sheriff was doing was in fact, the oldest trick in the interrogator's playbook. It was why the three of them had been separated as soon as they arrived here and kept that way ever since. They were playing the psychological game of trying to use the three of them against each other to make each one believe that the others had told more than they actually had. Eric wasn't going to fall for it, of course, but that didn't mean that he couldn't come up with something to make the sheriff think that he had.

"I don't know all the details of Beckman's mission. He's in a completely different Special Operations group and branch from the one I was in, as you are well aware. What I do know, is that there is a big force that's mobilizing to occupy this region and secure the entire Mississippi river navigation channel and adjacent lands, as well as those beyond. The kind of actions you've taken on that riverside sandbar are going to make it worse on you when they do. You're not going to be able to resist what's coming with your militarized deputies, no matter how well-equipped you think you are or how many men you have. It's nothing in comparison to what you'll be up against."

"What actions are you talking about? What makes you think I had anything to do with what happened on that sandbar?"

"Come on, Sheriff Farley! Did you think I would believe it was anybody other than your men? No one with any sense would buy that some random gang of armed civilians took out that Black Hawk and an entire squad of Special Forces soldiers! How many of your men did it take? Were you there yourself when it went down?"

"If I *had* been there, we wouldn't be sitting here having this conversation," Farley replied. "Beckman wouldn't have gotten away. But now that I know you had three more operators with you besides that young man you're calling your nephew, I guess the five of you had a different ride here. But regardless of any of that, I'm not worried about more federal troops coming, because I know how incapacitated they are by now. They're disorganized and lacking leadership. Troop morale is at an all-time low, because especially in the National Guard and reserves, the men are worried about their families at home, and rightly so. Why would they go off on long deployments, even in other parts of their home state for unknown periods of time and let their wives and children go hungry or worse? That's why we had to do what we're doing here and form our own local security forces for our county and the two that neighbor us. We can't depend on the government to do it for us; not now and not ever again! You know that as well as I do.

"But I still want every bit of intel you can give me regarding Beckman's unit. I'll cut you the same deal I did him if you come through. He saved his own skin by telling me about your three buddies, but he claims that because he's only a PFC, he doesn't know anything else about the extent of his unit's operations. But I know that when you Special Ops guys collaborate across different branches like that, you've got to know enough about each other's operations to get the job done. Most of the men that have sat across from me at this same table in this room were never offered a deal like the one I'm offering you. This was the end of the road for them, but I'm giving you a chance to get out of my county alive. You and your 'nephew' both if you tell me what I want to know."

"I can tell you anything you want to hear, but if I keep telling you the truth—that I know nothing of Beckman and the 26th Special Forces Group he's affiliated with, nor what their operational plans are—then what?"

"Then we go out to the special place not far from here where all the other men that sat there where you're sitting and lied to me went. You'll get to watch while your 'nephew' goes in front of my firing squad first. Then, you can watch your other three buddies follow after him, one day at a time. If that doesn't jar your memory and get you talking, then you'll get your turn too, at the end of the line. So, think it over, but don't take long doing it, because we'll be heading out tomorrow at first light. There are certain traditions to uphold regarding summary executions, and 'tomorrow at sunrise' has a nice ring to it, don't you think?"

The sheriff and his men left, and Eric stretched out on the table to get some sleep. He was still quite confident the man was bluffing, and that he would be back some time tomorrow for another round of questioning. As long as they used the threat of death in their attempts to extract information that he couldn't give them anyway, Eric figured he'd keep playing their game. If the interrogations became violent, then he'd have to rethink it, but he fell asleep with few worries, as he was too exhausted from being awake more than twenty-four hours to sit up and think about it any longer.

And so, it came as a surprise when the door to the interrogation room swung open again just a few hours later. There were two extra men with rifles pointed at him this time, and as he was led down the hall and out of the building, Eric saw that it was indeed just breaking dawn. And he saw that Lenny was standing at gunpoint beside the same waiting SUV that he and Eric had been brought there in the day before.

FIFTEEN

Jonathan, Willis and Trey had assessed the layout of the old landfill and decided on the best positions to take up after Eddie told them where he wanted to be in order to get his shot at Sheriff Farley. There was only one road in, so they didn't have to worry about the sheriff and his men approaching from any other angle. The only reason for them to come here at all would be to carry out another one of the firing squad executions that Eddie said happened here all too frequently. It was simply mind-blowing to Jonathan that an elected sheriff could amass a following that would support him in such measures, but Jonathan had seen a lot of crazy things in recent weeks and months, so the idea wasn't as far-fetched as it would have been before.

What *was* far-fetched, was that they even were here at all. If it hadn't been for finding Michael, who told them about Claude Busby, who then introduced them to Eddie Poole, Jonathan knew it was unlikely they'd have ever figured out where to find Eric, Lenny and Beckman, especially in time to do any good. As it was, they had just gotten here in the nick of time by Eddie's reckoning.

Of course, Jonathan couldn't dismiss the possibility that Eric and Lenny had somehow escaped, knowing Eric's capabilities, but they couldn't count on that. What was surprising was that Eric had been fooled in the first place. Jonathan had no way of knowing what the circumstances were at the moment of their encounter at the farmhouse, but however it happened, Eric had gotten himself into quite a dilemma if he was indeed in the hands of a madman like Sheriff Farley.

Jonathan had no illusions after seeing the aftermath of that attack on the Searcy's house that the sheriff and his men would show any mercy to their prisoners. And if they had anything to do with the attack on Beckman's squad, things could be even worse for him. If the sheriff and his men were actually fighting against federal and state troops, then they were capable of anything. They were liable to interrogate or even torture Beckman to get the information they wanted from him. Or they could use him as a hostage to make some sort of demands from the authority he served.

The same could be true if they found out Eric was a SEAL, which was quite possible because Beckman may have told them. For a moment, Jonathan regretted ever telling Beckman as much as he had about Eric's background. Eric had told him to shut up when he started talking about it, and he did, of course, when he realized his mistake. He didn't mean to compromise Eric's security by blabbing about it. He was just trying to let Beckman know who he was dealing with and that Eric wasn't some deckhand on a ship somewhere at sea while he was serving in the Navy. Beckman's claim of being in Special Forces himself didn't mean much to Jonathan. But Eric was the real deal and Jonathan had seen him prove his skills time and time again ever since he'd met the man. Beckman, on the other hand, may have broken down at the first threat of pain and told the sheriff and his men everything he knew, and that would have included the fact that Eric and Lenny weren't traveling alone.

Jonathan still didn't know for sure that the men they encountered in those two vehicles last night weren't looking for them specifically. If they were, he wondered now if that search would have changed the way the sheriff usually did things. What if he didn't bring Eric and Lenny and Beckman out here at all? It was possible that if Beckman told them the truth—that Eric and Lenny weren't alone—the interrogation could have intensified to the point they didn't need to bring them out here to shoot them.

Jonathan couldn't help feeling anxious about all the possibilities racing through his mind as he sat there on the edge of one of the dirt embankments overlooking the landfill. *Was he wrong to put all his trust in Eddie Poole?* As the gray sky of dawn became tinted with the yellows and reds of the impending sunrise and still no one showed, Jonathan's doubts increased. He worried that they were in the wrong place, or in the right place but at the wrong time. If so, he doubted they would get a second chance to save Eric and Lenny.

As he watched the sun slowly emerge from below the horizon of a distant line of trees, Jonathan's anxiety increased to the breaking point. He normally thought of himself as a laid-back and easy-going kind of dude. It was how he'd been raised, and it was instilled in him by his oceanside lifestyle growing up in south Florida. But since he'd been in all these tight spots and life or death confrontations he'd experienced since meeting Eric Branson, Jonathan's carefree attitude had undergone a gradual adjustment, and right now the tension was tearing him apart.

He glanced over at Willis and Trey, wondering if they too were feeling as apprehensive. Then he watched Eddie, some 75 yards away on the edge of a different steep bank. Eddie had his scoped rifle set up on a makeshift rest he'd assembled from some old car tires he'd found at the periphery of the dump. It was obvious the man wanted nothing more in life than to get Sheriff Farley into his crosshairs, and at this point, he was committed, and Jonathan doubted anything would change his mind. But still, after nearly another hour of waiting, when it became obvious there were no planned sunrise executions before a firing squad here today, Jonathan backed away from his position and circled around to climb up there and have a chat with Eddie.

"It's pretty clear they're not coming today, dude. I'm worried that we're in the wrong place! After what happened last night, everything may have changed. What if they found those five dead guys already? They may be torturing Eric and Lenny to death to try and find out where we were hiding, and where we may have gone. They may not ever bring them out here to shoot them like they do other people. They may just do it where they are right now!"

"Well, if they do, there's not a damned thing we can do about it," Eddie said.

"Why not? If we could take them by surprise here, we could do it there at their headquarters too. I know you haven't been doing the kind of stuff we learned from Eric, but you'd be amazed at what even two or three guys can pull off when they're working with the element of surprise, and there's four of us! You're obviously a good shot to have a rifle setup like that and you could still get the sheriff no matter where he is if we can just get you in range. I say we need to try, because we can't just sit here all day doing nothing!"

"Suit yourself if you want to leave, but I'm not. I know damned well that if Sheriff Farley has what he considers enemy prisoners, there's gonna be executions, and he'll do it out here because he wants folks in the county to know about it! He may usually do these things at sunrise, but that don't mean he *always* does! It could happen at any time today, and if it doesn't, then maybe it'll be tomorrow. I'm in this for all or nothing at this point, and I'm staying right here until he shows up; I don't care how long it takes! I told you before that it won't work to try and get him on his home turf. It would be suicide to attempt it and you'd accomplish nothing. I don't care if I die out here as long as I get Sheriff Farley first, but I'm not throwing away my chance by trying to get past all the men he's got on guard at his place! And I'm not telling you how to get there either, so don't ask. I've been waiting too long for this opportunity and I don't want to see it ruined when you and your buddies go down there and get yourselves killed. Sheriff Farley probably *would* just go ahead and shoot Eric and your other friends if that happened. So, if you want to go, then go for it! But you're on your own!"

"Well, whatever dude...."

Jonathan was pissed as he stormed off from Eddie and went back to his position. But he decided to give it another hour before going to talk it over with Willis and Trey. He couldn't blame the guy for wanting to avenge his brother and figured he would have felt the same way if he had a brother and somebody killed him like that. But his concern was getting Eric and Lenny out of wherever they were, and he could care less about revenge or ridding the county of a bloodthirsty tyrant, because that wasn't what they were here for. When that second hour passed and the sun was high above the horizon, he decided he'd had enough. He felt sure that Willis and Trey would agree with him and that they would be willing to go and try to find the sheriff's compound without Eddie's help. But just as he'd circled back down and was climbing up to Willis's position, he saw Willis turn back to him and point to something out on the entrance road to the east.

"Someone's coming!" He shouted.

"Is it them?"

"I think so! It's several vehicles! I count six of them; two pickup trucks, two SUVs and a couple of Humvees!"

ERIC HAD NO OPPORTUNITY TO SPEAK TO LENNY THAT morning before they put him into the back of the SUV he was standing next to. They took Eric to one of the crew cab pickup trucks that was also set up with a prisoner barrier between the front and rear seats. Eric scanned the other vehicles that included two Humvees, looking for Jonathan, Willis and Trey, but there was no sign of any of them. It looked to him like around a dozen men in total were loading up to go wherever it was they were taking him and Lenny. Whether or not it was all still a bluff, he couldn't be sure, but before they moved out, Sheriff Farley came over to the truck he was in and stuck his head into the open front window to speak to him. Eric's hands were unrestrained but there was nothing he could do from behind the wire mesh barrier anyway.

"If you're wondering where your other buddies are, don't worry, they're not going with us this morning; just you and your nephew. You'll find a notebook and a pen on the floorboards back there if you're ready to write down all the information I asked for regarding Beckman's mission and your own. It's a short ride out to where we're going, so I'd suggest you write fast. If you don't, you'll see your 'nephew' shot this morning, and then we'll work our way down the line every day after, starting with your other three men and then with Beckman. It doesn't make a lot of difference to me whether it takes all week or not, but you'll be the last to go if it comes to it, so you'll have to live with your decisions every minute of the last few days you've got left. So, just do yourself and everybody else a favor and get to writing. It's in your best interest, believe me!"

Eric glanced down at the notebook but didn't bother to pick it up. Another of the sheriff's deputies took the shotgun position on the front seat after the sheriff stepped away to get into one of the Humvees, and Eric remained silent as the vehicles began pulling out. When they formed a line as they turned onto the exit road, the truck he was in was fifth in line, behind the SUV in which Lenny was riding and in front of the second Humvee that brought up the rear.

After the long winding ride out to the front gate, the convoy stopped at the intersection with the paved road that they'd come there on the day before. After what seemed like at least a twenty-minute wait, they pulled out turning south, heading back the same way from which they'd come. As he watched the countryside go by out of the windows of the truck, Eric figured the place they were taking him and Lenny was somewhere back down there in the woods, as this exercise now seemed too elaborate to be a mere bluff or intimidation tactic. Maybe the sheriff's threat of executing Lenny was in fact, real, but if it was, then they'd already missed that sunrise window that Farley seemed to consider essential to the tradition. The sun had cleared the horizon while the convoy was still sitting there at the gate. Whether it really mattered or not, Eric didn't know, but they were going *somewhere*. If it was to the execution site, then Eric doubted there was much he could do to change the sheriff's mind, because he simply didn't have the intel Farley wanted. He knew next to nothing about Beckman's unit, other than what Beckman had told him in their brief conversations. None of it was useful info to this arrogant lawman that had essentially declared himself the dictator of his little corner of the world. Eric doubted Beckman and his superiors even knew of Sheriff Farley before that last, ill-fated Black Hawk flight or else he would have mentioned it.

Eric recognized houses and other landmarks he'd seen along the way there yesterday, and sure enough, the convoy made all the same turns in reverse, retracing the route along those long gravel roads leading away from that farmhouse where the assault had occurred. But before they reached the place where Eric and Lenny had first been forced into those vehicles yesterday, the convoy came to a stop again and most of the men got out with their rifles, leaving Eric and Lenny locked up where they were. Eric could see that they were gathering around an old-looking pickup truck that was halfway on the road and halfway in the ditch to one side, and as he studied it, he noted that there were bullet holes in the body and tailgate and that both of the rear tires had been flattened. Someone in that truck had been involved in a gunfight, and the sheriff and his men were clearly interested in investigating the incident. Eric saw them spread out and search up and down the road and the adjacent ditches, and he saw them picking up what he figured were spent casings and pointing at something in the road—probably tire tracks. They walked back and forth around the scene for a good half hour before finally, Sheriff Farley climbed back into the Humvee up front and the convoy began the process of turning around in the narrow road. As Eric glanced back one last time at the abandoned pickup he wondered if the owner was somehow connected to the occupants of that house the sheriff's men had raided. It seemed the only explanation that would generate so much interest, but now they were going back the way they came again, and after they hit the pavement, Eric once again watched the landmarks he remembered go by. But this time when they reached the gate leading onto the sheriff's property and headquarters, the convoy didn't even slow down. The drivers continued north for what Eric estimated was about five miles, and then turned west onto another hilly gravel road that ran through a large swath of old cutover now grown up in tangles of bushes and briar patches. On the far side of the cutover, the road ended at a large opening ringed by clay bluffs and pushed up mounds of dirt and debris. Eric knew at a glance that it was an old dumping site, but it looked like it hadn't been used for that purpose in years. The place was completely deserted, and there were no vehicles or heavy equipment parked there. When the convoy reached the edge of the clearing the drivers turned all the vehicles around and lined them back up in the same order to prepare for their departure. But it was clear to Eric that they weren't leaving yet. Off to one side of the main landfill area, he saw a vertical clay bluff, and in front of it, four large wooden posts set vertically into the ground about five feet apart and the same distance from the face of the bluff. Eric didn't have to guess what they were used for as the back door of the truck was opened and he was ordered out with two rifles leveled on him at point blank range.

It was now a good two and a half hours after sunrise, thanks to the side trip the convoy made all the way down there to check out the stranded pickup truck. But it appeared Sheriff Farley wasn't going to let that fact deter him. Maybe this was all still a charade, but Eric didn't think so as he studied the fresh pockmarks in the smooth face of the bluff behind the posts. Bullets had struck that surface recently, as they had the posts themselves, most of them around a height equivalent to chest level on a grown man.

Sheriff Farley was approaching him now, and in his hand, he held the notebook that one of his deputies had retrieved from the floorboards of the pickup. Eric hadn't touched it during the ride, and he didn't plan on touching it now, because he had nothing else to tell the sheriff, much less in writing.

"If you're itching to see somebody shot, then why don't you put me in front of that firing squad instead of an innocent young civilian who's done nothing to you or anyone in your little militarized jurisdiction! Let Lenny go and he'll cross that river and never bother you again."

"Oh, he's done something all right, so he's far from innocent. He's guilty of terrorism because he was caught carrying weapons of war openly in public in my county. The sentence for that is death, and it will be carried out momentarily!"

"Only cowards use the threat of death to retain power and control! You're a traitor to the Marine Corps and a traitor to the constitution you swore to defend, you worthless sack of shit!"

Before Sheriff Farley could respond, Eric felt the impact of a vicious sweep kick that buckled his left leg and dropped him hard to the ground. He knew it was one of the guards behind him that delivered the kick and he rolled to one side immediately upon landing in an attempt to evade the follow-up attack he knew was coming. But it was not just one, but three of the men closing in on him now, and though Eric managed to dodge the next incoming kick, a third one connected to the side of his head with a force that left him stunned and disoriented, and totally at the mercy of whatever came next.

SIXTEEN

Jonathan glanced back over to where Eddie was stationed and saw him frantically waving for him to get back to his original position.

So Eddie was right after all.... "I guess this is it then!" Jonathan yelled back to Willis. "Good luck!"

"Same to ya! Let's get these bastards! Every single one of them!"

Jonathan backed down around the hill and circled back up to where he'd been waiting before, crouching low as he moved. The line of approaching vehicles was moving slowly, but steadily, and he barely had time to crawl back to his vantage point and get ready to shoot before the first one was coming to a stop at the edge of the landfill. When he looked Eddie's way again, he saw him using a hand signal to remind him to hold off and wait. Eddie was determined to get the first shot, and Jonathan was fine with letting him have it. He'd been wrong to doubt the man, he now realized, and his impatience had gotten the better of his judgment. If those vehicles had arrived a half hour later, he would have already been foolishly leading Willis and Trey off on some fruitless search for Sheriff Farley's compound.

Jonathan watched as all of the vehicles pulled up behind the first one, and then the drivers began to maneuver them around to face back the way they came. It appeared they wanted to be ready for a quick exit as soon as they were done with their business here, and when the doors started opening and the occupants got out, there was no longer any doubt as to what that business was. A tall man wearing a cowboy hat and a khaki-colored uniform typical of a sheriff's department stepped out of the Humvee that had been in the front of the line in the little convoy. When the doors of the other vehicles began opening, Jonathan saw two figures emerge at gunpoint: one from the back seat of one of the pickups, and the other from the back of an SUV with gold star emblems on its doors. And he saw that the detainees were indeed Eric Branson and Lenny Polk!

The two of them were under the guard of several men, all of whom wore solid green BDUs. There was no sign of Beckman though, and Jonathan wondered if it was because his earlier theory was correct. *Had the interrogators beaten information out of him until he was either dead or in no shape to stand and face a firing squad?* Regardless of Beckman's absence, there were enough men here to carry out that sort of execution, and as soon as everyone was out of the vehicles Jonathan saw one man grab a coil of rope out of the bed of one of the pickup trucks. Two others approached Lenny and seized him by the upper arms from either side, leading him towards the four wooden posts planted in front of the clay bluff. Lenny made a futile attempt to resist, but when the man with the rope joined in to help the first two, they easily dragged him across the muddy ground despite his struggles and soon had him secured to one of the middle two posts.

Jonathan wondered why they weren't forcing Eric over there as well until he saw one of the men return to the truck in which Eric had been riding and then walk back to the sheriff with a notebook in his hand. It was impossible to hear the conversation at that distance, but it seemed to Jonathan, as he saw the sheriff wave it in Eric's face and then hold it out to him, that he wanted Eric to either read what it said or write something in it.

When Eric made no move to reach for the notebook, one of the men standing behind him swept Eric's leg out from under him with a vicious low kick that sent him hard to the ground. Eric rolled to one side as soon as he landed though, trying to defend himself from the follow-up kicks coming from two of the other men that joined in. He avoided the first one, but the second guy caught him with a roundhouse to the side of the head, knocking him back to the ground. Jonathan could see that Eric was still conscious, but clearly dazed and in pain. He had his M4 shouldered and was sweeping the red dot of his combat sight back and forth between each of the three men that had engaged in the attack. It was all he could do to restrain himself from pulling the trigger then and there, but he kept hoping Eddie would do what he said he was going to do and take out Sheriff Farley first. Jonathan had promised to let him have that opening shot, but he was cursing under his breath now as he wondered what in the hell the man was waiting for. The sheriff was standing right there in the wide open, where he was an easy target for Eddie's scoped .243. *But he still didn't shoot!*

By now, the three that had tied Lenny up were walking back over to where the sheriff and the others were clustered around Eric, who was still on his hands and knees on the ground. As they stood talking amongst themselves, Jonathan noticed five of the group move off to one side and begin manually checking their weapons as if they were preparing to use them. *So, those were the men that made up Sheriff Farley's firing squad!* Jonathan wondered if it was always the same five or if they drew straws or something each time to select the men for that duty.

Regardless of how they picked the shooters, it appeared they were getting ready to do their job and it was obvious that the plan was to execute Lenny first, right in front of Eric, probably in an attempt to get him to talk. *I'll be damned if I'm going to let that happen!* Jonathan thought to himself as he glared over at Eddie, who was still motionless behind his improvised rifle rest, studying the scene through his scope but doing nothing else. *Shoot the sheriff, dammit! What are you waiting for, dude?*

Jonathan couldn't will him to do it, so he moved his own red dot over to the sheriff's face. The optic on his M4 was designed for fast, close-quarters target acquisition rather than long, precision shots, but he was confident he could take the man down on the first try because the distance wasn't that great. The only problem was that it wasn't what they'd agreed on. If Jonathan fired first, he ran the risk of botching the whole ambush with the confusion it would create. The plan was for Eddie to take out the sheriff and for his shot to simultaneously signal Jonathan, Willis and Trey to quickly work their way through every other available target before the sheriff's men had a chance to react. It had to be done that way to have the best chance of getting Eric and Lenny out unscathed, but if Eddie waited any longer, it was going to be too late for poor Lenny. *The five men of the firing squad were already lining up and getting into position to await the sheriff's command!*

Jonathan was sweating even though there was a distinct chill in the morning air. He looked over to Eddie once again and then back to the sheriff and then the five on the firing line that now had their rifles at low ready. Jonathan's red dot was centered on the back of the nearest shooter's head now, but he was fighting the urge to swing it back over to the sheriff and do what Eddie still wouldn't. But before he could give in and do it, something totally unexpected happened. Sheriff Farley suddenly went down, but not from Eddie Poole's bullet, even though Jonathan finally heard the report of his .243 about a half-second too late.

To Jonathan's astonishment, Eric had managed to lunge from where he was still down on the ground and tackle the sheriff in what was apparently a kamikaze effort to prevent him from shouting that order to fire. Jonathan knew Eddie had probably already taken up the slack in his trigger to squeeze off the round that would exact his revenge before it happened, so he fired the shot anyway, even though his reaction was too late as his target was suddenly yanked out of his line of fire by Eric's attack. Eric's action and the unexpected report of the high-powered rifle echoing off the surrounding bluffs caused every man down there to turn towards either Eric and the sheriff or look around for the source of the gunshot as they tried to process what had just happened. It was during that moment of shock and uncertainty that Jonathan took out the first man in the firing squad and knew that Willis and Trey were following his lead as green-clad men began dropping fast amid a din of rapid, but controlled semi-auto rifle fire.

THE KICK ERIC BRANSON HAD TAKEN TO THE SIDE OF THE head rattled him badly, and it took him a few minutes to shake off the effects, which he did only through sheer willpower and the instinct to survive. He knew he couldn't fight all the armed men that surrounded him and hope to prevail, but it was clear to him that they no longer considered he was in the fight at all and were now focused on the spectacle of the execution of the young man tied to that post. It was the only shred of advantage Eric had, and he didn't intend to waste it. As he pulled himself together and focused on Sheriff Farley, Eric slowly drew one foot up beneath him to gain purchase on the ground without drawing the attention of his captors. Then he used that coiled position to launch a low, diving attack into the sheriff's lower legs, locking them both together in a powerful two-armed trap as his momentum slammed the man hard to the ground. The sheriff wasn't carrying a rifle, like most of the men he commanded, but he was wearing a full-sized Glock pistol in an open-carry holster on his right hip. Eric's goal was to obtain that weapon and use it as a tool to negotiate with the sheriff's men, gambling they didn't want to see him pull the trigger with the muzzle to their boss's head.

His audacious attack caught Sheriff Farley completely off guard, as Eric had expected it would, and getting to the man's gun should have been simple once he was down and pinned under Eric's weight. But the unexpected rifle shots that rang out from somewhere beyond the small cluster of men in the middle of the landfill came as a surprise to everyone there, including Eric. By the time he had a hand on the gun he was going for, Eric saw several of the sheriff's men fall as they were hit by what soon turned into intense incoming fire from several directions. Eric had no idea who the unseen attackers were, but it seemed apparent they'd set up a deliberate ambush. Whether they were specifically targeting Sheriff Farley's men or intended to kill everyone there, including him and Lenny, Eric had no idea. But there was nothing he could do at the moment because he had his hands full dealing with Sheriff Farley.

Even though Eric had gotten ahold of the grip of the man's sidearm momentarily, the sheriff had recovered from his initial shock at being taken down and was now working to prevent Eric from drawing the weapon from its holster. Farley appeared maybe ten years older than Eric, but he was strong and very fit and apparently skilled in the art of ground fighting, as Eric soon learned when he suddenly found himself in an iron-gripped choke hold. It happened in part because he was unable to both go for the man's gun and control both his arms at the same time, but also because Farley knew what he was doing. The Sheriff rolled Eric over as he completed his maneuver, pinning his hand between the butt of the pistol and the ground with the weight of both their bodies as he cut off Eric's air supply with his forearm. As he fought to regain his ability to breathe, Eric was aware of the ongoing onslaught of incoming fire. Some of the sheriff's men had managed to scramble for cover behind the nearby vehicles and some were returning fire with their rifles, aiming upward at the low clay bluffs surrounding the perimeter of the dump.

Eric fought to relieve the pressure on his windpipe as he saw one of Farley's men bravely coming to the aid of his boss despite the withering fire that had already cut down half their number. He recognized this man as one of the guards that had taken him at gunpoint at the farmhouse. The man was now pointing his rifle at Eric's face as he dropped to one knee to make sure his bullet didn't also strike the sheriff's torso when he pulled the trigger. Eric could do little to move out of the line of fire at that point, and he was certain that the muzzle of that M4 rifle, less than five yards away, would be the last thing he ever saw. But then there was a spray of red from behind that weapon as the man's head was struck with a rifle round before he could squeeze the trigger. Eric redoubled his efforts to break the vise-like choke hold that would soon put him out of commission, but then, just seconds later, he felt the sheriff's arm and entire body go limp. When he pulled away, drawing the man's pistol as he did, he saw that Sheriff Farley had likewise taken a rifle round to the head and was no longer a threat to anyone.

Eric knew he had to get to cover and do it fast, because he had no faith that those unknown shooters who were apparently quite good with their weapons of choice wouldn't make him their next target. The nearest option was the Humvee at the rear of the line, parked some thirty feet away. Two of the deputies were pinned down behind it, firing sporadically at the hillside and too preoccupied to notice that Eric was now in possession of Sheriff Farley's Glock. Eric took them out from where he was still flattened to the ground next to Farley's body. Then, he leapt to his feet, scooping up the M4 from the other fallen man on his way to the Humvee. As soon as he dropped low behind it, Eric glanced back out at Lenny and saw that he was still alive and apparently uninjured as he struggled to no avail against the coils of rope that bound him to that wooden post.

There was no way that Eric could get to him at the moment,

because even if the unknown shooters didn't open fire on him, there were still a few of the deputies left to contend with, and one of them had seen him just as he reached the cover of the Humvee. Eric had fired at him but missed as he dove behind the front bumper of one of the pickup trucks. To neutralize that threat, Eric crept forward alongside the Humvee until he could see under the truck's chassis between the wheels and target the man's feet and lower legs as he crouched there. Three quick rounds cut his base out from under him so that part of his torso was in view when he fell, and another rapid double-tap took him out of the fight for good.

Eric was pressed close to the side of the Humvee as he looked for more targets and tried to catch a glimpse of the unknown shooters. He could see that Lenny was still okay, and now that there were only maybe two or three of the sheriff's men left, the gunfire had tapered off significantly. It seemed to Eric that those men alone were the targets of the ambush, otherwise the shooters in their elevated and concealed positions could have just as easily taken out Eric before he got to cover, much less Lenny, tied up and helpless out in the open as he was. Eric wanted to go cut him loose, but he still couldn't be sure it was safe to do so until he heard a shout from atop the bluff during a lull in the shooting.

"ERIC! IT'S ME, JONATHAN!"

Jonathan? How in the hell could it be Jonathan up there, especially when Sheriff Farley said he and Willis and Trey had all been rounded up? And if they hadn't been, how would Jonathan know to come here, of all places, and who was up there with him, doing all that shooting?

There was no time to ask him that question directly though, because just as the kid shouted down to him, Eric heard an engine roar to life in one of the vehicles. It was one of the pickups that was parked nearest the front of the convoy, all of which were already turned around and lined up pointing out to the road. It seemed that at least one of the sheriff's men was trying to escape, and there was no way Eric could let that happen, because as far as he knew,

Beckman was still back at that compound, and Eric intended to get him out if he was alive. If any of these guys made it back there, that job would be far more difficult. Eric didn't know if Jonathan and those with him up there were aware that one of the trucks had started up though. There were still two other guys pinned down somewhere among the other vehicles, and that was probably where their attention was focused. Eric waved and pointed, hoping Jonathan would see him and understand what he was doing before he moved from the Humvee to the next truck where he'd shot the other guy trying to take cover in front of it. He would let Jonathan and those with him worry about the others they had pinned down. The truck he'd heard was already tearing out of the parked lineup now, fishtailing on the muddy road as its driver punched the accelerator.

Eric hopped in the cab of the other one and started it up. There was no time to back up and go around, so he drove right over the body of the man he'd shot and then punched it as he swerved through the mud around the other vehicles in his way. One of the sheriff's men who'd taken cover behind another SUV parked in the line stepped out and waved to flag him down. Eric saw the shock on his face when he realized it was one of the two prisoners, rather than another deputy behind the wheel, but he'd realized it too late to get out of the way. Eric swerved hard and smashed him between the side of the truck and the stationary SUV, then corrected his course to avoid ramming the parked Humvee at the front of the line. As soon as he was in the clear, Eric's sole focus was stopping the man who was attempting to escape in that other truck.

The rough road leading into the dump didn't deter the desperate driver from pushing to the point of disaster. Eric figured he knew the road well, as he'd probably been here many times with the sheriff and the others who participated in these ritualized murders. But though the man had a good head start and may have gotten away from a more cautious pursuer, Eric didn't let up until he was close enough to ram the other truck hard from behind. The road was too rough and too twisty to allow him to do any shooting while he was driving, even with the handgun he'd taken from the sheriff. Eric was going to have to do this another way, so as soon as he saw an opportunity in a place where the road widened slightly at the bottom of a hollow, he jammed the accelerator and pulled partway alongside. A sudden yank of the wheel brought the front quarter of his truck hard into the left rear quarter of the other, and both vehicles slid out of control and into the muddy ditches along either side.

Eric had been expecting the impact and sudden stop, of course, so he was braced and ready to jump clear as soon as his ride came to a stop. He saw the other guy scrambling to crawl out the passenger side door to exit the truck, so he rushed around the rear bumper and brought the front sight of the Glock into line with his center of mass. Eric was just about to pull the trigger when he decided to refrain. If he let this one live for now, he could prove useful in providing the information Eric needed to get Beckman out of that compound; along with Willis and Trey, if they were indeed there, as Sheriff Farley had said. Eric ordered the man to freeze and drop to the ground, and then he checked him for weapons and demanded answers.

"He's still alive as far as I know!" The man replied when asked about PFC Beckman. "I saw him late yesterday! Sheriff Farley wasn't planning to have him shot anyway, because he was going to use him as a hostage."

Before Eric could ask about other prisoners, he was interrupted by the sound of another vehicle approaching from the direction of the dump.

"Stay where you are and don't make a move, or you'll be the first one I shoot!" He told the man as he took cover beside the truck and shouldered the M4 he'd picked off the other guy.

When the vehicle he heard turned out to be one of the two Humvees parked back there at the dump, Eric focused his sights on the driver's side and waited. Whoever was behind the wheel had stopped immediately at the sight of the two wrecked pickups. But momentarily, a figure emerged from the passenger side, and it wasn't one of the sheriff's deputies, Eric confirmed at a glance. Instead, this man was dressed in hunting clothing and was carrying a scoped deer rifle. He moved quickly into the ditch to keep a low profile as soon as he left the Humvee. Eric didn't quite know what to make of him until the driver left the vehicle next, quickly taking cover in the other ditch on the opposite side of the road. Eric had no doubts at all about that one though. Even if he couldn't have recognized him by his slim build and thick, curly dark hair, the short lever-action rifle he carried was unmistakable.

"WILLIS!" Eric shouted.

SEVENTEEN

WILLIS INTRODUCED HIS COMPANION WHEN THE TWO OF them made their way down the road to where Eric was keeping an eye on his new prisoner.

"You made me miss my first shot!" Eddie Poole told him, after he and Eric shook hands. "What were you thinking, jumping the sheriff like that all by yourself? They would have killed you for sure if we hadn't been there, and you didn't know that we were!"

"I was thinking that at that point, I had nothing to lose," Eric said. "If that sheriff was willing to put a young man in front of a firing squad for no other crime than carrying a weapon, then I figured I'd be facing the same fate whether it was today, tomorrow or the next day. I thought there was a slim chance that by putting a gun to his head, I could negotiate an understanding with his followers. After all, I knew they had to hold the man in high regard to obey the kinds of orders he was giving. But you're right, I had no idea that Lenny and I would have outside help; especially not in the form of a coordinated ambush like you guys pulled off. That was great work!"

"You can thank Eddie for every bit of it!" Willis said. "We

would have never found this place without him, especially not this soon."

Eric said he wanted to hear all about it, but first, they had to get PFC Beckman out of that compound. Now that he knew Sheriff Farley had been bluffing when he told Eric he'd detained the other three men of his team; Beckman was the only remaining concern here. Eric knew Willis didn't particularly like the man, and probably blamed him for all that had happened since they met him, but Eric was still convinced Beckman's intentions were good.

"We're still going to need his help to accomplish what we came here for, and it sounds to me like that Colonel Rencher he spoke of is just the man I need to meet."

"Well, if you're gonna try and get him out, it'll be a lot easier now than it would have been," Eddie said, when Willis told Eric that Eddie had said rescuing them from the compound was pretty much impossible. "With Sheriff Farley and nine of his men at the dump dead, plus this guy here out of action and no telling how many of the rest down there in the woods looking for me besides the five we killed last night, the number still on duty at the headquarters is probably as low as it'll ever be."

Eric had told Eddie that the convoy had detoured back to the south this morning after a long wait near the gate. He figured Sheriff Farley must have gotten a radio call about something of interest down there, just as they were pulling out. At the time, Eric thought Jonathan, Willis and Trey had already been captured, because that's what the sheriff had told him. When they turned onto the same gravel road that led to the farmhouse they'd raided yesterday and stopped to examine an old pickup truck that was stuck in a ditch and riddled with bullet holes, Eric assumed it had some connection to that raid. But now he knew the truck belonged to Eddie Poole and that the sheriff's men were still searching for him and Eric's three companions. Eric smiled at the thought of their confusion this morning when the sheriff's convoy pulled up to the scene of last night's gunfight. According to Eddie, the sheriff knew the truck well, and would not have forgotten what he'd done to the owner's brother. Seeing the evidence that Eddie had been in a violent encounter sometime during the previous night and knowing he was missing two of his vehicles and five of his men must have been perplexing for the sheriff. Now he had not only the problem of finding the three mysterious members of Eric's team that PFC Beckman had told him about, but also a local backwoodsman that was hellbent on revenge and possibly had something to do with his missing men. Farley would have thrown a lot of resources at the problem, Eric was sure, so Eddie was probably right. *The time to go get Beckman was now!*

"Do we really need him?" Eddie asked, nodding at Eric's prisoner, who was the only surviving member of the sheriff's execution detail.

"Possibly. He'll help us if he wants to live, because if he doesn't, he'll die like the rest of them."

"I'll go back and tell Jonathan and Trey that you caught him before he could get away," Willis said. "They've probably got Lenny cut loose and are already heading this way now."

"Don't just pick them up in the one Humvee," Eric said. "If the other vehicles are drivable, bring them too if you can. Oh, and one other thing: grab that cowboy hat the sheriff was wearing! I'm thinking we'll just drive right in there like the sheriff and his men would if they were returning to base!"

As they waited on Willis and the others to return, Eddie gave Eric a brief account of why he held such a grudge against Sheriff Farley. His only brother had been murdered for nothing more serious than violating a curfew the sheriff had imposed right around the time he began restricting firearms and free movement in his greatly expanded jurisdiction. Kirby hadn't even been carrying a gun at the time, but he'd gotten into a drunken fight in town with two other men that were, and all three were arrested because they were out on the street after dark. Eddie figured Kirby had probably attempted to resist the arrest as well, because he knew his brother, but anyone would have in that circumstance, because they all knew the penalty. Sheriff Farley rarely made exceptions once he enacted new decrees, and all three of them suffered the same punishment, which was designed to serve as a warning for the rest of the local population. The rogue sheriff had gotten bolder and more merciless with each passing month, but today he got the payback he'd long had coming. After hearing his story, Eric was glad Eddie Poole got his vengeance, and he owed him his gratitude, because in the process, he'd saved both Lenny and Eric from certain death, as well as reunited his team. Eddied just shrugged it off and said he was glad to help, and that he was ready to kill even more of the bastards that followed Sheriff Farley's orders. As it turned out, he got his next opportunity much sooner than he expected.

When they heard the sound of vehicles approaching from over the hill again, Eric saw that Willis was driving the same Humvee as before and the two SUVs and the other Humvee were following, which had to mean that Jonathan, Trey and Lenny were all accounted for and able to drive. Having four of the six vehicles was great, because it meant they could leave both of the pickups where they were and not waste time pulling them out of the mud. But in the brief moment that Eric and Eddie were distracted by the approaching vehicles, Eric's prisoner decided to seize the opportunity to leap to his feet and bolt for the woods.

Eric turned at the sound of him crashing into the brush and ordered him to stop, but the fleeing man ignored him, no doubt counting on Eric's desire to keep him alive as a useful hostage and hoping he wouldn't be shot in the back. What he didn't know though, was that Eddie Poole had no such desire. Eric hadn't considered this at first, because Eddie didn't say a word as Eric repeated his shouted command once again, ordering the running man to halt. When his words had no effect and the fellow continued on, busting through the waist-high brush and young pines of the long-neglected cutover, Eric hopped across the narrow ditch to take off after him. But he'd barely gotten started before he was stopped short by the thunderous crash of a rifle report from just a few feet behind him. The running man pitched forward into the brush carried by his momentum into a tumble, and Eric turned to see Eddie standing there with his deer rifle still shouldered as he watched through the scope for any indication his target might get up and run again.

"What in the hell did you do that for?" Eric asked, knowing the answer before he did. Eric knew the man was among the five shooters on Sheriff Farley's firing squad. Eddie knew it too, so he didn't need an excuse to kill him, but his escape attempt gave him a good one and apparently, that was all the explanation he felt he owed Eric.

"It'd be a waste of time for you to run him down, and we don't need him anyway. I didn't trust that he wouldn't try to pull something once we got to that gate, even if we had him at gunpoint. And besides, I know he was one of the sons of bitches that shot Kirby because he was in the line-up getting ready to shoot your friend, Lenny!"

Eric didn't argue. Forcing a hostage to comply in a situation like the one they would soon get into was always iffy anyway, and the man's value to them was limited after Eric had already questioned him. Eddie had verified with his riflescope that the man was down for good when Eric asked him, and so the matter was dropped. When Willis and the rest of Eric's team pulled up and stopped the four vehicles, Eric walked over to check on Lenny. He was still a bit shaken up from his experience in front of the firing squad, of course, but he was unhurt and ready to get into the action against those responsible.

"I don't know why you wanted it, but I brought that cowboy hat you asked for," Willis said.

"I was going to have our man that tried to get away in the pickup truck wear it," Eric said. "I'd planned to have him drive up to the gate with it on, so that from a distance it might fool the guards into thinking their sheriff was behind the wheel. But since he's no longer with us, I guess I'll wear it myself." Eric took the hat from Willis and put it on, adjusting the brim so that it was low enough to shade the details of his face. "What do you think?"

"I think it might fool them from a quarter mile away, but I wouldn't bet on it working any closer."

"That's good enough, considering we've got quite the sniper with us now." Eric nodded at Eddie, then laid out a revised version of his original plan to take out those guards and then proceed onto the property and approach the compound. Eddie liked the plan and said he could do his part if they did theirs. Anything that would give him an opportunity to put more of Sheriff Farley's men into his crosshairs was okay by him.

"You're good with that rifle, I'll give you that," Jonathan said to Eddie. "But I want to know what in the hell took you so long to shoot Sheriff Farley! I don't understand it, because you had a wide-open shot when he was just standing there before Eric took him down. I didn't think you were ever gonna do it and I was about to shoot him myself. I thought he was going to give the order for that firing squad to shoot Lenny while we were all waiting on you to pull the damned trigger!

"Yeah, I'm sorry about that. I thought it would be easy too, but I guess I let my emotions get the best of me. I've been dreaming about an opportunity like that ever since I knew what Sheriff Farley did to Kirby. But that was the first time I'd been that close to him since it happened, and I was so upset and pissed off and full of hate all at the same time, I guess it just messed me up. The first time I put my crosshairs on his face I was shaking so bad I couldn't keep a lock on him. I was afraid I'd miss and blow the whole ambush! I had to catch my breath and try to calm down. I was just about to get there when Eric jumped him. I'd already half-squeezed the trigger and when it happened, I jerked it on that one round without thinking. I knew I missed as soon as I sent it, but seeing Eric wrestling with him for that pistol snapped me right out of my funk. When he had him in that choke hold, I was getting ready to shoot again until I noticed that other guy run up and take aim at Eric. So, I had to shoot him first and then wait until I had a clear shot at Farley. Sorry to cause all of you so much stress, but it was the best I could do at the time!"

"Better late than never!" Eric said. "It was still good shooting, and I expect you to do more of the same. Now, if you guys are all ready, let's go get Beckman out of there!"

Eric had intended to deal with the two gate guards up close and personal, using the hostage they would have recognized as a distraction to get them into that sort of range. But now, he thought the better plan was to let Eddie take care of them from a distance while the rest of the team kept them distracted enough that they wouldn't realize they'd become his targets.

Eric climbed into the lead Humvee wearing Sheriff Farley's hat, as he knew it would be visible from a distance and add to the illusion of normalcy when the convoy approached the gate. Eric doubted the guards would be overly concerned about the two missing pickups, as it was feasible the sheriff may have diverted them elsewhere, or they were otherwise delayed in returning with the others. Willis was riding shotgun with him, while Jonathan and Trey followed in the two SUVs, and Lenny brought up the rear in the other Humvee, with Eddie riding with him.

After they pulled out onto the paved road and made their way south, Eric maintained a slow, but steady pace until they rounded the last bend and came into view of the gate. The distance from there to the small guardhouse was about 200 yards, which was plenty far enough to make it difficult to discern why the last Humvee in line was pulling over to the shoulder and coming to a stop. Eddie would have time to prepare for his first shot while the rest of the vehicles proceeded on ahead. And just as Eric hoped they would, the guards spotted the approaching small convoy and stepped out into the open to wait for them. Eric was sure they were the same two men that had been posted at the gate earlier, when he and Lenny were first taken out that way in the sheriff's entourage.

Both were dressed in the same olive-drab uniforms that all but Farley's top officers wore, and these two were also wearing helmets and rifle plates. As they waited to greet the returning convoy, the guards had their weapons in hand, but appeared relaxed and unconcerned anything may be wrong. Eric was approaching at a steady ten miles per hour and was only a few vehicle lengths out when one of the two men suddenly collapsed in his tracks without warning, leaving his companion momentarily frozen where he stood splattered with the fallen man's blood.

What a perfect face shot! Eric smiled, as Willis, who had his short 30-30 in hand and ready to bring into action, immediately shouldered the weapon and put the second guard down with one of his 190-grain Buffalo Bore hog hunting rounds that appeared to strike him in the center of his throat, just above the protection of his front plate. The guy had taken too long to process the unfathomable thing that had just happened to his buddy, and in his moment of hesitation, he'd met the same fate. These backwoods hunters from Louisiana and Mississippi could put some of the best operators Eric had worked with to shame, and they were making this almost too easy, or so it seemed. But getting past that gate was just the beginning. Eric had no idea what they'd be up against getting Beckman out of the compound, but he knew that if they were going to succeed, they had to act now while they still had the advantage of surprise. And the only reason they had that advantage was because they'd given none of the sheriff's men a chance to grab a radio mic. Eric intended to keep it that way, and once all the vehicles were inside, he took the handheld clipped to one of the dead guard's vest and then he and Willis and Jonathan and Trey dragged the two bodies out of sight into the bushes.

EIGHTEEN

PFC Beckman turned instinctively to the direction of the door on the other side of the room at the sudden sound of gunshots that seemed to come from just outside the building. The lone officer who'd been in there questioning him yet again leapt up from the bench behind the table and yanked it open to look out into the hallway. The sudden interruption was as much a surprise to him as it was to Beckman, who had no idea what was going on out there but recognized an opportunity when he saw it.

Until that moment, everything in his world was going downhill now that he was in the hands of these men whose intent he was finally beginning to grasp. After this morning's interrogation, Beckman understood that Lieutenant Pickett, this same man standing with his back to him in that doorway, and the same man who'd led the assault on that civilian-occupied farmhouse, was also responsible for the ambush and murder of his squad and the crew of their helicopter! Pickett had told him point blank that he and his assault team had done it, and he'd justified it by claiming that federal troops were targeting civilians in Sheriff Farley's jurisdiction. That was ludicrous of course, as the Army didn't consider the terrorists and river pirates attacking vessels on the Mississippi to be anything less than enemy combatants. In no instance did the members of Beckman's 3rd Battalion engage unarmed and peaceful civilians.

But this officer and the sheriff he worked for insisted they had and claimed they were acting in defense of their citizens when in reality, they'd engaged in an act of war against the same nation they'd both sworn an oath to defend. Both men claimed to have served tours of duty in foreign wars in the service of that nation, yet now they were openly attacking soldiers still serving active duty.

It was mind-boggling to Beckman, but after seeing this property where the sheriff lived and based his operation, and hearing Lieutenant Pickett brag about their heavy-handed enforcement of law and order in their jurisdiction, he understood that all these men wanted was wealth and power. Most of that wealth they'd acquired was in the form of thousands of acres of private lands they'd commandeered in exchange for the questionable security they were providing the local population. And the power to which they'd ascended and endeavored to keep came through intimidation of that same population. But while fear and intimidation where tools that worked for now, Beckman failed to see how they expected to retain all that newfound wealth and power given the ever-deteriorating situation around them. They'd dismissed the intel Beckman relayed to them regarding Eric's report of the invasion happening west of the river. And somehow, they were in abject denial of the fact that if the rest of the country didn't pull out of this downward spiral of dissolution and destruction, all their ill-gotten gains would be of little use.

After learning the truth of what happened to his friends and fellow squad members, PFC Beckman wanted nothing more than to kill the man who led that ambush, and this unexpected distraction presented an opportunity he wouldn't have dreamed he'd ever get just moments before. The lieutenant had told him when he first entered the room that Lenny, the younger of the two men taken into custody with Beckman yesterday, had already been taken out at dawn to face Sheriff Farley's firing squad.

"Your Navy SEAL buddy had the honor of being the witness today. But you'll get to watch when it's his turn," Lieutenant Pickett had said.

"You won't get away with this," Beckman replied. "Did you really think you could destroy an Army helicopter and kill the crew and a whole squad of Special Forces soldiers without repercussions? Colonel Rencher has probably already sent combat search and rescue aircraft out to overfly the river and look for that missing Black Hawk. It'll be easy to spot, sitting there in plain view on that wide-open sandbar. And as soon as it's confirmed, he'll throw everything he's got this way and you and your sheriff will have nowhere to hide."

Lieutenant Pickett had just laughed it off, saying he knew they didn't have the resources to do a damned thing about finding one missing helicopter, much less hunting down those responsible. It would be written off as a win for the insurgents, which was just another way to avoid admitting they didn't even know who their enemy was. Beckman knew he was mostly right, but didn't show it in his reaction, of course. At best, Colonel Rencher would send a fixed-wing aircraft out to have a look. If the crew spotted the wreckage, which was quite likely, given the location right there on the river, then he would perhaps send out one of the other two Black Hawks they had at Camp Hurley. But the most another helicopter crew could do was land there and assess the aftermath of the attack. They would be able to account for every man aboard that flight but one, and then they'd recover the bodies and return with their report. This location was simply too far away to send sufficient resources to follow up on it and hunt down those responsible, because at the moment, the colonel had his hands full just maintaining control of the coastal areas closer to home. So, Lieutenant Pickett was right to assume he wouldn't be punished, but that was before this totally unexpected eruption of gunfire just outside cut short their conversation.

Beckman had no idea why the shooting started or who might be involved, but an open door and the lieutenant standing there with his back to him presented a temptation too enticing to resist. He already knew there was no way out of here that would end well for him, because he was the only survivor of the ambush on that sandbar. Now that he knew the truth about what had happened, they would never let him return to his battalion with that information, even if they planned to use him as a hostage somehow to make more demands. Beckman refused to allow himself to be dragged in front of a firing squad, so he decided then and there that if he was going to be shot, then it would be in battle and not as the victim of an execution.

He was on his feet as soon as Pickett had his head out the door. Beckman knew he had to act fast, because the man would either turn and come back inside the room or exit completely and lock the door behind him. There was no time to go around the end of the long table, so he went over it, stepping up first to the bench and then onto the top, from which he literally dove onto the lieutenant's back, driving him out into the hallway through the three-foot-wide opening.

Lieutenant Pickett never saw it coming, of course, and Beckman's weight and momentum carried him hard to the floor. Beckman heard the loud thump as the man's head bounced upon impact with the smooth concrete. Somehow, he was still conscious, but not for long, after Beckman pulled himself up so that he was sitting astraddle the man's back and could slam his head into the floor again, using his upper body weight behind a two-handed grip.

Beckman glanced both ways in the hall as he drew Pickett's pistol from its holster and momentarily ducked back into the doorway behind him. The shooting outside was still going on, but from the sound of it, someone was returning fire from within the front of the building with a rifle. Beckman still had no idea who could have launched such a bold attack on the sheriff's headquarters like that, but he didn't care. Whoever it was, they were the enemy of his enemy and that was reason enough to help them.

Beckman checked that the Colt M1911 had a full magazine, and that a round was chambered, then he slipped quietly down the hallway towards the entrance, pressing close to one wall as he advanced. When he reached the end of the corridor, where it opened out into what was essentially a lobby area between the sheriff's office and some other administrative offices, Beckman saw the shooter prone on the floor behind the shattered glass of one of the front windows. Taking advantage of the two-foot-high brick and concrete wall below the windowsill, the green BDU-clad deputy was firing sporadically with an AR-15 in the direction of the front gate. Beckman could see two of his dead associates sprawled on the gravel parking lot outside. It appeared this one man was the last defender holding out against whoever had attacked the place, and he had no idea that he now had an enemy behind him as well. Beckman braced his left forearm against the corner of the wall and used it to steady his right-hand pistol grip. He knew his first round struck the man directly in his upper torso as soon as he fired, and that a hit like that from the .45 ACP would no doubt do the job, but he moved the front sight to his target's head anyway and squeezed off an anchoring shot just to be sure. There was no indication that any other defenders remained in the building, and Becket still couldn't see who the attackers were, so he decided his best option was to retreat and try to find another way out. When he passed the still unconscious and maybe already dead Lieutenant Pickett on the way back down the hall, PFC Beckman shot him in the back of the head with his on pistol.

"That's for my buddies, Henderson, and Jacobs, and for Sergeant McHenry and all the rest of the men of my squad, you traitor!"

∽

Eric knew the distance from the front gate to the headquarters compound on Sheriff Farley's property was great enough that the two rifle reports that killed the guards wouldn't likely be heard. And even if someone was nearer to the front of the property and did hear them, the sight of the four vehicles returning at a relaxed and normal speed would dispel any concerns those sounds may have raised. The tactic of letting Lenny drive for Eddie so that he could stop some distance back and use his rifle had worked so well that Eric saw no reason not to use it again. Eddie could take his first shot while still seated in the Humvee and if necessary, could then bail out to get in a better position for any possible follow-ups.

When they passed the horse corrals and rodeo arena, Eric didn't see the young woman from yesterday or anyone else with the animals, but up on the hill on the front porch of the palatial ranch house, a different woman turned and waved at them as the four vehicles went by.

"Probably Sheriff Farley's wife," Willis said.

"Nope, not a chance," Eric corrected him. "But she could be his *widow!*"

Eric wondered if any of the deputies were perhaps posted up there at the house to provide security for the sheriff's family, but he figured probably not, considering the gate guards and the proximity of the rifle range and headquarters. When he drove around the last bend and into view of the compound, Eric adjusted the brim of the sheriff's hat low on his forehead and eased on up to the gate, with the two SUVs following close behind. One man with a rifle was standing there waiting to greet them, as was a large mixed-breed dog that ran up to the wire fence and began barking. As Eric slowly closed the gap, it seemed obvious that the dog had figured out something wasn't right, and he thought he could see confusion on the man's face too as he squinted to better see through the windshield of the lead Humvee. Whether he realized the man in the cowboy hat wasn't Sheriff Farley before Eddie's bullet struck him in the forehead, Eric didn't know, but if he did, he'd had no time to sound the alarm. Instead, the report of that rifle was the first warning those inside had, and by the time the first of them emerged from the building, Eric and the rest of his team had exited the vehicles and dropped to prone positions beside the roadway to engage them in a direct offensive. The initial exchange resulted in three of those men from inside the headquarters getting cut down before they realized the nature of the attack. The dog broke and ran for cover behind the vehicles that were parked to one side of the building, and Eric was relieved to see it because he didn't want to have to shoot it. Their biggest problem now seemed to be the one rifleman that was still inside and returning fire from his position low under one of the front windows. He would have to be eliminated before they could go in and clear the building and search for Beckman.

But Eric and his companions couldn't get a clear shot at him from where they were, so he asked Jonathan if he'd go with him in an attempt to circle around back to look for another way in. Willis and Trey kept the shooter occupied while they moved, and Lenny and Eddie remained out there where they had stopped the Humvee farther out, so they could watch the road for anyone else returning to the compound. But by the time Eric and Jonathan found a way inside the fence and reached the back of the building, the gunfire out front had stopped. The two of them were on either side of the single metal door they found in the rear, whispering back and forth about the possibility of breaching it, when they heard the sound of a deadbolt rolling back and then saw the doorknob turn. Eric was on the side with the knob, so he motioned to Jonathan to drop low to his knees so as to get out of his line of fire as he shouldered his rifle to shoot whoever emerged from point blank range. But the man that cautiously stuck his head out only to find himself looking into the barrel of Eric's M4, wasn't one of Sheriff Farley's men at all. Instead, it was Private First Class Robert Beckman, alive and unhurt, attempting to slip out the back of the building while carrying the pistol that he told Eric and Jonathan he'd used to take out that last shooter at the front window.

~

Eric, Jonathan and Beckman did a sweep of the building to check that there were no more of the sheriff's men hiding out inside. In the process of clearing it, they came across their confiscated gear in one of the offices: the M4s and handguns Eric and Lenny had been carrying, along with Beckman's combat knife and Eric's custom blade and the night vision monocular that had come in handy so many times.

"What now?" Jonathan asked. "Do we wait here and get the rest of them when they come back, or haul ass for that Camp McCall place we were gonna walk to?"

While Eric would have preferred to remain there long enough to set up an ambush for the sheriff's other returning men, he decided it was too risky. They didn't know who else was in the house besides the woman they'd seen on the way in, and they had no way of knowing whether the men out looking for Eddie Poole and the three men Beckman had told them about would return all at once or in staggered groups. It was also possible there was a two-way radio station in the house and that whoever was up there could have already used it to report all the gunshots they heard from the direction of the compound. The last thing Eric wanted was to get pinned down here in a protracted firefight. They had an opportunity to getaway clean and they had vehicles available in which to do it, so he told Jonathan what he had in mind.

"Neither. We'll head back south down to where Eddie lives and when we do, we'll take the sheriff's Humvee and one of the better trucks. Any of his men we encounter will be just as clueless as these were until it's too late to realize their mistake. We'll take out any we can along the way, because they all deserve the same fate, but like Eddie says, without Farley and his top deputies, this little private army is finished. Once the locals realize he's dead, and Eddie plans to spread the word, they'll take matters into their own hands and hunt down the rest. But we can't let Eddie go home alone, knowing there's at least a dozen of those guys looking for him. And while we're down there in that neck of the woods, I want to meet Michael Searcy, and thank him for leading you guys to that Claude Busby fellow's house. And then I want to thank Mr. Busby for introducing you to Eddie. Beckman and Lenny and I wouldn't have gotten out of this one on our own, and we all know it. While we're down there, we'll get our rucks from where you hid them on the Searcy place. If Michael wants some of his clothes or other things from that house, we'll get those for him too; it's the least we can do.

"Beckman wants to go back to that sandbar and see if there's any evidence Colonel Rencher sent one of the other Black Hawks out there to recover those troops. If not, there's enough of us that we can bury them and then we'll head directly for Camp Hurley. It's a lot farther than Camp McCall, but we know it's operational and that it's the home of Beckman's unit. With the sheriff's vehicles, we've got solid transportation and there's plenty of fuel here to top off the tanks and auxiliaries before we go. Now that we know who ambushed Beckman's squad and can report to Colonel Rencher that they've been eliminated, I may be able to get his attention regarding the bigger problems he's got coming from the west."

FERAL NATION
TENACITY

SCOTT B. WILLIAMS

ONE

Matt Griggs shook off the heavy blow that almost knocked him unconscious as he pushed himself up to his hands and knees from the muddy, leaf littered ground upon which he'd fallen. The low murmur of whispered comments and chuckles among the other recruits compounded his humiliation. Griggs wanted to kill Keith Branson then and there, but he knew that any attempt to do so, even if he had the ability, would be futile. Branson had the full support of nearly all the other twenty-two men there, and he had the backup of the other two trainers, his father, Bart Branson, and another older man named Sam Necaise, both of whom carried rifles as they stood there watching the spectacle alongside the recruits.

That final vicious punch was the third time Keith Branson had effortlessly put him down hard after Griggs took his first swing at the man, and by now, Griggs admitted he'd had enough. Ignoring all the eyes that he knew were locked upon him, watching to see what he would do next, Griggs staggered the rest of the way to his feet and moved to the perimeter of the circle of onlookers. The men in his path stepped aside, and Griggs walked a short distance away to stare into the surrounding empty woods as he fumed.

"Anyone else?" Griggs heard Branson demand of the group. "Anyone else think they've got better ideas than I do about how to run this outfit? Anyone else man enough to step up here and prove it? If so, speak up now! If not, then shut up and fall back in line!"

Griggs didn't expect anyone to make a move, and they didn't. Some of the other guys had grumbled and complained, but none had the nerve to call Branson out the way Griggs had. They just followed orders like it was their only option and went right back to running the drills Branson had them working on out there in the expanse of bottomland hardwoods that bordered the nearby bayou. Griggs hated this environment almost as much as he hated Keith Branson. He hated the mud and stench of the swamp even more than he'd hated the scorching deserts in which he'd served most of his time in the Army. Matt Griggs was no stranger to the woods, but he was from the northwestern corner of Georgia, a region where the higher elevations at the southern end of the Appalachians made the air cool and refreshing, even in the summer. On those wooded slopes, the ground was rocky and solid beneath one's feet, and the streams ran cold and clear, in stark contrast to the stagnant brown sloughs of this river-bottom lowland that stank of rotting vegetation, dead fish and mud.

Griggs missed those rugged hills and had figured all along that if he could make his way back there, he'd be a lot better off there than just about anywhere else he could think of in this country gone mad. He'd been attempting to do exactly that when he got caught up in all the chaos after finding himself stranded in Houston when it became impossible to get a flight back to Atlanta the moment things took a sharp turn for the worse. That was so many months ago it seemed like another life to him now though. Griggs still wasn't sure how he would get to Georgia, but after he and most of the other men here with him were liberated from that C.R.I. work camp and talked into coming here, he knew the folks running this militia weren't going to help him do it. Keith Branson and his cohorts were dug in here in the

Atchafalaya Basin, and it was obvious they weren't planning to leave.

From what he gathered, they had quite a few more people and considerable resources in the form of boats, weapons, and other supplies at some secret base camp nearby they called *Sierra Zulu*. Griggs didn't know exactly where this hideout was located, because none of the new recruits were allowed to go there. The handful of refugees from the work camp that were taken there were all women and children that had nowhere else to go. But Griggs and those here with him hadn't seen any of them since. Those like him, who volunteered to join the militia, were mostly unattached, or were at least separated by circumstance from the families they'd had before. Some of the detainees freed from that camp still had homes or family holding out in the region, and most of those folks chose to leave and go back to them, despite the warnings from Branson and the other leaders that it was a bad idea. While Griggs acknowledged that maybe that was true, after what he'd seen here, he thought being a part of this outfit was a far worse idea, and he had already made his decision to leave even before this most recent confrontation with Keith Branson today. It wasn't their first dispute, but it was the first time one of their clashes had come to blows, and for Griggs, it was the final straw.

He was fed up and thoroughly done with this situation and there was no way he would stay there and put up with more of what he considered to be not only idiocy, but downright treason. He was confident of the illegitimacy of this so-called militia that Keith Branson, along with his brother, Eric and his father, Bart, had put together. While all three men were allegedly military veterans with extensive combat experience, as far as Griggs was concerned, they were also traitors to the nation that he himself had once served with honor.

It seemed to him that the Bransons and their co-conspirators were more interested in establishing control of the region for their own interests, despite what they told the new recruits to the contrary. To Griggs, that made them little different from the mercenaries working for the private contracting organization into whose hands he and his companions had fallen before. While this new 'militia' that rescued them hadn't confined them or forced them to do hard labor the way the C.R.I. thugs had, they *had* expected them to fall in line for rigorous training and follow orders as if they were new conscripts that just landed in boot camp. And through it all, Branson and the others with him were talking of the dangerous operations in which they would soon be expected to participate—operations against forces that were far stronger and far better equipped than they could ever hope to be out here, hiding out in this swampy backwater.

Like the rest of the men there, Griggs was grateful to be away from that C.R.I. camp, and grateful to be armed and provided ammunition, provisions and the other basic essentials. He'd had high hopes for the entire enterprise at first, because he was as eager for revenge against those mercs that had detained them as the next man. But since they'd relocated here and got the training camp and routine established, Griggs quickly figured out he was going to have trouble fitting in. For one thing, Griggs felt like he knew as much or more about military operations as any of these three in charge now. He'd served in the U.S. Army for four years as a combat engineer, working his way up from the bottom to the rank of specialist. Moreover, most of those years were spent on deployments to the Middle East, where he'd seen his share of real combat against a determined enemy. It didn't sit well to be taking orders from a couple of Marines, one of which hadn't worn the uniform since the early 1970s, and the other that same man's son who was a deputy here after doing his own short time overseas. The third guy working with them as an instructor was an old local backwoodsman named Sam Necaise, who had no military experience at all.

But worse still was the former Navy guy they all deferred to for everything. The son of the old Vietnam vet and brother of the deputy, Eric Branson was the one who'd decided to organize a militia in the first place, and not just for defensive purposes, but to actually engage the enemy on missions outside the isolated Atchafalaya River Basin. Eric was in charge of it all because he was supposedly a former Navy SEAL—*weren't they all?* Griggs had seen little of him since their rescue though, because not long after the training camp was established, the Navy guy had left on some mission none of the recruits were privy to. In his absence, Deputy Keith Branson and his old man, Bart, were calling the shots.

Now the two of them were claiming that the same private military company that had been running that detention camp was working in conjunction with remnants of actual Army National Guard units! They claimed that those units were no longer serving the United States they'd sworn to defend, but Griggs didn't buy it. He didn't believe it possible for entire garrisons of soldiers sworn to serve their country to be subverted or coerced into treason, no matter what these two jarheads and the other locals fighting with them claimed to have seen. Griggs knew individuals might do such a thing, but all the enlisted men and NCOs, as well as *their* superiors too? *How was he supposed to believe that, coming from these two Marines that were actively discussing and planning operations against uniformed troops?*

They were seriously preparing the recruits to set up ambushes and sniper hides, telling them that these rogue troops would be returning in larger numbers to the area and that it was imperative to go on the offense against them before they could establish a foothold in the river basin. Griggs understood how most of the civilian men among the recruits could be persuaded by this. They'd been displaced and mistreated by men in uniform and were ready to lash out at whoever they thought was responsible. But Griggs wasn't having any part of it! He couldn't imagine firing on soldiers wearing the same uniform he wore when he served in the Army. That was just madness, and besides, they wouldn't stand a chance of success anyway, whether those soldiers were the good guys or the bad.

Griggs was determined to get away from it before any of those plans came to fruition, but he knew he couldn't leave immediately that afternoon. He had planning to do, and besides, he didn't intend to go alone. There was one other man in their small group that somewhat saw things the same way he did, and Griggs knew he wasn't among those cracking jokes or suppressing laughter while watching him take that beating from Keith Branson. That one man was named Boyd Moreau, and after talking it over with him quietly that evening after they returned to camp, Griggs was certain Moreau would be willing to go with him when the time came.

"I'm with you on leaving. I want to get away from this mess too," Moreau said, "but the thing I'm most concerned about is whether we'll ever find anyone out there we can trust."

"Don't worry about that," Griggs assured him. "With my background in the Army, I'll be able to figure out who's who when the time comes. It's not hard to tell the difference between jokers like these guys running the show here and the real deal."

"What if there aren't any that are the real deal, though? What if they never send any more actual military troops to this area? If it's like Branson says it is, that mercenary outfit already controls everywhere west and north of here. You know that's why his brother went east to look for help. Maybe we should go that way too."

"I don't think so, even though I'll have to go east eventually to get back to my hometown. Going that way right now isn't feasible. It's too far, and it involves crossing the Mississippi River. There's no bridge anywhere near this area, so we'd have to steal one of the boats, and if we did that, it'd be easier for them to come looking for us than if we just bug out of here on foot.

"Besides, there are no military bases that I know of near the river over there anyway and even if there were, there's no way to know if they are still operational, considering the situation. I think we're better off going up there to that outpost where we know there were soldiers, whether Branson thinks they were legit or not. If they really killed as many of those men as he says they did and they *were* legit, I can guarantee you it won't be long before more troops come rolling in there to investigate and figure out why they lost contact with them! Things may be chaotic right now, but all wars are chaos, and that's what they're trained to deal with."

Griggs had expected it would take a bit of convincing to get Moreau to see his reasoning. He was just glad there was at least one man among the recruits that was open to considering what he had to say. He would go alone if he had to, but it was much better to have a companion. Two men could keep watch better than one, and when they did encounter the authorities, the two of them could vouch for each other, backing up each other's stories if they were subjected to interrogation, which Griggs figured was probable.

While it was true that Moreau's concerns were valid, Griggs didn't believe this C.R.I. outfit controlled as much territory as Branson claimed. He didn't doubt they'd set their sights on taking over this part of Louisiana, because he'd already seen evidence of that. They'd done pretty well at rounding up people and putting them in those detention camps, but Griggs knew it couldn't last long. The real military would be coming in to set things straight. He was sure that the only reason they hadn't yet was because they had their hands full everywhere else at the moment and hadn't been able to spare the resources to secure this region yet. And the main reason they had their hands so full was that people exactly like Keith Branson and his gang of outlaws were taking the law into their own hands and making up new laws as they went along. Griggs didn't know if reporting what they knew would do much good right now, but he knew that eventually, men like Keith Branson would be rounded up and brought to justice. And he had to convince Moreau that he didn't want to be there among them when it happened, which proved simple enough.

"The way things have been in this situation; I wouldn't be surprised to see them line all these guys up and execute them on the spot. That includes the leaders and their followers. The last thing you want to do is get caught with a bunch of insurgents like them in a time of war. They will be considered enemy combatants in the field, and POWs if taken captive. But this isn't a normal war and any NCO in this situation won't have the time or resources to handle them, as a group or on a case-by-case basis. They'll be interrogated to gain any intel that can be extracted from them to help round up their associates, and then they'll be taken care of then and there."

Griggs knew Moreau was convinced once he put it to him like that.

"Look, you'll be serving your country by turning your back on this band of terrorists. I'd be willing to bet we'll both get rewarded for any intel we can provide on these guys. We'll get protection and a place to go, if nothing else."

"We still don't know where Branson and the rest go every time they leave here, though. Any soldiers we report to are going to want to know that."

"We won't get it by hanging around here any longer either, and you know it. But you also know it can't be far from here. You said it yourself, that you figure it's somewhere in the maze of bayous and canals to the southeast, and we know from hearing their boat motor every day that they're coming and going from downriver. We don't need the exact location. We can provide them enough to go on, and it'll be easy enough for them to hunt them down."

Moreau's familiarity with the local area was another tremendous advantage to bringing him along. Moreau had told him he'd spent his childhood in Morgan City, which was located on the Atchafalaya some distance to the south, and he had spent a lot of time on the river back in those days. He knew many parts of the vast swamp and he knew something of the local culture even though he'd hardly been back in his adult life, and it was just an unfortunate circumstance that left him stranded there a few months prior.

When it was settled that Moreau would for sure go with him, the two of them quickly made a plan that would enable a smooth exit. Since no one among the recruits had seniority over the others, Keith Branson himself made the assignments for the night watch and other duties they would carry out after he and the other trainers left each day. Griggs' challenge to Branson's authority had put him on bad footing, of course, so he wasn't scheduled for sentry duty anytime soon, but Moreau was, and that would work well in their favor.

Griggs knew they had to quickly put some distance between themselves and the militia camp before Branson returned the next day for training, or there was a chance he and the other men would come after them. Branson would consider it a security risk to let them simply leave, and besides, he would be pissed to learn they had taken all the ammunition and supplies they could carry when they left. But Griggs knew too that they didn't have the resources or the time to mount a long, drawn-out pursuit and figured they would give up quickly if they didn't find them in the immediate vicinity. At least that's what he was betting on.

The fourth night after his altercation with Branson was the night he'd been waiting for. He and Moreau had been talking and making their plans every evening prior and had managed to sneak the supplies they needed into the surrounding woods little-by-little each time one of them left the camp to go make use of the nearby latrine. Moreau was already out there, standing watch on the west side of the sole gravel road that led into the property from the north. Another recruit named Reggie was on the other side of that road, far enough that he wouldn't see Griggs leave if he skirted wide around that area, keeping near the banks of the bayou.

Griggs made his exit an hour after dark, carrying only his rifle as he excused himself from the group to make another visit to the latrine. After a quick detour to his hiding spot to grab his ready-to-go backpack full of stolen goods, he made his way to Moreau's position and the two of them disappeared into the woods to the north.

TWO

It took Griggs and Moreau four days to make the trek from the militia camp to the Red River Wildlife Management Area compound that was their destination. They had pushed hard as planned on that first night, making it well north of the Interstate 10 Bridge before daylight. If Branson and any of the men from the camp came looking for them, Griggs and Moreau never knew it. They kept to the woods as much as possible over the following days, and Griggs found himself more grateful than ever that Moreau had come along. Moreau knew most of the gravel back roads near the river, and they used those where possible and made detours through the swamp when necessary to skirt around places that appeared to be still inhabited. By doing this and traveling mostly at night, they managed to avoid making any contact along the way.

Moreau knew exactly where the outpost Branson had told them of was located, and when they finally reached the labyrinth of gravel roads winding through the wildlife management area, he led them right to it. Griggs figured it would've taken him twice as long to find the place alone, if he ever did. When they circled around through the woods to check it out before going any closer, Griggs was both disappointed and relieved to discover that the compound was deserted. While it would have been great to find an active garrison there to welcome them in, he'd known all along that it was also possible that other insurgents or desperados could have taken up residence there. Finding the place abandoned gave the two of them some time and the option to assess the situation and figure out what to do next.

He and Moreau kept within the woods and moved around the entire perimeter of the property, looking for any sign of movement or life inside the fenced compound. It was obvious even from a distance that there had been quite a battle on the grounds. They could see a shot-up Humvee outside the gate, and beyond it, the makeshift fortifications that had failed to protect the defenders within. Bullet holes in the sides of the buildings and shattered glass in every window told the story of an intense onslaught of incoming fire. They found abandoned vehicles beyond the rear of the perimeter, near the banks of the Red River. When they slipped down there for a closer look, Griggs and Moreau were horrified to find the decomposing corpses of several men dressed in green Army BDUs piled haphazardly in the back of an old, armored truck. Several more were strewn about on the ground nearby.

"This tells me that no one connected with this unit has been here since those men were killed," Griggs told Moreau. "They wouldn't leave fellow soldiers there to rot like that."

"Well, we know Branson was telling the truth about taking down this place. Either that or he and his bunch came along and found it like this and claimed they did it."

"They did it," Griggs said. "I don't know how they pulled it off, but they did."

After they were quite certain no living souls remained in or around the compound, the two men moved inside the perimeter to investigate closer. It appeared that no one else had been there since the time of the battle. But Branson and his men that were in on this savage attack had apparently moved all the bodies out of the compound before they made off with the weapons and supplies that were on hand there. He didn't know whether they did it because they were planning to use the place at some later time, or for another reason, but Griggs was glad that the gruesome task wasn't left to him and Moreau. Those soldiers deserved to be buried, but that was more than the two of them could do alone.

"What they did to the men posted here is exactly what they were going to ask us to do soon enough if we hadn't left, Moreau! Now, do you see why I wanted to get the hell out of there?"

"Yep. You were right. It looks pretty obvious from the uniforms those men were wearing, and the trucks and the Humvee and everything else here, that this was a real National Guard or Army outfit. I just don't see how they managed to do it. I mean, this place was barricaded and surely the soldiers on duty here were trained and well-armed!"

It was true. Looking around the place, Griggs had to wonder just how Branson and his bunch did it. It wouldn't have been easy, but with the right kind of planning and trickery, he knew it was possible. If that brother of his really had been a SEAL operator, then he was a specialist at planning high-risk missions with a minimum of assets.

"Pulling this off is what gave them the confidence to think they can keep doing it. Maybe they know what they're doing, or maybe they got lucky, but they won't get away with this kind of thing for long. There's going to be some payback coming their way as soon as this massacre is discovered. It's just pretty obvious to me that it hasn't yet."

"And I wonder why that is. Maybe no one is coming to check on this post after all. Do you really think we ought to stay here and wait around, not knowing?"

"I say we give it a few days at least. We can be thinking of an alternate plan while we wait, but we should at least give it a shot. It's not a bad place to hole up. We'll have a good view from up there in that elevated lodge building. We can alternate watches and bail out in a hurry to the woods if we see something suspicious."

"I guess. It just gives me the creeps, knowing what happened here."

Griggs understood. It was harder for a civilian like Moreau, who hadn't seen the aftermath of real war, to process a scene like this. He didn't like it either, but he'd seen worse. He figured if they hung around long enough, he would have to get that truck started and drive it somewhere farther from the compound. If nothing else, they could dump those bodies in the river or some slough off to the side. It was better than leaving them piled in the back like that. It was a damned shame what had happened to those soldiers—men who sacrificed their lives trying to restore law and order in a place where civilization had broken down. Griggs knew it was happening everywhere, and that it would surely continue for who knew how long, but this was hard to take, because both he and Moreau had fallen in with the perpetrators who did this, thinking *they* were the good guys.

The first night they were there seemed to drag on forever and Griggs was almost as uncomfortable as Moreau at the prospect of spending the night in the abandoned lodge. They'd mostly been sleeping in the daytime and moving at night during their trek anyway though, so staying awake all night was no big deal, aside from the boredom. All was quiet in the surrounding woods and on the river nearby, and by the end of the second night Moreau was starting to really get impatient about just sitting there doing nothing, leading the two of them to debate again the merits of staying versus going somewhere else.

"The thing about leaving here," Griggs said, "is that I don't have a clue where to even start looking for another Army unit elsewhere. The logical place to find one is where they already had an established post like this. It could be a hundred miles to the next outpost or base of any sort. There's just no way of knowing.

"I think we ought to wait here at least a couple more days just to be sure. Beyond that, I don't know what to tell you. I suppose at that point I may decide to try to make my way back to Georgia, one way or the other."

Griggs hoped it didn't come to that, because he didn't want to have to travel alone. He knew Moreau had no interest in going to Georgia because his home was in California. He'd been stranded here the same as Griggs, during a short trip to his hometown of Morgan City to settle his father's estate. That was before the shit hit the fan, of course, and if he hadn't been in Louisiana for that reason he would not have been caught up in any of this, at least not here. But Griggs reminded him that things in California were probably as bad, if not far worse. They simply had no way of knowing. Likewise, Griggs had no way of knowing what the situation on the ground in north Georgia was like. He knew he couldn't stay here indefinitely, but the prospect of the long, dangerous trek all the way home to his familiar mountains wasn't something he was ready to think about yet. Griggs had enough experience to know that the odds weren't in favor of a lone man traveling that far considering all that was going on now.

But the very next day, the solution he had hoped for seemed to present itself before he had time to really consider other options. He and Moreau were walking around the woods out back of the compound, discussing again the possibility of moving the old truck with the dead soldiers when they heard it. It was the sound of several vehicles approaching on the single gravel road leading in. There was no mistaking the sounds of engines and the popping of gravel under tires, growing louder as they closed in.

"Over here!" Griggs shouted. "Let's get down out of sight behind these bushes and wait. It's better that we weren't inside the compound! This way we can get a good look at whoever it is before they know anyone's around!"

They barely had time to get to a position of concealment before the first two vehicles rolled into view. Much to Griggs' relief, he saw that both of them were indeed green Army Humvees. More green and one Desert Tan truck followed behind them, and all appeared to be standard government-issue hardware.

"Would you look at that?" He whispered to Moreau. "I think we're in luck!"

"How do we know they won't just shoot us as soon as they see us? What if they think we were in on what happened here?"

"Let me do the talking. I know the lingo and I'll let them know my name, rank and old unit number right off. Better to let them know we're here now before they get set up and start finding all those dead guys back there."

Griggs and Moreau waited until all the vehicles pulled inside or parked out in front of the compound. Then, they watched as soldiers with their weapons at the ready fanned out inside the perimeter and secured the buildings. Griggs knew that in a matter of minutes they would sweep the grounds farther out and the two of them would be discovered whether they revealed themselves or not. He decided now was the time to do it.

"Come on man," he told Moreau. "Let's leave our weapons here and just stand up and walk that way. Keep your hands over your head and walk slowly right beside me. Follow my lead and remember to let me do the talking!"

Moreau did as he was asked, and just as Griggs had expected, as soon as he shouted out and made their presence known, rifles were turned on them and they were ordered to freeze in place where they stood. It was a tense moment, especially for Moreau, who expressed his fears in low whispers to Griggs. Griggs was nervous too, but he was doing his best not to show it. He knew that things could go either way at this point, but what else were they to do? They'd come looking to make contact with a military unit and now they had their chance. It was either that or try and sneak away and continue hiding out, trying to survive on their own. No, Griggs knew they were doing the right thing. They just had to accept the risk and get it over with.

When the NCO obviously in charge of the detachment

stormed out there to join the soldiers already holding them at gunpoint, Griggs was surprised to hear him barking orders at them in Spanish. When the man turned to Griggs and Moreau, sizing them up but not raising his own weapon, Griggs saw that he indeed appeared to be Hispanic, but that everything about his uniform and equipment, and those of his companions, was U.S. Army. Griggs stated his name and rank and the name of his own former unit without being asked, adding that he had served most of his time in the Army on deployments in Afghanistan and Syria. Then he stated that Moreau was a civilian with local knowledge that had helped him find this place.

"Why were you looking for it? Why are you here in this restricted area?" The corporal asked, in heavily accented English.

"Because we were hoping to find a unit exactly like yours. We heard about what happened here, and we have valuable intel regarding the party that is responsible for it."

"You knew of this massacre before you came here? Where were you when it happened? How were you involved?" The NCO demanded.

"We knew of it, but we were in no way involved. This happened weeks ago. We just got here the day before yesterday. We know who is responsible for it, and that is why we are here. I knew I had to come here because I knew that men who swore allegiance to the same flag that I fought for were murdered here. They were murdered by the insurgents that are terrorizing the residents of this region and everyone else in their path!"

Griggs went on to explain that he and Moreau had been held captive, along with more than 20 other men and an unknown number of women and children, in a work camp run by a private contracting company that he now knew was called C.R.I. Griggs said that they were freed from that detention camp by this group of insurgents, but that he later found out the group was rounding up local civilians and anyone else they could find to recruit into their militia. After they were taken there with them, he and Moreau had learned that the leaders of this so-called militia were planning even more attacks like the one they had carried out here at this remote outpost. Griggs told him that this militia leader had claimed that the men stationed here were no longer soldiers in service to their country, but were really working with C.R.I. to overthrow it. He told him this man used that lie as an excuse to attack this same outpost. Then he told him that the man's name was Eric Branson.

After hearing all this, the NCO turned to the men who were still pointing their rifles at Griggs and Moreau. He gave them orders in Spanish and pointed to the metal building in the compound that Griggs and Moreau had already determined had once been an office building when this place was still a wildlife management area headquarters.

"Commander Reyes will have many more questions to ask you when he gets here, and I will be there to hear your answers as well as soon as I am done assessing the damage here."

Griggs tried to stop him with more questions of his own as they were led away, but the officer was uninterested now. He was intent on surveying the aftermath of the attack, looking for more evidence of what had happened there.

More than an hour passed before Griggs and Moreau saw the NCO again, this time accompanied by another Hispanic-looking man who was clearly in charge, even though he was dressed in a non-standard BDU-type uniform that bore no rank insignia or unit information.

"This is the man I told you about, Commander Reyes. He is the one who claims to be a soldier, and who mentioned the name *Eric Branson*."

Griggs gave his name, rank and unit name again, but the new officer was more interested in the other information he had than who he was.

"How do you know Eric Branson? Do you know where he is right now?"

Griggs repeated what he'd told the corporal of how he and

Moreau and the others in the C.R.I. camp had been freed by Branson and his associates, and then coerced into joining their militia, which he said was currently being run by Eric Branson's brother, Keith, and his father, Bart.

"Eric has been gone for at least two weeks. He took some men with him and went east over to Mississippi to try to make contact with some forces he'd heard about over there, probably more insurgents. I don't know if he made it or when he'll be back, but I do know where the militia camp is, and I know that Keith and Bart Branson are there almost every day, training the recruits for their planned operations."

Commander Reyes was especially interested in that last bit of intel, although the disappointment on his face was obvious when Griggs told him Eric Branson was not at that camp and that he had no idea when he'd return. It seemed that finding Eric was a top priority to him, and Griggs sensed the commander knew more about Branson than he was letting on. The more he observed of Reyes and his men, the more Griggs began to think that something seemed off, and it was more than just the commander's non-standard uniform. Almost all the soldiers in the detachment were Hispanic, and other than Reyes, all he'd heard speaking English did so with a heavy accent. It made sense that a lot of soldiers from Texas and other parts of the Southwest might be of Mexican heritage, but it seemed strange that so many of them were using Spanish rather than the official language of the country they served. Commander Reyes was the only one who spoke English with little to no accent, but Griggs heard him converse with the NCO in perfect Spanish as well. Griggs began to piece together the answers to some of his questions when Reyes continued the conversation about Eric Branson.

"This fellow that you have been associated with has told you many lies," Reyes said. "I know that you must have been grateful to him for getting you out of that labor camp, but everything he has told you was misguided. The truth is that C.R.I. is not your enemy and is not the enemy of the people here in Louisiana, either. The only enemies are those who are participating in the organized insurgency as well as some random bands of outlaws taking advantage of the situation.

"I apologize for any inconvenience you may have suffered while you were detained at that camp, but you are a soldier, and you know how these things happen sometimes in the fog of war. Until security is reestablished in a conflict of this nature, everyone is a suspected insurgent. Sometimes innocent people are swept up in the effort to achieve that objective. Sometimes it is by mistake, and sometimes it is deliberate because it is for their own good and protection. Of course, if you are one of those involved, it seems like a bad thing at the time, but in your case, all of that is in the past because you and your friend are here now, talking to me. If I understand you correctly, Specialist Griggs, you came here for the purpose of helping us set things right. And you did so after learning the truth about the men who caused all the death and destruction you can now see with your own eyes right here."

Griggs nodded in agreement with the last part, but he was full of questions regarding the rest. "So, you're telling me that CRI is really aligned with National Guard and Army troops?" Griggs asked. "I can't see how that would ever happen...."

"Why not? You said that you served your country in foreign wars. Were you blind to all the private contractors that were also employed during those wars to carry out certain tasks that the people calling the shots wanted done quietly, and off the official reports?"

Griggs didn't reply. He just glanced momentarily over at Moreau as Reyes continued.

"The thing is, the Army and the National Guard here in the CONUS are no longer even structured the way they were when you knew them. Things had to be completely re-organized in the wake of all this domestic unrest. A new, comprehensive military branch has evolved from it, and it is called the North American

Interior Defense Force. And yes, most of the men you see here today, as well as those who died here at the hands of the insurgents, are a part of it. We at C.R.I. are working with them and they with us."

Griggs was stunned. "So, you're with C.R.I.? *You're a C.R.I. commander yourself?*"

THREE

Griggs didn't know what to make of what Commander Reyes had just told him. An alliance between the private military company known as C.R.I. and the soldiers that established this outpost was the last thing he'd expected to find here. *What in the hell was going on?* Moreau was just as shocked and was visibly shaken upon hearing it. He was urging Griggs not to say any more.

"The two of you came here because you knew that the organization you were training with was up to no good, am I right? Reyes asked.

"That's what we thought," Moreau said. "But whether that's true or not, CRI is definitely up to no good! It was C.R.I. that first came through here and forced residents out of their homes, rounding them up and moving them to those detention camps. We know because we were among them. They even made some of us do hard labor, like criminal convicts! How can anyone who experienced that be expected to trust anything a C.R.I. operator says? There's no way I'll ever believe that any legitimate branch of the U.S. military is working with C.R.I., whether it's some new branch or not."

Moreau had a point. But while Griggs agreed with everything he said, they were in a touchy situation now and it wouldn't do to sit here and challenge Commander Reyes, given the position they were in. Griggs knew they had to figure out a way to extricate themselves from what they'd just walked into, but he soon found out that Commander Reyes wasn't having that.

"Since you came here with this intel regarding the militia training camp," Reyes said, "you must realize that I will require your services to take me and my men back there so we can take care of the problem. Eliminating the resistance that Eric Branson has built here is my number one objective in this region. It is the one thing standing in the way of all my other projects, and it is the reason I am here. I won't be leaving until the situation is taken care of, no matter what it takes."

"Well, we're not going to help you!" Moreau said. "You can figure it out on your own. I'm not going back down there to that camp for any reason, but even if I had a reason, I wouldn't help anyone associated with C.R.I.!"

Griggs managed to stop him before Moreau said too much, but Commander Reyes just laughed and appeared unfazed by it anyway. Griggs knew the man had the upper hand and there wasn't a lot they could do at the moment. But he didn't want Moreau digging the hole they were already in any deeper.

"I'm going to give you two a chance to talk this over between yourselves. I've got other work to do here, but I don't have a lot of time to waste either. I need you two to get this resolved and get on board, because I will be ready to move out as soon as the rest of my men arrive and bring the boats we will be using for the work we have to do on the river."

When Reyes and those with him left the room, Griggs and Moreau were able to talk freely for the first time since they had made contact here, since one of the guards had been assigned to watch while they were waiting on Reyes earlier.

"We really screwed up coming here!" Moreau said. "I guess I should've known better."

"Known better how? Either you believed Keith Branson, or you didn't! Branson told us that these people were working with CRI and that the troops they've killed here weren't really U.S. soldiers, or that if they'd once been, they'd been tricked into believing they were doing the right thing now. Maybe he was telling the truth after all? But if it *was* the truth, it's too late to do anything about it now. We *did* come here and now we've got to figure out how to get ourselves out of this mess. I can tell you from experience with men like Reyes though, that it won't do any good to just flat-out refuse him. He's used to people who follow orders, and he expects us to do the same."

Griggs found out how right he was a couple of hours later, when Reyes sent a couple of his men in there to take him away, leaving Moreau behind. He was led up to the first level of the elevated lodge building where Reyes was waiting for him on the back porch overlooking the Red River.

"So how did your conversation with your indignant partner go?" Reyes asked him. "Were you able to convince him of the importance of cooperating with us so that we can accomplish the task we came here to do?"

"Boyd Moreau is a civilian, and he always has been. He doesn't understand the sort of operation you're involved in, and you can't expect him to. Like most of the people here in this river basin, he is stressed out and afraid and is just trying to survive. Hell, that's all I'm doing too. It's been years since I got out of the Army, and I never had any intention of going back. That's why I got the hell away from Branson's outfit when I did. Even though they promised us security and all the provisions and everything else we needed to survive, it wasn't worth it to me to go down that road again.

"Now, had it been a genuine civilian militia of people banding together for the purpose of self-protection, that would have been one thing. But as soon as I found out they were planning offensive operations, I was out of there. Moreau was the only one among the men there I could talk sense to and convince to leave with me. I'm sure most of the other guys there would have probably felt the same way if they had really understood what they'd gotten themselves into, but they didn't. Look, I get why you want to go after Eric Branson. I know he is the one that instigated all of this, at least from your point of view. But those other folks are just innocents caught up in it all who are trying to hang on to what's left of their lives. A lot of them have lost everything they had, including their homes and their families. They are not your enemy."

"My enemy is anyone who is standing in my way," Reyes said. "You should know that. It is also anyone with information that could help me, but still refuses to cooperate. Now, I don't think you fall into that category, do you, Specialist Griggs?"

"I came here to bring my intel to the proper authorities. I expected to find an Army or National Guard unit to deliver it to, not some new 'branch' of the military I've never heard of before, and certainly not the same private contracting company that kept me locked up and forced me into slave labor for weeks! I don't know what to believe any more when I see troops in U.S. Army uniforms that can barely speak English. But seeing that no other unit has arrived here since, I have my doubts one will. Like I said, I'll give you the intel I have, but I really don't want to get involved any further in this. I'm not from Louisiana anyway, and I don't know any of these people here beyond spending time with them in mutual confinement. I was never here to fight for or against anyone! I was simply stuck in Houston, Texas, when all these troubles began to unfold. Then, my problems got worse when I tried to cross this wretched state in the aftermath of a hurricane that had taken out the power grid and destroyed most of the infrastructure. All I wanted to do was get back home, but it didn't happen. I was at the wrong place at the wrong time and so I got caught up with all those other guys and ended up in the camps your company built."

"That is truly unfortunate and as I said, I apologize for the inconvenience, but what is done is done, and you are still alive, so there is always hope that you will find your way home, is there not? So, tell me, Specialist Griggs, where *is* home for you?"

"North Georgia. Near a small town called Dahlonega."

"Well, I have never been to Georgia, and I cannot help you get back to Dahlonega right now, but after I am finished with this mission here, and if it is successful because of your assistance, I can assure you that I will do everything in my power to connect you with the right people who *can* help you get there. I don't know what the situation is like there either, of course, but if it is where you want to go, then I can make it happen!"

"I want to get home as soon as possible, I really do. But if it means going back down to the Atchafalaya Swamp first, then no thank you. I don't want to get involved in any more fighting and I won't have a part in anything that I know will result in the deaths of more civilians there. And I know for certain Moreau doesn't want that either, just as he already told you."

"Well, the fact of the matter, Specialist Griggs, is that there are few who do want conflict, yet here it is. And like it or not, everyone is involved. Do most of them enjoy it? Probably not. But they also know that they have to do what needs to be done. I think you can understand that, and I know that with your military experience, you can grasp those concepts. If Moreau cannot, then that's going to be a problem. So, make sure you clarify it for him. We move out tomorrow afternoon!"

"There's nothing we can do while we're here, surrounded by all of Reyes's men," Griggs told Moreau when they were back in the same room together that evening. "The only thing I know to do is to pretend to be agreeable and go along with them and then see if we can find an opportunity to escape into the woods somewhere along the way. You know how far it is down there to the camp. We're a lot more likely to get our chance out there in the middle of nowhere. It won't happen here."

"Maybe, but I still think he'll back down if we stand our ground about it. I think he's just bluffing, hoping that we'll cooperate and give him what he wants. He doesn't really need us to show him the way, because it's easy enough to draw him a map that will guide him to that camp. But if we do have to give him one, we should make it all up and send him and his men off on a wild goose chase now that we know who they really are. Those guys we were training with back there don't deserve what he's planning to do to them, even if Branson may. They think they're doing the right thing and I'll be damned if I'm going to have any part in getting them all killed! And you know that's what's going to happen, isn't it, Griggs? They aren't going there to put them away again in a work camp this time. It'll be a slaughter and you know it."

Griggs did know it, and he knew that Moreau was right about the innocence of those other men. It was a damn shame to think of this mercenary force coming down on them like that and killing them all, as Reyes surely planned to do. Although he claimed his main objective was to get Eric Branson, Griggs knew it was more than that. He was going to get everyone connected to the Bransons and stamp out any opposition to the plans of whoever was directing all this. If he'd been with C.R.I. long enough to be the commander of a substantial number of their mercenaries, then Reyes was surely a ruthless killer-for-hire himself. He would delight in taking out those recruits and interrogating any survivors he could get his hands on for information that might lead him to Eric. It was obvious he didn't know the location of Sierra Zulu, and that was one bit of intel that neither Griggs nor Moreau could give him, because they didn't have it either.

"I don't think it's a good idea to flat out refuse to go tomorrow," Griggs reiterated. "I do think Reyes is serious, and I doubt he's going to let you simply walk away from this. For one thing, they will not want word to get out that they have moved troops back in here. I doubt they'd let either of us walk out of here for that reason alone now. So, the choice is either go with them, or find ourselves detained here indefinitely. Refusal may even get us shot. I don't have to remind you of the reputation C.R.I. has. You've seen it firsthand."

"Yeah, and they'll probably shoot us both anyway when they're done with us, even if we do cooperate."

"You're probably not wrong. We are indeed in a tight spot, buddy. I'll give you that. And I feel like it's my fault because I talked to you into coming here with me."

"Don't blame yourself. I was ready to split anyway, and if you hadn't had the idea to come here, I probably would've run into trouble anyway trying to find somewhere else to go. I wasn't going to go along with Branson on any of those raids he was talking about. I could see setting up an ambush if our camp was about to be invaded or sniping some of the C.R.I. guys if they came back into the Atchafalaya looking to round up more innocent people. But I wasn't going to sit out there watching some highway for an opportunity to shoot any uniformed troops rolling by. It just didn't make sense to me at the time, but maybe Branson was right."

Griggs and Moreau didn't have to wait long to find out how serious Reyes was about the urgency of his operation. Throughout the following morning, they watched through the partially boarded window of the small room where they were confined as more trucks with more men rolled into the compound. Griggs noted that three of the trucks were towing trailers carrying 20-foot-long commercial fishing skiffs with big outboard motors on their transoms. He knew that Reyes intended to use the boats to seek out Sierra Zulu, and he noted that they had installed tripod mounted M60 machine guns on the forward platforms of each of them and had reinforced the center console steering stations with welded steel plate. The boats weren't built for war, but they were making do with what they could get their hands on, and it was obvious they were getting ready for a serious offensive in the Atchafalaya swamp.

It wasn't until shortly after noon that they were led outside and confronted by Reyes again. This time, there was no room for discussion. Reyes was ready for them to tell him that they were going to cooperate and lead the way to the militia camp. But despite Griggs' warning, Moreau flat out refused yet again.

"I'm not going back there!" He said. "I won't have anything to do with what you're planning, because I spent months locked away with some of those guys in that camp and I know that they are all good men doing what they think they have to do to make the best of bad times. They don't deserve what you have planned for them, and I won't be a part of it!"

Griggs studied the C.R.I. commander's expressionless face, waiting for his reaction to what Moreau just told him. It was an act of defiance on Moreau's part that surprised Griggs with its utter disregard of the consequences. While Griggs agreed with the sentiment, he would never have expressed it so strongly in the present situation, and he immediately wished he had done more to convince Moreau that he shouldn't have either. But what was done was done, and there was no way to unsay what Moreau had already said. Griggs broke the silence that hung over them after his friend made his statement by telling Reyes that he would go with him if he would just let Moreau leave.

"We don't need him with us because I know exactly where the camp is and there is no reason for both of us to go. Like I told you before, he's an untrained civilian and he has no business there, anyway."

But Griggs knew he had failed when Reyes just looked at him with a still expressionless face and casually drew his pistol. There was nothing else he could do to intervene, whether the commander intended to use the weapon for stronger persuasion or for its designed purpose. Griggs had little time to wonder, because as soon as the muzzle came into line with his friend's face, the trigger squeeze came with no hesitation. Griggs winced at the sudden report and saw the bullet hole appear between Moreau's eyes just before he collapsed where he stood. The hapless guy was dead before his body hit the gravel of the compound yard.

As much as instinct tried forcing him to react by taking a step back or even turning to run for his life, Griggs stood his ground unmoving. He knew it was futile to do otherwise as he waited to see if Reyes was going to simply do away with him as well. But the commander holstered his weapon as casually as he'd drawn it before acknowledging Griggs was even there again.

"I warned you both. I told you that I had no more time for discussion when I explained to you that I needed your help. Now, are you going to do what I have asked of you, Specialist Griggs?"

Griggs nodded. He couldn't quite find the words to respond, so he didn't try. *Poor Moreau...* It was such a shame that he had to die that way, but there was nothing he could do about it now. All Griggs could think about was making sure he didn't end up the same way.

FOUR

Griggs had known it would be difficult to extricate himself from this situation, but he couldn't see a way out at all now. After seeing Commander Reyes casually execute Moreau right before his eyes, Griggs doubted he'd survive this, whether he cooperated or not. Even so, staying alive for as long as he could was the goal, and for the moment, that meant going along and doing whatever he could to push the inevitable farther down the line. He figured there was always a slim chance something could happen along the way that might give him an unforeseen opportunity, so he resolved to do everything he could to remain alive long enough to see. And if and when such an opportunity presented itself, Griggs would be ready to take advantage of it.

Just as Reyes had told him the day before, the convoy was ready to roll out later that afternoon. He had watched as the trucks pulling the trailers backed up to the nearby ramp on the Red River to launch the three boats, and he'd overheard talk among the men that more boats were coming to the post soon. From what he understood, the plan was to rendezvous somewhere upriver of the militia camp before they made their move to attack. Griggs didn't know whether they planned to use the boats in that operation or not, but he had told Reyes of the small bayou that led into the property from the south, and how it connected to the main channel of the Atchafalaya farther downriver.

When they finally moved out, Griggs was put into one of the Humvees at the front of the convoy and Reyes assured him he would be the first to die if the route he directed them on led them into an ambush or some other surprise along the way.

"These men you are riding with have orders to shoot you the moment we receive any incoming fire. If you have any second thoughts about the route you laid out for me, now is the time to speak up!"

Griggs didn't know of another route. He wasn't even sure of the one he'd pieced together, because he and Moreau had traveled off-road much of the way. The only part he was certain of was the section closer to the militia camp, where he'd been out on frequent training maneuvers with the other recruits since he'd first arrived there. Directing this convoy back there was a hell of a position to be in, Griggs knew, because it had been long enough since he and Moreau left that Branson could be up to anything by now. There actually *could* be an ambush or at least a sniper or two set up somewhere along those backroads on the way to the camp. Griggs had no idea how Branson and the other leaders had reacted after he and Moreau deserted the way they did. He didn't know whether they set out to look for them or not; all he knew was that he and Moreau never saw any sign of them if they did.

Those same backroads were just as deserted now as they had been then, and to Griggs' relief, the convoy made it to the first destination without incident, arriving just before dark. It was a place not far north of the Interstate 10 Bridge where they could rendezvous with the boats that were coming downriver. Reyes seemed pleased after checking it out with some of his men. Like Griggs had told him, the small slough that connected to the river close behind a dead-end road provided a good place to hide the boats and plan the assault.

The team that would take the militia camp consisted of around thirty-five men, including Reyes and Griggs. They set out on foot the next day to close the gap and get into position to launch their attack shortly after dark. Griggs had given Reyes all the details he could think of regarding the normal movements and routines of the trainees, including the positions and watch schedules of the sentries. Griggs knew all of it was subject to change, but he was keeping his fingers crossed that the recruits were still there and still following the same patterns. It was certain that they would still be posting a night watch if they were, and considering the way he and Moreau had slipped out unnoticed, the numbers of those sentries may have doubled or more.

Reyes' plan was to eliminate the sentries first, of course, and then take out the rest of the camp. Griggs knew that all the intel he provided meant he was directly involved in getting those men killed, but he knew he'd be dead like Moreau if he refused or gave Reyes false information. He justified it by reminding himself that he wasn't going to be pulling any triggers, as he'd been given no weapon and was not an active participant in the assault. He also told himself that Reyes and his men would have come there with or without his help, and that none of those recruits had a chance anyway, considering the forces that were aligned against them. Griggs simply had to focus on his own survival now, because he didn't want to end up like them and Boyd Moreau. And because the only way to do that was to comply, that's exactly what he did. There'd been no opportunity to attempt an escape since they left the Red River outpost, as he'd been under close observation the entire time.

Griggs was kept back with the bulk of the men waiting alongside Reyes as a small advance team slipped off shortly after dark to take care of the sentries. Griggs figured they would do it without firing shots if they could, and the long wait in silence that ensued had him wondering if it was done or if some change meant bad news that would come back on him for misleading them. It was an agonizing hour or more before he finally learned that Reyes had gotten the radio signal that all was clear for the assault. At that point, Griggs was brought along with a small detachment in the rear as Reyes' assault force slipped through the woods on both sides of the gravel road leading to the camp.

Once the first shots were fired, the intensity of the attack ratcheted up with bursts of full auto, punctuated by the louder explosions of grenades that ripped through the deep silence of the remote swamp. Griggs first thought the men on the receiving end of all that hellfire surely didn't suffer, but he knew he was wrong when he heard the screams of the wounded when the shooting finally stopped. The sounds of men yelling orders and then several more shots that he figured were follow-ups to finish off the survivors came next, and then Griggs was rushed along to where Reyes and the rest were assessing the aftermath. When they reached the clearing, he saw numerous bodies strewn about the camp area, as he'd expected. It appeared that all but two of them were dead, and he watched as both were dragged over to the top bank of the bayou at the back edge of the clearing.

Some of Reyes' men were sweeping the cattail marsh below that bank, apparently looking for something there, when Griggs heard a shout about some of their men being down. He didn't know exactly what was going on among all the confusion as Reyes left him there under the watch of the two soldiers guarding him and disappeared down to the bayou to see what had happened. When Reyes came back moments later, he zeroed in on Griggs and confronted him with a barrage of accusations.

"Two of my men were shot down there at the water's edge and we don't know where the shooters went. You said they didn't have boats here at this site at night, and that all the sentries would be out to the north, watching that road!"

"They didn't have boats when I was here! Branson and his old man and the other old guy, Sam, came and went every day in that big gunboat I told you about. They wouldn't have left it here, and if it was here, your men would have seen it when they moved into position to launch the attack. The only big boat around here is that sailboat that's sunk out there beside the dock—the one Eric Branson brought here that I already told you about as well. It'll never float again, as anyone can see. The only other thing around here that *would* float is a little beat-up aluminum johnboat with no motor on it that you'll find pulled up in the reeds down there on the far side of the dock. Some of the guys used it to set out hooks for catfish, but they never went far from camp in it; just up and down the bayou nearby."

"A fishing boat? I asked you if there were any boats here, and you said no. How is it that you forgot to mention that one?"

"Because I'd hardly call it a boat, that's why. It's not something they could move troops in or use to launch a counterattack. It's just a piece-of-crap 14-foot johnboat with no outboard!"

"And yet someone here apparently did use it to make a getaway, after killing two of my men, because there is no boat to be seen down there! I should shoot you right now, the way I shot your companion who refused to follow my orders!"

"Are you sure the boat isn't there? I will show you where they kept it if you want to see."

Reyes did, and when Griggs led him to the spot where the little boat had always been pulled up on the bank, he saw that it was indeed gone. Griggs wouldn't admit it now, of course, but he realized he'd made a terrible mistake by failing to mention the boat. He'd certainly known it was there, and he knew that two of the recruits in particular, Eli Landry and Seth Guidry, were avid fishermen and were often out in the johnboat whenever they had a break from their duties. He should have remembered this detail and passed it on to Reyes, but at the time he'd been more focused on the locations of the sentries and the camp itself. It was obvious to him now that one or both of those guys had been out in the boat after dark when the attack occurred, and from the looks of it, they'd indeed managed to kill two of Reyes' men and then get away before the other members of the assault team spotted them. But he doubted they'd had time to get far and said as much to Reyes.

"If someone did get away down the bayou in that little boat, they weren't moving fast and couldn't have gone very far with just a paddle," Griggs said. "It should be easy enough to catch up to them."

"If we had a boat of our own!" Reyes was furious. "But we don't, because you assured me that we would surprise these men in their camp here with no means of escape! Now, my men have no way to go after them until daylight, because that's when I told the boat crews to show up here. I wanted them off the river until after we'd secured the militia camp and the plan was to have them arrive at dawn in time to get them into position to pursue Branson's gunboat if for some reason he didn't enter the bayou in the boat and fall into our trap. Now, it could all be ruined. If even one man managed to escape downriver in that little fishing boat, he could meet Branson on the way in, and warn him away!"

Griggs understood. The place where the boats were tied up north of the interstate was out of range of the handheld radios that Reyes' officers carried. He had no means of notifying the men waiting up there at that slough north of the interstate that there was a change of plans. There was no use trying to follow along the banks of the bayou either, as Griggs had already explained to Reyes that the land just downstream of Branson's property gave way to swamp that was impossible to traverse on foot. Looking for whoever left in that johnboat would indeed have to wait until morning, when they had boats in which to do it. But the next thing that happened did not have to wait, much to Griggs' dismay.

The two wounded militia recruits that were still hanging onto life were being questioned over at the spot where they'd been dragged to after the attack was over. A couple of Reyes' men were trying to get information from them about the whereabouts of

Sierra Zulu, but said that both men claimed to know nothing about it. Griggs knew they were telling the truth, because like him, they'd never been there. As far as he knew, no one from the recruit camp had. Branson and his closest associates were keeping the location of their main hideaway secret. Reyes knew this too because Griggs had already told him before they arrived here.

Reyes knew he would get nothing of use from the two men, and Griggs doubted he was interested in taking prisoners, especially prisoners in the shape they were in, unlikely to survive their wounds even until morning. He assumed that he was about to see them shot then and there, the way Reyes had shot Moreau. It never crossed his mind that Reyes would have a different idea, so Griggs was stunned at what he was ordered to do next.

"I want you to shoot them, Specialist Griggs! You are the reason that we found these men and their companions, and I want them both to know it before they die. They made the decision to join a terrorist organization and unlike you, they made the decision to stay even after they learned the true purpose of their training.

"Now is the time to prove that you are willing to earn the help you asked me for. If you expect me to assist you in getting home after we are finished with our work here, then do what has to be done so that we can prepare for the next step."

Griggs knew even before he opened his mouth to protest that it would do little good. This was exactly the sort of thing men like Reyes delighted in, the ability to exert control over a man like him and further demonstrate to the rest of his troops that those under his command were subject to the whims of his will without question.

Griggs truly regretted that he had ever gone to that Red River outpost in the first place now and knew the two of them should have done as Moreau suggested and just gotten the hell out of the area, leaving all this fighting to those who were involved in it. Instead, Griggs had foolishly believed he could make a difference. He had foolishly believed he was doing the right thing, and that

Branson was truly an insurgent or a terrorist, just as Reyes claimed he was. The more he saw of all this, the more Griggs questioned everything he thought he believed. The truth was that Reyes and the company he worked for were the terrorists. Griggs had known that when he was in that detention camp, but he'd refused to believe Branson's claim that the military forces at that outpost were really working with them. He'd refused to believe that those troops were no longer loyal to the United States until he went there and saw for himself. And now that he was here among them and the C.R.I. commander, Griggs knew there was no way those forces were really former National Guard or Army regulars.

Most of the men appeared to be foreign anyway, which made sense because they had apparently displaced the actual troops whose equipment, weapons and uniforms they'd somehow acquired. Griggs figured he would never know the whole truth, but he did know that what was left of the U.S. military here at home was a fraction of what it had been during the years when he was serving overseas. Recruitment rates were down to all-time lows long before all this unrest began to unfold, and the troops that were killed fighting not only in the Middle East but later in Europe and Asia weren't being replaced.

Griggs figured that what was left of the reserves still at home had their hands full, maintaining their immediate AOs. Like everyone else, they also had to look out for their own families in the absence of organized law and order. He doubted that many of them would relish the thought of marching off to fight in different regions, leaving their families to fend for themselves, no matter what they had signed up for. This was a complete breakdown of every functional system, and no institution, even the military, was strong enough to stand on its own.

What he had to do next was the hardest thing Griggs had ever faced, but he knew that war was horror for all involved. There simply wasn't another option, aside from sacrificing himself, that could get him out of it. And while Griggs may have done that at one time for some of the men with whom he'd served as a younger man, he was well past that now. Besides, it was obvious to him that these two were going to die soon anyway, so he had to consider that maybe he was doing them a favor.

Griggs took the Beretta that Reyes handed him and opened the slide enough to check that a round was chambered. Then, he took two steps closer to the two men huddled there together on the ground and resolved to make it as quick and painless as possible. Griggs knew their names, but he put that out of his mind even as one of them called him by his own and accused him of being a deserter and a traitor. When the deed was done, Griggs lowered the weapon and gave it back to Reyes.

"I hope you're satisfied now with what you've forced me to do. And I hope you are going to honor your promise to get me the hell out of here and back to Georgia as soon as possible."

"I will keep my promise," Reyes said. "But your work is not finished here yet. When the boats go downriver in the morning, you will be with them, because you have seen more of this river than any of those men, and also because you can identify the boat that Branson will come here in if you see it along the way. You can also identify the little boat that you claim was kept here. I want whoever is in it taken care of and then after Branson is taken care of too and we clean out the terrorist nest that he has built in this place called Sierra Zulu, we will talk of getting you home to Georgia."

Griggs was actually glad to hear that Reyes wanted him on board one of the boats. There was nothing he wanted more than to get away from this camp again, and the sooner he could do so, the better. He didn't know what would happen out there on the river, but he didn't want to be here when Branson and the rest of his crew arrived on that gunboat. While it was true that Reyes had the upper hand and would probably pull off a successful ambush if Branson arrived unaware, Griggs also knew it wouldn't be as simple as killing all those untrained militia recruits in the middle of the night. Branson and the rest of his core group had been in plenty of action since all of this started, and some of them knew what they were doing. Griggs had seen proof of what they were capable of when he and Moreau first reached the Red River outpost. Whatever happened here tomorrow, Griggs knew it would be intense, and he hoped like hell he wouldn't be a part of it.

He was delighted to learn that he didn't even have to wait until morning to get out of there. Since Reyes couldn't reach the boat crews by radio, he ordered a small detachment of five men to take Griggs to the river right away. Reyes didn't want to wait for those boat crews to find their way up the bayou in the morning. Instead, the men with Griggs would hail them on the radio from a sandbar south of the bridge as soon as they heard them coming. They would pick him up there to save time. Griggs had no choice but to comply for now, but it was a huge relief to be out of the commander's reach, if only for a few hours.

FIVE

THE DULL WOOD-AGAINST-METAL THUMP THAT SHAUNA Hartfield heard shortly after daybreak was unmistakably manmade. None of the animal inhabitants of the Atchafalaya Swamp, aquatic or terrestrial, made such a sound, and even if she hadn't been certain the first time it got her attention, Shauna had only to wait another minute or so before she heard it again. *Her mind was not playing tricks on her... It was the clunk of a wooden paddle or oar bumping against the gunwale or hull of an aluminum boat....*

The sound was coming from somewhere out there in the thick morning mist that hung low over the river, making it impossible to see more than a few yards beyond the bank. Even though they carried easily to her ears in the stillness of that quiet place, each of the occasional bumps was subdued and Shauna could tell they weren't deliberate. She heard no voices or other noises to accompany them, so she knew that whoever was out there was trying to navigate the river quietly. She was certain that the boat was either a canoe or a small johnboat, if it was being propelled by paddle power alone, and Shauna knew from experience that even the most careful paddler couldn't avoid bumping their boat at times. There were currents and snags everywhere in the river, especially near the banks, and any obstruction suddenly looming into view in the reduced visibility of the fog would require a quick reaction.

Any paddler might have to make a sudden maneuver and inadvertently bump the hull in conditions like that, and Shauna wanted desperately to believe that it was indeed an experienced paddler making those sounds. She wanted to believe that it was in fact the most experienced boatman she'd ever known even, but she didn't dare call out his name or hail the unseen vessel from where she stood hidden on the bank among a stand of hardwood trees. Instead, Shauna remained silent, waiting and listening because she knew that in reality, it could be anyone out there in that boat. And anyone who wasn't a part of their group was as likely an enemy as not. If the mystery boat continued down the river without turning into the bayou she was posted there to guard, Shauna would likely never know who had passed. But if it entered the cutoff, then she was ready, whether friend or foe.

Before this unexpected interruption, Shauna's thoughts had been wandering that morning as they always did when she was out there alone on security duty. She welcomed the brief hours of silence that allowed her mind to drift away like that, free of the demands of conversation and camp chores that were a constant back at Sierra Zulu. The predawn watch was her favorite shift when it was her turn to come here to the junction of the cutoff bayou that connected their well-hidden refuge to the main channel of the Atchafalaya River. She had arrived at 0400 to relieve Marcus Thibodeaux, putting her in position to experience the full transition from predawn darkness to the rising sun of a new day over the course of her four-hour watch. Out there to greet the coming day alone like that, in the silence of that vast bottomland forest, Shauna sometimes allowed herself to succumb to the illusion that all was at peace again. The reality, of course, was that nothing was farther from the truth. Although it had been quiet for some time now in the immediate vicinity of their secluded deep woods sanctuary, there was no way of knowing that wouldn't change again at any moment. Shauna and the others living there were acutely aware that their security depended on maintaining a low profile and keeping a vigilant watch. Guarding this entrance into the cutoff bayou was perhaps the most critical part of that vigilance, as this waterway was the only reasonable route in there. As such, it required an active watch twenty-four seven, even as a two-person perimeter security detail patrolled the areas of deep woods nearer the camp.

When she was out there by the river alone, Shauna's thoughts were usually drawn back to the twisted sequence of events that led them all to this unlikely place. She sometimes let her mind wander over the memories of fear and uncertainty that had dominated her life during the days, weeks and months of not knowing how or if she'd ever reach her daughter again. But those worries were behind her now, despite the impossible odds and the thousands of miles that had separated the two of them. Megan was here with her now, safely in the camp down that winding bayou behind her. And they were together because of the efforts of Megan's father—Eric Branson—a man Shauna had once given up on. The divorce and the life she'd lived for a while with another man seemed so far from her present reality she sometimes wondered if it was ever even real. If not for the presence of her stepson, Andrew, who was the best thing she'd gotten from that marriage, she might soon have forgotten.

Now, as she stood there and searched for movement in the fog that obscured the river from her view, Shauna wanted nothing more than to see Eric Branson emerge from that smokey mist. *Was he still paddling one of the three aluminum canoes he and his team had left in? If so, then maybe it was Jonathan, Willis, Trey, or Lenny who had bumped their paddles against their boats....*

Shauna knew it was quite possible. She'd been telling herself Eric could return at any time of any day, whether she was posted here to greet him or not, and she wanted to believe it. But as the days turned into weeks, she also couldn't help but wonder if Eric's luck had finally run out. For as long as she'd known the man, his life consisted of one dangerous mission after another, each taking him far away and leaving her behind to wait and worry. Her only respite from it had been those brief years after the divorce, during her marriage to Daniel Hartfield, but now Eric was back in her life, and Daniel was gone forever.

The difference in the waiting this time and all those times before was that the sort of dangers Eric once faced in distant lands Shauna would never visit were everywhere around her now, even here at home. Shauna finally knew firsthand what Eric had lived through each of those times he'd gone away. And ironically, Eric had concluded that leaving his family and going away wasn't something he wanted to do anymore. In the past, she'd never really believed him when he told her such things. But now she knew that he meant it, as she could see it in his eyes when he said goodbye to her and Megan before setting out on what he promised was his last mission away.

"You know I wouldn't do this for any of the old reasons I justified it before, Shauna. I'll never fight someone else's battles again; not for duty or money. And I won't do it simply because it's what I'm good at either. I've had all of that I ever want. I came back here for my family, and everything I do now is for family first. You know my number one goal when I made landfall in Florida was to find Megan, whatever I had to do. And I was able to do it because of your help, and all the help I had from my dad, my brother, and all my new friends like Jonathan and so many strangers I met along the way. Now, not only do I have my little girl, but I am surrounded by family and friends. And best of all, I have you in my life again, Shauna. Do you think I'd trade all that for anything? Well, I wouldn't! I don't want to be away from you and Megan even for a day, but you're both aware of the situation here and you know what we're facing. Someone has to go and try to make contact with friendly forces if we expect to hold out here, Shauna. You know there's no one more capable of leading the sort of expedition that will entail than me."

Shauna wanted to believe that Eric meant everything he said, and she *did* believe that he thought he meant it. She knew he was indeed motivated by the reasons he stated, but the one thing she no longer *could* believe was that this was the last time he would leave like this. Eric had done the same thing so many times now she would never believe him when it came to that. Eric's last mission would be the one he didn't come back from, and that was an outcome Shauna didn't want to think about. But that thought was always in the back of her mind and it was there today, just as it had been every other time he had left her to participate in some dangerous operation.

Shauna knew their small band of mostly civilian refugees couldn't hold off the threats they were facing without outside help; she'd seen enough to convince her of that. Her only argument against Eric's proposed excursion was that she didn't fully see the logic of staying there and *trying* to hold out. She knew this swampy river basin and the surrounding farmlands and small towns were home to their many new friends and allies and to Eric's brother, Keith, but she wasn't convinced any of them should remain there. Shauna thought they should all go east if there was a reasonable chance that somewhere across the river, in Mississippi or beyond, they might find military forces still loyal to the country they'd enlisted to serve. Eric wouldn't hear of it though, saying the intel he had was too sketchy to rely on.

"What I got from Sergeant Davis was enough to convince me it's worth taking a small team over there to find out, but it's not convincing enough to put all of you at risk. Nowhere is truly safe, but it's safer staying put here in the middle of nowhere than trying to move about, not knowing what we'll run into."

It was hard to argue with Eric's logic. Shauna had seen plenty of the dangers that could be encountered out there, whether traveling by water or overland. The other thing Eric had pointed out, and that she knew he was right about, was that even if there *were* friendly forces over there east of the river, it was questionable whether they would be willing or able to take on a large group of refugees that would put a strain on their resources. It simply didn't make sense to expose everyone in the group to the potential risks and disappointments such a journey would entail. And so Shauna had reluctantly dropped her opposition to Eric's decision and prepared herself for yet another period of waiting and worrying when the time to say goodbye finally came. She'd coped after then by keeping herself busy, which wasn't hard, considering the challenges all of them at Sierra Zulu faced every day. Living in primitive conditions deep in the swampy woodlands of the Atchafalaya Basin demanded plenty of hard work, aside from the necessities of keeping watch and maintaining readiness to fight.

Keith and his father, Bart, along with Sam Necaise, were working with the militia recruits and were usually away during most of the daylight hours conducting training. For security and logistical reasons, they had established a separate camp for that operation, located on the property where Keith had once lived with his wife, Lynn, before she was killed, and their house later burned to the ground. The decision to do things that way was voted on by all the core members of the group at Sierra Zulu, primarily due to the sheer number of new recruits. After the successful mission to rescue Sam and the others at the Red River Wildlife Management area outpost and the subsequent liberation of numerous detainees at the C.R.I. labor camp farther west, there were far more volunteers than they could accommodate at Sierra Zulu.

"We can't work with that many people out here in a place that's only accessible by boat," Eric had said when he and Keith brought it to a vote before the group.

"Aside from the numbers, not all the folks that were detained in that camp are from around these parts. Some were taken while they were attempting to travel through the area. We can't know their level of commitment or whether we can fully trust them all until we've worked with them for a while, and that's why I recommend keeping things separate. The supplies we took from that camp at the Red River post will sustain the recruits for at least a couple of months, even after setting aside what we need for everyone here at Sierra Zulu. I hope to be back long before then. In the meantime, turning all those new volunteers into trained fighters should be the top priority. They're motivated after what was done to them and what they've seen done to others. We've got the weapons and ammo to equip them, and I'm betting most of them are eager to use them to get the payback they crave. But let's keep them away from Sierra Zulu. This place is for family and the friends that we know we can trust with our lives."

Shauna had agreed with Eric's assessment regarding the new trainees. There were more than enough folks at Sierra Zulu, and she could not imagine more than doubling that number with a bunch of strangers. They were already living in close quarters with little privacy, even though they were deep in the woods. Everyone in camp had to pitch in and work together and the more people involved, the more complicated coordinating all those efforts became.

The other problem for Shauna and Megan and the other women and girls in the camp was that most of those new recruits were young or middle-aged men. The last thing they needed was the hassle of fending off the advances of some of those single guys who would surely direct their attention to them in their down time. Shauna had met a few of the recruits when she went with Keith and Bart up to the training area one day, and she had felt the eyes upon her the entire time she was there. Having all those men living there in the same camp with them would be nothing but trouble and everyone knew it.

"My property will do just fine for the purpose," Keith had said. "Even though it's accessible by that one road, as well as by way of the bayou, it's still quite remote as you all know and with that many men, maintaining security shouldn't be a problem. The best thing is that it's also close enough to Sierra Zulu that we can quickly run back and forth to carry out the training they're going to need."

The militia didn't have a specific mission at that point, other than to bolster their overall numbers and make things difficult for C.R.I. and their allies to move in and occupy the Atchafalaya River Basin. Eric wanted every willing and able volunteer they could recruit, because larger numbers meant they could set up more observation points in the beginning and later, conduct patrols and sniper operations to counter whatever enemy incursions occurred. If Eric was successful and managed to find and elicit the help of real trained soldiers, the militia's operations might be limited to security duty only. But regardless of that possibility, Keith, Bart and Sam were doing their best to get the recruits ready for anything. In another hour, Shauna expected to see the three of them pass by aboard the gunboat, with Ronnie Ferguson at the helm, on their way out of the bayou to head upriver for another day of training. They had been making the trip six days a week since Eric had left, and today was the first day of a new week after they'd given the guys a well-deserved Sunday break.

Shauna would use the handheld radio clipped to her backpack nearby to notify Bart and Keith of the boat she'd heard before they left camp, but only after she was certain the occupants were beyond earshot of her voice downriver—assuming they didn't enter the bayou instead. She listened intently as she waited, hearing nothing now but the usual birdcalls and other natural background sounds of the swamp, and soon she began to think maybe the boat had indeed drifted on past the turnoff along the broad river channel. In another hour, the sun would burn off most of that morning mist, and if Keith wanted to investigate, it would be easy for him and the crew to spot the slow-moving boat with a quick detour downriver. Shauna was quite disappointed though, because if the boat did go on, it was because Eric Branson wasn't in it, and her daydream of a joyful reunion would remain just that. But just as she began to think about going over to get the radio from her nearby backpack, a new sound from much closer this time brought her full attention back to the direction of the fog-shrouded river. That sound she heard this time was the sound of a man's voice, speaking at a low volume that just barely carried through the fog to where she was listening from the bank.

"I think this might be it! It's pretty much got to be. I can't tell in this fog, but it looks like a wide channel."

Shauna could hear someone reply in agreement, and then, after a brief moment of silence, she heard the distinct dipping of paddles in the water, even though there were no careless bumps against the hull now. Raising her rifle to her shoulder, she braced her forearm against the trunk of the big sycamore beside her and strained to see movement through the cloaking mist. When at last the boat materialized, she saw that it was a square-nosed aluminum johnboat, and not a canoe, as she'd hoped before. Two men wielding wooden paddles propelled it from the bow and stern, while a third was lying unmoving in the bottom between the front and middle seats. Both of the men paddling had rifles close at hand, leaning against the edges of the flat metal seats from which they guided the little boat into the bayou. Shauna studied their faces in turn through her rifle optic now that they were clearly in view. She didn't know either man, and it was time to put a stop to whatever they had in mind here.

"THAT'S FAR ENOUGH!" Shauna shouted as she kept her rifle shouldered, ready to take out either or both of them if they reached for their weapons. "KEEP YOUR HANDS ON THOSE PADDLES AND PULL OVER TO THE BANK! DON'T TOUCH THOSE RIFLES IF YOU DON'T WANT TO DIE!"

SIX

Eli Landry was so startled at the sudden sound of a woman's voice from such a short distance away that he nearly dropped his paddle. He was glad that he didn't though, as she repeated her command. She wanted him and his buddy, Seth Guidry, to keep both their hands on their paddles while using them to move their boat over to the nearby muddy bank. For a brief second, Eli Landry considered the alternative, glancing down at the Colt M16A2 propped on the metal seat beside him while wondering if he might have to go for it. Eli already knew that was a bad idea, though. The voice was close, but the woman it belonged to was completely hidden from view in the dense woods that grew right to the edge of the bank, giving her all the advantage. From her cool, confident tone, Eli had no doubt she would make good on her threat if he or Seth failed to follow her orders. And though there was a chance she would shoot them anyway, Eli planned to do his best to give her every reason not to. They had nothing of value other than their rifles and the boat itself, which was a battered old 14-foot aluminum johnboat with no propulsion other than the weathered wooden paddles each man wielded. While their weapons were in plain view, it was obvious to anyone that the third man in the boat, James Andre, was in no shape to be a threat to anyone. In fact, James was in so much pain from the two bullet wounds he'd sustained that Eli doubted he was even aware they were once again facing the possibility of getting shot.

"Easy now, we're pulling on over!" Eli called out in answer to the unseen woman, as he glanced over his shoulder to make sure Seth was in agreement.

"Yeah, we're not looking for trouble!" Seth added. "We've had our share of that last night!

Seth had that part right, Eli thought grimly. The three of them were lucky to be alive, and James wouldn't be at all if he and Seth hadn't managed to carry him to the boat and get him out of there. They'd been paddling for hours in the dark ever since, desperate to put some miles behind them before daylight and to find the cutoff that would take them to safety, if indeed this was the right one. Eli figured they'd know the answer to that soon enough. He'd expected to encounter security if it was, of course, and the fact that the woman had even ordered them to stop at all, rather than killing them outright gave him hope that maybe she was part of those security measures, rather than a member of some gang of desperados.

The trouble all started the evening before for Eli and Seth, when they'd taken the johnboat a short distance down the bayou from camp to check and re-bait the drop lines they'd set out along both sides of the waterway in hopes of supplementing their boring freeze-dried rations with some fresh-caught catfish. It was obvious the area was over-fished compared to the way things were before so many people had been forced to retreat into the swamp to survive, but Eli and Seth knew what they were doing, and if anyone could eke out subsistence from what the Atchafalaya had to offer, those two lifelong outdoorsmen could. Ever since they'd been freed from the detention camp and brought there with the rest of the men for militia training, the two of them had made frequent nighttime excursions in the little johnboat, bringing in everything from crawfish to the occasional small gator.

Last night had started much like so many before it since they'd been living in the camp there. Yesterday was a Sunday, so they'd had their one-day-a-week break from the militia training, and Eli and Seth were feeling great and were eager to get out in the boat and away from all the other guys in the camp for a while. The two of them had pretty much laid claim to the johnboat, as they were the most enthusiastic fishermen there, so no one said a thing when they set out just as it was getting dark, as they so often did. Both men had lived in the river basin their entire lives, and both had worked as full-time commercial fishermen in years prior. Going back to a small, engineless johnboat wasn't ideal, of course, and neither man had worked from such a craft since they were kids, but still, it was a boat, and any boat was better than no boat.

Eli Landry never had the slightest interest in joining the military, even though both his older brothers had signed up for the Army as soon as they each graduated high school. Eli couldn't imagine a life of following orders, nor one of shipping off to some Middle Eastern desert where he could neither fish nor enjoy the freedom of disappearing down a winding bayou in his boat. He'd never dreamed, of course, that he'd become part of a militia unit engaged in combat training right here at home along those same bayous, yet here he was, living in a militia camp along with a couple dozen other volunteers who now found themselves with little choice but to fight for their lives and their homeland. The shooting and firearms handling part came easily to Eli. He'd done his share of hunting since he'd been old enough to shoulder a single-shot .410 shotgun, and he'd later acquired plenty of experience with rifles, hunting everything from squirrels to deer and wild hogs. But like most of his companions in the militia camp, Eli Landry had never hunted men before. Now, they were being taught how to do just that—learning how to go out on patrol and to set up sniper hides and preparing to take out armed men who would surely kill them if they didn't shoot them first.

Eli didn't have a problem with that, because like the other men there, he'd been detained and made to do hard labor by the same forces that would surely be sweeping through the area at some time in the near future to finish the job they'd started. Eli knew the only option was to stand and fight or leave his homeland for good, and he had no intention of going anywhere. The training he and the others were getting was legit, as it was coming from men with real combat experience, and he felt confident they could hold their own as the tactics of guerrilla warfare were laid out and explained to them, then reinforced by endless drilling and simulations. Eli knew that in time, the militia would have to employ those tactics for real, but he didn't think that time was now. Eli's mistake was assuming that the leaders of the militia would make the decision as to when they were ready to engage the enemy. What he didn't consider, was that the enemy would come to them, bringing the fight unexpectedly to their training camp way out there on the secluded bayou. And it happened just an hour or so after he and Seth had paddled away in the johnboat.

The first shots fired startled both Eli and Seth, but neither of them realized what was actually happening until those reports were followed by the rip of machine gun fire and several explosions that were surely detonating grenades. When the intensity of that onslaught tapered off, they heard the unmistakable sounds of men screaming in pain and terror, and Eli and Seth knew that this was no surprise drill devised by their instructors; the camp had been attacked for real!

The two men tied their boat to an overhanging branch at the bayou's edge and grabbed their rifles to race back through the woods towards the camp. They were on the opposite side of the waterway from the camp itself because the other side was too swampy to traverse on foot from that far down. This gave them the advantage, because from the willow thickets on the far side, they were able to see what was going on in the moonlit clearing, while staying out of sight of whoever it was that had launched this sudden assault.

As they slipped through the dense trees until they were close enough to see the old dock on the other side, near the place where they usually kept their boat pulled up in the reeds, Eli and Seth knew that they were too late to make a difference in the outcome of the battle, even if just two additional men *could* have made a difference. Most of the shooting had stopped by that point, but Eli and Seth saw a man running in the shadows behind the dock, then stumble into the water and fall with a splash when someone began shooting at him from farther up on the top bank of the bayou. It was obvious to Eli and Seth that the fallen man was one of theirs and the two shooting at him were with the unknown attackers.

"Cover me! I'm going after him!" Seth whispered as he slid down the bank and waded into the bayou.

Eli opened fire in the direction of the muzzle flashes he'd seen, emptying at least half of the thirty-round mag of the M-16 Deputy Branson had given him. He didn't know for sure whether any of those rounds found their mark, but for the moment, there was no more incoming fire directed at the man in the water. Seth had reached him momentarily and Eli covered him as he swam back across, pulling the wounded man with him until he reached the near bank, where Eli helped drag him up into the concealment of the willows at the top. Eli had seen then that the man was James Andre, one of their fellow recruits who'd grown up along the river in the next parish to the south. He and Seth quickly determined that Andre had been hit twice. The round to his lower leg had caused him to go down first, but appeared to be a flesh wound only. The other one had penetrated his right shoulder from the rear, breaking his collar bone upon exit and leaving a ragged hole from which the man was losing a lot of blood.

"You're gonna be okay, buddy." Eli whispered. "We've got the boat tied up just down the bayou. We're gonna get the hell out of here!" Eli told him, as he pressed a folded-up bandana over the bloody hole and told Andre to do his best to hold it there. But there was no time to move him back downstream to the boat before more men came into view across the bayou.

"I think you killed two of them!" Seth whispered, as he and Eli watched them gather around something at the water's edge below the opposite bank. "I saw them go down when you opened up on them. They're gonna know now they didn't get everybody in the camp!"

Eli quickly saw that there were too many of them to engage. He and Seth were going to have to wait it out where they were, hoping they wouldn't be discovered while doing what they could to keep James Andre from bleeding out.

"Unless they decide to swim, they won't find us over here. And if they try that, they'll be easy pickings!"

Eli hoped they didn't try it though, as he saw even more men fan out along the far bank and the area around the adjacent dock. They were close enough now that he could even make out some of their conversation, and he watched as one man led them to the area of reeds just past the end of the dock, pointing to the very spot where Eli and Seth usually kept their little boat. This man clearly knew about the boat, and the longer Eli studied him, the more he thought he seemed familiar. And then, hearing him speak again, as he pointed down the bayou and gestured with his hands, it suddenly dawned on Eli that the man was Matt Griggs! Seth had realized it at the same time.

"I should shoot him right now!" Eli whispered, even though he knew he couldn't do so without bringing the entire force of attackers down on them, making it unlikely they'd get out of this alive. Instead, he and Seth just watched and waited until Griggs and the men he was talking to turned to walk back in the direction of the camp. *None of us saw this coming,* Eli thought. *Who would have believed that the malcontent deserter who'd done nothing but complain would go off and join forces with some unknown group and then lead them straight back to the location of his former comrades?*

Like almost everyone else among the recruits, Eli hadn't really liked Matt Griggs. He was a loud know-it-all who thought that his former Army experience made him better than the rest of them, and he even argued with Deputy Branson until it finally got him a beat down in front of all the men. Griggs had said little to any of them after that, other than the one friend he had among them. It was just two evenings later that he and Boyd Moreau slipped away while Moreau was on watch duty, taking all the weapons and supplies they could carry in the two backpacks they also stole. When it was discovered that they were gone, the rest of the men took it as good riddance and thought little more of it. They all figured it was the last any of them would ever hear of those two, but apparently, they were badly mistaken. If Moreau was there with him, they didn't see him, but Griggs' presence proved he was responsible for the sudden attack. And as far as Eli and his companions knew, the three of them were the only survivors.

"We have to try and find our way to Sierra Zulu!" Eli whispered, as he and Seth quickly carried James through the woods to where they'd left the johnboat. "I know we have orders to stay put, but in this circumstance, we've got a hell of a good reason to disobey those orders. It's too late to help the rest of the guys, but it may not be too late to make Griggs and whoever he brought with him pay for what they've done!"

"Yeah, but to do that, we've first got to get down the bayou and then down the river. We'd better hope that whoever those people are that Griggs brought with him didn't come by boat!"

Eli knew that Seth was right. The johnboat was their only hope of escape and their only hope of reaching Sierra Zulu, if they could even find it. But with no motor and many miles to paddle in the slow, flat-bottomed aluminum boat, they'd be easy targets for anyone coming after them with a motorized vessel. Even so, any boat was better than the alternative of trying to travel on foot through the swamp, which was virtually impossible carrying a wounded man. At least with the little johnboat, they could stick close to the bank, keeping to the shadows where possible. Since the night was still young, they had time to make quite a few miles under the cover of darkness if they didn't waste it. Like Eli and Seth, James said he hadn't heard the sound of any motors, so that seemed to indicate that the attacking force was land-based and had approached the camp by way of the single gravel road leading in from the north. If that were true, then escape downriver was a viable option.

Eli and Seth carried James down the bank and got him situated in the bottom of the boat, then paddled as quickly down the bayou as they could until they reached the broad expanse of the Atchafalaya River. After waiting a few moments to listen for the sounds of outboards or other marine engines, they set out downstream, taking advantage of the currents where possible, while keeping the boat near enough to one bank so that they could bail out into the woods if they came under fire.

It was a long, exhausting, and nerve-wracking night, as the two men were constantly looking over their shoulders in the dark while whispering reassurances to their wounded companion that it wouldn't be much farther before they found help. When the morning mist began to build in the cool air over the river just before dawn, they crossed to the east bank where they expected they would find the cut-off and forged on blindly, hoping they wouldn't miss it in the low-visibility conditions. The only thing that prevented that from happening was the subtle current that carried the boat with it as it diverged into the narrower bayou. Eli noticed it when he was forced to sweep the paddle hard from the bow to miss a stump protruding from the surface dead ahead, banging his paddle hard against the gunwale as he did. When it seemed obvious that this current was flowing almost due east, he whispered back to Seth that it was possible this was their turn.

"Well, we won't know until we follow it a ways, but it's worth checking out," Seth agreed.

Eli was hopeful as the two of them paddled into the smaller waterway, leaving the broad river behind. While they'd been invisible out there in that heavy mist, he knew the morning sun would burn that off fast, and those wide-open waters would offer no place to hide if the enemy they'd escaped during the night had boats and came looking for them. Because he and Seth had killed two of their men at the edge of the bayou, Eli figured the attackers were aware that some of their targets had escaped.

Since it seemed obvious that Matt Griggs had brought them there, he would have also told them that not all the militia were based at that one training camp. Griggs knew about Sierra Zulu, because all the recruits there did, but he didn't know where it was, because he wasn't from around there, and Deputy Branson and the other trainers were purposefully vague about its location. Eli understood their reasoning for that, and didn't question it, but he knew the river well, and could extrapolate from what he'd overheard well enough to have a good guess that it was somewhere in the maze of waterways to the south and east of the main river. And to reach that area, one had to first turn off on a bayou big enough to accommodate the gunboat and the other vessels Branson and his companions operated from. This one seemed adequate to do just that, so Eli had determined it was worth checking out. And now that he and Seth had been stopped short as soon as they turned into it by the sudden command from a woman hidden there, overlooking the entrance, it seemed all the more likely they were on the right one.

As the johnboat came to a stop in the mud at the water's edge, Eli called back to the still hidden woman, hoping to assure her they had good reason to be there. He had no way of knowing whether she was with Branson's outfit, but he'd heard there were a few women among their ranks, some of them even fighting alongside the men in some of the clashes they'd had to date. If this woman was one of them, then Eli knew she would know what he was talking about when he told her what they sought.

"We are looking for Sierra Zulu!" He called out, as he held his hands high, the shaft of the paddle still gripped firmly in both.

SEVEN

SHAUNA HARTFIELD WAS RELIEVED TO SEE THE MEN IN THE johnboat comply with her orders. The one who had spoken appeared to be in his late 40s, judging by the mix of gray in his heavy beard. He wore a faded camo hunting jacket that appeared to be stained with blood. The second man was a good bit younger looking, probably in his early 30s, and tall and lean like his companion. Shauna took them both for Atchafalaya locals, not only because of their appearance, but for the ease with which they handled the old johnboat. The third man in the boat with them was lying there unmoving and maybe even unconscious, so it was difficult to make out his features, but she could see that he had a scruffy beard too, as well as long, wild hair. Like his companions, his clothing was stained and dirty, and the makeshift bandages on his shoulder and leg were soaked through and through with blood.

Shauna was glad that neither man reached for the weapons beside them because she didn't want to have to kill them before she found out who they were. But now that the boat had nudged into the soft mud of the bank, and the man that spoke said that they were looking for Sierra Zulu, they really had her attention! *How did they know the name of the hidden base camp that only she and her tight-knit group of friends and family were aware of?* Shauna had no idea, but she was determined to find out.

"Keep those paddles in your hands and step out of the boat! Get away from those rifles and stand out there in the open where I can see you!"

Shauna waited as the two awkwardly got to their feet without the assistance of their hands. Both men kept a tight grip on their paddles just as she insisted and when they were standing there beside the boat, she ordered them to hold them over their heads with their arms outstretched as high as they could reach. Glancing back at the third man still in the boat to confirm that he was indeed incapacitated and not a threat, Shauna took a couple of steps away from the trunk of the sycamore tree from behind which she'd been watching.

She was also dressed in camouflage and blended in well with the background, but when she moved, she knew both men suddenly spotted her and were now watching intently to see what she was going to do. She could tell they knew she had the advantage, standing there with an M4 leveled on them while they stood helpless in the wide open. Shauna took a couple more steps closer and then stopped to ask her next question:

"What did you say you were looking for?"

"*Sierra Zulu!*" The same man that had spoken before replied. "Does that mean anything to you?"

The man who asked this seemed to get a little more nervous when she didn't reply right away. Shauna moved a few steps closer still, walking along the top of the bank until she was standing nearly directly over them and could get a better view of the third man, still lying unmoving in the bottom of the boat.

"What happened to him?" She asked, indicating the other man with a nod. "Is he hurt?"

"He's been shot; hit by rifle rounds in the shoulder and in the leg."

"Why was he shot? Who are you and why did you turn off the river here? What is this Sierra Zulu that you are speaking of?"

Shauna knew the man was caught off guard by her questioning, but she wanted to know how he knew the name of their base camp before she said any more. No one without inside knowledge of their operation could possibly know that name, and she had to know who these men were before the conversation went any further. The man was hesitant to answer, and Shauna understood that the two of them were wary of her as well, considering that she had the drop on them and that they had no idea who she was or why she was there. But it was up to them to provide an explanation first, not her.

"This bayou is off-limits to outsiders," Shauna continued. "I want to know why you're here and where you think you're going!"

"We don't mean to trespass," the man answered. "If this is your private property, just let us turn around and go back to the river and you'll never see us again. I'm sorry we bothered you."

"That's not going to happen until you tell me about Sierra Zulu —what it is—and why you are looking for it!" Shauna made sure that her tone left no doubt that refusal to answer wasn't an option. And though she didn't say so, she wasn't about to let these men leave without telling her, even if they tried.

"Sierra Zulu is the headquarters for a mil..." The man hesitated as he fumbled for the right word. "For an *organization* we are a part of."

Shauna knew he'd been about to say 'militia', but then thought better of it and changed his mind.

"An organization? Organization for what?"

"For safety and security. If you've been around here any time at all, you know how dangerous things are now. People have to stick together for protection, that's all. Look, things are so dangerous, the people in charge of the organization haven't even told us exactly where their headquarters is located. My buddy, Seth, and I have a good idea, because we know the river basin pretty well, and we know it's on a bayou west of the main river channel. But if we're on the wrong bayou, we'll move on, like I said."

"So, who are these people that are in charge of this place you call Sierra Zulu?"

"The main one is a fellow named Keith Branson. He was a deputy sheriff in this parish before things went south. He and his father and a fellow named Sam Necaise are in charge, as far as we know. They're the ones we see most days when they come to our camp upriver. Have you ever heard of them?"

Shauna studied his face, then answered with more questions of her own. "Can you tell me what this Keith Branson looks like? And what his father's name is?"

The man did, and then he described the location of the camp where he and the others had been living, telling her it was on property belonging to Keith Branson, the same property where the deputy had once lived with his wife, before she was killed, and their home was later burned to the ground. At this, Shauna lowered her rifle and relaxed, confident these men hadn't come here with ill intent, especially since there were only three of them and one was wounded badly enough to be incapacitated.

"So, you guys are with the new recruits Keith moved up there to his old home place... You were with the bunch that had been detained at that C.R.I. work camp?"

Both men nodded. Keith wouldn't have told them how to get here, but they would have surely heard mention of Sierra Zulu during their training, and if these two were from the local area, as they certainly appeared to be, it wouldn't be too hard for them to figure out where to begin looking for it.

"You *do know* Keith then? You know about the militia too?" The man asked.

"Of course I do. Keith Branson is my brother-in-law. It was my husband, Eric Branson, that led the rescue operation that set all of you free to join the militia. And putting together the militia was his idea in the first place. So, what happened? Why did you leave the camp and how did your friend get shot?"

Shauna listened as Eli and Seth gave her their names and then a detailed account of what had happened the night before. The story they told was bad news, and that news would be a devastating blow to everything Keith, Bart and Sam had been trying to achieve, not to mention Eric. Shauna glanced out over the river beyond the entrance to the bayou. The morning mist was beginning to thin, but it was still impossible to see beyond the middle of the channel.

"Are you sure you weren't followed last night on the river?"

"We didn't hear or see anything," Eli said. "There were no boats in the bayou, and we didn't hear any farther away on the river either. I don't think the men that did this came by boat at all. I think they came by way of that gravel road leading in there. That's how Griggs and Moreau left, and they'd have known just how to lead that bunch back in there to set up that attack."

"You did the right thing, coming here to look for Keith. And he needs to know about this, ASAP!"

What Eli and Seth had told her was truly disturbing. Two disgruntled militia recruits had left nearly two weeks ago, and then at least one was seen with an unknown band of attackers that crept up on the militia camp in the dark and murdered everyone but these three men who were fortunate enough to escape. To pull that off was no easy feat, because even though it had only been a few weeks since they started, the recruits were getting excellent training and Keith and Bart would have made sure they had solid security protocols in place to safeguard the camp. This attack took devious planning from someone familiar with those protocols—and it also took someone with a serious grudge.

Shauna remembered Keith talking about the deserters after they left. The trouble with them had started not long after Eric left on his expedition to the east. One was a know-it-all Army combat veteran who argued with Keith and Bart over almost every detail of the tactics and skill sets the two of them were attempting to teach the mostly civilian volunteers. But there was apparently more to it than that. It seemed unbelievable that those men not only left the militia, but somehow joined forces with another group and then brought them back there to wipe out their former comrades. Shauna had no idea who the marauders were, and neither did these men who survived it, apparently. But if the three of them hadn't made it here when they did to tell their story of what happened, then Keith and the others who were going there this morning to resume their training after a Sunday break might have run straight into an ambush! This was bad, and Keith and the rest of the group had to know about it right now. Shauna knew it couldn't wait even the remaining half hour or so until Keith and the others came by in the gunboat on their way to what was supposed to be another routine day. She'd never had to use the handheld radio that whoever was keeping watch here always had available, but now was the time. She told Eli and Seth what she was doing and walked back to her lookout position near the big sycamore tree and unclipped the unit from a side pocket in the small daypack she'd left there.

Then, she pressed the transmitter button and called out to the gunboat, knowing that either Bart or Ronnie Ferguson would be aboard even if Keith wasn't yet, as one of the two was always on watch there in the pilothouse. When a voice crackled back through the speaker, it was Ronnie's.

"Ronnie, this is Shauna, and it's urgent! Tell Keith and Bart we've got a big problem! Three men just arrived here at the cutoff, and they've got bad news—*really bad news!* The militia recruit camp was attacked last night, and as far as they could tell, everyone there was killed except for them. They think that the two men that deserted a while back were involved, and that maybe they joined forces with some other group and led them straight there to the camp!"

There was a brief pause before Ronnie replied. "I'll go pick them up, Shauna, and we'll be right there!"

Shauna took a deep breath and switched off the radio. She knew that aside from Eric, Keith was one of the most level-headed and experienced leaders a resistance group like theirs could hope to have. He would come up with a plan to deal with this, but as she walked back down to where Eli and Seth had landed, and waited for the gunboat to arrive, Shauna couldn't shake the feeling that everything was about to change again. The attack on the militia camp was bad enough, but the fact that it was carried out by men associated with those deserters only added to her sense of unease. Who were they? And how did those two find them so quickly and get them to do their bidding? And more importantly, what did they know of Sierra Zulu and the rest of the group still hiding out there? None of the recruits were supposed to know about this place, and yet Eli and Seth did, and if they found their way here, those deserters leading those unknown enemy forces could just as well do the same!

"A ride to Sierra Zulu is on the way, but let's get your boat out of sight of the river while we wait for it. That fog is burning off fast, and it won't be long before anyone coming down that river will be able to spot the entrance to this channel."

Eli nodded, and he and Seth hastily pushed their boat away from the bank and climbed in. As they paddled it farther down around the first bend in the bayou, Shauna followed from the bank above, asking Eli more questions about the deserters.

"Do you think they have an idea of where to find Sierra Zulu? I know Keith didn't share the specifics on the location, but you two had enough to go on to find your way here. Is it possible that they could have overheard enough to do the same?"

Eli glanced back at the river behind them before he spoke up. "It's possible, yeah, for sure. They were with the rest of us there for a good three weeks before they split, so they could have figured it out. Everybody there knew it was somewhere downriver, of course, because we could hear the gunboat coming from that way every morning and going back every afternoon. We talked about it, of course, because we were all curious and were wondering what it was like there."

"Those two fellows weren't from around here though. At least Griggs wasn't," Seth said. "Moreau said he lived in Morgan City when he was a kid, but I don't know how much he knew of the river."

"The Atchafalaya Basin is huge, as you probably well know," Eli added, as the two of them continued talking while tying up the boat in the spot to which Shauna had directed them. "It would take them weeks to search all the bayous, channels and canals one-by-one. But of course, they could get lucky and come straight to it on the first guess, like we did. All I can tell you is that we didn't talk to either one of those guys about it. We barely talked to them at all, because it was obvious to everyone in the group that neither one of them really wanted to be there, and neither one was on board with what Deputy Branson and the other trainers planned to do once we were ready."

"Especially Griggs!" Seth added. "Keith probably told you he had to whip his ass one day when Griggs kept pushing him."

Keith *had* told her that, and at the time, Shauna thought it was just the normal stuff that happened when you put a bunch of men together and started giving them orders. But now she couldn't imagine the reaction that Keith and Bart were going to have when they got the full story from these two. They were going to be furious and would want to go and hunt down everyone who was responsible for that attack, but whether that was immediately feasible or not, she didn't know. Eli and Seth had no idea of the numbers involved, but it was obvious that it was a significant force to so thoroughly overwhelm a camp of more than twenty armed recruits who had an established security routine and were somewhat prepared to defend themselves. Of course, Shauna had seen enough to know that a cunning assault leader could accomplish a lot with just a small team, too. Regardless of their numbers, this was an enemy that couldn't be taken lightly, especially since they had obtained an unknown amount of intel from the two traitorous deserters who led them there. Shauna's thoughts of how Eric would handle this if he were here were interrupted by a sudden low whistle from Seth, who had walked back up along the bank to the place where they'd first landed the boat when Shauna ordered them to stop. He was waving frantically for her and Eli to join him, and that's when Shauna first heard the sound of a motor.

She turned and glanced back in the other direction along the bayou to confirm her ears weren't playing tricks on her, and that it wasn't just the gunboat approaching from Sierra Zulu. She didn't expect it to get there quite that fast; but that depended on how long it took Ronnie to run back to the camp in one of the skiffs to pick up Keith and Bart and then bring them back out to where the gunboat was moored in the deeper part of the bayou. But no, there was nothing coming from that direction, and the motor she heard sounded different, anyway. It was the sound of a big outboard, and as it grew louder, she realized it wasn't just one either. *It sounded like two or more boats were approaching and they were definitely coming from upriver!*

Shauna and Eli crouched down in the concealment of the low bushes from which Seth was watching when they reached his side, just in time to hear the boats suddenly throttle back and slow as they came into view in the middle of the river adjacent to the entrance. The mist had thinned enough that they could clearly make out the shapes of three big center-console skiffs and see that there were several men in each of them. As the engines idled there and the boats drifted, it became apparent the occupants were discussing this very side channel they couldn't miss seeing from where they stopped. And as Shauna and the two men beside her watched, one of the three boats turned and slowly came their way, even as the other two sped away and continued downriver.

EIGHT

Keith Branson began his morning looking forward to the boat trip upriver to go and work with the recruits again. He looked forward to it most days, but especially on Mondays, when he was always ready to get away from the crowd at Sierra Zulu again and go spend some time on his old homestead.

Keith was glad that it worked out the way it had to establish the militia training camp there, because it gave him an excuse to go there most days and he always felt closest to Lynn when he was on the property where the two of them had once built their dream home together. Keith wished he could rebuild and live there full time again, but it wasn't really feasible at this point. The group needed the seclusion of Sierra Zulu as their main refuge because it wasn't safe for all of them to remain in such an exposed location, considering everything that had happened recently.

For the recruits, though, the property was just about ideal, and Keith thought the training was going quite well. He and Bart were close to having them ready to go out on patrols farther afield, so they could expand their watch for enemy activity. They hadn't seen any C.R.I. contractors or other organized groups operating on the river or nearby roads since Eric had left, but Keith knew it was only a matter of time before they were back. Any day could be the day they could be called into action again and when he saw Ronnie Ferguson come tearing up the bayou as fast as he could safely negotiate the shallow water in one of the little runabouts, Keith knew something was up, and that maybe this was that day.

"I got a radio call from Shauna!" Ronnie said as he hopped out and tied off the skiff. "The militia camp was attacked during the night! Three of the men made it down there to the mouth of the bayou, where she's standing watch. She said something about the two deserters being involved. I don't know anything else. She just wanted me to let you know ASAP so we can get down there!"

Keith sprang into action, immediately yelling for Bart and Sam to grab their weapons and gear and come with him. Greg Hebert asked if he wanted him to come too, but Keith told him no.

"Not yet, man! Let me get a handle on what's going on because there's no telling what we're going to need to do, depending on what actually happened. Get Hal or Elroy and come on down there to Shauna's position in my patrol boat as soon as you can. Keep the radio on in case I need to reach you, but we've got to go now!"

The three men hopped into the skiff with Ronnie, who sped back to the gunboat as fast as possible. Keith's mind was churning over the implications of Shauna's call as Ronnie started the engine and got on the helm of the bigger boat. As soon as he and Sam cast off the mooring lines, and Bart was at his station behind the Browning, Ronnie swung the vessel around in the narrow bayou and headed out towards the river.

What did Shauna mean, there were only three survivors, and that the two deserters may have been involved? Keith tried to call her on the VHF before they got there, but she didn't answer. *How did something like that happen out of nowhere? Who could have attacked the camp with such devastating results, and why now? If the two militia deserters were involved, who had they fallen in with so soon that had the will and the capability to pull off such a thing?*

And if the three who told Shauna about it were the only survivors, how did they manage that?

Keith knew he'd have to wait and get the answers to those questions directly from Shauna and the three who brought her the news, because she hadn't given Ronnie any further details. He didn't know who the three survivors were, but he couldn't wait to get there and ask them just what in the hell happened. This was a devastating development, considering all the work and time that had gone into putting that militia together. And if it were true that so many of those men died there last night, then it was truly a tragedy. Most of those guys were just local civilians who were volunteering to help defend their fellow citizens in a time of need. They hadn't taken any action against anyone since they'd assembled there, and he doubted anyone could have known of their location or what they were doing there unless the deserters had indeed told them.

Keith immediately regretted not going after Griggs and Moreau now. But at the time they were discovered missing, it hadn't seemed worth it. It wasn't like he could force them to stay and fight for the militia, and besides, if they didn't want to be there, he damned sure didn't want them there and neither did the other men. He'd already had plenty of trouble with Griggs, culminating with the day he had to physically put him in his place in front of everyone in the unit. Keith knew that didn't sit well with the man, and that, of course, things would never be the same between the two of them after it happened. Griggs was clearly a hothead and his limited amount of Army experience more than two decades prior gave him the delusion he knew far more than he really did. At the time, Keith thought it was best for all of them that the know-it-all was gone, and if Boyd Moreau felt the same, then it was good riddance to him as well. *But how could he have ever foreseen that Griggs and Moreau would return with people willing to do what had apparently been done last night?*

While Keith had no idea how they'd accomplished that so soon, he knew that Griggs had vehemently disagreed with him every time he brought up the raid on the Red River outpost. He simply couldn't accept the notion that the soldiers there were no longer loyal to the United States and were, in reality, working with C.R.I., the same mercenary organization that had imprisoned him and the rest of his fellow recruits. Stuck in that way of thinking, it was likely he would blindly trust anyone in uniform if he happened to find someone. If Griggs had really done this, then Keith had made a terrible mistake that led to the death of most of those men and the destruction of the militia he and his father had been working with such diligence to build. The thought of it tore him apart as Ronnie drove the gunboat as hard as he could along the winding bayou.

When they finally rounded the last bend before the bayou joined the main river, Keith was surprised to see a strange motorboat idling slowly towards the entrance to the cutoff. It appeared to be an aluminum center-console commercial fishing boat, the type of working craft Ronnie Ferguson had once owned before it was destroyed the day Eric and Jonathan took it up to Simmesport. The boat was more than a quarter mile away when they came into view of it, but Keith could see that there were several men aboard it.

Whoever was at the helm had obviously spotted the approaching gunboat at the same time, because the boat immediately circled into a tight U-turn at the mouth of the bayou as the helmsman opened up the big outboard to speed back out to the open river. Keith glanced back at Ronnie to wave him forward, but he didn't need to because Ronnie had seen everything that was going on. As they passed the point where Keith knew Shauna was standing her watch, he saw her step out into the open accompanied by two men to wave them down. Ronnie saw them too and backed off on the throttle enough that they could shout back-and-forth as the boat drifted by at reduced speed.

"You got here just in time!" Shauna yelled. "That boat just turned off to come in here, but there were two more just like it that kept going down the river! They are definitely looking for something, and I am sure that it's these guys that escaped from the militia camp last night."

Keith glanced over at the two men beside her and instantly recognized them as Eli Landry and Seth Guidry.

"This was all Matt Griggs' doing!" Eli shouted. "We saw him last night with those men that shot up the camp!"

"What did the men look like?" Keith shouted back. "Do you think they were soldiers? Private contractors? Or just members of some random gang?"

"Soldiers for sure!" Seth yelled. "Most of them were wearing regular green Army fatigues. Griggs was too, but as far as I could tell, he didn't have a weapon."

"We didn't see Moreau, so I don't know if he was with them or not. But it was definitely Griggs; I am sure of it!" Eli added.

"We'll go with you if you want!" Seth yelled. "We're ready to do our part to make them pay!"

"Not now! Stay here with Shauna. Greg and one of the other guys are on the way in my patrol boat, so it'll be best if all of you hang tight here while we go after that boat!"

"Be careful, Keith," Shauna warned. "It looked to me like they had some kind of small machine gun mounted on the bow of that one and the other two may come back to help them if they have radios!"

"We'll worry about that when it happens! But we're not going to let them get away. Bart is on the M2, so don't worry about us!"

Keith turned his attention back to the job at hand as Ronnie steered the gunboat out to the river. When they were in the main channel and heading south, there was no sign of the smaller boat ahead, but there were still patches of mist here and there and the next bend was less than a half a mile below the cut off. Ronnie pushed it until the gunboat was running wide-open and by the time they rounded that bend they caught a glimpse of the open boat heading into the next bend below it.

It was soon obvious that the smaller boat was able to match or exceed their maximum speed and that they weren't really gaining on it, so they were going to need different tactics. Keith glanced over at Bart behind the M2 and saw that he was already preparing to open fire while they still had a clear view of the target. Keith watched as the first burst of 50-cal kicked up a line of huge splashes in the water in front of the fleeing boat, causing it to veer hard to one side.

When the men they were chasing spotted a side channel to the east, the boat swerved again and entered it. Keith smiled because he knew the fleeing men were hoping for an exit to get out of the line of fire, but this channel was nothing more than a dead-end slough that formed a large horseshoe lake because it was once the old river channel. He knew that there was nowhere for the boat to go and that they had them trapped now.

The men they were chasing obviously did not know that or they wouldn't have turned in there. They were still running full speed as Ronnie cut in behind them, sealing off any possibility of escape. It was only when they had made it all the way around to the closed end of the horseshoe that they realized their mistake, and the boat suddenly slowed.

Instead of giving up, however, the helmsman of the other boat circled it around to face them and in the next moment, Keith and Sam had to dive to the deck of the gunboat to take cover behind the reinforced steel bulwarks. The machine gun Shauna had warned them about was real, and the incoming rounds were hitting too close for comfort. Keith thought it sounded like a smaller 30 caliber weapon, but even so, he knew they were well within range. Bart was protected by the armored turret of the Browning, so he responded with a heavy barrage of 50-cal and when he let up, the enemy gun was silent.

"They're not going anywhere!" He yelled to Keith. "I shot the hell out of that outboard too!"

Keith dashed back to the pilothouse to grab a pair of binoculars so that he could try to determine the status of the men aboard the disabled boat. He could see movement behind the low gunwales and knew the occupants were staying down even though Bart had stopped firing. That any were alive at all was a matter of luck, because there was nothing on that boat that would even slow down those rounds. If he wanted to, Bart could shoot the aluminum vessel to pieces, but it wasn't necessary.

"Hold off a minute!" Keith yelled. "I'd like to take one or two of them alive if we can. We need to find out who in the hell they are!"

Keith directed Ronnie to circle wide to the east side of the slough where they could approach the boat while keeping it in full view with the sun behind them. As he kept the binoculars focused on the boat, he saw two men stick their heads up just enough to aim their rifles over the gunwales. Keith ducked once again in anticipation of the incoming rounds, but the old man made the would-be shooters forget about it when he let loose with another burst from the M2, cutting up another line of splashes in front of them.

Then Ronnie closed the gap until they were inside of a hundred yards. From there, Keith could see that there appeared to be two men inside the boat, and that they were locked in a struggle in the bottom, just forward of the console, fighting like they were trying to kill each other!

The scene was so unexpected Keith didn't know what to make of it, but as he kept the binoculars on them, he saw one of the two men suddenly get to his feet after hitting the other with a barrage of punches. Then, in the next second, the same man bent to pick something up from the deck and Keith saw that it was a pistol. As soon as he pointed it at the other man, Keith heard the shots as he fired three times before dropping the weapon and raising both hands high over his head as he turned to face the gunboat. Now, he was shouting in their direction, begging them to please not shoot him and insisting that he wanted to surrender.

Keith hadn't expected anything like it, but he waved Ronnie forward and as the boat closed in and he once again focused his binoculars on the lone man's face, he suddenly understood exactly why he had just done what he had. The man standing alone there in that boat was none other than Matt Griggs!

Keith and Sam both had their rifles leveled on Griggs as Ronnie brought the gunboat alongside the disabled vessel. Griggs had recognized them from the beginning, of course, as he well knew the gunboat and could clearly see all four men aboard it once the chase was up. He was talking nonstop now, trying to explain himself and pleading with the two of them to stop pointing their weapons at him. Griggs had his hands up over his head and was saying that he was forced to go with these men and that he was so thankful when he saw the gunboat coming down that bayou when it did, because he knew it was theirs and that Keith, Bart and Sam would be aboard it.

"Who are these men?" Keith demanded, looking at the four lifeless bodies in the bottom of the boat. "They are obviously in uniform, and it is the same uniform you are wearing now as well! It looks to me like they are the same stolen Army uniforms that those North American Interior Defense forces at that Red River outpost were wearing! I know what happened last night at the militia camp, and I know that you were there because you were seen there with men in uniforms just like these!"

"Yes! I was there," Griggs said. "But only because I was forced to go! Please! You've got to hear me out, and you don't have to hold me at gunpoint to do it, because you can see that I am unarmed!"

"I don't have to hear anything!" Keith said. "But I have every reason to shoot you where you stand, because you are in the uniform of the enemy that attacked the militia camp and killed most of the men posted there last night. Now you are literally in the same boat with them, and I know that you and your dead comrades were looking for the men that escaped last night and brought the message of the attack to us."

"I'm in this uniform because I was forced to wear it! And yes, I'm in the boat with them, but you just saw me shoot the last one that was alive to stop him from firing at you! That's why you've got to believe me. None of this was my doing!"

"I have reason enough to shoot you for desertion alone! My biggest regret is that I didn't hunt you down and do it immediately after you and Moreau left! So, where is he? Is he in one of the other two boats that went downriver?"

"No, Boyd Moreau is dead! I'm telling you, neither one of us wanted to have anything to do with this. Yes, we *did* desert the militia, and I wish we hadn't now, but I felt like we weren't wanted there anyway. We didn't fit in, and it wasn't working out, and you can't force someone to fight when they don't understand what they are fighting for."

"I thought you just said you were forced to do just that, for these men you brought back here to kill your fellow recruits! You hadn't even been asked to fight yet before you deserted, but you knew exactly what we were training for. You knew the mission was to stop the same outfit that locked all of you up in that labor camp before my brother led the raid that got you out!"

"Yes, I get that now. And I get that we made a mistake by leaving, and Moreau paid for it with his life when we were captured by people working with C.R.I. all over again."

"C.R.I.? So, was C.R.I. behind what happened at the recruit camp last night?"

"Yes. It was a man named Commander Reyes, who was in charge of it all. It was Reyes who forced me to come here, and he did that by executing Moreau right in front of me the day after they captured us!"

"Reyes? Are you sure about that name?"

Griggs nodded and then described the man. It was indeed the same Commander Reyes Keith and Bart and some of the others had met in Texas, the same Commander Reyes who'd once helped them, but now was apparently in charge of the C.R.I. operation to seize control of this part of Louisiana.

"You saw Commander Reyes execute Moreau?"

"Yes! He shot him in the face with his pistol at point blank range because he wouldn't help lead them back to our camp—the militia camp on your property."

"And yet Reyes found it anyway because *you* obviously did lead him there, Griggs. Is that about the way it worked?" Keith was furious, and it was all he could do to refrain from squeezing the trigger as he shouldered his rifle again and pointed it directly at Griggs' face.

"I was forced to go along with them! I had no choice! It was either that or they would've shot me the same as they shot Moreau!"

"Maybe you thought you had to comply because you were afraid for your life, but you didn't have to lead them to the camp. I thought you were a soldier once, Griggs! But you have proven that you are nothing but a coward, a deserter, and a liar! You could have led them somewhere else and then tried to escape if what you are telling me is the truth, but I don't believe it is. I don't believe it because I saw you aiming a rifle at us too before you realized that it was over and that Bart's M2 was going to cut that boat to pieces with you inside it if you didn't do something different!"

"He's told us what we need to know, Keith," Sam interrupted. "Let's shoot him now and get it over with. We've got two more boatloads of fellows like those down that river that need killing just as bad!"

"Please!" Griggs pleaded again. "I can help you if you don't. I swear I can! I can tell you what Reyes is planning next, and you can figure out how to stop him! No one else could do that but you, but you're going to need my help to do it!"

NINE

Keith decided to let Griggs live for now. Whether the man had more useful intel for him was questionable, but if he did, Keith would get it out of him. Aside from that, though, he'd already thought of an immediate use for him, and that was to draw in and take out the crews of the other two boats. He knew they had to hurry and get prepared in order to make it happen though, because for all he knew, they were already on their way back.

"There was no answer," Griggs said, when Keith asked him if anyone aboard the boat he was aboard had radioed the other crews upon spotting the gunboat. "I don't know if our radio wasn't working or if it was theirs, but if they got the call, they didn't reply."

Keith figured Griggs was telling the truth or the boats would have turned back right away. Regardless of that, they would return soon enough, when they didn't find what they were looking for. He ordered Griggs to move back to the center console and put his hands on the metal wheel. Then he jumped aboard and used one of the handcuffs he still carried on his belt to secure Griggs' wrist to it. Then, he ripped the microphone cord out of the VHF and threw it overboard, just to make sure Griggs couldn't try it whether or not it was working. With that taken care of, he and Sam heaved the bodies of the four dead men over the side.

"I'm telling you that I can give you all the information you want about Reyes and what he's planning," Griggs said. "Well, I don't know everything he's planning, but I know that he's got lots of men on hand there at your place and a lot more on the way and he was expecting you to arrive there this morning for the training, unaware of what happened."

"So, he's prepared an ambush?" Keith asked.

"Yes. They're waiting for you and Bart and Sam to show up like you always do when you come up that bayou to the dock."

"And who was it, exactly, that told them we always do that, you son of a bitch?" Sam demanded.

"I had no choice!" Griggs answered. "But I'm telling you about it now, so that ought to count for something! Whether I told them that or not, they already knew about the militia and that you had some hidden camp way down here in the swamp. Their number one priority, according to Commander Reyes, was to hunt down Eric Branson and everyone he was associated with, because they said he was the leader of a terrorist insurgency down here. It was just a matter of time before they found that camp!"

"Reyes may have his ambush in place, but he knows there were survivors that escaped the attack last night. That's why he sent you and the others down here in the boats. He must know the survivors would try to warn us."

"He knew someone got away, yes. He would have sent boats after them right then if he could have, but he didn't have any because they weren't supposed to get there until dawn. The boats were coming to help with the ambush and make sure the gunboat didn't leave the bayou once you brought it in there."

"Well, Reyes will never know if his boat crews found the survivors or not, because he's never going to hear from any of you now. I intend to make certain of that!" Keith said.

Bart tossed the end of a long mooring line over to Keith and then uncoiled a hundred feet or so from the stern deck of the gunboat after Keith secured it to the bow cleat of the fishing boat. Then Keith and Sam hopped back aboard the bigger vessel and Ronnie pulled forward to take out the slack.

"What are you doing now?" Griggs wanted to know.

"Don't worry about it. You'll have your role in it, though. You can bet on that!"

With that, Keith and the others ignored Griggs, who was still shouting to them about something as Ronnie steered out of the dead-end slough and back into the river. After checking to make sure neither of the smaller boats or any other vessels were visible upriver or down, Keith directed Ronnie to head north and return to the mouth of the cut-off bayou, where they could prepare for the next phase of his new plan.

When they arrived there with the smaller boat in tow, Keith saw that Greg Hebert was also on site with the patrol boat, which was pulled up to the bank near the spot where Shauna, Eli and Seth had spoken to them on the way out. When the group watching them return saw that someone was standing locked to the wheel of the small fishing boat, all eyes were upon him until Eli screamed Griggs' name in fury upon recognition.

"Where in the hell did you find him?" Eli wanted to know. "He was on that boat?"

"I'm really glad you brought him back alive!" Seth yelled, "Because I want to shoot that son of a bitch myself!"

"Not yet!" Keith countered. "Griggs has got a job to do, and he's about to do it right now. If he fails, then you will have my permission to shoot him. You can be sure of that. But I think he'll comply because Griggs is a coward, as we all knew already. He's also a traitor who will turn his back on anyone if it serves his purpose at the time. We just got a demonstration of that when he shot one of his new buddies just as we caught up with him!"

"You're saying this is the same Commander Reyes we met in Texas? The one that let Jonathan go so that he could come and find you and bring you to pick us up?" Shauna asked, when Keith told them the rest he'd learned from Griggs.

"One and the same," Keith assured her.

"First, he helps us, and now he wants to kill us all."

"He's following orders. We already knew he was a career C.R.I. man, so I can't say I'm surprised. Seems like now he's got a personal vendetta against Eric since he sees Eric as the main obstacle to his entire operation over here. Now he even knows Eric's gone. Griggs told him that and no telling what else. But I intend to keep him guessing when it comes to what happened to his three boat crews this morning."

After Keith told them what he had in mind, he learned from Shauna the identity of the third survivor, James Andre, and that Greg and Hal had quickly moved him back to Sierra Zulu right after they arrived, so he could get the best care they could give him with what they had on hand there.

"I think he will make it," Shauna said. "Eli and Seth got him here in time. With antibiotics and a little luck, his wounds won't get infected. Both rounds that hit him passed all the way through, so there are no bullets to dig out. He's lost some blood, but Eli and Seth did a good job of slowing that down too."

Keith knew that what Eli and Seth did last night was truly heroic. When they could have just as easily turned and disappeared down that bayou, ensuring their safety and avoiding the certainty of pursuit by not shooting those two men that were trying to kill James, they had done the opposite. Eli had taken two shooters out and Seth had risked everything by swimming across that bayou to haul James back over to the other side with all those armed men in close proximity. Then, they had carried them all the way to their little boat and brought them down the river to safety by paddling through the night. Those two men were everything Keith and Eric were looking for in militia recruits and were the polar opposite of despicable cowards like Matt Griggs.

"How are we going to do this?" Greg Hebert wanted to know. "Do you have a plan, Keith?"

"We'll pull that boat out there into the river just off the mouth of the bayou, just far enough so it'll be easy to see when they're coming back up the river, but close enough that they'll be in easy rifle range when they close in on it to see why it's still there."

"We could just use the M2 and take them out before they get that close." Greg said.

"Or hit them with the grenade launchers when they do," Shauna added.

"No, I want those two boats intact, if possible. They could turn out to be useful to our operations. They are perfect for some of the things we might need to do later, and they may come in handy even sooner when we work out a plan to stop Reyes."

"Sounds good, Keith." Greg agreed. "I just hope we can lure them close enough so we can get them all."

"That's where Griggs comes in," he said. "He will get them to come close, or he will be the first one I shoot."

"Do you think he will do it?" Shauna asked.

"He doesn't have much choice. He's going to be locked to the boat and standing out there in the wide open. All we need him to do is wave them in and once they're in range, it'll be up to all of us to do the rest, so pick your targets carefully! Let's take out the guys at the helm of each boat first and then aim for anyone else that tries to take it after they go down. Make sure they don't get a chance to bring those 30-cal machine guns into play either, because they may get lucky if they start spraying lead. If either one of those boats gets away before we kill them all, then we've got the gunboat and the patrol boat to go after them."

The plan was set. The gunboat would be tucked back into the bayou at the top of that first bend, with Bart on the M2 and Ronnie at the helm. Sam would stay aboard with the two of them. Keith would be near his patrol boat, which Greg would take just upriver from the cut off, where he could tuck in close to the low clay bank in a spot where the willows grew right down to the water's edge. There it would be out of view from where Keith planned to anchor Griggs' boat. Keith would have a clear line of fire from a spot a bit closer atop the bank and could run back and hop aboard with Greg if they needed to give chase. The rest of the group, consisting of Shauna, Hal, Eli and Seth, would be concealed in shooting positions near the mouth of the bayou, waiting with their rifles until Keith gave the signal by firing the first shot. He hoped that shot would be directed at one of the two helmsmen in the other boats, but he was damned sure prepared to use it on Griggs if the man did anything other than follow his strict instructions.

Griggs had already told Keith that there were four guys in one of the boats and five in the other. He said that they both had the same M60 machine guns mounted on the forward platforms, just like the one aboard the boat he was in. Those guns at the bow made for a pretty good set up, but Keith wasn't going to give them a chance to bring them into play. The key, as in most such situations, was to take out the enemy using the element of surprise. They would lure them into an ambush just like the ambush that Reyes had planned for him.

When the plan was understood by all, the next step was to get Griggs into position. Keith and Greg towed the captured boat out there with the patrol boat and secured it to the riverbed with one of Keith's anchors. Then, Keith removed the handcuffs from Griggs' wrist and, combining them with a short length of chain wrapped twice around one of his ankles, secured him to the base of the steering pedestal instead. That way, he could stand there and wave with both hands without looking suspicious. *And he would do it or else!*

"Remember what I told you," Keith warned him again. "Any gesture you make other than straightforward signals for those guys to come over to you will get you a 5.56 in the head. I'll be right over there on that riverbank just a hundred yards away with my rifle and believe me, I won't hesitate to scramble your brains if you screw this up!

"And even if you do manage to screw it up, it's not going to do Reyes and his men a damn bit of good. If those guys take off and try to run away at this point, we're going to run them down and obliterate those boats. So just keep doing what you've been doing all along—thinking of no one but your own sorry ass! Do what you've got to do to save it, and right now that means complying with us and getting your new best buddies to come up close and personal so we can shoot them without messing up two good boats! You got that, Griggs?"

"You don't have to worry about me." Griggs said. "I'll get them to come over here. I don't have anything to gain by helping them anymore. I know you don't believe me, but I *really do* want to help you avoid Reyes and all his men. It makes me sick what they did there at the militia camp and I really didn't want to have any part of that."

Keith ignored that last part. He didn't give a damn how many times Griggs apologized or how many excuses he concocted for what he had done. There was nothing he could do now to absolve himself of his guilt for what happened up there at that militia camp last night. How he would ultimately deal with him, Keith hadn't decided yet. It would probably come to a decision between all the members of the group, but however they arrived at their verdict, Keith knew that Griggs would pay.

Keith had time to think about all the things he had done wrong as he sat there on the riverbank with his rifle, waiting for the other two boats to return from downriver. Not only had he made a terrible mistake by failing to go after Griggs and Moreau when they left, he had also failed to establish an adequate security protocol to protect all those inexperienced militia recruits. Hell, it was a mistake and a failure to set them up in a location like that property in the first place! He and Eric had discussed it at length and they both knew it was a risk, but at the time they'd deemed it one they could manage. They had thought that with the numbers there, the men could protect themselves from anything other than a major assault. A major assault was the last thing either of them had expected to occur, yet now it had, though Keith knew it was highly improbable had it not been for a traitor like Griggs bringing the enemy straight to them.

Keith didn't have any reason to believe Griggs was lying about the execution of Moreau, because it sounded exactly like something a motivated C.R.I. commander like Reyes would do in order to force Griggs to give up the camp. But Keith didn't believe their encounter with Reyes, that led to their capture, was just some random accident. It seemed far more likely that they'd run into him because they'd gone looking for what they thought were the real authorities. The two of them had been so disgruntled with the militia when they left, they were willing to take anyone in uniform at face value.

Keith wasn't completely surprised to hear that Mitchel Reyes was in charge of the operation, either. Although Reyes had helped them before, assisting Shauna, Megan, Vicky and Jonathan in returning to Louisiana from his post in Texas, that was months in the past now, which was an eternity considering all that had happened in the meantime. That meeting with him was long before C.R.I. was ordered to start moving assets into the state of Louisiana. At that time, the Atchafalaya Basin was beyond Reyes' area of concern or authority, but he *had* stated that the plan was to eventually relocate all civilians to refugee centers. Until that happened, the vast swamp was a no-man's-land of scattered refugees and survivors. When the contractors moved in, they quickly began building detention camps rather than refugee centers, however, and soon after, they were rounding up civilians from their farms and homes to get them out of the way and keep them under control. Eric had learned Reyes was involved with that operation when they freed all the men from that work camp. But he and Keith both figured he was still based in Texas and unlikely to get personally involved here. But if so, that had clearly changed now, because Griggs' description of the man left Keith with no doubt of his identity.

Keith really hoped he didn't have to shoot Griggs when the boats arrived, because there were still answers he could get from him if he had more time to extract them. At the moment, though, the focus was on making sure none of those boats reported back to Reyes to let him know they'd encountered anyone from Sierra Zulu. It was crucial to keep him guessing and waiting, but for all Keith knew, he could already have more boats on the way downriver, even though Griggs said he hadn't seen any but the three. Keith was sure that Griggs knew very little of the operation in reality, because Reyes was only using him for a limited purpose, and it was surprising the man was still alive at all after he'd accomplished his primary task of leading Reyes to the camp.

What Keith really wanted more than anything right now was his brother's help. He was extremely disappointed that Eric still hadn't returned after so many weeks away, and it didn't bode well for the success of his mission that he hadn't. Keith hadn't been unduly concerned about Eric's safety, considering that he took with him four of the most competent and gung-ho young men they had among them. But it had been long enough now that the worry was starting to creep in. Keith knew no matter how good Eric was, there were a hell of a lot of dangers he could run into out there. There was no way of knowing what his brother had found on the other side of the river, but he still held out hope that he would return and that when he did, he would have help or a new solution to show them the way forward.

Until then, Keith's immediate concern was how to respond to what had just happened last night. Losing the majority of the militia recruits changed everything. Sure, they still had their core group at Sierra Zulu, and that group had been successful at taking down that Red River outpost and liberating all those new recruits in the first place. They could accomplish a lot without extra help, but Keith had known all along that C.R.I. and those aligned with them, including the cartel thugs, and this new illegitimate paramilitary force would come in larger numbers when they came the next time.

It was why Eric had left to seek help, of course, as well as the entire purpose of recruiting the militia. Eric knew they had to turn that situation around and get out of defensive only mode and take the fight to the enemy. It would be nice to not only hold their own, but to expand their secure zones and then eventually gather more of the local civilians into the fold and grow the resistance into a force that would be very difficult for an outside enemy to defeat. All of that would take time, of course, and Keith and Eric knew it when they began. But what happened last night was a setback that was almost too much to bear. Losing that many good men who had come so far in their training was a devastating blow to all of them, and Keith couldn't imagine Eric's reaction when he got the news, assuming he finally made it back.

Now, a large force under Reyes' command was right there on his own property, and an even larger one was on the way to reinforce them. Keith didn't have the resources to fight against odds like that, but the alternative to fighting was to be chased even deeper into the swamp with little hope of peace or a life worth living. He had to think of something, but the first priority was preventing any of those boats from returning upriver.

TEN

Griggs could feel the eyes upon him as he stood there in the open boat, waiting. He knew those who watched him were doing so through weapon optics or over the tops of rifle barrels pointed his way, and he had no doubt that most of them were hoping he'd give them a reason to center their sights on his head and pull the trigger. Griggs was surprised, in truth, that they'd let him live this long. The fact that Keith didn't shoot him as soon as he discovered him in that boat with Reyes' men gave Griggs a faint ray of hope that he might talk his way out of this. But at the moment, he knew he had to get through this first hurdle—that of surviving being used as live bait—before he would even get a chance to try.

The morning seemed to drag on forever as he stood there leaning back against the steering pedestal of the open boat, listening for the sound of outboard engines, but hearing nothing but the gurgling rush of the river running under the metal hull beneath his feet. It wasn't until the sun was nearing its midday peak that he finally heard what he'd been waiting for. The distant sound was definitely that of a boat motor, but Griggs knew it could be most any boat until it gradually grew louder, and he could at last tell that it wasn't just one, but in fact two motors he was hearing. He knew too, that they were coming his way from downriver even before the two center-console skiffs rounded the big sweeping bend nearly a mile to the south. The moment Griggs was put there for had finally come. The crews of the other two boats had given up and turned back empty-handed in their search for the escaped survivors.

He knew they had probably split up somewhere downriver and then regrouped after finding nothing. Now, they had to be wondering if the men aboard this third boat that left with Griggs somehow had better luck. They knew the crew had turned off into this first big cutoff to the east, and they had to be hoping that despite their own failure, they wouldn't have to return and report to Reyes with nothing to show for a wasted day. Griggs knew they'd zero in on him whether he waved them over or not as soon as they spotted the boat anchored there near the same place they'd seen it last.

He was more nervous than ever now, but he stood up straight, fully alert and focused, with his arms already moving back and forth above his head to get the attention of the two crews. Griggs was confident that they couldn't miss seeing him there, the boat stationary as it was in the wide-open river, far enough from the bank that it couldn't blend into the background of trees and bushes. *But what would they think of the sight of him alone there in it, with no sign of the four-man crew that was supposed to be there with him?*

Griggs didn't know, but he figured there was a chance they would open fire on him if Keith and those ashore didn't shoot them first. He really was in a hell of a fix, caught between two groups of people that couldn't care less whether he lived or died. The only use Griggs was to any of them was the information he could provide, and he knew both parties could well have decided they'd already gotten all of that he had to offer.

When he saw both boats change course to come straight in his direction, Griggs knew they'd spotted him, and he was beginning to think the ruse would go exactly as Keith Branson planned. Those boat crews coming to investigate were about to unknowingly put themselves squarely in the rifle sights of the resistance fighters they'd come here to hunt. But just as he thought it was inevitable that the trap would be sprung, Griggs was dismayed to see one of the two skiffs slow slightly and peel away towards the middle of the river on a course that would give a wide berth to the anchored boat to which he was shackled.

Griggs kept waving anyway while looking directly at the men in that more distant boat, doing all he could to keep their attention and make them think it was urgent enough that they come over to where he was also, but it didn't seem to be working. The four-man crew of that one had made the decision to stay well away for some reason, and Griggs could only assume it was from an abundance of caution. He could tell that at least one of them was looking his way through either binoculars or a rifle scope too, because he caught the sharp glint of the sun's reflection on glass as the boat crept upriver, now at near idle speed.

The other crew was still advancing directly towards him however, their boat moving at a slow but steady clip as all but the helmsman stood forward of the console with their rifles at ready as they studied him and glanced now and then to the riverbank and bayou entrance to see if they could determine what was going on and where the missing crew members might be.

They began shouting out to him as soon as they were within hailing distance, asking him what in the hell had happened to the rest of the guys and why he was just standing there doing nothing while the boat was anchored in place. Griggs didn't know what to tell them. Any story he could concoct would seem over the top and suspect, so he just kept quiet and kept waving, pretending he couldn't hear what they were saying as he motioned them onward as if he had something to show them that required them to come closer.

Griggs was waiting any second now for the sounds of the rifle reports that he knew were coming, and had his fingers crossed that it would happen soon, because if it didn't, he could be the one taking incoming fire from these men that were the intended targets. He was so nervous at this point that he was literally shaking when at last he saw the man at the helm of the closing boat suddenly collapse and let go of the wheel just as the sound of a rifle report reached his ears. And almost before he could process that, two more men at the bow dropped without warning, the one nearest the machine gun tumbling over the side and into the river with a big splash.

By then there was a literal barrage of rifle rounds ripping into the remaining two men on that boat, and Griggs saw them go down as well. But when he glanced out at the other, more distant boat, he saw that some of the men aboard it were firing back towards the riverbank now, even as the motor suddenly revved to high RPMs and pushed it up to speed. Griggs doubted the shooters aboard it could see a target from way out there because he knew that Keith and all his team were well concealed ashore.

But what came next was exactly what he'd feared. Some of the incoming rounds were directed at him for lack of a better target. And Griggs was certain that other crew connected him and the boat to which he was shackled with the ruthless slaughter of everyone aboard the one that had just approached the spot where it was anchored.

The restraints on his leg didn't prevent Griggs from dropping quickly into the bottom of the hull, so that's exactly what he did as he heard the incoming rounds rip into the aluminum sheet metal all around him. All he could do was curl up down there in a fetal position and try to make himself as small as possible while hoping like hell that Keith and the others would do something about the other boat and make the shooting stop.

But the shooting did *not* stop with those first few rounds. It seemed to go on and on at a full-auto rate of fire and Griggs figured it was because someone had brought the M60 into play as the boat sped away. Griggs expected at any second to feel the burning sensation of bullets tearing through his flesh, but by some miracle, despite the countless number of rounds striking various parts of the hull all around him, he remained unscathed when it finally ceased. Griggs understood the reason it had as he heard the heavier bursts from the 50-cal Browning aboard the gunboat. He smiled to himself as he considered how lucky he was to have survived that onslaught of incoming lead. Maybe it was because some of those rounds had been deflected by the steel plating that had been added to parts of the console, or maybe today just wasn't his day to die, but either way, he'd take it!

After the shooting tapered off, Griggs could hear the sounds of other boat motors running at speed now too, but he was afraid to look up until he was sure they were too far away to shoot at the anchored boat again. When he finally raised his head just over the gunwale, he could still see the other boat racing north up the wide-open river, and behind it in pursuit, the patrol boat he knew Keith Branson and his partner were in. Following in the wakes of both was the bigger gunboat that had been hidden back inside the mouth of the bayou.

Griggs didn't know what would happen next, but he knew that third boat had a bigger, more powerful outboard than the one he was aboard. The men in it had a decent head start, but it was a long way back to the bayou by the militia camp where Reyes and his men waited. The outcome of the chase would be determined somewhere beyond sight of where he was now, so Griggs figured he'd have to wait a bit longer to learn how it went. That didn't bother him at first, but then he realized he was still shackled to that steering pedestal in a boat that was riddled with bullet holes both above and below the waterline, and it was leaking like a big aluminum colander someone had tossed out into the river!

Griggs looked back to the riverbank and the wooded area near the mouth of the bayou and began waving and yelling to get the attention of the other shooters he knew were still hiding there, desperate to make them aware of his predicament. After the sounds of the boat motors faded away in the distance, he knew they could hear him, as the boat was anchored well within shouting range.

If someone didn't come out there fast and tow it back to the bank, the leaking metal boat was going to sink and take him down with it. As he waited for a reply to his calls for help, Griggs scanned the interior of the hull around him, looking at all the holes that were the source of the incoming water. He found several of them within his limited reach and began stuffing them with bits of rags and the ends of some pieces of rope and anything else he could find to slow the river's ingress. But though he managed to plug a few, the boat continued to slowly fill. *Would it actually sink to the bottom if it took on enough water, or did it have sufficient flotation built into the compartments under the seats to keep it half-awash?*

Griggs didn't know. All he knew was that one of the men in the crew that morning had told him all three of the boats were hand-crafted somewhere in the local area by a welder who used to build them for commercial fishermen working the river and marshes. It was obviously constructed to be strong and capable of handling the conditions of those waterways on which it was designed to operate, but Griggs was unsure whether it met the safety standards of more modern recreational craft, with all their government or insurance mandated requirements like positive flotation. Griggs doubted it, because the vessels were purpose built for needs of customers who used them to haul their catches of crawfish and other seafood to the market. Foam-filled compartments would be nothing but wasted space in that type of vessel.

Fully realizing the urgency of his situation now, Griggs got to his feet again and waved and yelled some more. He could now see two of the men that he knew had escaped the attack last night—Eli Landry and Seth Guidry—standing there on the bank at the edge of the woods, along with the woman named Shauna and another man he hadn't met, but who also came from Sierra Zulu with Branson and his partner. Griggs shouted to let them know that the boat had been riddled with bullet holes and that it was slowly sinking. He told them he needed help and that he needed it right now.

"Does it look like we have a boat to you?" Eli yelled back at him. "You saw both of the boats that were over here take-off up the river after those guys that ran away and left you there! It seems like we're fresh out of boats to come out there and get you! Sorry about that, but there's not much we can do about it now!"

"It's not that far!" Griggs screamed back at him, more worried than ever after hearing the cold indifference in Eli's tone. "One of you could swim out here and just help me get loose from these shackles! If I don't get them off, this boat will pull me to the bottom, and I'll drown!"

"That sounds like a personal problem to me!" Eli shouted back. "It sort of sounds like you made a bad choice when you got in that boat in the first place this morning!"

"Shauna here says that we don't have a key to those handcuffs anyway!" Seth yelled. "Keith and Greg are the lawmen in this bunch. Those handcuffs belong to them and they're the only ones that have the keys to them, so we couldn't get you loose even if we could get out there. Maybe if you're lucky, they'll get through with their business upriver pretty soon and make it back before you sink and start sucking water!"

"Or maybe they won't!" Eli shouted.

"Please! I've got lots more information for Branson! There's a hell of a lot I can tell him about Reyes that he'll never get if I don't get out of this boat!"

"Branson has other sources of intel and can piece together the rest on his own, I imagine!" Eli said. "He's managed this far without your help, and after what you did, there's no way he'd ever trust you again, anyway!"

Griggs was desperate to the point of panic now. The water was still slowly seeping in, and it was already several inches deep around his feet. and the low gunwales of the boat were visibly much closer to the surface of the river than before. He glanced downriver at the other boat, now drifting slowly away in the current with the bodies of the dead crew inside it.

"Hey!" He shouted to those on the bank again. "Branson wanted that other boat! Are you just going to let it drift away like that? One of you could swim out here and catch it and then use it to tow this one back to the bank! It wouldn't matter if I was still locked to it if it sinks in shallow water. But that way, Branson can decide if he wants to unlock me or not when he gets here!"

"That river's too damned cold to swim this time of year!" Eli yelled back. "That boat ain't gonna drift too far down. It won't be no big deal for Branson to run down there and put a towline on it when he gets done with his business upriver!"

Griggs flipped him off and sat back down in the pool that had formed around his feet, both angry and frantic as he began probing around the bottom of the pedestal for any possibility of breaking himself free of the chain and cuffs that shackled his leg securely to it. Branson had first wrapped the short length of three-eighths-inch chain twice around his left ankle and then he'd used one of the handcuffs locked through the links to hold it in place there. Then he'd locked the other cuff to the inch and a half diameter aluminum tubing of the steering pedestal, which was joined at its base to the inner hull of the same material by expert welds.

Griggs already knew from the first time he'd tried pulling free that even though he could work a bit of slack into the chain with his fingers, he'd couldn't make the opening nearly wide enough to slide the loops over his ankle. Breaking or bending either the handcuffs, chain or the aluminum tubing could not be accomplished without the right tools, and now Griggs was desperate as he searched around every part of the boat within his grasp for any such object or implement that might help.

There was a compartment under the stern seat in front of the transom to which the outboard motor was attached, and inside it he'd already found half empty containers of oil, several spare spark plugs and other engine maintenance items, along with bits of line, wire leaders and other fishing gear. But the only tool of any kind he found in there was a slender Phillips head screwdriver, probably used for adjusting something on the outboard and far too flimsy to provide any leverage with which to break himself free.

By the time he'd exhausted all possibilities of finding something he may have overlooked, Griggs saw that the boat was lower still in the water. As he got to his feet again, the pool he was standing in was nearly up to his knees, and the gunwales were mere inches from the surface of the river around him. Most of the big Mercury outboard was submerged as well and Griggs lost all confidence that there was sufficient flotation or air trapped inside the various compartments of the hull to keep it from going deeper. He turned back to the riverbank to scream again at those who were watching, yet still making no move to come to his aid.

"You sons of bitches could do something to help me if you wanted to! To hell with all of you!"

Griggs knew his words had no effect on them. He knew that what he had done to the other men by betraying them to Commander Reyes was something that could never be forgiven, as far as Eli and Seth were concerned. And even though he had never met the woman with them before, Griggs now knew that she was Eric Branson's wife—the wife of the actual founder and ultimate leader of this entire resistance operation. The hard truth was that no one among those watching him cared that he was about to be dragged to the bottom of the river by a sinking boat, and as Griggs looked back upstream to the direction in which the other boats had disappeared, he could no longer even hear the sound of motors in the distance. The racing boats were all already far to the north, and the chase was likely still on. At the rate at which the sinking boat was going down beneath him now, Griggs knew that even if the patrol boat or the gunboat turned around and headed straight back, it would be too late for him, even if Branson actually wanted to intervene. He wasn't getting out of this one, and he was beginning to realize that was a fact.

Griggs was so desperate to escape certain death by drowning at that point that he would have cut off his shackled leg had he been able to find a knife, but even that last-ditch option had eluded him. He didn't want to die this way. He never even liked the water much, and swimming was something he only did on rare occasions here and there. He had been afraid of the water when he was a child because he'd watched his cousin drown while playing too close to the rapids in one of the fast-moving creeks near his home. As a result, Griggs was much older before he even learned how to swim. Now, as he felt the boat continue to settle lower into the river, Griggs wondered what it would be like when he could no longer draw a breath of air into his lungs. He wondered if it was going to hurt, when after he'd held that last breath as long as possible beneath the river, he would finally have to expel it to take in only water in exchange. *How long would he suffer beneath its murky surface before he finally lost consciousness and faded away into the oblivion of nothingness?*

Griggs was still cursing and struggling against the shackle when he felt a final surge, like the floor of an elevator beginning its descent. The doomed hull finally shrugged off the last of the trapped air within it in an eruption of gurgling bubbles. With no buoyancy remaining at all, its descent to the bottom was quick and unstoppable. Griggs felt the water rapidly rise to his waist, then up past his chest and shoulders as he flailed with both arms in a futile attempt to tread it, as if that would somehow make a difference. He took the deepest breath he could force into his lungs as he turned his face as high above the water as possible, determined to stare up into that infinity of sweet, pure air for as long as possible before he was pulled from view of it forever beneath the dark Atchafalaya.

ELEVEN

THE LONG WAIT FOR THE OTHER TWO BOATS THAT HAD GONE downriver had Keith wondering if maybe they had somehow already slipped by them on the way back north, perhaps when they had turned off into the dead-end slough to pursue the other one they found Griggs aboard. Keith had heard no motors at the time, though, and the only time he thought it possible to miss them was during the exchange of gunfire that took place in the brief running battle with the crew of Griggs' boat. If the other two crews had been within earshot of all that shooting, he figured they would have suddenly turned in to investigate, considering the purpose of their mission. Griggs had told him that their orders were to go downriver and check out all the side channels and anywhere else they might find the men that escaped during the night in the little johnboat.

Realistically that was impossible, given the immense size of the river basin, but Keith didn't expect them to give up without looking pretty hard. He figured they were probably still downriver, but after nearly four hours of waiting, he was growing impatient. He wanted to get this over with so he could focus on a plan to deal with Reyes and the rest of his bunch that he now knew were occupying his property upriver. Keith still didn't know how many other boats Reyes had at his disposal, but he had to assume he had more and that he would send them down there if those first three didn't make it back when he expected they should. So, as he waited there listening, Keith knew he might hear boats approaching from any direction.

That's why it came as an immense relief to him, when right around noon, he finally heard the sound of outboards off in the distance to the south. The other two fishing boats were returning, and Keith yelled over to alert Greg, who was waiting a short distance upriver along the bank with the patrol boat out of view. When two boats similar to the one they'd captured finally appeared, running nearly side-by-side at a decent clip, Keith saw Griggs begin waving his arms as instructed. He had recognized them as the remainder of the search party, and Keith had high hopes that the ambush would go smoothly, and that this necessary step could be wrapped up in short order.

At first, it was obvious that the men in the two boats had spotted the anchored one, and it looked as if both were coming straight for it, which was the ideal scenario. But Keith cursed under his breath when he saw one of them slow and suddenly veer off on a course that would take it much farther away from him, following close to the bank on the opposite side of the river instead. *The crew of that one was being careful, dammit, and that was going to make his job much harder!* Still, Keith and the others with him were already prepared to deal with surprises. That's why he had Greg waiting with the patrol boat nearby and Bart, Ronnie and Sam on the gunboat, ready to barrel out of that bayou at a moment's notice.

Keith wouldn't let a deviation on the part one of the targeted boats stop him from taking out the crew of the first one, so as they came closer to Griggs, he prepared to fire that first shot that would be the signal to the others to join in and finish them off. It seemed Griggs was really trying to comply and not screw it all up, which was certainly a help. Keith had been watching him closely and doubted anything he'd done had warned the crew of that other boat to veer wide, so he didn't feel compelled to waste his opening shot taking out the traitor. Instead, he centered his reticle on the face of the man steering the approaching boat and without further hesitation, squeezed the trigger as the vessel closed within about fifty yards of Griggs.

Keith was pleased to see the remainder of the crew begin to fall within seconds of his first shot, and he barely had time to shift his aim to the last man standing before they were all down and out of the action. But there was no time to celebrate that success. The men in the other, more distant boat were now firing wildly towards the riverbank. Keith doubted they knew exactly what they were shooting at, because it would've been difficult to see muzzle flashes in the midday light and all his companions were as well concealed and motionless as him.

Regardless of whether they could see a target or not, those men clearly knew the gunfire had come from this side of the river and that the anchored boat had been placed there to lure them into a trap. Their realization of that was obvious when Keith saw them direct their fire towards the boat as well. He'd known all along that Griggs could get caught up in the crossfire if the ambush didn't go off perfectly, but Keith could do little about that at this point. Griggs had it coming, and he'd mostly served his purpose with the intel he'd provided. When Keith saw him drop to the bottom of the big skiff, he figured he'd taken a fatal round, but he had no time to give it another thought.

Someone in that distant boat was on the M60, but the shooting stopped when Keith heard a long burst from the bigger M2 aboard the gunboat. By then, the other boat was already speeding away to the north. Keith was on his feet and running and didn't hesitate long enough to look back and see if Bart, Ronnie and Sam were bringing the big boat out of the bayou because he already knew they were. He ran north up the bank to where Greg was waiting with the twin outboards running and leapt aboard as Greg cast off.

"We've got to stay on them, but not too close!" He shouted to Greg as he slammed the throttle handle forward and sped out into the river in pursuit. "The guy on that M60 may move it to the stern and turn it on us if we press too hard. I hope Bart can get them from farther out before they get out of range, but Ronnie's got some catching up to do, and it looks like that's a fast boat!"

Keith knew the crew would head straight for the bayou leading into his property. Their best chance of escape now was to make it there and rendezvous with Reyes, where they would have the backup of the full assault force he already had on site. Keith and Greg both knew it was crucial to prevent that from happening if they could. This wasn't simply a matter of stopping the boat crew from getting away. It was about preventing Reyes from knowing they were onto his plan for as long as possible. Keith still wasn't sure what he was going to do next, but he knew that whatever he came up with would work better when coupled with the element of surprise when it was time to make a move.

But his immediate problem was that the other boat was fast, and its crew already had a good head start since they had taken off as soon as they realized there were boats coming at them from the west side of the river. Keith's patrol boat with its twin Mercury 150s was fast enough to keep up, but the slower gunboat was still far behind in the wakes of both, and even with the advantage of the longer range 50-cal it couldn't make a difference unless Bart had a clear line of fire in one of the long, straight stretches between the river's big bends.

As Greg drove the patrol boat onward, Keith readied their extra weapons, which included two M4s with M203 grenade launchers attached. He wasn't sure if there would be an opportunity to use them, but it was good to have options. That M60 machine gun those guys had that was light enough to move to the stern was the one thing that could effectively make them keep their distance, forcing them to trail the boat from so far back they couldn't engage with their own rifles. But it was still a few miles to the cutoff and the important thing was staying on the other boat and keeping it in sight, thus giving the crew no quarter and no opportunity to turn off into a different side channel or otherwise evade them.

The bigger concern was that once they were in range, someone aboard the boat might call in by radio to notify Reyes and his men they'd run into trouble. Griggs had told him Reyes had more forces coming from the Red River outpost, but he couldn't tell him how many or what kind. As a captive they had brought him along only for his knowledge of where to find the militia camp, Griggs would know little of the operation aside from what he'd seen firsthand. Reyes could very well have an entire fleet of similar fast runabouts or even larger, fully armored gunboats, for all he knew. Keith didn't want to blindly run into the same kind of ambush he and his companions had just pulled off, but weighing the risks against simply letting that last boat go, he decided it was worth it to give chase. They simply had to prevent Reyes from getting an early warning that they were onto his plans by way of a detailed report from that boat crew on what they had seen.

The problem with stopping them though was that with every mile they were leaving the gunboat farther behind. The heavier inboard-powered vessel simply couldn't keep up with the top speeds of the two much lighter skiffs with their big outboards. It wasn't built for that, so the chase had left Bart few opportunities to use the M2 before the target boat disappeared around each sweeping bend, and after the first couple of miles, it became hopeless. The few bursts he'd let loose at the elusive target failed to connect, and now, when Keith looked back, the bigger boat was no longer in sight.

But Griggs had given Keith one other bit of information that gave him reason for optimism. No one aboard any of the three boats, aside from Griggs, had ever even seen this part of the river before today. As he said, the crews had just arrived from another staging area north of the I-10 bridge at daylight that morning. Keith got it out of him just where this place was, in a dead-end slough that was well hidden from the river but would offer no hope of escape if they returned there. Griggs had said that most of Reyes' men in the area had participated in the assault on the camp, so Keith knew it was likely the guys on this last boat would go there, rather than try to run all the way back to that more distant slough where they'd have less help in fighting off their pursuers if they even reached it.

But they'd never been up the narrow, winding bayou that led to the militia camp because Reyes hadn't expected them to arrive there until after dawn and didn't want them to waste time looking for the cutoff so they could make their way up it to the camp. Instead, he'd sent Griggs back by way of the road under guard of a small detachment of men to rendezvous with the boat crews on the main riverbank south of the bridge. Griggs told Keith how it had been a grueling double-time march in the dark to get there in time, but once the boats were in radio range just before first light, they'd made contact and one of them landed to pick him up from a sandbar. Griggs said he figured they would easily catch up with the men in the johnboat early that morning. The escapees were to be captured or killed and the three boats would report back to the destroyed militia camp after their mission was complete. Griggs had pointed out the cutoff to the crews of all three on the way downriver, so Keith figured they wouldn't have much trouble spotting it now, and it was only logical that when they did, they would turn off into it.

"We're not going to stop them before they get to the bayou," Keith told Greg, as he stood next to him at the center console.

"No, probably not," Greg agreed. "So, what do you want to do?"

"Keep pushing them hard. Force them to keep the hammer down so that when they *do* turn in, they do it at full speed or close to it. They don't know the channel at all, if Griggs was telling the truth."

Keith saw the smile on Greg's face as he understood. There was no guarantee it would work, but if those guys took that cutoff fast enough, they would have to be damned lucky to avoid what both men knew lurked beneath the surface in several places just upstream of the junction. For Keith and Greg and the others with local knowledge, those underwater obstructions left in the aftermath of the hurricane months prior were easily avoided. Keith had long since sounded the bayou and charted the danger areas. Most of them consisted of submerged trees felled by the storm, some in large, entangled clusters invisible just beneath the surface. Keith had used his chainsaw to cut away the logs and branches protruding into the parts of the channel he needed open and had winched some of the submerged sections out of the way where necessary as well. His efforts made the bayou passable, but only for those who knew the locations of the larger hazards that were beyond his means to move. With care, the little bayou was navigable, even for vessels as large as Eric's schooner that was now submerged next to Keith's dock. But even a small, shallow-draft skiff could run into trouble if its skipper didn't know where to look for the dangers, and that's exactly how Keith wanted it.

Keith could have called Ronnie to let him know what they were doing, but it wasn't necessary, because he knew he and Bart would figure it out, and it was best to maintain radio silence at this point. It was nice to know backup was coming, even if it arrived later, but Keith knew they couldn't slack off now. They had to press that boat crew into taking that exit and taking it at high speed when they did. That meant he and Greg had to stay on their ass so they'd have no other choice. From the river, especially approaching from the south, he knew the bayou entrance would appear wide-open and enticing, with no hint of all those hidden dangers that lurked under the opaque muddy water. The men in that boat would see that the smaller channel curved quickly out of view and would place their bets on being able to continue eluding their pursuers until they led them directly into an ambush by Reyes and the rest of his team. Keith knew they may have already made radio contact with them, and if so, Reyes would have a heads-up whether they stopped the boat crew or not. But even so, there was only so much they could convey over a quick radio call and stopping that last boat would deprive Reyes of his river access unless the additional boats Griggs said he had coming had arrived in the meantime today.

"It looks like they're going to take the turn, Keith!"

Keith braced himself against the console and studied the boat crew through his binoculars. The man at the helm had adjusted course from mid river and was now veering left into the channel opening that angled in from the northwest. It appeared he barely reduced speed, if at all, which was perfect. Greg didn't either until the crewman that had moved that M60 aft opened up with a long burst to discourage them from following the boat into the turnoff. But the fire was wild and ineffective as the boat was already carving into the next sharp bend to the left, and Greg lost little ground by backing off to avoid it. He made a show of accelerating hard again before they disappeared from sight around the bend, but that was only to let them know the chase was still on. Once Greg knew they couldn't see what he was doing, he abruptly throttled back so he and Keith could wait and listen.

"I predict their joy ride is about to come to an end!"

Keith hoped he was right. Their only chance of stopping the boat now was out of their hands, because there was simply no way to close on it without facing that machine gun at a range far too close for comfort. And chasing it all the way to the militia camp would be suicide. He knew the answer would come quickly, and it did.

Keith could tell by the sound of the engine that the boat had only rounded that first bend and was approaching the next hard loop back to the north when it happened. There was a terrific thud as the metal hull struck something solid in the water, and then the scream of the engine spinning up to even higher RPMs as the prop either broke away or was momentarily running free of water resistance because the hull had gone airborne. That first impact was followed by the sound of breaking branches and another heavy crash as the boat landed hard, probably in the dense willow thicket that grew almost to the edge of the muddy bank there. Then, the engine went silent, and Keith looked at Greg with a huge grin on his face.

"YES!!!! They drove the damned thing right into that logjam! It couldn't be more perfect if we'd set it up on purpose!"

"Except that it sounds like they didn't all break their necks...."

Greg was right. They could hear yelling and cursing now, which wasn't really surprising. Even if some of the four-man crew had been injured or killed, he hadn't expected the crash to be the end of this. Maybe that boat wasn't going anywhere, but that didn't mean all the crew and their weapons were out of commission, and the machine gun especially was still a threat if they hadn't lost it in the wreck, so it wouldn't do to just cruise around that bend in the wide open to find out.

"Sounds like we've still got work to do. I say we land right here on this side of the point and then cut across through the woods on foot. We can sneak up and finish them off while they're trying to pick up the pieces. Even if they got ahold of Reyes, there's no way his men could reach them down here before we get there. We can finish this business and be back in the boat and out of here before that happens."

"Unless they have other boats up at the camp that we don't know about." Greg reminded him.

It was true that more of Reyes' men might show up shortly because they were close enough that the sound of gunfire would carry there, but Keith wasn't especially worried.

"If they do, Ronnie and Bart will be here by the time that happens," he said. "They will see our boat tied up here, and I'm sure they'll investigate if they hear gunfire. If there's a problem, Bart will be able to help us out with the Browning."

"I'm with you," Greg said as he steered for the bank, keeping the engine just above idle so the stranded men they were going after wouldn't hear it. When they reached the bayou's edge and hopped out into the mud, Keith tied off the boat and the two men set out through the dense woods, each of them carrying one of the M4s with the mounted grenade launchers. If that boat wasn't out of commission already, it would be when they were done, and they intended to make sure neither it nor anyone aboard it made it back to the site of the militia camp.

They slipped through the woods in silence, hearing only bits of muffled conversation now as the angry shouting had ceased. When they reached the other side of the narrow point of land across the sharp bend minutes later, the scene before them was pretty much what Keith had envisioned.

The boat had struck the mass of submerged logs that were just inches under the surface there on the outside of the turn. Anyone who knew about it, like him and the others that navigated the bayou often, knew they had to hug the right bank when going around that particular bend because all the underwater debris had piled up on the outside. These guys *didn't* know that, of course, and had hit it running at least 60 mph, resulting in an impact which destroyed both the boat and the outboard, flipping the hull upside down before it landed in that thicket.

The wreck had done a number on the crew as well, of course, and Keith could see only two of them still moving about. Another was face down in the mud and possibly dead, and the fourth appeared badly broken up, moaning in pain at the top of the bank where his companions had apparently carried him after the crash.

Keith and Greg didn't hesitate to do what they came for. Each man took careful aim at the two survivors that appeared unhurt and fired simultaneously on Keith's whispered count, taking them out with a single shot each. Keith then switched his aim and finished off the wounded man as Greg fired an anchoring round into the still one, just to be sure. It was obvious the boat was totaled, so there was no reason to use the grenade launcher as Keith had planned. Gunfire was one thing, as it was frequently heard nearly everywhere nowadays, but an explosion so near would certainly get the attention of Reyes and his men, putting them on high alert to a serious threat, and so it was best avoided.

"Let's get the hell out of here and let Bart and Ronnie know what's happening!" Keith said.

TWELVE

On a normal day by this time, Shauna would have been back at Sierra Zulu, likely spending time with Andrew while taking a break after her morning watch. Shauna had never told her stepson the truth about what happened to his father, Daniel Hartfield, and still wasn't sure when or if she eventually would. The boy didn't ask her about it or even mention him very often anyway, because as far as he knew his dad had bailed on them because he couldn't cope with living out there in the swamp and was determined to find comfort and safety in one of the refugee camps he believed were nearby in Texas. Andrew had been through a lot since they all left Florida with Eric and Bart on the schooner, but he'd adjusted well to this new lifestyle deep in the woods. As long as he had his stepmom and his stepsister, Megan, and Bart to take him fishing in the bayou as often as possible, Andrew was quite content.

But this was anything *but* a normal day and Shauna wasn't sure now when she'd be returning to camp again. The sound of that paddle bumping against a boat that first got her attention had changed everything. And though at first it had excited her for the possibility of Eric's return, discovering its true source quickly led to a string of events more intense than anything she had experienced in weeks. Now, she was lying prone on the riverbank in the concealment of the woods with her rifle in hand, flanked on either side by two men she'd never met before today. When Eli Landry and Seth Guidry had found their way there that morning and told her the story of the militia camp, all that happened after had led to her participation with them in a hastily prepared ambush that had gone at least partly to plan.

Shooting the four men remaining in that approaching boat was a relatively simple task after Keith took out the one at the wheel. Shauna was certain that her own first shot found its mark when the guy standing nearest to the mounted machine gun collapsed and tumbled over the side. And she saw that all his companions were cut down just as efficiently by the hail of rounds directed at them from Eli, Seth, and Hal, who was also in on the ambush but positioned some twenty yards farther downstream from them on the same bank.

But despite the ease of taking out the crew of the one boat, it was incredibly frustrating that the other one had swung so far wide that its crew was too far away to engage it with any accuracy. Sure, she and her companions had sent some rounds their way, but they'd failed to stop them from getting away. They'd taken wild incoming fire in their direction too, as the men aboard that boat knew the shooters that killed their comrades were somewhere on that west riverbank, even if they couldn't see them.

Shauna had heard the machine gun bursts coming from the boat and heard the rounds hitting trees and branches above her head, and after that, she saw splashes in the water around the boat where Griggs was shackled. The sound of bullets pinging into the aluminum hull was unmistakable, and when she saw Griggs drop to the bottom, Shauna was sure he'd been hit. But it wasn't until after Keith and Greg left in the patrol boat and Ronnie, Bart and Sam joined in the pursuit that she turned her attention back to the anchored fishing craft. Sweeping the interior with the magnification of her rifle optic, Shauna expected to confirm Griggs was dead.

But much to her surprise, not only was the shackled prisoner still moving, but he was also apparently unscathed! He was clearly shaken up, though, and was looking about here and there within the boat in a state of panic. Shauna didn't realize what his anxiety was about until Griggs shouted over to the bank that the hull had been shot up badly and was rapidly taking on water! He was begging them for help, and both Eli and Seth were livid at the very thought of it. Eli's first reaction was to raise his rifle and take aim at the traitor, but Shauna managed to talk him out of pulling the trigger. But as he lowered the weapon, Eli correctly pointed out that there was no boat there with which to go and rescue Griggs, even if they were so inclined.

Even the johnboat he and his companions arrived in was unavailable. When Greg and Hal had first gotten there in Keith's patrol boat after Ronnie relayed her radio call, their immediate concern was getting James Andre back to Sierra Zulu where he could get some attention to his wounds. To do so, they thought it best to just tow the little johnboat back there with him still in it, so they wouldn't have to move him into the patrol boat, causing him more discomfort and pain. And after they did exactly that, they left the little boat there when they returned to Shauna's post in Keith's boat. So now, with the patrol boat and the gunboat in pursuit of the enemy boat that got away, there were no boats available to those left there on the bank to wait.

That meant Griggs was out of luck, although he had another solution that he pitched to them when he yelled to suggest that one of them could swim out there and simply free him before the sinking boat went down. That wasn't an option either, Shauna knew, because just like Eli told him, only Keith and Greg had keys to those handcuffs. Without bolt cutters or some kind of heavy pry bar which they didn't have, breaking Griggs loose before the boat sank to the bottom was hardly possible.

Griggs then countered by saying someone could simply swim to the other boat that was now drifting downriver with its dead crew and use it to tow the one he was shackled to over to shallow water where he would be safe even when it went down. Shauna knew it could be an option, assuming one of them could do all that fast enough. But that boat had drifted quite far already, and catching up to it as the current carried it downstream could take more time than Griggs had.

Assuming the engine was still idling in neutral as it had been before the shooting started, a swimmer could board the drifting boat and quickly run back up to where Griggs was anchored, but then it would take a minute to cut it loose, attach a tow line, and pull it to safety. All the while, it would be taking on more water through no telling how many 7.62mm bullet holes. Shauna was a strong swimmer who was totally at home in the water, and if anyone in their ambush team could pull off such a feat, it was her. But she had to ask herself why. *Was going to all that effort to save a deserter and a traitor like Griggs worth it, even if Keith wanted to question him further?*

She knew Eli, Seth and Hal didn't think so, and none would have lifted a finger to help him after what Griggs had done. Shauna couldn't care less if he drowned either, but she was tempted to do it for Keith, until Hal gave her another reason why she shouldn't bother.

"I've been fishing out there off the mouth of this bayou with Bart more times than I can count since we've been here. There's a deep channel farther out, but right there where Keith dropped that anchor, there's a big old submerged gravel bar that's around four or five feet deep in most places until you get out past the drop-off. As long as that son of a bitch is standing up, he won't drown when that boat settles to the bottom. I'd leave him right where he is until Keith and Greg come back."

"Are you sure about that?"

"Yep. I've been out there plenty in one of the skiffs. It's shallow where he is."

Shauna thought about it as she glanced back out to Griggs and then at the distant, drifting boat. His was filling faster now, and it was clear that she didn't have time to help him anyway if Hal was wrong. That boat would be underwater before she even got started good. *Griggs better hope that gravel bar is real,* she thought, as she turned back to her companions, handing Hal her rifle before squatting down to unlace her boots.

"What are you doing?" Eli demanded. "You heard what Hal just said!"

"I did, but just cover for me! I'm going to go grab that other boat, anyway. I know Keith wants it and we don't know how long it'll be before he gets back."

"That's a long swim and that water's cold!" Seth said. "Are you sure you're up for that?"

"Don't worry about me. I know what I'm doing. This won't take long."

"She used to swim in those triathlons or something like that," Hal told him.

Shauna was in the river without another word. Her strokes took her straight downstream with the current, giving the sinking boat with Griggs in it a wide berth. She didn't think he was even aware that she was in the water, as he was out of her sight now, down in the hull, probably still trying to find a way to break free on his own. Once she was past him, Shauna didn't look back. Her focus was on the single goal of reaching that other boat.

She still had her doubts about that submerged bar that Hal had assured her was under the river where Griggs' boat was anchored, though. While Hal could be right, she didn't think that water depth was Keith's primary consideration when he decided where to drop the anchor. What he was really looking at was putting the boat into the ideal location to draw the crews of the other two into rifle range.

He wanted it far enough off the bank so it wouldn't be obvious that it was a trap, while also making it impossible to miss, even if those other boats were near the opposite bank when they returned upriver.

The other thing that crossed Shauna's mind as she swam was that even if the boat sank in just a few feet, it could roll over once submerged or shift in some other way that might prevent Griggs from keeping his head above water. But it wasn't her problem if he drowned. Griggs had put himself in that position by doing what he did and she knew that those two guys that came here this morning to give her the news wanted nothing more than to see him die, preferably in the most terrifying and painful manner. And while she knew Eric and probably Keith too could devise many imaginative ways to make that happen, she had to admit that Griggs' predicament at the moment was about as grim as possible from his own unfortunate perspective, considering he had no clue of the river's depth there. The small size of the holes through which the river was filling the boat gave him plenty of time to contemplate what would ultimately happen—time to taste the fear and dread as he wondered when he would take his last breath.

It took Shauna a good 20 minutes to reach the other boat, and as she grabbed hold of the rail a couple of feet forward of the transom, she already knew the outboard was no longer running. She hoped it wasn't damaged from the gunfire, because if she couldn't get it started, it would mean a tough slog through the woods along the riverbank to get back to the mouth of the bayou, as there was a bit too much current to contemplate swimming upriver.

When she pulled herself aboard, she found exactly what she expected, lots of blood that made for slippery footing and four of the five dead crew still sprawled where they fell. Two of them near the bow were already hanging partway over the gunwales, so it was easy enough for her to lever them over the side and get them out of the way. The dead guy at the helm presented more of a problem, however, and it took her several tries before she was able to haul him up onto one of the seats and then work his legs over the edge until she could finally push him over. By that point, she was too exhausted to bother with the last one on the forward sole ahead of the center console. The guys could get him out when she got back to the bayou.

Shauna turned her attention to the engine, and to her relief, the big Yamaha started right up when she pushed the ignition button. What she saw ahead of her after putting it in gear and pointing the boat back upriver was almost exactly what Hal had predicted. Nothing of Griggs, but his head was visible in the spot where the boat had been. And she knew that the only way that could have happened was if it had actually settled on the bottom in water less than six feet deep. She headed straight in his direction, knowing there was nothing she could do to help him but curious if he was indeed in a stable condition for the moment and able to keep his head above water.

Griggs heard the motor and began screaming for help as he turned his head to face her, no doubt thinking her purpose in coming was to save him. But Shauna couldn't do that even if she wanted to. Freeing his leg now would require diving under the muddy brown river water and releasing the handcuffs by feel alone. Doing that without a key wasn't going to happen, and neither was towing the sunken boat, which was now a huge anchor, with the weight of its outboard and all those under seat compartments that were now filled with water. She doubted even the big gunboat could drag it to the bank. But Griggs was certain there was a way.

"I thought it was all over when I felt the boat begin to drop once it went completely under. I thought I'd taken my last breath, and I couldn't believe it when I felt it hit the bottom under my feet and I realized my head was still clear! It was like a miracle, and I knew it wasn't my time to go yet! You've gotta get me out of here. There's got to be a way! If you do, I'll do everything in my power to help you and your friends! I'll go up there and take on Reyes by myself if I have to!"

"I already told you," Shauna said. "I don't have a key. No one has the key to those handcuffs but Keith Branson and Greg Hebert. They were both Sheriff's deputies here, and that's the reason they had them. Without a key, I can't unlock them."

"There are other ways to get them off, like with a hacksaw or something! Maybe you can find some bolt cutters or a big pry bar; something that will break the chain! Look in the compartments of that boat under the seats. There may be a toolbox. I tried to find one in this boat but couldn't find anything within reach that would do me any good!"

"It wouldn't matter if I *did* find a hacksaw or something like that," Shauna said. "I'm not going to hold my breath and work underwater there long enough to use a tool like that to cut hardened steel! And even if I had the key to those cuffs, I still wouldn't do it alone because I can't trust you enough to get within reach of you that way."

"You don't think anyone could be that stupid, do you? Do you think I would try to do something to the one person that could free me from drowning?"

"It doesn't matter whether I think you're stupid or not, but I definitely believe you would do something like that to someone trying to help you, because you've proven it already. You deserted the militia and then you went and found the one enemy who wants us all dead and led them straight back there to kill men who trusted you—men you lived with and trained with for weeks!

"You're lucky to be alive now at all, I'll tell you that. If I hadn't stopped them, those two guys that escaped the attack last night and came here to tell me the story would have shot you as soon as Keith and the others left. They would have done it long before the boat even sank!"

"That's because they don't understand why I did what I did. They don't understand that I had no choice!"

"There's always a choice," Shauna said, "and the choice you go with always has consequences. For you, the consequence resulted in getting you locked to the very boat you came here on with men looking to hunt down and kill even more of your former fellow recruits.

"No one can unlock you from it but the man who put those cuffs on your leg. You are very fortunate that he didn't shoot you himself, and I know the only reason he didn't is because you had intel he could use. Whether he thinks you have more is something he'll decide when he comes back. I don't know if he'll set you free or not. He may just as soon shoot you or he may leave you there. If I were you, I'd rather be shot." Shauna looked off into the distance, pointing at the sky across the river. "Did you notice those clouds that are building off to the northwest? Keith said a front was coming through, so that means rain—lots of steady rain—and when it rains, the river rises. It may take a while, but it *will* rise, and I'll bet when it does, it'll be more than a few inches!"

She saw Griggs look in the direction of the gathering clouds and watched the fear come over him again as he realized she wasn't just making it up. Shauna wasn't trying to taunt him; she was just telling him the truth, and the truth was that she really couldn't help him.

"Keith wouldn't want that to happen, and he wouldn't shoot me either, because there is a *lot* more that I can tell him about what Reyes and his men are planning! In the meantime, that anchor on this boat could drag, or something in the current could sweep the whole thing downstream into a deeper hole or something. If it goes even six inches deeper, I'll drown, rain or no rain!"

"No, I doubt that'll happen. My friend, Hal, over there on the bank said he knows this area of the river from fishing here, and he said there's a big gravel bar under here, so it's only about four or five feet deep in most places. So, you were lucky Keith put that anchor where he did. Like you said, another six inches or so and you wouldn't be breathing now."

"You see why I'm worried, then! Please! While we wait for him to get back, can't you just bring the boat over here close enough so that I can hold on to the side of it? I'm standing here neck deep in this river and I can feel the current pulling on me now. I don't know how long I can stand here like this. Right now, I've got one hand on the steering pedestal two feet under, but if the boat moves even a little, I could lose my balance and fall and if that happened, I don't know if I'd be able to get my head back above water in time. If you could just bring that boat alongside, I could hold on to it. You know I can't hurt you or do anything to get in the boat as long as my leg is chained to this one, but if I could just hold on to anything above water, I wouldn't feel like I was about to drown any minute!"

"It wouldn't do you a lot of good to be holding onto it if that boat you're chained to started moving. I couldn't do anything to stop it."

Shauna was looking around inside the storage compartments under the seats as she talked, finally pulling out something she'd expected to find there.

"Here you go! I found a life jacket I can toss you. That'll keep your head above water if you get too tired to stand there. I can't hang around out here in the open on this river like this, because I don't know how many more boatloads of armed men may be coming my way."

"Reyes doesn't have any more boats, I swear! The three we were in are it!" Griggs said, as he grabbed the lifejacket when it landed in the water near his head.

"Keith said you told him there were lots more, and lots more men on the way as well."

"Maybe later, but not now. After Reyes interrogated us and made me agree to lead him back to the militia camp, he sent someone back somewhere for more, but he knew it would take more time for them to arrive. That's why he didn't wait. He wanted to go attack the camp right away. But he wasn't ready to start looking for Sierra Zulu until he had all his other forces in place."

Shauna realized this might change things for Keith, if it were indeed the truth. She didn't have anymore time to waste here, now that she had a fast boat and a message to take him.

"This life vest won't do me much good if this boat moves."

"If you're not satisfied with it, there *is* another option I just thought of, if you really can't stand to wait on Keith and Greg to bring those keys."

Shauna circled the idling boat around until she was about 10 feet away from him now, knowing he was watching her every move and waiting to hear what she was going to suggest. She made sure he saw her as she reached to her belt and withdrew the large, fixed blade knife she always wore there. It was a 7-inch-long Marine Kabar with a partially serrated edge that she'd found among the supplies taken from the Red River outpost. Shauna had honed it to a razor's edge and kept it that way, as she used it daily around camp.

"I'd be willing to loan you this while you wait, in case you get impatient and decide you want to cut yourself free. I'll even give you my belt to go with it so you can make yourself a tourniquet when you're done. Just be sure to hang onto one of the straps of that life jacket while you've got your head underwater using it, and when you're finished, the flotation will help you make it over to the riverbank, since you'll have to swim mostly with your arms, you know! Or, if you're ready now, I'll take you myself, but you need to hurry, because I'm not waiting any longer."

"Are you serious? Do you really think I want to cut my leg off to get out of this boat?"

"You tell me. I'll bet you would have done it twenty minutes ago, when that boat was still filling up and you didn't know the bottom was just five feet down! Am I right?"

THIRTEEN

Griggs took the knife and the belt from her, and although Shauna doubted he would actually use it, she didn't have a problem giving him the Kabar. It wasn't like it was anything special that she couldn't replace, and she got some satisfaction just knowing the mental anguish such a choice would present, especially after she had pointed out to him those gathering clouds on the horizon.

There really wasn't anything else she could do for him, even if she'd wanted to. Considering how he was shackled to that boat, freeing him while working underwater in zero visibility would be difficult and dangerous, even if she had the key to those handcuffs. To attempt it by any other means would be exponentially more so. Even if he was one of their own and she was willing to try by any means necessary, success was far from certain. But Griggs *was not* one of their own—not any longer—and his desertion and betrayal had cost the lives of nearly two dozen men and put everyone associated with them at risk. Griggs deserved to die; there was no question of that, especially since he'd even confessed to what he'd done. But Shauna gave him the option of the knife because she knew that if he used it, he wouldn't get far, and if he survived at all, he would hardly be in any shape to be a threat to anyone. Shauna doubted he would do it anyway, because he'd already proven himself a coward. But whether he bled out from an amputation or drowned in rising water, his death would not be as merciful as the rifle bullet both Eli and Seth had been so eager to send his way. Griggs would simply have to watch the sky and weigh the odds. *Would Keith return in time, or would the imminent threat of rain force him to act?*

When Shauna motored back over to the bank, she asked the men waiting there to help with getting that last dead guy out of the bottom of the boat. After they dumped the body into the river and she told them of her conversation with Griggs and what she'd given him, Eli and Seth were more or less satisfied.

"That'll give the son of a bitch some time to think about what he's done," Eli said.

"Yeah, even if the river doesn't get up, he's going to think it will," Seth agreed. "It'll drive him crazy!"

"It'll get up," Hal said. "That's not just an afternoon shower coming. It'll be raining before dark and when it starts, it'll set in for days. It's just that time of year. If Griggs isn't willing to use that knife, he better hope Keith comes back with the key, and that if he does, he still has questions he wants answers to bad enough to dive under that river and use it!"

"I think Griggs has said enough already," Shauna said. We can't wait around here for Keith. He just gave me more information about the situation up there at the militia camp. He said he's sure there aren't any other boats at that slough north of the interstate, where those three came from this morning. He said if there were, they would have gone downriver by now too, if not this far, at least far enough that Reyes could have reached them by radio. And then he would have sent them down here to see what was going on. The other thing is that Griggs said those three were the only boats of any kind he saw at the Red River outpost before the convoy moved out to head south and prepare for the attack on the camp. He said Reyes talked about how he'd sent for more, but he didn't want to wait for them to arrive before making his move. He thought he could wipe out the entire recruit camp at night and then take out Keith and Bart in an easy ambush when they arrived the morning after. But Griggs forgot to tell him about that johnboat that you slipped out of there in, and it ruined everything for him and caused him to send the only three boats he had down here to try to find you. Assuming Keith and the others managed to stop that last boat, Reyes is stuck now with no boats until more arrive from the Red River outpost. When and if they do, they'll first go to that staging area in the slough Griggs told Keith about. He said Reyes planned to regroup there after the ambush and organize the next part of his campaign to locate Sierra Zulu."

"So, what you're saying is that Reyes is essentially cut off now that he's waiting at the militia camp for those three boats that aren't coming back?"

"It sounds that way to me, yes. I'm thinking that now that we have this boat that's still in perfect working order, we should go upriver and meet Keith and Bart before they come back here. This may be the only opportunity we have to isolate Reyes before he gets his reinforcements and more boats. Griggs says there's only a handful of men up there at that slough where they left all their vehicles. He also said Reyes was unable to reach them by radio, so unless he sent someone from his assault force back there to tell them, those men don't know what happened there last night. They don't know that Eli and Seth escaped with their wounded buddy, and they certainly don't know we intercepted those boats. It would be the perfect time to hit them out of nowhere when they don't expect it! I know that's what Keith will want to do if we can find him in time."

"Well, what are we waiting for? Let's go do it!"

"No, not you, Hal. I'm sorry, but you know someone has to stay here and keep watch because we can't leave the entrance to Sierra

Zulu unguarded. I'll take Eli and Seth with me if they're willing and feel up to it after all they went through last night."

"I'm damned sure up to it!" Eli said. "I can't wait to get a shot at some more of those assholes!"

"Count me in too!" Seth agreed. "I feel perfectly wide-awake and won't be sleeping anyway until all those hired killers are dead!"

"I can't promise you Keith will be on board with it, but he knows the place because he already got the location out of Griggs before he left. It's a slough off the river not far above Interstate 10. If we can get there by way of that other navigation channel, Reyes will never hear the boats go by from where he is."

"The Whiskey Bay Pilot Channel," Eli said.

"Yes."

"I know it well. Keith will be on board with it, you can bet on that. What you're talking about is exactly the kind of thing he and Bart and Sam were training all of us for. It makes me sick to think that all those guys were murdered up there last night before they got a piece of the action against those thugs, but I can tell you that I'm ready to do more than my share to make up for it! And so is Seth."

"Let me behind that M60 at the front of that boat. I'll lay into them until I either run out of ammo or melt the barrel!"

"I see one minor problem with your plan."

"And what would that be, Hal?"

"Well, you're going up that river to meet up with Keith and Bart in a boat that looks just like the one they just chased up that way. I figure there's a slight chance they might think there was a fourth boat with that bunch they didn't know about, since they're not expecting you. You'd better make sure you approach them in a careful manner and give them time to see who you are. You wouldn't want to make Bart nervous and have him aiming that M2 your way as soon as you come around a bend!"

"We could just call them on the radio, assuming the one on this boat works." Eli said.

"Yeah, you could, but on that open VHF band, you'd run the risk of letting Reyes and everyone else up there at that camp in on what you're doing!"

"No, we can't risk that. We need to maintain radio silence," Shauna agreed. "What I got from Griggs may be good intel, but I still don't trust him. We don't know what else Reyes may have or what may be coming. I think we'll be fine if once we spot them, I do something obvious, like slow down to idle and turn broadside to them. We'll all wave like crazy, and with any luck at all, Keith or someone will put binoculars on us before they open fire. They should be able to figure it out, even though they assumed we'd stay put until they got back."

"You're probably right," Hal said. "Just be careful and good luck! I'll hold things down around here while you're gone."

As it turned out, they spotted both the patrol boat and the gunboat running together and coming their way about halfway between the cutoff they'd left and the other bayou leading up to Keith's property. Since both boats were on their way back, Shauna hoped it meant they'd been successful. She was at the helm of the fishing boat, so she did exactly what she'd suggested to Hal and immediately slowed and turned, presenting the boat broadside to the approaching boats smack in the middle of the channel. No one who didn't recognize them would be so stupid. At least that's what she hoped they'd think. And as she and Eli and Seth stood there waving, she kept her fingers crossed that Bart would refrain from pressing his thumbs into the Browning's butterfly trigger until one of them recognized who they were.

Her gamble paid off, and minutes later both the gunboat and the patrol boat were alongside. Shauna relayed to Keith what else she'd learned from Griggs and explained why she thought it imperative that they make a move now, rather than wait for a better opportunity that might never come.

"We got that other boat," Keith told her. "But not until they were already in the bayou. Reyes and anyone else that was on my property would've heard all the shooting, especially the long burst from that M60 when they opened up on us before they went around the first bend."

"They thought it would keep us from following them in there," Greg added, "But we didn't have to, anyway." He told her how they had tricked the fleeing boat crew into running that first bend at nearly wide-open speeds.

"After they piled up on the bank, it was a simple matter to slip through the woods and finish them off. But like Keith said, Reyes couldn't have missed hearing the gunshots, including our own. We knew from what Griggs said that he had too many men there for us to deal with, even if we waited for Bart and Ronnie to catch up. There was no way for just four of us to outmaneuver them, and we had to assume they were set up and waiting to ambush anyone coming up that bayou to the camp."

"I'm sure they are," Eli said. "Ambushing folks is what they're good at."

"Griggs talked some more," Shauna said, after telling Keith that he survived all the gunfire directed at him, but then ended up in an even more terrifying predicament, shackled to a sinking boat.

"He would say anything in a situation like that," Keith said, after hearing her out.

"Yes, but most of what he gave me was just stuff he would have given you too if you'd had more time to question him. That's why we came here to meet you without delay since we had a boat in which to do it. Griggs swears there were only these three boats at the Red River outpost when Reyes' convoy moved out to come down here. He heard Reyes and his men talking about the many more that were apparently on the way, because he'd sent for them, but he hadn't wanted to wait for them to get there. Now that we have this one and we know the other two are out of commission, we know that Reyes has no boats at all and that he is cut off from the other men he left at that slough up there north of I-10. Griggs said that place was definitely out of hand-held radio range, because

Reyes couldn't reach them last night to get the boats down there right after they discovered some men from the camp escaped. I thought you'd want to take advantage of that intel and hit them now, while we have a chance. Those other boats may already be on the way, but if they're not, they'll probably be there tomorrow. If we can take out that small detachment that's there now, we may even be able to ambush those boats when they do come. We may not get a better opportunity to intercept them and prevent Reyes from using them to find and attack us at Sierra Zulu."

"She's right," Bart said. "We can go around by way of that Whiskey Bay Pilot Channel and Reyes will never know we're upriver. If those men posted at that slough don't have any additional boats on site yet, we can come down on them from upriver, which they'd never expect, and take them out. Then we control their staging area, so we will be the ones greeting their reinforcements when they arrive!"

"In theory, that could work," Keith said, "but we're going to be stretched pretty thin with just the eight of us."

"We may not have the numbers in our favor, son, but we've got three boats and the element of surprise."

"Our idea was for me and Seth to go straight there from downriver in this boat," Eli said. "That way, when they hear it coming and then see it, they'll think it's just a couple of their guys coming back. We can stay down low and now that it's starting to rain, they won't be able to tell who we are as long as Shauna's not with us. We're both wearing dark colored camo anyway, so they won't notice that we aren't in uniform."

"Shauna won't be with you if I have anything to do with it!" Keith said. "Eric would kill me if I let anything happen to her by putting her in that kind of situation."

"It's not up to Eric!" Shauna reminded him. "Eric's not here, so he's not in charge."

"No, but his little brother and his old man are, at least as far as security decisions go, and you know it!"

"He's right," Bart told her. "You'd be better off coming with us, anyway. Having more than two people in that boat isn't the best use of our limited resources. Eli and Seth are basically going to use it as a distraction. If Keith agrees to do it, you and Sam need to go with him and Greg when they slip ashore, because Ronnie will have to stay at the helm of the gunboat, and I'll be up there on the Browning."

"I think it could work," Keith agreed. "We know exactly where that slough is if Griggs was telling the truth and that's really where they're staging all this from. If we approach it quietly from upriver in the patrol boat and tie it off to the bank somewhere before we're heard or seen, we can slip up on them easily there, because it's heavily wooded on the north side of the slough. They'll be focused on the other boat coming up from downriver, where they know it went this morning, and they'll never guess there's danger from the other direction."

Keith looked at Eli. "Maybe when you get close enough for them to see the boat, but still too far for them to identify you or ask questions, you can act like you're having engine trouble or something. That may lure most of them out there to the bank to see what's going on. Then, you can lay into them with that M60 like you said. Any of them you don't get, we will, because we'll be hitting them from the opposite side while they're trying to take cover from your angle. Bart and Ronnie can come in at that point too and engage any survivors and maybe disable their vehicles with the 50-cal. We've got grenade launchers to help with that, too."

"It sounds like a plan to me," Eli said, "if that traitor wasn't lying about them being there!"

"We won't know that until we go see."

"Griggs didn't have anything else to lose when he told me all that," Shauna said. "But I don't think he expected me to come upriver and talk you into going there today. I'm sure he was hoping you'd get back down there ASAP with that handcuff key!"

"Screw him!" Seth said. "He's right where he ought to be, and when the river gets up, he'll get exactly what he deserves."

"Unless he works up the nerve to use Shauna's knife," Eli said.

Keith just shook his head and looked at Shauna. "That was a hell of a thing, you know, giving him a choice like that! I can't wait to see the look on Eric's face when he hears that story."

Shauna knew there were two ways to look at it. On the one hand, it was a cruel gesture, offering a trapped man such a grim choice, but on the other it was an act of mercy, because she didn't have to give him a choice at all. Griggs had a way out now, if he chose to use the knife, and if he didn't, then it wasn't because she hadn't given him one.

"Eric won't have a problem with it, but I'd rather you not mention it to Megan or Andrew," she said.

Keith agreed and said that if they were going to go through with this, it was time to move. He turned to Eli and Seth and asked them again if they were sure they were up to what they'd proposed.

"I know you both went through a hell of a lot last night, and I want to make sure you understand that if you go through with this and we come up against more opposition than we're expecting, you two are going to be a couple of sitting ducks out there on the river in that open boat."

"I'm damned sure up to it," Seth said. "There's nothing I want more than to kill as many of those human scum as I can. I'll do whatever it takes to make it happen!"

"Me too," Eli agreed. "We've learned enough from the training you put us through to understand how it's supposed to work, and maybe even what to do if it doesn't. Either way, I'm ready. We'll provide the distraction and if the rest of you do your part, we'll wipe them out. It may even be easy!"

"Don't ever make the mistake of thinking that any real operation like this is going to be easy," Greg warned. "This isn't a drill. It's combat, and combat can go sideways in a hurry!"

Eli and Seth nodded. Shauna knew that nothing Keith or Greg

said could dissuade them from doing what they wanted to do, so with the plan set, the three boats turned and headed upriver until they reached the confluence of the Whiskey Bay Pilot Channel. Ronnie and Keith steered into the right fork while Eli kept to the old river channel. Keith had warned him to keep his speed low and to hug the east bank as much as possible to reduce the chances of Reyes and his men hearing the outboard when they passed by the vicinity of the militia camp. While it was well to the west of the river along the little bayou and hidden from view of the river, it wasn't so far that someone there couldn't hear an outboard running at speed up the channel. They didn't have to hurry anyway, as Keith had asked them to time it so that they arrived at the mouth of the slough in about an hour and a half, giving them time to get into position while leaving about an hour of daylight in which to get the job done.

As Keith drove the patrol boat, following behind Ronnie and Bart in the gunboat, Shauna, Greg and Sam discussed with him the next step they'd be taking after they reached the main river again north of I-10.

"We'll tie up a good quarter mile above that slough. The gravel road that dead ends there is on the south side of it, so chances are that's where their camp will be. In this weather, most of them will be in their shelters if they have them, and it should be no problem to slip up close to the opposite bank where we'll be in easy rifle range. As soon as Eli and Seth come in and they go out there to see what's going on, we should be able to take out most of them."

"All assuming Reyes' reinforcements haven't arrived," Greg said.

That was a possibility, Shauna knew, especially if some of those reinforcements had arrived by boat and had the means to intercept them on the river. To avoid letting Eli and Seth run into a trap, they'd all agreed that the signal for them to turn and run back downriver would be a burst from Bart's 50-cal on the gunboat. It was the only reason he would fire first, and it would mean they'd decided to call the whole thing off.

But when they arrived at the north end of the pilot channel and doubled back down the Atchafalaya, there were no boats in sight. Keith and Ronnie both steered their vessels across the river to hug the west bank as they turned south to approach the entrance to the slough. Keith didn't want to take any chances by trying to take the boats too close, so he stopped perhaps a little farther from the objective than he'd planned, but going the rest of the way on foot was the surest way to avoid detection. After they tied the patrol boat off to the bank, he set out with Shauna, Greg and Sam, as Bart and Ronnie hung back aboard the waiting gunboat. When Shauna looked back at it over her shoulder before they disappeared into the woods, the big gray vessel was surprisingly hard to pick out against the drab backdrop created by the darkening sky and drizzling rain.

It took them less than twenty minutes to close the gap to the edge of the intersecting waterway they were looking for. When they came into view of it Shauna saw that the slough, with its stagnant greenish brown water, intersected the river at nearly a right angle and that it was about 20 to 30 feet wide. It was the perfect place to tuck away a few good-sized boats, hidden from view of the river, but there were no boats in sight there now. There were several vehicles parked along the gravel roadway on the other side though, and she saw that they were a mix of military trucks, pickups and Humvees. Several tents were pitched nearby, and from the look of it, all the men occupying the camp were inside them, sheltering from the rain, as there was no activity to be seen without.

Maybe this is going to be easy, just as Eli suggested, Shauna thought, as she heard the sound of an outboard motor off in the distance, approaching slowly but deliberately from downriver. It took another minute for the men inside those tents to hear it and realize what it was, as they were probably deep in conversation and perhaps playing cards and passing around bottles, but as the boat drew nearer, they began to emerge one-by-one, checking their weapons as they moved in the direction of the river. Shauna knew that she and her companions could have killed several of them right then if they wanted to, but that wasn't the plan, because it was far better to lure everyone in the encampment into the kill zone before the first shot was fired. As she watched them stream out of the tents, she realized there were quite a lot more than Griggs had thought, and wondered if it was because some of Reyes' reinforcements were already here. It was impossible to tell in the gloom of the woods beyond, but there could very well be more vehicles parked farther out along the road, and for all she knew, even another cluster of tents.

If that were the case, then it was too late to change the plan now. Eli and Seth had gotten no warning shots from Bart's M2, and Shauna knew they were quite close from the sound of that motor. She heard it cut out and rev up several times in a row, and knew Eli was messing with the throttle to make it seem as if he had engine trouble, and a moment later, she heard some of the men from the camp shouting out at the two men in the boat. Shauna was certain that the fight was about to be on any second now, when a new sound from out of nowhere changed everything. She glanced over at Keith, who was just a few feet to her right before they both looked back out over the river to the south of their position, searching the gray sky beyond the tree line. There was no mistaking that sound. *It was a helicopter, and it was coming in fast and low, straight in their direction!*

FOURTEEN

C.R.I. COMMANDER MITCHELL REYES WAS FRUSTRATED beyond words. He had been waiting all morning and still he'd heard nothing. The men he had sent during the night to escort Griggs to the river in order to rendezvous with the boats had returned by midmorning. They assured him Griggs had boarded one of those boats and that all three had gone downriver in search of the missing men that escaped from the militia camp.

But Reyes didn't understand what was taking them so long. According to Griggs, the boat those men got away in was a little 14-foot aluminum johnboat with no motor. It was unlikely they'd gotten far with nothing but paddles, but Reyes had seen enough of this river to realize there were endless smaller waterways and possible hideouts into which they could have ducked to avoid being seen. The long wait obviously meant the search crews hadn't found them yet, and he had to accept that it was possible those men would never be caught after killing two of the soldiers under his command.

That was bad enough, but it was far worse that this turn of events had completely botched the ambush Reyes had counted on to eliminate Eric Branson's brother and father. Both men should have arrived early that morning, as Griggs said they did every morning to commence a new day of training, and killing them should have been as simple as killing the recruits the evening before had things gone the way they were supposed to. But, of course, things hadn't. The ambush was ruined because of the one little detail that Griggs forgot to mention: the existence of that damned little boat!

At this point, Reyes had to assume that those escapees likely made contact with the Bransons or someone else from the hideout they called Sierra Zulu. He wondered if perhaps the place was even closer than Griggs had estimated. If so, the men in that boat may have arrived there during the night. Whatever had happened to them, something had clearly changed, because neither the Bransons nor anyone else came up that bayou all morning, and Reyes was beginning to think that he was waiting around there for nothing. He had more than thirty men on hand and ready for the perfect slaughter but now there was no target to engage.

The other small detachment left guarding the vehicles up at the slough north of the interstate were out of hand-held radio range, so it was impossible to reach them and learn whether they'd yet heard from the expected reinforcements that should be arriving from the Red River outpost later that day. The men had been left there with orders to remain until those additional troops arrived, and he and his assault team returned. As soon as the staging area was established when they got there yesterday, and Reyes deemed it suitable for the purpose, as Griggs had assured him he would, Reyes had sent a vehicle with four soldiers back to the Red River outpost. Their mission was to lead the next convoy in and to provide the coordinates to the crews of the additional boats he'd sent for as soon as they arrived at the compound on their trailers. Like the first three that he was waiting for to report back to him, the boats had been modified and fitted out specifically for the operation at hand here, and Reyes couldn't wait to see them in action.

His plan was to gather all his forces in that one place that was near enough to the objective, and then begin conducting search and destroy missions from there until they located and eliminated this place called Sierra Zulu and everyone associated with it. That was his primary objective for this entire operation on the Atchafalaya River, and getting rid of Keith and Bart Branson early on would have eliminated a major obstacle. It seemed too good to be true when he found Griggs and his fellow deserter already waiting at the old outpost, disillusioned with what they'd been doing and willing to give up the location and the routines of the militia recruit camp where they'd been training. Reyes didn't hesitate to act on that intel even before he had all his resources on hand. It was at least a partial success. That training camp was under his control now, and most of those recruits were dead, but he'd failed to finish the job because of Griggs' stupid little omission.

Reyes had already planned to shoot the man just as he had shot his partner before they left. He couldn't stand a deserter or a traitor, even though Griggs had deserted and betrayed his primary enemy and given him vital intel. Reyes knew a man who would do what Griggs had done would do the same to him or anyone else who made the mistake of trusting him, so men like him were best disposed of once their usefulness expired, which Griggs' about had. The only reason he was alive right now was because Reyes thought it wise to send him downriver with those boat crews. Griggs was the only one among them who had even a smidgeon of local knowledge of this place, and he would recognize on sight the boats that Keith and Bart Branson were using if they encountered them along the way.

But with every hour that passed and still no word nor sign of those three boats, the more Reyes began to think something may have really gone wrong down there. If Keith and Bart Branson did get a heads-up about what happened here last night from whoever had escaped, it was quite possible they'd set up an ambush of their own and turned the tables. If so, Reyes realized he could be waiting there for nothing while exposing himself and his men to a situation that would leave him few options, considering he was still without backup. The lack of even a single boat was the most serious concern, because operating in this wretched river bottom swamp environment without boats was virtually impossible. Cross-country travel on foot was severely limited here, even for soldiers experienced in a variety of terrain. Reyes hated the place personally, as he was a man of the drier, more open country found in his old stomping grounds of west Texas and northern Mexico.

It was a long and strange journey that brought him here to this place, and though he would have preferred to stay in Texas, he did relish the challenge and adventure that hunting down a worthy adversary would entail. When he had first been ordered to an assignment in east Texas, as commander of the C.R.I. operations concentrated along Interstate 10, Reyes had thought the state line was as far east as he would ever have to go. In retrospect, he should have known the occupation of all this territory would not go as smoothly as he'd hoped. And the irony of what he was doing here was that when he was still in Texas, he'd actually met and aided some of the men he was hunting now.

He remembered how the three women, accompanied by a young man from Florida, had arrived there at his post. They'd been sent back east under C.R.I. protection by orders from Major Langley, in New Mexico. A deal had been cut with a man named Eric Branson, who was a former Special Forces operator Langley had made an arrangement with to help him with a problem down near the Mexican border. The major had promised Branson that he would get his family back to their place of refuge in Louisiana, and at the time, Reyes had been ordered to assist. No one expected any trouble to result from the seemingly insignificant gesture, because Eric Branson and his companions weren't supposed to survive to get in the way. As it turned out, not only did Branson survive, but he also made his way back to Louisiana where his family was holed up on the Atchafalaya, and once there, set to work building up a resistance to everything C.R.I. and its allies had planned for the region.

If only he'd foreseen such a thing could have happened, Reyes could have prevented Eric Branson's wife and daughter from ever leaving Texas. He'd helped them instead, and in doing so had even met Eric's father, Bart, and his brother, Keith, the same two men he'd hoped to ambush and kill this very morning.

That meeting seemed like a very long time ago now, and much had changed for all of them in the interim. Reyes had known C.R.I. would eventually move east into Louisiana, but from all the reports he'd heard at the time, there was nothing to indicate that doing so would become so problematic. Reyes regretted that he hadn't done the one thing that would have changed everything back then, but all of that was out of his control now. So, here he was, on the ground in the midst of this vast swamp, trying to fix all the things that had spiraled into chaos.

As the morning wore on until it was finally past midday, Reyes was still waiting there with the rest of his men when he was suddenly yanked from his thoughts of past mistakes by the sound of speeding boats and a long burst of machine gun fire. Judging by the long duration of the sustained burst, Reyes knew he was hearing a belt fed weapon rather than a rifle switched to full auto. Reyes thought it must have come from one of the three boats with their mounted M60s, but when the gun stopped, the echoes of those reports were followed by the sound of what he was sure was the sound of a heavy impact. Reyes didn't know what it meant, but he heard no more engine noises either.

"That was somewhere down this bayou, by the sound of it," he told one of his corporals. "Griggs said it's impossible to follow along the bank, but we need to try. I need you to get eight or ten of the men to come with us. We're going to cross over to the other side and see if we can get down there that way. It sounded like that boat may have wrecked to me!"

Reyes hated to get wet, but judging from the gathering clouds that had turned the sky gray, he knew they were all going to anyway, whether they waded and swam that bayou or not. He wasn't the kind of leader to wait at the rear for a report from his troops, either. Reyes was here to be in the action, and his curiosity at that point wasn't about to let him wait any longer to find out the source of what he'd just heard.

It was still quiet from that direction until he and all his small team were on the other side. Then, out of the silence, they heard rifle reports, the first two nearly simultaneous, followed by two more a few seconds apart. After that, there wasn't a sound, and Reyes set out to lead the men through the thickets along the bank, all of them moving as quietly as possible as they had no idea what they would encounter down there. As they made their way through the briars and mud, Reyes realized it wasn't impossible to follow the bayou, as Griggs had led them to believe. Although it did appear far swampier on the other side, where the camp and dock were located, at least over here they were able to wade through the wet spots until finally, they came upon the sight of what they were looking for.

One of the custom-modified aluminum skiffs he'd ordered was upside down on the bank ahead, where it had come to rest completely clear of the water in a cluster of small willows. Reyes and his men paused to look and listen for signs of the crew or whoever had fired those last shots, and when they were satisfied that it was clear, they moved in to discover that the four-man crew had all been shot to death. As he stood there looking over the scene, Reyes tried to imagine just how it happened. He assumed the killers had been in another boat that had quietly left the bayou with its engine running at idle speed, as there were no footprints in the mud to indicate they'd been ashore there after the shooting. It seemed that whoever had done it was gone, but still, it made him nervous standing there where these men had all died, surrounded by enough greenery to conceal an entire platoon of riflemen that could be watching them that very moment. Reyes doubted the killers were still that close, since he and his men weren't already dead, but the evidence they'd been here was right before him, and he knew that what happened here would not be the end of it.

"We need to go back up to the militia campsite and get ready to fall back and rendezvous with the incoming reinforcements," Reyes told his corporal. "It's obvious that some of Branson's people intercepted those boats. If this is the only one that even made it back to the bayou, that doesn't bode well for the other two. We may be dealing with a much larger group than Griggs let on; there's just no way of knowing. Still, I want you and nine or ten volunteers to hang back and watch the camp area. Be prepared to engage anyone coming up this bayou if you have to, but use your judgment and stay out of sight if there are too many to get them all in one decisive counterattack. If they don't show by dawn tomorrow, meet us at the staging area and we'll go from there."

Commander Reyes had suffered a serious setback and Reyes didn't like setbacks. He had known it was bad news as soon as he discovered that someone had escaped the attack last night, but he had had no idea it was this bad. Reyes had made the mistake of trusting Griggs not only the first time when he'd assured him he knew where all the recruits would be before they launched the assault, but also he had let Griggs convince him that it was impossible to follow the bayou on foot. Now he knew that wasn't completely true. While it may have been very difficult to get down there through that slop in the dark, it wasn't impossible, and if he'd sent some men right away to attempt it from both sides of the waterway, they may have gotten a shot at whoever was making off in that little boat.

But like a series of falling dominoes, each bit of misinformation Reyes took at face value led to a mistake, and each mistake created yet another problem. Now, it appeared he had lost the only three boats he had on hand, along with their crews! Reyes wouldn't have believed it possible had he not seen it for himself. *How in the hell did this backwoods, mostly untrained civilian resistance group get as organized and efficient as they appeared to be in such a short period of time?* He had certainly seen evidence of their competence when he and his men arrived at that Red River outpost and discovered the absolute massacre of the troops that had been on duty there. Eric Branson had pulled off that assault despite the fact that those men were dug in and in a defensive position. Reyes still didn't know how he'd done it, but he knew for sure that he was dealing with a worthy adversary indeed.

Even so, Reyes relished the thought of going against him. He had no fear of Eric Branson, and he had the full support of C.R.I. and its vast resources, along with that of their allies in the cartels and the new defense force. All of it gave him a massive amount of manpower and equipment to draw from if he needed it. And Reyes would use whatever it took to crush this opposition and obliterate Eric Branson and everyone and everything associated with him.

But he knew it made little sense for the entire assault team to remain there watching that campsite and doing nothing, especially now that the enemy was onto them. He would leave a few men here to watch and wait and report back to him, but it was pointless to expose any more of them than necessary to the risk of remaining there. Reyes knew the enemy would eventually come there to survey the aftermath of the wiped-out recruit camp and retrieve their dead, but he couldn't wait for that to happen. He needed to get back to that staging area where he could coordinate with his incoming reinforcements and make a new plan for dealing with all the new difficulties he faced.

Earlier that morning, while they were waiting for the boats to return, he'd had his men drag the bodies of the dead recruits out of the clearing and pile them up on the other side of a ditch within the edge of the woods. The men had also buried the two of their own who died there last night, so now if anyone came down the gravel road and turned in there, the campsite would first appear merely deserted. Reyes instructed the corporal and the handful of men he left with him to keep an eye on the clearing and the surrounding woods, and then he wished them luck and set out on foot with the balance of his force heading north.

While he sincerely hoped those men left behind would get an opportunity to kill a few of Branson's men, he wasn't betting on it. They would send someone there, for sure, but probably not before they spent some time carefully planning how they would do it. Eric's brother and father, who were in charge now, had to know that it must have been a sizable force that came there to attack the camp. Reyes doubted they would rush in half-cocked and bent on revenge, especially after what he'd seen of their tactics so far.

It was already late afternoon by the time Reyes and the men he took with him departed the camp. The rain he'd known was coming had finally arrived, in the form of a cold and uncomfortable drizzle. Reyes was grateful for the cover it provided though, because it meant they could move faster through the woods without making much noise. They were doing exactly that, but before they'd gone half a mile from the militia camp, they all heard another, most unexpected sound from somewhere off in the distance to the south.

It was the sound of something coming at them from down the Atchafalaya River, but it was no boat! What Reyes and his men heard, much to their disbelief, was the sound of a fast-approaching helicopter. Reyes doubted it could be any friends of his, because C.R.I. didn't have any helicopters on hand in the area and he didn't know of any other forces allied with them that did. It seemed incomprehensible that Branson's resistance could be operating aircraft of any kind, much less helicopters, but Reyes wasn't taking any chances by betting it would just keep flying by, following the Atchafalaya upriver. He motioned for his men to look for cover and concealment among the trees and to get down and stay down while they waited to see what this was about.

It quickly became obvious that the helicopter wasn't just flying the river when they heard it circle back in exactly the area where the bayou merged into it. After that turn, it was clear from the sound that it was heading straight for the militia camp they'd just left, and Reyes could tell that it was coming in low and fast. In the next second, he heard the unmistakable whirring roar of a minigun raining down bullets at a rate of fire so fast that the individual reports were lost to the ear. Reyes wondered why in the hell his men back there had allowed themselves to be seen, if indeed they had, because why else would the gunner have fired? There was no return fire to be heard as the helicopter circled wide and strafed the ground down that way again, and then began flying a methodical search pattern over the surrounding woodlands, the crew no doubt looking for survivors of their hellish onslaught.

Reyes knew his present position was too close for comfort, but there was no time to get his men moving again before he saw the helicopter coming in over the treetops, passing directly overhead. Reyes had kept his face down after that first glimpse, but before it disappeared, he'd seen enough to recognize the unmistakable profile of a UH-60 Black Hawk. Where in the hell such an aircraft had come from, Reyes had no idea, but it was clear that whoever was manning it had zeroed in on the site of that militia camp for a reason. And from the sound of it, they'd spotted his men there and had fired without hesitation. It was as if they knew who was there and had come to target them specifically.

On a mission that had been plagued by unexpected developments, this latest surprise was the most unexpected of all. Reyes didn't know what to make of it, but there was nothing he could do at the moment but wait and see whether the Black Hawk would leave the area or land nearby and put boots on the ground. As he waited there frozen in position with his remaining men until it finally flew away to the northeast, Reyes concluded that the only option they had left was to escape and evade. Their entire operation had been compromised, and for all he knew that Black Hawk was now headed straight for the staging point where he'd planned to go before it arrived. And Reyes had to consider that if there was one such aircraft working against him, there might well be more, and no telling what else besides. He was in a tough spot out here, cut off and out of radio range of anyone else in his outfit. And as he thought about his limited options, Reyes knew the only thing he and his small band of mercenaries still had going for them was the deteriorating weather and the coming darkness that was now little more than an hour away.

FIFTEEN

Eric Branson could barely contain his anticipation as the helicopter pilot came in low over the Atchafalaya River, following the winding bends up from the south and rapidly approaching the junction of the cut-off bayou leading to Sierra Zulu. He had been away for weeks, with no contact with anyone in Louisiana. Eric knew everyone here was probably wondering if he and his team were ever coming back at this point, and he couldn't wait to surprise them with the good news he was bringing when he arrived there today.

Of course, they weren't expecting him to return aboard a Black Hawk helicopter, and the last thing he wanted to do was alarm everyone in the camp with the sudden appearance of an unmarked military aircraft that could mean the arrival of either friend or foe. To avoid that, Eric intended to have the pilot stop at the checkpoint out at the mouth of the bayou so he could make first contact with whoever was on watch at the time. There was nowhere to land at the base camp proper anyway, because of the heavy tree cover within which it was hidden. The only way to get into the campsite directly from the helo was to fast-rope down, which, of course, he and the members of the 26th Special Forces Group that were with him were prepared to do.

But as they closed in on the junction, flying just a couple hundred feet above the water, the first thing Eric spotted as he scanned the river in the direction of the cut-off, was a bright orange PFD about a hundred yards out from the bank. The pilot and the rest of the team saw it too, and at Eric's direction, they circled around and dropped in lower to get a closer look. From that distance, Eric could see that there was someone in the lifejacket. It was a man, and he was looking up at the helicopter while shielding his face with one hand against the spray of water kicked up by the rotor. Eric didn't recognize him as one of their number from Sierra Zulu, however, and he was puzzled as to how he got there and why, but he intended to find out ASAP.

Eric signaled to the pilot that he wanted to go even lower, and one of the other soldiers readied a rope to drop down within the man's reach. The man in the water was waving at them with one arm now, making gestures that seemed to indicate that he couldn't use the rope. Eric couldn't see his other arm, as it was underwater, and he wondered if perhaps the man was injured and was trying to tell them he couldn't hang onto the rope.

Eric hauled it up as fast as he could while the pilot kept them in a steady hover, then he quickly tied a large loop in it so the man in the water could get it over his head and shoulders. Using hand signals to show him what he had in mind, Eric demonstrated the loop and then dropped it back within his reach. Still, the man kept yelling something Eric and the other soldiers couldn't hear over the noise of the helicopter engine, and he seemed unwilling to even try to get the rope into position for the lift. Eric was quickly getting frustrated because he didn't have time for this kind of nonsense.

"He's being difficult, so I'm going to go down there," he told PFC Beckman, who was crouching there in the doorway beside him.

"I guess he's injured or something and can't get into the loop, huh?"

"Either that or he's too stupid to figure it out."

"Hey look over there!" One of the other soldiers said, tapping Eric hard on the shoulder. Eric looked where he was pointing and saw a man standing on the riverbank near the junction of the bayou. The man was waving and motioning urgently for them to come over there. Then, he pointed at the man in the water while shaking his head vigorously back and forth and making a big horizontal sweeping motion from side to side with one arm. Eric didn't know for sure what he meant, but he seemed to be telling them 'no' in regard to the man in the water. He grabbed a rifle from one of the other men who had a high-power optic mounted and zeroed in on the man ashore to get a look. Eric saw him step back and raise his hands over his head at the sight of the weapon pointed at him, but by then Eric lowered it, as he knew who he was. The man's name was Hal, one of Sam's group that he and Jonathan had met after their first encounter with Sergeant Davis' men and the gunboat up at Simmesport. He was now part of the core group at Sierra Zulu, and Eric figured he was the one on duty to stand watch there at the moment, since he was right near the bayou entrance when he emerged from the trees.

When Eric looked back down, the man in the water had grabbed hold of the looped end of the dangling rope, which had a few feet of slack in it now, but he'd still made no effort to get into it. Eric yelled and motioned to him to either put it around his body or let go, because they were moving to the bank where Hal was standing. But the man didn't let go until the pilot began to slowly lift off, and when he finally did, Eric saw he was still yelling at them, although he couldn't hear a word of what he was saying. The one-finger salute from his now-empty hand was all too clear though, and Eric returned the gesture before directing the pilot to a spot past Hal and just around the first bend in the bayou channel, where he knew there was a mud bar wide enough for the Black Hawk to set down and let them disembark.

Eric and Beckman and three other soldiers leapt to the ground from about five feet up before the aircraft touched down and ran over to where Hal was waiting. Eric had to know what he'd been so urgently trying to convey.

"Man, am I ever glad to see you!" Hal told Eric as they shook hands. "I didn't know who in the hell it was when I saw that helicopter coming in, but when it hovered over that guy out there in the river and I studied all of y'all in the open doorway through my riflescope, I couldn't believe my eyes when I saw it was you! I saw what you were trying to do, and I knew I had to get your attention, because you were wasting your time."

"What do you mean, wasting my time? What the hell's going on here? Who's that guy in the water and why didn't he want us to pick him up?"

"It's not that he didn't *want* to be picked up. It's that he *couldn't,* because your brother, Keith, locked him by the ankle to a boat, and now that boat's on the bottom of the river!"

"What do you mean it's on the bottom of the river? What boat, and who is that guy, anyway? He looks vaguely familiar, but it's hard to tell because he's soaking wet."

"It's an aluminum fishing boat he came down here on with a bunch of Reyes' men. They attacked the training camp up at Keith's place last night and only three of the guys there made it out alive. Reyes sent three boats down here this morning to hunt them down, and Keith found that son of a bitch in one of them. He didn't kill him right away because he was using him as bait, to catch the rest of them in the other two. It kind of worked because we wiped out the crew of one boat, but the bunch in the last one got away. Keith and Greg and your dad and Ronnie took off after them, but not before they shot up the one boat anchored there with that son of a bitch in it. Lucky for him, there's a gravel bar out there where it sank in about five feet of water! Six more inches, and he'd have drowned."

Eric was dumbfounded at all of this. "So, who is he? And Reyes? Do you mean the Reyes that's the C.R.I. commander from Texas?"

"He's a traitor, that's who! A deserter *and* a traitor, and yeah, he brought Reyes and his C.R.I. hired killers right back there to the militia camp last night! His name's Griggs. He looks familiar to you because he was in that bunch we busted out of that C.R.I. work camp way out there in the middle of nowhere. Like most of those guys, he joined up with the militia afterwards. But then he and another fellow deserted because of disagreements they had with the way Keith was running things. Keith thought that was the end of it, but boy was he wrong! Somehow, Griggs hooked up with Reyes and told him everything, and after he caught him, Keith got it out of him that he and his men were up there at the militia camp waiting to ambush him and your dad when they got there this morning for training!"

Eric vaguely remembered this Griggs guy now that Hal had reminded him. He hadn't interacted with him enough to have a clue of his true character, as he'd been busy planning his expedition and had left the work of training the recruits to his dad and brother. Now, Hal was telling him most of the recruits were dead and all that training had been for nothing!

It was hard to believe that just two deserters had caused this much disruption and death, but Eric had seen enough lately that nothing really surprised him anymore. There'd been no realistic way to vet all the new recruits before bringing them into the militia, but at the time it didn't seem necessary because after freeing them from that labor camp, those guys hardly needed persuasion. They were gung-ho and eager to get free training and weapons so they could go back and get their revenge against the people that had made their lives a living hell.

"Keith came back to Sierra Zulu one night and told us about his problems with that guy and how they'd finally reached a breaking point. Griggs got right up in his face that day, and Keith had to make an example of him in front of the rest of the men to maintain discipline. He knew Griggs didn't like him, but he'd still hoped he would come around. Of course, he didn't, and just a couple of nights later, he split with the one buddy he still had left there.

"Keith was beating himself up pretty good today for not going after those two as soon as they deserted back then, but how could he have known Griggs was capable of what he did last night? None of us were expecting anything like that. Besides, at the time, Keith's natural reaction was to be glad he was rid of him and his buddy if they didn't want to be there. It wasn't like he could force them to stay."

"No," Eric said. "I would have done the same. Desertion is serious, but these guys were just volunteers and they'd barely gotten started with the training at that point. Keith isn't to blame. Some people are just rotten to the core, and Griggs is surely one of them. I'm glad you were here to stop me from trying to save him, because now that I know how he got there, I know he's exactly where he should be. There's no time now, because it sounds like I'm needed upriver, but I intend to have a word with him when I get back."

"Don't be gone too long then," Hal said. "With all the rain we've got coming in, this river's getting up. It'll be over his head by morning, unless he uses the knife Shauna loaned him to save himself from drowning by cutting off his leg!"

"Shauna did that?" Eric grinned.

"He was begging her to help him, but of course, she couldn't, even if she'd wanted to. Keith and Greg are the only ones with handcuff keys, and there's no telling when they'll be back. Shauna just gave him the option."

It was more than the man deserved, Eric thought, but Shauna knew that Griggs would pay the price for what he'd done, one way or the other. Eric hoped to interrogate him if possible, but there was no time for that now. With his wife, brother, and father all upriver where Reyes had an unknown number of assets in both men and equipment, Eric knew he had to go and go now. He knew the slough Hal was talking about when he told him that Reyes had more men stationed there and that Shauna, Eli, and Seth had gone to meet Keith to convince him they needed to try to take it. What they had in mind made sense if it would prevent Reyes from coordinating with his expected reinforcements, but it sounded to Eric like they were stretching themselves thin, trying to pull off something that risky with just eight people. They needed help, and Eric had the means at his disposal if he could just get there in time.

The news of what happened at the militia camp last night was devastating, but Hal had good news too, telling him that until then, all had been quiet here during his absence, and that Megan and everyone else at Sierra Zulu were doing just fine.

"I want you to stay put here and keep watch, Hal, but if you hear from anyone at Sierra-Zulu, be sure and get the message to Megan that I'm back and will see her soon!"

"Shauna and the rest of them upriver won't be expecting a helicopter, just like I wasn't, but once they figure out it's you in it, they're sure going to be glad to have that kind of help." Hal was gazing at the fearsome miniguns mounted on either side of the Black Hawk.

"Yeah, Reyes won't be expecting it either, I don't imagine. We'll pay him a quick visit on the way up, since we've got to go almost right by Keith's place anyway to get to that slough!"

When Eric and the rest of the team were back in the air and flying low over the river, his mind kept replaying all that Hal had just told him. He had learned after they liberated that last labor camp that Commander Reyes was in charge of the operations there. He knew that Reyes had his orders to clear out the civilian population in that part of Louisiana, locking the remaining residents down in relocation camps while they seized control of the waterways and highways and everything else of strategic value. Only Eric and his civilian resistance force were standing in the way, and he knew that

Reyes had already made it a priority to hunt them down and eradicate them.

At the time, it seemed pointless to stand and try to fight them off with the limited resources he had, and that was why he'd left to go east to Mississippi, seeking extra help. It had proven to be a long journey fraught with obstacles and setbacks, but he had more or less succeeded in the first phase of what he had in mind. Getting a ride back here in a Black Hawk with a small team of Colonel Rencher's Special Forces operators from Camp Hurley was clearly a step in the right direction, if only the beginning. Eric had expected to disembark at Sierra Zulu with those men that included his new friend, PFC Robert Beckman. The new team would bolster the militia force and assist with the training, while the Black Hawk crew would return as soon as possible with Jonathan and the other three young men that were part of his original expedition team.

All that had changed now though, and instead of the anticipated reunion with his family at Sierra Zulu, Eric and the men with him were on their way to surprise them by joining them in the fight against Reyes. The Black Hawk would take them there quickly, and its onboard weaponry would give them the ability to make a difference, assuming it wasn't already too late.

Eric scanned the river from bank to bank as the pilot followed the big, sweeping bends that took them to the junction of the bayou leading to his brother's old homestead. The pilot stayed low over the treetops when he turned off at Eric's direction, and when Eric spotted the clearing, he saw a small group of uniformed men scattering for the cover of the woods. Eric knew they weren't the militia recruits because Hal assured him all but three had been killed the night before, having gotten the eyewitness account directly from Eli and Seth. Those men running on the ground were either C.R.I. contractors or troops from the other mercenary force working with them that Eric had already encountered. They were here because they were in on the murder of most of his militia, and Eric intended to give them no quarter. At his signal, the gunner on the starboard

M-134 Minigun let it rip. Eric watched as the streams of tracers cut through the shadows of the sparse late fall canopy below. Those men could try to run and hide, but there was no cover against that hail of 7.62mm bullets raining down on them from above. Eric and the other soldiers joined in on the action with their rifles as well and after the pilot circled around for one more pass to give the man on the port gun a taste of the action too, they couldn't find any more moving targets left to shoot.

"I think we got them all!" PFC Beckman said, as the pilot flew a pattern for a few passes before leaving the scene to head north to that slough.

"I doubt it," Eric said. "I saw maybe a dozen men down there. There must have been more last night, but whether we got the ones responsible for that ambush or not, they won't hang around here any longer. We'll worry about hunting the rest of them down after we rendezvous with my folks up there at that slough!"

Eric, and all the men with him, were scanning the river below once the Black Hawk intersected it again and followed it north. When they crossed the Interstate 10 Bridge, there was no sign of life there, only a few abandoned vehicles that had been there the last time Eric had seen it. It was on the river to the north of the bridge that Eric expected to encounter both his friends and foes, and minutes later, he was not disappointed. The third aluminum fishing boat Hal had described was the first thing he spotted. It appeared nearly stationary when he saw it, its bow pointed towards the mouth of the slough from where it seemed to be idling mid-river. Eric knew Shauna had left on it with Eli and Seth, but he could see when they passed overhead that only two men were aboard it now, and both were looking up at the unexpected sight of the aircraft.

Eric also spotted a small group of armed and uniformed men at the edge of the woods on the south side of the slough. They'd looked up at the helicopter too, of course, dropping down as it passed, and behind them, among the trees, Eric could see a line of military vehicles and some tents along the gravel road there. He knew they were Reyes' forces, but Eric had insisted before they arrived here that no one aboard the helicopter should fire until he gave the word. He wanted positive identification with his friends and family so close, and to get that, he had to know where they all were first. The pilot circled back as soon as they passed the mouth of the slough, and that's when Eric spotted the gunboat waiting there in the river a short distance away. Not far from it, tied off to the west bank, was Keith's empty patrol boat. Eric realized immediately that he'd arrived neither too early nor too late, but rather, just in time to interfere with what was clearly a clever plan to take out the men camped at that slough. But as he saw Bart on the deck of the gunboat begin to track the Black Hawk with the barrel of that M2, Eric realized his family and friends were far more likely to assume the helicopter crew was with Reyes, rather than someone that was on their side. As he hung as far out the side door as he possibly could, waving to his father, he could only hope the old man would take the time to look closely before pressing that trigger with his thumbs.

SIXTEEN

Keith returned Shauna's shocked stare just before the helicopter came into view, flying low over the treetops as it followed the river. Until it arrived on the scene out of nowhere, everything about their hastily prepared plan was coming together with perfection. They were all in position, including Eli and Seth, who'd just arrived in the boat. The men they'd come here to target had left their tents to go out in the rain at the sound of the outboard and were walking right into the trap they'd set. In a few more seconds, Keith knew most of them would be bunched up together near the riverbank, and when the shooting started, they'd be caught in a crossfire from two sides.

But now the roar of a fast-moving helicopter demanded they shift their attention to the sky instead. Keith was in utter disbelief when he saw it was a military aircraft. *Did Reyes have helicopters as part of his operation here too? If he did,* Keith wondered, *why hadn't he sent them down the river instead of the three boats? And why hadn't Griggs mentioned it?* It didn't make sense, but then again, this helicopter had come from downriver, so it was possible it could have just arrived in the area from somewhere to the west, probably Texas, and had made a sweep up the Atchafalaya from the south.

"Stay down and keep your faces down!" He whispered to Shauna and the others with him. "They'll be focused on the boat out in the river and those guys on the bank. If we're lucky, they won't see us over here on this side."

Keith hoped he was right, and that the undergrowth they were hiding in was dense enough to conceal them from above, but he felt bad for Eli and Seth, as they had nowhere to go, sitting in a boat out there in the wide-open river like that. He expected at any moment to see them cut to pieces by whatever armament that helo was carrying, but instead, it passed over their position and circled back away from the river to the north. Keith knew the crew couldn't have missed seeing the gunboat waiting in the river up there, as well as his own boat tied off to the bank nearby. As it went by at about 50 feet above the trees, he saw that it was a UH-60 Black Hawk, and on the port side that he could see, there was a gunner on the mounted M-134 Minigun as well as several soldiers visible through the open door.

Some of the men out on the riverbank had dropped to the ground upon its approach, while about half of them retreated back into the woods. Their reaction didn't tell Keith a lot, because even if the Black Hawk was part of Reyes' operation, its arrival may have been unexpected. Keith wondered if perhaps someone had sent it to follow up on the ambush at the militia camp. If so, it may have landed there and even picked up the commander himself.

But when the Black Hawk made that turn on a path that Keith knew had taken it directly over the gunboat, yet still didn't engage, he wasn't quite sure what to think. Bart would have fired as well if he felt threatened, but Keith knew his dad had to be as surprised as everyone else at its arrival.

"It's coming back around from the west now," Sam whispered. "Eli and Seth should've turned that boat around and ran while they could!"

He was right, but Keith knew they wouldn't do that. Eli and Seth had come here for a purpose, and that purpose was to kill as many of these men associated with the massacre at the militia camp as possible. And it was at that moment that Seth decided to act, helicopter or no helicopter. While the men on the riverbank were cautiously getting back to their feet, their attention focused through the treetops to the skies off to the west, Seth let loose with a long burst from the M60, just as he'd planned to do.

Keith saw all the men in the cluster go down, some hit and others diving to the ground for cover before scrambling to return fire. That's when he raised his own rifle and shot the first one he could get in his sights. Seconds later, he heard Shauna, Sam and Greg doing the same. They quickly eliminated the rest of the group that was out in the open, but it wasn't what Keith had planned, because now their cover was blown. There was still an unknown number of adversaries out of sight back there where the vehicles were parked among the trees, and he wasn't sure how they were going to deal with them, not to mention the helicopter.

He was sure those that were back there in the woods were caught off guard by what just happened, but he didn't expect that it would take them long before they would regroup and launch a counterattack. The helicopter would be upon them again too, leaving Keith and his companions no time to retreat to the boats, if that were even an option against this new threat from the air. He glanced back towards the river, hoping to see Eli and Seth taking off in the boat while they still could, but to his surprise, they were now entering the mouth of the slough, and they weren't alone. The gunboat was right behind them! *Why would Ronnie and Bart take a chance like that, making themselves an easy target for the gunners aboard that Black Hawk?*

He got his answer when Bart began firing on the parked vehicles with the M2. At the same time, Keith heard the unmistakable buzz of an M-134 spitting hellfire from the air. It was hovering somewhere just out of view over the trees to the west, so he knew the fire was not directed at any of them or either of the boats. The gunner on that helicopter was instead engaging Reyes' men and vehicles along the gravel road!

After three or four more bursts from that terrifying weapon, the helicopter circled back around right over the river where it was in plain view of all of them, including Eli and Seth and Bart and Ronnie. Keith saw Bart signal to the crew with a big thumbs up and then watched puzzled as it slowly descended to the small opening next to the bank until it was near enough to the ground for seven soldiers in full battle gear to jump out.

One of them was waving and yelling at Bart, and Keith saw the old man point directly to where he was concealed on the other side of the slough with Shauna, Greg, and Sam. The soldier was clearly looking for them now, and as Keith stared back, wondering why Bart had revealed their location, Shauna suddenly leapt to her feet and shouted in excitement.

"ERIC!"

She was right! Keith could hardly believe it, but the man standing there with those other soldiers was his own brother, Eric!

There was no time to greet him though, or even shout back and forth. Eric motioned to them to follow from their side of the slough as he moved into the woods with his small team, their weapons at ready and their intentions clear. The Black Hawk climbed back above tree level and followed them west over the woods. It was time to hunt down and kill any survivors they didn't get with the first onslaught, and Keith saw that Eli and Seth had landed on their side of the slough and were coming with them as well. Only Bart and Ronnie would remain behind, and Keith knew the old man was probably cussing about being stuck there on the boat at that gun, missing out on the opportunity to go hunting again with his two boys.

Keith was bursting at the seams with unanswered questions. *Where did that helicopter come from and how did Eric know to come here at precisely the right time?* It was all impossible to fathom. As far as he could see, the Black Hawk had no markings on it whatsoever. It was all solid green—not the usual olive drab, but a dark, almost black, forest green—so it was impossible to tell what military branch or organization it belonged to.

Eric had surprised him before when he returned in a float plane sent there to the Atchafalaya from the Gulf coast of Mexico by a cartel boss, but the men that had bailed out of that helo with him didn't look like cartel enforcers, contractors or civilian militia. They had every appearance of active-duty soldiers, from the way they were dressed and equipped to the way they moved once they were on the ground. If Keith had to guess, they were Special Forces operators at that. Eric had surely found them somewhere on his quest to the east, but if so, *where were Jonathan and the other three young men he took with him?*

Keith had to wonder if there was more than one helicopter, or if perhaps more troops were on the way by boat or some other means. If so, perhaps Jonathan and the rest of the team were with them. Regardless of how he managed it, Eric's arrival here couldn't have been timed any better if they'd all sat down to go over it in meticulous detail. Visibility wasn't great in the steady, light rain and there was barely an hour of daylight left, but Eric and those with him aboard the helicopter had managed to assess what they saw on that first pass and accurately target the enemy. How they knew that Seth or Eli out there in the smaller boat weren't on Reyes' side, Keith couldn't imagine, but he was glad neither man fired at the helicopter. Hell, even Bart must have been tempted, because it was just logical to assume it was with the enemy, especially considering no one here on the Atchafalaya had heard from Eric in weeks.

But as he considered all this as they were spreading out into the woods, making their way west the short distance to the end of the slough, Keith heard the buzz of a minigun again. He knew it meant one of the helicopter gunners must have spotted additional targets farther out along the road. There was small arms fire coming from the ground, too. Eric's team was in on the action, and it was likely that whatever enemy remained was returning fire if they could.

All this told Keith that there were clearly a lot more of Reyes' forces here than he'd thought at first, and he realized now that their ambush probably would not have succeeded without outside help. Griggs was either lying when he told Shauna how few men were posted here or else the reinforcements Reyes expected had arrived today. But with the aerial firepower of the Black Hawk preventing anyone from leaving by way of the road and Eric and the rest of his team sweeping the woods between there and the river to pin them down, the extra numbers weren't going to matter.

Keith quickly lost sight of Eric and the soldiers once they were in the woods, but he could tell from the direction of the gunfire that some of them had worked their way around to the south of the tents and vehicles. He turned to Eli and Seth as soon as they caught up.

"Follow Sam and circle up to the north so you can cut off any of those guys that may try to make it back to the river! They know they can't use the road, so following the river north is the only other option they really have to escape. It looks like Eric and his guys went the other way to stop them from going south."

Keith, Greg and Shauna moved directly to the west, taking advantage of the big hardwood trees for cover along the way. When they had a clear view of the road, Keith could then see there were at least two dozen trucks and Humvees parked along the edges. Dead men wearing those same green camo uniforms were scattered among them, most of them probably victims of the Black Hawk's miniguns, but from where they approached, they could see a group of three or four survivors pinned down underneath one of the large trucks. Those men were no doubt focused on the threat above and were unaware of a new, closer danger. But when Greg fired the M406 high explosive grenade that landed under that truck with them, they were out of the fight before they ever knew what hit them. Keith heard a few more sporadic shots from the direction in which Eric's men had gone, and all the while the Black Hawk circled the area, its gunners looking for targets until there were no more to be found.

It was several more minutes before all the shooting finally ceased, and then Keith spotted Eric making his way over to their position, accompanied by one of the soldiers on the team working with him. Eric was as nonchalant as if they did this every day, and it was no big deal at all.

"PFC Robert Beckman, I'd like to introduce you to my brother, Keith Branson, and his partner, Greg Hebert, of the St. Martin Parish Sheriff's Department. And this badass warrior lady with them is Shauna, my wife."

"Ex-wife, technically, Eric Branson!" Shauna said, as she rushed up to Eric and threw her arms around him.

"I don't know where the hell you came from or how you knew to find us here at precisely the right moment, but I hope you've got an explanation for it, because it's really blowing my mind," Keith told Eric.

"Why are you surprised? I told you I was going to get help and here I am. Yeah, it took a little longer than I thought it would, but better late than never, right?"

"A day earlier would have been *a lot* better, at least for our militia. You're not going to believe this, but Commander Reyes, the C.R.I. guy from Texas, is behind all this. He moved his forces in here before we knew it and last night, they hit the recruit camp at my place. They killed all but three of our guys there. Two of them that made it out came to tell us and found Shauna this morning. They're the same two that were out there in the fishing boat when you and your guys first flew over. Eli Landry and Seth Guidry."

"Yes, I got the news from Hal. Hal is the one who told me where to find you and told me what was going on. I truly regret that we didn't get here a day earlier. It's despicable that those guys were murdered like that."

"What's even more despicable," Greg said, "is how Reyes knew where to find them."

"Yeah, I know about that, too. Hal told me and I also saw that guy out there in the river myself. In fact, he's the first thing we saw when we came in low to the bayou cutoff on our way to Sierra Zulu. We were going to land there and notify whoever was on watch of our arrival so that we wouldn't frighten anyone at the camp with the helicopter. But there he was, someone in the water with an orange lifejacket on. I had no idea that he was locked to a boat that sank to the bottom, because you know how muddy the Atchafalaya is. Even though it was only five feet deep, according to Hal, it was impossible to see that a boat was there. We even tried to rescue him before we knew who he was. The pilot dropped us down low over him and I threw him a rope, but he was yelling something and refused to get inside the loop, and it wasn't until we landed and I talked to Hal that I found out why."

"I gave him that lifejacket," Shauna said.

"And a knife too, from what I understand," Eric said, grinning at her.

"It was the least I could do. I doubt he's got what it takes to use it, but we'll know soon enough, I suppose."

"Well, I hope I get to have a chat with him before he does, or the river gets over his head. But the first thing I want to do is check all these dead guys here and make sure Reyes is not among them. Both of you met him before, so you can identify him if he is."

"He can't be here," Keith said. "Not unless he left there early this morning, and I really doubt he did, considering what Griggs told me. But he may well have left later, after he heard the chase and the gunfire when Greg and I ran down that third boat."

Eric told them what he'd seen when they flew over Keith's place, where the militia members had been massacred. He told them they'd spotted a group of maybe a dozen men there that scattered at the sight of the helicopter and that they had strafed them in several passes, killing all that they could see.

"Maybe Reyes is one of them then, but we won't know until we go and check."

SEVENTEEN

"You can ride with us," Eric told Keith as the other soldiers climbed back aboard the Black Hawk. "We don't have long before dark, but I'd like to determine whether or not we got Reyes when we first opened fire on the group we saw on your property. You met him, so you can identify him if he's among the dead."

"Maybe. Unless that M-134 did too much damage."

"We didn't let up until we got everyone we saw moving down there, that's for sure, but since we only saw a dozen at most, I know we didn't get everyone involved in the attack last night."

"No, not according to Eli. He saw a lot more men than that while he was covering for Seth when he brought James Andre back across the bayou. Some of them may have returned here, but if so, they had to leave this morning to get here before we hit them, and I doubt Reyes was with them."

Eric nodded. They'd already checked the dead here after the mop-up and there was nothing to indicate the commander was among them. Keith hadn't expected to find him here anyway, after what he'd gotten out of Griggs about the planned ambush. Reyes wouldn't have left that to just a dozen or so of his men, and he wouldn't have wanted to miss out on it anyway, as killing some of Eric's family members was personal to him and would have been the highlight of his operation here. Eric doubted they'd been lucky enough to take out Reyes with that strafing run either, but it was best confirmed while they still had transportation to get there quickly.

"Have Greg and Bart meet us there at your place because we're going to need a ride back to Sierra-Zulu in the boats. The Black Hawk can't land there and besides, the crew had orders to return to base as soon as they dropped us off. They're already going to be overdue after all the surprises we found here. I'd hate to see Colonel Rencher blow a fuse over this because he already lost one Black Hawk recently.

"So, the rest of those guys with you that aren't part of the crew are staying?" Shauna asked.

"Yes, and more are on the way. I'm not sure if they'll get the next ride out or if Rencher will send Jonathan and my other guys, but either way, we've got help coming, and not just by air. I had no idea Reyes would be on the offensive here already, and I certainly didn't expect to have to deal with him the very first day I got back. Rencher and I have been making plans though, and I'll fill you in on the details later. But we're running out of daylight now, so we've got to go."

"Let me ride down there with you too," Shauna pleaded.

"Sorry, but there's not enough room. Just come on the boat with Greg. We'll ride back to Sierra Zulu from there together afterwards and we can talk more then. I can't wait to hear about everything else that's been going on here, and I can't wait to see Megan!"

"She'll be as happy as I am to see you," Shauna said. "She's been looking for you to show up again every day, but I sure hate it for Vicky. She's really going to be disappointed when she finds out Jonathan isn't with you!"

"She should be happy to know that he's okay, though. All the guys are. I can promise her that he'll be here soon. I wish I could have brought him today, but I had to have a team of trained operators for this first trip. It was the only way Rencher would send the Black Hawk out here."

Eric would tell them later of his meeting with Colonel Rencher and the 26th Special Forces Group, and all they'd gone through to get to him. But first, he really wanted to know the status of Commander Reyes and the men he had with him down at Keith's place.

When they flew over the property to make another observation pass before setting down, it was less than a half hour before dark. The Black Hawk pilot touched down just long enough for them to hop out after they confirmed no signs of movement in the area, then Eric, Keith, PFC Beckman, and the rest of his team spread out across the scene of the strafing, where they began checking the bodies. The M-134 had wreaked havoc on those men, of course, considering they had no available cover besides the trees, and many had been caught in the open before they realized what they were facing. Still, Eric knew it was possible there'd been some survivors, so they were cautious as he and his brother moved together among the dead, looking for one that Keith might recognize as Reyes. But after they had examined all the bodies they could find, it appeared none of the men who died here were C.R.I. commanders. All wore the same green camo standard-issue uniforms that Sergeant Davis' men had worn at the Red River outpost, and Eric figured they were all part of that organization that was pretending to be the new force for restoring and defending national order.

"I'm not surprised he's not here," Keith said. "He probably just left these men here on the off chance that we'd still come up that bayou. He already knew we were onto him though, because like I told Shauna, there's no way anyone here wouldn't have heard us chasing that last boat, and the gunfire that went with it. He couldn't reach those guys we took out up at the slough, because it's out of handheld range. He probably set out that way on foot, but didn't have time to get there before we hit them. Wherever he and the men he took with him are though, there's no way they could have missed hearing that helicopter going over between here and there. You can bet that wherever they are out here in the swamp, they'll be moving fast again once it gets dark. Reyes will want to cover as much ground as he can before morning. He may be headed up that slough or he may strike out to the west or somewhere else hoping to escape and evade. It'll be hard to track them down in the dark, especially in these conditions, so what do you want to do, Eric?"

Eric knew Keith was probably right about Reyes. He was likely out there, and probably not that far away from here, but they'd lost the daylight, and what had started out as light rain had turned into a steady downpour now. Finding Reyes and his men tonight would be practically impossible, even if he'd had his Jicarilla tracking buddies from northern New Mexico.

"Let's go to Sierra Zulu for the night. I want to see my daughter and I want to have a word with that Griggs fellow before the river gets up. In the morning, I'll get you to bring me and my team back here at first light, rain, or no rain, and we'll see if we can pick up the trail then. You and Bart and Greg can go back upriver and wait there, near the slough, in case he shows up. If we don't find him between here and there, we may have to wait until we get the additional help Rencher is sending here. We'll need it anyway, because it sounds like we're going to need to take down that Red River outpost all over again. I regret now that we didn't just burn the damned place to the ground when we had a chance, but I didn't figure on being gone long enough for Reyes to get this organized."

While they were waiting for the boats to arrive, Eric filled Keith in on a few of the key details of his long and eventful expedition to Mississippi.

"Wow! It sounds like you were almost done before you even got started good, running into that Farley guy. Do you think he was really the elected sheriff there?"

"I'm pretty sure he was. Family money got him into office a long time ago, and it helped him stay there. He had enough influence and power by the time the shit hit the fan everywhere that things just fell into place for him to become the tyrant of his little realm. Beckman and I screwed up and got ourselves and Lenny in a jam. If it wasn't for Jonathan, Willis, and Trey, I wouldn't be here talking to you right now. That's a fact."

"Yeah, and it would be a damn shame to end a career like yours shot like a dog at some backwoods county landfill."

"I'd prefer to go out a different way when it's my time, but at least the trouble we got into helped out some other folks. We did the people in that part of Mississippi a real favor by getting rid of that asshole and his little private army. After what we went through there, crossing the entire state to get to Beckman's base was more like an afterthought."

Eric went on to explain that although getting there was the easy part, convincing Colonel Rencher to help him was quite another. Eric and his guys had found themselves waiting and wondering day after day and had about given up when they finally got the answer that brought him here today. He gave Keith the short version, and then when the boats arrived, it was Shauna's turn to get the answers to her own questions. Eric told her as much as he could on the ride downriver in the dark, and listened to her stories of what life had been like there in his absence, and how she'd been hopeful every morning when she was on watch that he would return.

"After all that's happened today, it's hard to believe it was just this morning that I heard someone bump a paddle against a boat. I couldn't see a thing in the morning mist over the water, but I really thought you'd finally made it back today."

"And now I have," Eric pulled her close to him, and kissed her.

When they neared the entrance to the bayou leading into Sierra Zulu, Keith steered straight for the area where he had anchored the boat to which he'd shackled Griggs by the ankle. But though they scanned the river with flashlights as he motored slowly back and forth, there was no sign of the orange lifejacket or the man's head above the water.

"Without a working GPS, I can't be sure of the exact spot where I dropped the anchor, but we've got to be close to that sunk boat right here."

"Yes, this is where it was," Shauna said. "But I'm not sure the river has gotten up enough that his head and the life jacket would be completely underwater. It doesn't look that different from what I can see of the bank over there."

"It's not," Greg said. "It hasn't been raining long enough to have an effect on the river level yet. It'll be tomorrow before it rises that much."

"Griggs didn't know that though," Eric said. "All this rain probably freaked him out. It looks like he may have gone ahead and used your knife after all, Shauna!"

"If he did, then he may have made his way to the bank. He had the life jacket, if he didn't lose it."

They motored over to the mouth of the bayou to where the gunboat and fishing boat Eli and Seth were in were both pulled up to the bank. Eric saw that Hal was still there at his post, and now he was talking to the others on the boats, including Eric's new friends from the 26th Special Forces Group that had caught a ride with Bart and Ronnie.

"I didn't even know he was missing," Hal said. "I couldn't see a thing out there once this rain picked up like it has, especially after dark. If he cut himself loose, there's no telling where he is now."

"Do you think we should go look for him?" Shauna asked.

"Not tonight." Eric said. "If he actually did it, he's not going far on one leg before morning."

"If he cut his own leg off, he probably went into shock and passed out before he even made it to the bank," Keith said.

"Yeah, and even if he didn't pass out and somehow dragged himself out of the water, it was probably only far enough to bleed out. We can make a quick sweep downstream at daybreak when you take me and Beckman and his buddies back up there to look for Reyes."

"I gave him my belt to make a tourniquet with when I gave him the knife."

"But you didn't think he'd use either one, did you?" Eric asked her.

"No. I just wanted him to have to think about it. I wanted him to suffer the mental anguish I guess, after what he did—the kind of anguish Eli and Seth must have suffered after watching what happened at that camp while knowing there was nothing they could do about it."

"Well, you accomplished that," Keith said. "I wouldn't have thought he'd have it in him to use that knife either, but I'm like Eric. I imagine he'll be dead by daylight if he's not already, but even if he survives the night, he's not going anywhere."

"They wouldn't let Jonathan come with you?" Vicki Singleton asked Eric in disbelief as Megan put her arm around her and then hugged her close. The tears were already streaming down her face at the news Megan's father brought as she clung to Jonathan's folded letter he had given her.

"No, not today. I'm sorry, Vicki. I did my best to convince Colonel Rencher to let him come, even if the other guys couldn't, but he insisted on filling every available space aboard that Black Hawk besides mine with a soldier from his unit. But Jonathan and the rest of the guys will get a ride, I can assure you of that. I have Colonel Rencher's word. In the meantime, they're all getting some valuable training. He insisted on putting them to work on drills and exercises with some of his operators. They're going to come away from that with new skills and knowledge that will give them the edge for what we may have to do next."

"From what you told us about how they rescued you and Lenny and Private Beckman, I can't imagine there's much else they need to learn," Megan said. "How many times does Jonathan have to prove himself? How many times do any of them have to? From what you've said about Lenny, Willis, and Trey, I can't see that they need to either."

"Everyone can benefit from extra training and learning new skills, Megan. You should know that. And besides, it wasn't up to me. Things are different on a functioning military base. The colonel has his protocols and ways of doing things, and I had to go along with him if I wanted his help. Getting help is the reason we went over there and Jonathan and the rest of the guys all knew that the mission was uncertain and subject to change at any time. I can assure you they're all cool with it though, because they're just happy that the colonel is willing to help. I doubt we would've had as much success in persuading him had it not been for finding Beckman out there in the woods and bringing him back, along with word of what happened to that other Black Hawk he was aboard."

"It's just this waiting!" Vicki said, after she'd dried her eyes and composed herself. "It's already been a month. How much longer do I have to wait? You can't even tell me if they're coming the next time the helicopter returns?"

"No, I can't tell you that for sure, but if it's not the next time, it'll be the one after or another one soon. Rencher is going to get a full debriefing from the crew when it returns to base tonight. Once he finds out what happened over here and that we're already facing a new C.R.I. incursion on the ground in the Atchafalaya Basin, he'll be even more motivated to act."

"And that could mean sending more soldiers before he sends the guys," Megan said.

"That's possible," Eric admitted. "But if that's what he does, it will be to our benefit as well. You see what we're facing now after all that happened today."

"Well, actually, we didn't see it, because absolutely nothing happened out here at Sierra Zulu. We had no idea all of this was even going on until we got word from Elroy when he went out there to relieve Hal, and Hal sent him back to tell us."

"And that's just further proof that we picked a great spot for our ultimate refuge," Keith said. "This place is hard to find and is relatively defensible compared to anywhere else in the area. As long as we can keep the conflict far enough away from camp that no one here even knows it's going on, I call that a win."

"The bottom line," Eric said, "is that Reyes has decided to make his move, and even if we got lucky somehow and find out he was killed today, it won't matter because C.R.I. and their allies will replace him with someone else. This is why we need Rencher's help, but I can tell you that he isn't going to help us stay here long term. Anyone that wants security and safety will have to migrate east to the vicinity of Camp Hurley, where they are maintaining control of the situation, and there's still law and order.

"This area of Louisiana is about to be a war zone for the foreseeable future. Whether Rencher has the resources to stop the enemy here before they cross the Mississippi River remains to be seen, because it's impossible to know exactly what we're up against. But at least I managed to convince him it was worth the effort to send that Black Hawk out here to see, and to leave Beckman and his squad with us. Once the colonel gets that debriefing from the crew, he'll see why it's better to fight this battle here rather than on his home turf."

WHEN ERIC WAS FINALLY ALONE WITH SHAUNA AT THE END of that long and exhausting day, he reminded her that she'd played a key role in thwarting Reyes' plans. She had heard Eli and Seth approach before she could even see them, and she'd gotten their warning to Keith in time to prevent him from running into a fatal ambush. Then, she'd gotten even more intel from Griggs by talking to him one more time when Eli and Seth had wanted to just shoot him.

"Griggs still got what he deserved, but because of your quick thinking in getting that other boat, you were able to get that new information to Keith and my dad before Reyes could reconnect with his men up there."

"We probably would have been wiped out if you hadn't shown up when you did though," Shauna said. "There were a lot more troops at that place than Griggs thought."

"Well, now there are none, until more come by road or by boat. Reyes is on the run, and the men he left at Keith's place are all dead. I know that doesn't bring back all those civilian recruits that died there too, but Reyes' botched massacre exposed his operation. Those men signed up to fight for their homeland, and even though they died before they had a chance to really fight, their sacrifice wasn't in vain. Many more will probably die before this is said and done, but we will prevail in the end, because the enemy is fighting for power and control, but we are fighting for our way of life."

BOOKS IN THIS SERIES

1. Feral Nation - Infiltration
2. Feral Nation - Insurrection
3. Feral Nation - Tribulation
4. Feral Nation - The Divide
5. Feral Nation - Perseverance
6. Feral Nation - Convergence
7. Feral Nation - Sabotage
8. Feral Nation - Defiance
9. Feral Nation - Alliances
10. Feral Nation - Retaliation
11. Feral Nation - Opposition
12. Feral Nation - Tenacity

1. Feral Nation Collections 1-3
2. Fera Nation Collections 4-6
3. Feral Nation Collections 7-9
4. Feral Nation Collections 10-12

ABOUT THE AUTHOR

Scott B. Williams has been writing about his travels and adventures for more than thirty years. His published work includes hundreds of print and online magazine articles and more than two dozen books. His interest in trekking, sea kayaking and sailing small boats to remote places led him to pursue the wilderness survival skills that he has written about extensively in both his fiction and nonfiction works.

A solo sea kayaking odyssey of nearly two years, undertaken at age 25, set Scott on his path to becoming a storyteller when he authored the account of that adventure in his 2005 travel narrative: *On Island Time: Kayaking the Caribbean*. That journey and countless others that took him far off the grid for extended periods gave him the inspiration to delve into his passion for fiction and to write action and adventure tales like the ones that shaped his own desire to travel and explore.

With the release of his first novel, *The Pulse*, in 2012, and the subsequent sequels to it that became a popular post-apocalyptic series, Scott moved into writing fiction full time. Later and ongoing projects include the *Darkness After* series and the *Feral Nation* series, with more new works currently in development. To learn more about his upcoming books or to contact Scott, visit his website at: www.scottbwilliams.com

Made in the USA
Las Vegas, NV
18 January 2024

84542838R00308